CAGED IN

E.P.WRITER

COPYRIGHT

This novel is subject to copyrights. Not to be copied, used, or taken in any way, characters or plots, without written consent from the author, Elizabeth Pearl Writer, aka, E.P.Writer, aka, Elizabeth.P.Writer, aka, E.Pearl.Writer.

Not to be reproduced, transferred, shared or recorded, in any forms on any platforms both electronically or physically. No uploading or distribution via text or audio/ video or photo, by anyone living, dead, undead, missing, or lost.

All rights reserved.

Copyright © E.P.Writer 2023
Released December 2023
Reformatted November 2024
ISBN: 978-1-923109-12-4
Imprint: EPWriter prison
e.p.writer.newsletter@gmail.com

Copy Editor;
Lynne Lloyd Moss of LLOYD MOSS publishing
www.llydmosspublishing.com

Cover Design;
E.P.Writer

SOCIAL MEDIA

You can individually search my social accounts or scan the QR code to be effortlessly taken to a link for all my social pages. Or search my linktr.ee for the same link as the QR code.

Linktr.ee:
linktr.ee/e.p.writer

TikTok:	e.p.writer
Etsy:	epwriter.etsy.com
Instagram:	e.p.writer
Facebook Page:	E.P.Writer
Facebook:	Elizabeth PearlWriter

You can also find links to ARC signups (when they become available) in the QR link.

DISCLAIMER

This is a work of fiction, loosely based around the representation of life in prison. None of the events or characters are based on real life or real people, either living or deceased.

The Satanism in this novel is not based on facts, but a fictional version to match the aesthetic of the story.

This novel is to enter into a fictional world, consent is required in real life, so stay safe and make sure you ask before you touch. It is a NO unless it is an enthusiastic yes. Consent and permission.

Remember my readers. Play safe. Get their consent or don't do it. The following story is not a representation of what BDSM or safe sex should look like. Unless all people involved give their;

Consent.

Enthusiastic yes.

Boundaries

Safe words/Signals.

This is a fictional story. I do not condone rape. Always ask for consent. Play safe and play fair. Safe words are there for a reason.

Don't be an asshole, get their C.E.B.S

Happy reading my fellow friends.

CONTENT WARNINGS

(Contains but is not exclusive to)

Blood-play/ Knife-play/ Breath-play/ Pain-play
Biting/ Marking
Stalking
Forced Proximity
Manipulation
Death/ Murder/ Serial Killer
Possessive/ Obsessive Behaviours
Attempted Sexual Assault/ Rape/ Non-Con
Violations/ Abuse/ Cruelty
M/M
Gang Assault/ Attempted SA/ Non-Con
Mild Non-Con/ Assault
Gangs/ Violence/ Blood/ Fights
Attempted Blackmail/ Threats of Violence
Drug Use
Tattoos/ Needles
Dom/ Sub
Masochism/ Sadism
Semi-Public Sex
Emotional Hurt/ Comfort
Predator/ Prey

CHAPTER TIMELINE

Chapter -------------- Date ----------- Day --------- Title

Chapter 1 ----- 15th May 2022 ----- Day 1 ----- Caged In
Chapter 2 ----- 15th May 2022 ----- Day 1 ----- Meet the Cellmate
Chapter 3 ----- 15th May 2022 ----- Day 1 ----- Cut the Line
Chapter 4 ----- 15th May 2022 ----- Day 1 ----- Serial Killer?
Chapter 5 ----- 15th May 2022 ----- Day 1 ----- First Shower
Chapter 6 ----- 16th May 2022 ----- Day 2 ----- Meeting the Locals
Chapter 7 ----- 16th May 2022 ----- Day 2 ----- Counsellor
Chapter 8 ----- 16th May 2022 ----- Day 2 ----- Not Polite to Stare
Chapter 9 ----- 17th May 2022 ----- Day 3 ----- Day Three
Chapter 10 ---- 17th May 2022 ----- Day 3 ----- Fight or Flight
Chapter 11 ---- 18th May 2022 ----- Day 4 ----- Prison Job
Chapter 12 ---- 19th May 2022 ----- Day 5 ----- A New Day in Hell
Chapter 13 ---- 19th May 2022 ----- Day 5 ----- Serving
Chapter 14 ---- 19th & 20th May 2022 ----- Day 5 & 6 ----- SC-Ghost
Chapter 15 ---- 31st May 2022 ----- Day 17 ----- Back from The Hole
Chapter 16 ---- 1st June 2022 ------ Day 18 ----- Discovery
Chapter 17 ---- 2nd June 2022 ----- Day 19 ----- Visitation
Chapter 18 ---- 2nd June 2022 ----- Day 19 ----- Filing Room
Chapter 19 ---- 2nd June 2022 ----- Day 19 ----- Seeking Help
Chapter 20 ---- 2nd June 2022 ----- Day 19 ----- Can't Hurt to Ask
Chapter 21 ---- 4th June 2022 ----- Day 21 to 26 ----- Lockdown
Chapter 22 ---- 9th June 2022 ----- Day 26 ----- A Date
Chapter 23 ---- 9th June 2022 ----- Day 26 ----- Not my Cell
Chapter 24 ---- 10th June 2022 ---- Day 27 ----- Curiosity
Chapter 25 ---- 11th June 2022 ----- Day 28 ----- Tattoo
Chapter 26 ---- 11th June 2022 ----- Day 28 ----- Storm Out
Chapter 27 ---- 11th & 12th June 2022 ----- Day 28 & 29 ----- Alive
Chapter 28 ---- 12th June 2022 ----- Day 29 ----- Love Struck
Chapter 29 ---- 12th June 2022 ----- Day 29 ----- Sin
Chapter 30 ---- 13th June 2022 ----- Day 30 ----- Sin's Cell
Chapter 31 ---- 13th June 2022 ----- Day 30 ----- I'm Broken
Chapter 32 ---- 14th June 2022 ----- Day 31 ----- Relax
Chapter 33 ---- 28th June 2022 ----- Day 45 ----- You Trust Me
Chapter 34 ---- 28th June 2022 ----- Day 45 ----- Ruined

Chapter 35 ---- 29th June 2022 ----- Day 46 ----- Knife-on-Skin
Chapter 36 ---- 29th June 2022 ----- Day 46 ----- Med-Wing
Chapter 37 ---- 29th June 2022 ----- Day 46 ----- Choices
Chapter 38 ---- 29th June 2022 ----- Day 46 ----- The Letter

CAGED PRISON SERIES

A prison world where secrets run wild. Where no one is as they seem, and nothing can be trusted.
Book 1 and 2 interlock in their timelines:
Book 1, Caged In, follows a new inmate, Jasper Marcelo, as he learns what life is like behind bars. And tries to survive in this new world of lies, manipulation and betrayal.
Book 2, Caged Killer, focuses on, Sinn'ous, a serial killer with a love for satanic worship, and a rooted desire to possess anything he craves. And what he craves is the naive new inmate, Jasper.
Caged Killer, coming 2025.

CAGED IN
CAGED KILLER
CAGED SECRETS
CAGED DEATH

This series will be linked with, A Serial Killer's Life Series. An overlap that won't take away from either story if you don't want to read the other series. But it will hold more background insight into Sinn'ous.

Feel free to follow my social media pages (see front of book) to keep an eye on their progress.

PRONUNCIATIONS

Sinn'ous (Sin – oss)
Sinj (Singe)

DEDICATION

To all the naughty boys in cages.
This one's for you.

1

Sitting alone in the transitional cells, Jasper Marcelo—or, Izz, as most people call him—is contemplating his life choices.

Does he feel guilty for stealing? No. Does he regret transitioning from houses to pickpocketing? Yes.

Izz never should have tried it, never should have changed his tactics. He's good at robbing, good at breaking in and getting out without drawing attention to himself. He never takes too much, only a few items, most owners chocking it up to them misplacing things. But then he had to go and screw it all up.

And he screwed up big time. He's excellent with houses, exceptional with locks. He's an idiot for changing to pick pocketing. Less than a dozen people, and two weeks after he started, he was caught. He should have just stuck to buildings, to what he is actually good at.

All of this is happening because he listened to Cole. Why did he have to listen? His friend is an impulsive reckless lunatic, he knew it, yet he still followed Cole's instructions.

E.P.WRITER

Izz had a good thing going. He was working—alas, a crappy, low paying job, but at least it was a job—and he was robbing on the side. He had no choice on the latter, he had to keep his sister in school. To help his mum keep a roof over their heads, to prevent them from starving or freezing to death. They needed their rundown apartment and the crappy heating. Most of all, they needed more money than what he and his mum were able to earn at their jobs. Their mum was working her terrible barber job, with an asshole boss, pulling in double shifts, for shitty pay checks. She was still paying off the countless doctors' bills. His sister was recovering from cancer. After his father's death, all the insurance money was used to pay for chemo and all her other meds and treatments.

Izz's not going to be there for her birthday, in three months, she will be eleven. And he isn't going to be there to help her, or their mum. Now that he's in prison. With no way to provide for his family.

How are they going to stay in their little apartment? They'll be evicted—be out on the streets, freezing in the snow, and there is nothing he can do about it.

I screwed up.

I failed them.

Why do I have to be such a mess? A terrible brother and a lacking son.

He rubs his hands over his face, trying to scrub away his emotions before they get the better of him. He isn't sure about much in prison, but he knows crying will be a very bad, very dumb idea. If he falls down the emotional hole, he may as well slap a target on his ass with the words 'Bitch Boy' flashing neon pink.

CAGED IN

He already has it bad. His petite features. His warm, tan coloured skin. His soft hazelnut hair—long on top, shaved short around the sides. Eyes a rare forest green, brilliant and bright, demanding everyone's attention. He usually wore contact lenses during his . . . extracurricular activities. To keep his noticeable, and noteworthy, feature from becoming stuck in people's memories.

He's a mixed blood. He may as well have no race, with the amount of blood from multiple different races coursing through his veins. He's basically a glorified mutt. A mix-and-match puzzle of genes scrambled together.

He's not sure if it's going to help him in prison or make him more of a target. Being all and none of the races at the same time. For some reason people still see race in today's society, even with so many people like Izz in the world.

He hopes he can get by without anyone realising he doesn't belong to an ethnic group—he has a few tattoos, dotted here and there, maybe he can join in with a tattooed prison gang—

If it's not like the movies where everyone in prison is covered head to toe in ink . . .

He doesn't have very many tattoos, only a few small ones. He wouldn't get into the prisoner roles in the movies with his ink work.

A skull on his ankle, which he regrets now, worrying it will label him as a bitch boy or something, not that his petite features won't do that already. He's sure ankle tattoos are considered girly? For his sake, he hopes not.

He has another tattoo on the back of his neck, the date of his girl's death. She was killed in a fatal car wreck with her family when he was thirteen. They knew each other from birth, lived right next door their whole lives. They were always talking about their future, playing families, and make-believe marriages. She will forever be close to him, he'll never forget her. As soon as he hit fifteen and could find a decent artist to bribe, he had her birth date and death date permanently marked in his skin. His mum had not been happy, to say the least, but she understood why he wanted it so badly.

His third tattoo is vines and branches, interwoven with a snake skeleton that wraps around his biceps—well, his girlish biceps. He is muscled, just not overly so. He's not a rough tough bad ass dude who people will take one look at and back off from, with zero contemplation on starting any fight. He's more . . . delicately muscled. Skilled enough to hold his own in a fight, against one, who isn't overly skilled in hand to hand—

Okay. Okay. He's more of a run-the-fuck-away kind of fighter. When fight or flight kicks in, he picks flight. In prison, that's not really an option. You can only run so far in this caged in Hell-hole. He's been in this prison for the better part of three—or four—hours, and he already wants out of it. He has yet to meet the other inmates and already hates it.

So, in comparison to pretty much every inmate he has seen on television shows, Izz may as well call himself a clean-skinned push over, or whatever the term is that tattooed prison peeps use on non-tattooed peeps. Do they say peeps? Best he doesn't say that out loud to them, to be on the safe side—

It's not really *them*, now, is it? He's a part of the *them*. An inmate. Someone society throws into the same bag of bad

CAGED IN

people, treating them—us—like we're disgraceful, disgusting degenerates. A plague on society. Not worth caring about.

If only they cared enough to listen to our stories. To see the world through our eyes, live the world in our shoes. Sometimes, you don't have a choice in what you do. Sometimes, life throws you under the waves and holds you down, and you find yourself taking drastic measures to pull free from the depths.

His ass is beginning to go numb, his mind blank with boredom—he needs something to focus on, to distract himself—

Izz jerks to his feet and walks over to the bars, squishing his face against the cold metal cage. He can't see very far down the corridor. All he can see is more of the same—plain whitewash brick walls and a lumpy ass concrete floor. Like whoever they hired to lay the concrete hadn't been interested in wasting their time smoothing things out. Criminals live here, after all. And who cares how they live—

Man, he has to get out of his head. His thoughts keep spinning into morbidity. Morbidity? Morbidly? Morbid? He's not sure which is the correct term. Are they all correct? Does it matter?

A clank to his left catches his attention, he angles his head around in the tight space between the bars. The distraction is a good thing, he hates being left alone with his thoughts. Better to be surrounded by people and distractions, than alone.

He can hear heavy footfalls—boots thumping on hard ground, echoing off empty corridor walls. The jingling of keys tells him it's a guard approaching.

Finally, I can get out of this stupid, boring, cell.

He's not thrilled at the concept of meeting his new house-mates—cage-mates?—but he is going to die of boredom if he's left here any longer. He needs to get out and move around, stretch his legs, interact with others.

Do they have an outdoor area with enough space to jog? Like a football court? He frowns as the thought crosses his mind. He hopes they have some sort of grassed area. Not sure he can last his whole sentence without access to fresh air. Being stuck inside a stuffy prison, all day, every day, for months on end . . . it's a terrifying thought.

"Inmate," a deep voice booms, announcing the guard's arrival. "Turn around. Hands behind your back. Walk backwards to the bars."

The guard's a tall, hulking man, with long blond hair pulled into a ponytail. Weird that they would be allowed to grow long hair working in a prison. Wouldn't it be, like, a safety risk, or something?

Izz complies. Excited at the prospect of leaving the tiny transition cell. Doing his best to keep his happy little jig to himself. Pressing his back to the barred door, and patiently waiting for the guard to finish cuffing his hands. He groans under his breath at how tight they're fastened to his wrists.

It would be a bad idea to complain. Pissing off a guard on the first day, he can imagine isn't a hot idea—

The cell door clunks open, without the guard touching it. Sliding away from the wall, removing the barrier between himself and the guard.

CAGED IN

Must be electronic? Would explain the weird clunking noise he hears every time a door unlocks and opens. Some sliding, some opening like your regular push-pull doors.

His upper arm is grabbed in a crushing hold, and he's dragged down the corridor—it's a long corridor to be manhandled down, with an unflattering grey door awaiting their arrival at the far end.

More clunking—this time the blond guard pushes the door open—no sliding back for this electronic mass. Someone must be watching them from a control room? Surely the guard doesn't have one of those sensors to open the doors? Like the dogs have in their collars to open those expensive electronic doggy doors. Those had made it very easy to break into someone's house. He had a way with dogs, they all seem to love him—a happy, tail wagging bundle of joy, easily manipulated into opening their owners' home for him.

The room beyond the grey prison door is small, with a glassed-in cubical off to one side—in what looks to be bulletproof glass. It's extremely thick, like something you would find in a bear enclosure, thick enough to keep those fuzzy balls of teeth and claws locked away from people with nothing better to do than stare at them.

Behind the glass, a cheerful red-headed woman is putting some sort of pack together, as he's pulled over to the cubical. The guard doesn't say anything, he just stands there, holding Izz in place.

Izz watches the woman stuffing a pillowcase with a towel, toothbrush, toilet paper roll, soap, second set of orange prison assigned clothes—twins to the orange prison outfit he is currently sporting. And will be sporting for some time. He hates orange, his least favourite colour. Another way for them to stick it to him, he supposes.

"There you go, sweetie," the red-head chirps, a smile gracing her lovely face. She slides the well-stuffed pillowcase under the slit in the glass wall. Offering it for him to take.

"Thank you." Izz smiles back at her. Not sure how he's going to pick up the offering, with his hands secured like they are behind his back.

The guard solves the problem. Grabbing the case, and shoving it behind Izz, where he has a split second to grab the cotton material before the guard lets go. He barely manages to grip it and save it from hitting the floor.

Do not snap at the guard, you do not want to go to solitary confinement on your first day. Izz grits his teeth. *The least the guard can do is treat me like a human being and not garbage.*

He's led over to another door on the far side of the little room. More electronic locks clicking open, this door being another one the guard has to push open—

And they're back in another boring white corridor. It's a shorter distance to the door at the other end—in the same unflattering grey colour. Only change this time is the noises he can hear, muffled voices drifting out of the door's seams.

Here we go.

Izz takes a deep breath as the next door is swung wide—

A bombardment of loud voices barrelling in, bouncing off the walls, drilling into his skull, spiking his anxiety. The hot air racing to follow, clogging his lungs, and prickling his skin in warning.

Prison life here I come.

2

The prison is massive. Izz had admired its size from the outside, now he's within its walls, it is daunting. Even with a ten-foot ladder and a dozen inmates playing '*stack the criminal*', you wouldn't come close to touching the ceiling.

He steps into a two-story, rectangular room—crowded with inmates. Every space he can see, there are inmates clad in grey prison shirts and pants, with white sleeveless undershirts—a few inmates wearing blue prison clothes, and the occasional is in a black version. Everyone's shirts showing a combo of black letters and numbers stitched to the front—except the black shirts, those are grey, or perhaps white, at one point in their life before years of wear and tear stained them grey. It's dehumanising to be reduced to nothing but a barcode.

I wonder what the different colours mean?

He has to assume his orange uniform is for the new arrivals as he's the only one sporting the nauseatingly bright colour. He prays he won't have to wear it for long.

Bring on the grey.

E.P. WRITER

Izz follows along next to the mute guard who has a permanent scowl etched onto his face, and a grip like steel. Why do they feel the need to drag him around? He's in a cage, where exactly is he going to run?

Lining the fringes of the room are cells with barred doors, and brick walls to divide each cell, blocking you off from your neighbours. They are a decent size—for what he expected to get for cells. Although . . they do look kind of cold and lonely . . .

He passes by a small round table, identical to the others sparsely scattered down the room's centre. The metal tables are bolted into the concrete floor, inmates surrounding each one, sitting on them or on the round stools—that are likewise anchored into the ground.

He figures there has to be more sections in this prison containing cells. His view from the prison transport bus had shown a large spread out facility. Definitely big enough to hold more than the couple hundred inmates in this room. No doubt about it.

If he has to guess, he will say there are a hundred—or so—cells, if he combines both top and bottom floors. The second level is accessible by two metal staircases—one on either side of the room—and is also wrapped in cells, with metal rails to keep you from stumbling off the platforms edge—

Granted, you can still climb the rails and jump off the ledge—to the concrete floor below—if you truly desired to end your life . . .

He's led straight through the room, dragged in the direction of one of the staircases. Where he immediately catches the attention of all the inmates. He feels like a bug

CAGED IN

in the spotlight, being scrutinised and sneered at. He certainly doesn't want to draw so much notice, but his bright orange clothes make it virtually impossible to blend in.

He holds his head high as best he can, keeping his body facing forward, tension tingling his spine, and a cold sweat building. He allows his eyes to scan the room. Portraying confidence he doesn't possess, showing everyone he isn't going to be easily intimidated, that he isn't an easy target. Deep down . . . deep down he fights the urge to run and hide.

Don't let them see how terrified you are.

Inmates are huddling in groups or wandering alone. Some stopping their conversations to turn his way, others pausing their card games to glance over. Emerging from their cells to get a look at what all the fuss is over.

All the attention is amplifying his growing anxiety. He tries to ignore the lewd comments, the catcalls, the wolf whistles, the nasty suggestions and slurs thrown his way. He knows they're doing it to get under his skin. And he refuses to let them rattle him, allowing the words to roll off his shoulders as best he can—or perhaps . . . suppressing his external reactions to them is a better description? Because internally . . . Internally he's freaking out.

His march through Hell ends at the base of the stairs on his left—

How will he manage to navigate them with his hands cuffed behind his back?—

The guard solves the issue by half carrying him up them. It's the only time he's grateful for the guard's constricting hold. His stumbling and slipping, on the metal stairs, does little to slow the guard down—he's a rag doll along for the ride.

This is not at all humiliating. Izz mutters sarcastically in his head, loathing the silent guard more than before. Why does he even need the cuffs? No one else has them on.

There are inmates on the second floor too. Leaning back on the railing, milling around outside the cells and clustered within them. Sitting or lounging on bunks. Reading, or chatting. A few sleeping? Or perhaps passed out. A couple empty cells scattered among the lively ones. An inmate taking a dump in a metal toilet at the back of a cell—

Izz turns away immediately. Wanting to give the guy privacy—and he isn't interested in watching another man use the toilet. He could have gone his entire life without seeing it. The quick snippet he caught is now forever ingrained in his mind.

Thank you prison system. Not.

It isn't long before the guard stops outside an empty cell. And he finds his hands freed from the cuffs—

Izz pitches forward—a hand between his shoulder blades shoving him into the cell. His grip automatically tightening on the pillowcase as he catches himself. Pivoting back to the guard, he barely suppresses the urge to snap at them. Good thing they leave before his will to stay out of solitary confinement crumbles, due to the disrespectful treatment. He may be a prisoner, but that doesn't give them the right to treat him like shit.

Uptight A'Hole. Izz bristles, glaring at the empty spot the guard vacated.

Guess this is my cell . . . ? Whatever.

CAGED IN

Weird ass guard.

Izz inspects the two single metal bedding platforms protruding from the cell's brick walls. One neatly made bunk, blankets and pillow arranged respectably. And one with a bare mattress—if you can call it a mattress—maybe *'foam paper'* would be a more apt title for the flat thing. The mattress has no padding whatsoever. Might as well sleep on the metal bedframe, wouldn't make a difference.

He dumps his pillow-pack on the paper mattress. Peering up at the little shelf sticking out of the wall above his bunk. A good place to place possessions, photos perhaps? The other bunk has one as well, holding a few books and other items—he hopes his cellmate isn't a crazed lunatic or something worse.

He braces his hand on the smooth metal bunk, leaning to the side to check out under it—no legs or stand, they're embedded in the walls. He's not sure how he feels about this arrangement. Is there a weight limit? Before they bend and sag, causing you to roll off the slippery metal like a slide.

Righting himself once more, he inspects the rest of the cell. At the head of both bunks are short square cupboards. He opens the doors to the one near his bunk—three shelves greet him, with enough room to fit his spare clothing items, towel, toiletries, and maybe a few other little bits and pieces.

Down from the cupboard—on his side of the cell, against the wall—is a sink, with a mirror made from a reflective hunk of uneven dinted metal. No glass mirrors in prison, it seems. A metal toilet sits beside the sink, a little metal friend to keep it company in the corner. He does not look forward to using it—ignoring the cold metal on his ass—it's out in the open, anyone walking past will see him using it.

No privacy in prison . . .

The back wall holds a miniature window, set unevenly in the middle of the white bricks. He doesn't have OCD, but even he's pissed off at the lopsided window. The mini square trapping a thick protective glass shield, with bars on the outside—kind of pointless, considering the window is so small, even without the bars and glass in the way, he wouldn't be able to fit his head through it, much less his entire body in an escape attempt.

He sighs, sitting down on the bare mattress, ass sinking in to hit the metal below. He reaches over to begin unpacking his makeshift pillowcase bag—along with the items he watched the red-head pack, it also contains sheets and a thin pillow. The flat pillow is more inviting to sit his ass on than the paper-thin mattress. And that's saying something considering the pillow contains an insignificant handful of feathers, like they plucked a pigeon for the stuffing—

"Hey, I'm Reni. Sticks said you're in need of a tour and a rundown of the rules."

Izz startles at the hyper-excited voice piercing the cell, heart stuttering behind his ribs, his eyes flashing over to the barred door.

The inmate occupying the space in the doorway is a well-built man—similar to Izz's height. Short brown hair—laced with red highlights, flickering when he shifts his head. Tattoos ringing his neck and wrists—some sort of detailed

CAGED IN

intricate swirling design, not something Izz suspects would be possible to have inked in prison.

"Sticks?" Izz frowns at the man, unsure what to make of the name? If it is a name?

"A guard." When Izz shows no signs of understanding, Reni tucks on. "Long blond hair. Hates talking to inmates. We call him Sticks, 'cause he has a stick up his ass."

"Oh. Yeah. Him." Izz mulls the description over. "Makes sense." The guard had been stiff, and their expression did have a fuck-off-and-die vibe.

"Don't call him that though," Reni continues, the rest of his words spilling out in a rush, "Unless you want to be sent straight to The Hole, call him Sir, you call all the guards Sir. Some you can get away with a first name basis. Others you go into first names and they want second and third base, if you get my drift—handsy assholes—But anyways, call them all Sir, so you don't invite trouble."

Does this guy breathe when he talks?

He would laugh, but he isn't in a particularly laughing mood. This place oozes depression, an aura rubbing him the wrong way. A shadow of darkness creeping over him the longer he's within its walls. He has a bad feeling about this place. A fear he won't leave here with the same morals and frame of mind he came in with.

What had Reni said . . . The Hole . . . ? Must be what they call solitary confinement? He knows what it is from movies, a solitary place built for punishments. Filled with dark sunless cells, to sit in your own thoughts and drive you crazy.

"Alright—" Izz barely manages to get the word out, before Reni's voice floods right over him. Continuing in the same breathless speech.

"I'll be your guide, I usually guide all you newbies, not normally as easy as having the new guy in my cell, hate walking all around the prison to find wherever the fuck they put the new guys, guards are never any help." Reni thrust out his hand towards Izz, offering his palm for a handshake. "Sorry, if you haven't already noticed, I talk a lot, like a lot, a lot. My name's Reni, nice to meet you, and you are?"

Guess this is my cellmate.

"You told me your name already," Izz informs him, standing to shake his hand, "and I'm Jasper Marcelo, but everyone calls me Izz—long story."

"Well. Izz. Now you can't give me any excuses for forgetting my name," Reni makes a face like you better not forget, and Izz can't help but laugh.

His cellmate's energy level is way out there. He can see himself getting along fine with the man. The outgoing vibe matching and melding with his own—when he's comfortable and not internally panicking.

Maybe this prison stay won't be so bad after all? If I have Reni to keep me company.

Reni abruptly swivels, marching straight out of the cell. "Come on. Dinner should be getting served any moment now—oh, and don't shake people's hands, they pull you in and shiv ya. Unpleasant experience."

Izz absorbs the information, keeping it close in mind, so he won't screw it up and get himself killed—sounds like his cellmate is talking from experience?

CAGED IN

He follows after Reni, jogging to keep up with the man's long strides. He keeps his eyes on the tattooed neck, avoiding looking too closely at the many inmates staring at him. He's antsy enough as it is, without knowing precisely how many are judging him—or sizing him up . . .

Would they have a go at him to garner how tough he is? Or is that something strictly left for the Hollywood team to build tension and amp up violence in their movies?

"Come forth, newbie." Reni throws over his shoulder. "I will introduce you to The Gang—not really a *gang* gang. We tried clique or misfitted clan or coven, but it sounded weird and witchy, so we call ourselves The Gang. Makes us sound tough, even though we're just the random leftovers who couldn't cut it into the actual gangs that do all the shady stuff around here."

They hit the metal platform at the top of the stairs, taking them down rapidly. Not by his choice, Reni walks like he's on a mission with a time crunch breathing down his neck.

Izz perks up at Reni's words, specifically, *shady stuff?* Meaning drugs and contraband? He's hopeful that's what it means. And not some underground prison fight club. Another thing he isn't sure if it's a Hollywood fake or real life. This gang business could, however, mean he has a chance of scoring something to ease his nerves. To lift some of the stress off his back after the trial.

"You know anyone to get weed from?" Izz's not entirely sure why he asked. He doesn't have any money to offer, and he'd literally just met the man. For all he knows, Reni's an undercover cop—

I need to stop watching so many fake crime movies . . .

Reni swivels to face Izz, eyebrow raised, "you've been here ten seconds and you're already talking drug buys."

"Weed's not a drug." Izz scoffs, glaring at the other, he isn't some drug addict. He merely needs something to mellow his nerves. It's not like weed makes him see things or start eating people's faces off—like whatever drug that guy in the news report was on. Some nasty cannibal action was going on there—

"You sure 'bout that?" Reni's tone drips with sceptical mockery.

"Whatever." Izz laughs, waving his hand to dismiss his cellmate's remark. "I'm not seeing flying horses with it, so it's not going into the drug column for me."

Reni rolls his eyes. Turning to lead the way once more, shoving through the clusters of inmates. Blowing a kiss to one man who snaps at him. Izz has to admire loud mouths total lack of concern and fearless disregard for the many inmates with a larger muscle mass.

He follows along in Reni's wake. Trying to keep his smirk to himself, as he watches other inmates shoot daggers at his cellmate's back. Expecting a fight to break out at any second, but other than some slurred words and heated looks, nobody starts anything. He's not sure he wants to witness a fight on his first day, or be dragged into one . . .

3

Izz's cellmate pilots him away from the cells, through an archway, and into a wide-open corridor. He's greeted by blank white walls, a total lack of decorative paintings or anything really. Depression comes to mind once more. If he has to put a face to what depression looks like—in a mental image—it would be this brightly-lit white prison tunnel. Maybe that's the point? Prison isn't supposed to be a happy joyous place. Wouldn't be much of a punishment if everyone wants to be here.

They pass a few closed doors—one door with a label reading, *Cleaning Supplies*—and a collection of split-off corridors punching out at random intervals in the walls. He has no idea where they lead. He fears he will be here long enough to figure it out. With the time he has in this cage, he will eventually learn all the secrets held within this whitewash of depression. Not a concept he's thrilled by.

The two cellmates march along until the long corridor spills out into a huge, open cafeteria room with high ceilings. The space is crammed full of long tables lining the two outer walls—two dozen, at least. A clear pathway through the centre funnels the inmates to the food serving bar—if it's called that?—at the back of the room. A kitchen is visible behind the inmates' serving meals to the impatient men forming an ever-growing queue.

Bundled closely together, each table is big enough to seat thirty inmates—perhaps even more if they squish together. The starting table in each row is planted next to the wall on either side of the corridor entrance—the same entrance Izz stands frozen in, numbly gaping at the noisy chaotic mealtime in full swing.

The sheer size of the cafeteria is overwhelming. Multiple, large flapping double-doors are spaced out around the room. High above his head are windows, thick and lined with bars like every other glass window in this cage. However, these bars are on the interior, not the exterior. If you threw a chair at them—if you can find a chair not bolted into the floor—you wouldn't be able to break the glass. No doubt it's bulletproof too.

He blinks back into focus when Reni flies straight towards the line to collect food. Izz dodges in and out of the obstacle course of inmates and their food trays. A sea filled with tattooed men—the occasional odd one out with no visible tattoos.

He drags his feet, trailing slowly behind his cellmate. Not keen to find out how bad the food will be. Food he is required to eat during his stay here—unless he wants to starve to death—

Will the prison let him starve? Or will they strap him down and force him to eat? They're forcing him to stay in

CAGED IN

this cage, against his will, isn't too much of a stretch to imagine them shoving food down his throat—

Why don't they call this abduction? It feels abductiony, to say the least . . .

Prison, a fancy word for *abduction.*

His head twists—eyes scanning—to keep a watchful eye on the inmates brushing past him. So many of them everywhere, at least five hundred. The tables filling fast. The noise level rising as hundreds of voices compete for airtime. Adding on to the thick smells of men and multiple food choices.

The thick queue Reni lands in, is a decent length, with more inmates filing in by the second. Izz shuffles along the line to his cellmate, who is high fiving another inmate, and starting a rapid fire conversation. One Izz can't keep track of, too many confusing words and half sentences, which make no sense to an outsider. And that's exactly what he is.

For now.

No way is he living here for months and months without making friends, how boring would that be. He doesn't do floating on the outskirts of socialisation. He's more a dive headfirst—and make a fool out of himself, without a care in the world—type of person. He's liable to find out the waters are full of unexpected jagged rocks, tangling driftwood, and fast-moving predators, to snare and maim him. He has to be more vigilant of the way he interacts with people in here. Unless he wants to get stabbed— shivved? Do they still call it a stabbing in prison? Or is that only an *'outside-world'* term?

His focus is drawn away from his rambling thoughts—and his cellmate's hyper conversation—by an icy warning shooting up his calves into his ass and exploding through his stomach. As if he were electrocuted with a cold chill—

His eyes latch onto a tall, well-built, inmate, dressed in prison grey. 6'3, with a messily spiked mohawk—black sides, and a red stripe down the middle, reminding him of a redback spider.

He's curious with the way the sea of inmates' part to give the mohawked male a wide birth. Perhaps they too are experiencing the same assault to the little hairs on the backs of their necks, as he is.

He's drawn to the tantalizing male by something he can't put his finger on—as the male strides directly to the front of the queue. Cutting in front of the dozens waiting, and no one expresses any issues with it. No one speaks a word about it, the majority all around Izz deliberately avert their eyes.

The spikey-haired inmate collects a tray, sliding it along to select his food and moves on. Swallowed up in the sea of grey, as everyone once again parts to get out of his way—

" . . . this is Izz." Reni's voice spears into Izz's skull, a hand slapping down on his shoulder. He barely catches the ending of his cellmate's sentence—what is Reni talking about?—

Izz comes face to face with the inmate Reni had high-fived earlier. A little too close for comfort, considering they're strangers, and in prison.

This inmate is marginally taller than Izz. Black hair covering his ears to hang over a well-formed jawline. His

CAGED IN

skin pale white—vampire, in a dark cave, pale—resulting in the black tattoo, on the side of his neck, to stand off his skin, the colour contrast freakishly flawless. His eyes, a pale blue, soft and light, matching his skin tone.

Izz has to admit the vampire look-a-like is cute. Not his type but he can appreciate the allure.

The vampire inmate smiles at him, revealing a smooth set of teeth and no fangs, much to his disappointment. He would not have been surprised if the guy sported a set of permanent dental fangs. Those fake fangs dentists will stick to your teeth for the right amount of money.

"Name's Blake," vamps drawls, as he holds out his hand towards Izz.

He caught a glimpse of a black rose, on the vampire's palm, in the seconds before they clasp hands—

Izz scolds himself for not remembering the rule about shaking hands. Not greeting people in this way is going to take some getting used to—he better learn fast. He doubts his cellmate is exaggerating the warning. He will be disappointed in himself if he's sent to the . . . infirmary? . . . leaking blood, on his first day.

"Izz," he mutters, grinding his teeth in frustration—

Izz jumps out of his skin as someone's hand grips his shoulder firmly, as a collective weight drops down on him. A warm body half draping over his shoulders, to bellow right in his ear, "new guy. Hello."

He jerks his head away, wincing as his ears scream at him, yelling silent profanities at the loudmouth who nearly killed them. Squealing and ringing in protest, to drag his skull into the suffering right alongside them.

"Zid. Jesus, man," Blake reprimands, pulling his hand away from Izz, taking an offended step away from the inmate in question, "lower the volume."

"Oh, my bad. My bad," Zid shoves his face into Izz's personal space. Sticking his hand out, this time Izz remembers not to shake the hand and receives a devilish smirk from Zid as a result, "I'm Zidie." He breezes over the lack of reciprocation to the hand-on-hand action, "you can call me Zids, Zido, Zida, Z—"

"I think he gets it, man," Reni butts in, cutting off Zidie's long list of self-appointed nicknames.

The first thing Izz notices about Zidie, is his crazy blue-tinted blond locks, scruffy and wind swept, as if he ran to the cafeteria. With a tattoo under his left eye of some kind of little cupcake covered in frosting.

Why would you put a cupcake right there on your face?

Inwardly, Izz chuckles. Luckily, it's a well-done tattoo, and not some back alley, five bucks job by a colour blind crack addict. He must admit, it does suit the man. Even though they met a literal second ago, he's already sensing a playful child-like attitude from Zidie. Cupcake is going to be fun to hang around with.

"Hi," Izz responds, still fighting with his ears to calm down and do their job—their protest is painful. "I'm Izz."

"Izz." Zidie purses his lips, his nose scrunching as he scrutinises Izz, "why Izz?"

Apparently Zidie has no filter from his brain to mouth, either. To go along with his loud boisterous energy.

"Dude," Blake cuts in, glaring daggers at Zidie, a displeased noise escaping his throat.

CAGED IN

"What?" Zidie asks with an innocent expression plastered on his face, his devilish grin growing wider by the second, "it's a weird name."

"And yours is normal?" Blake shoots back, crossing his arms over his chest. Presenting awfully close to a disapproving older brother.

"Never said it being weird was wrong, us weird named individuals gots' to stick together. Ain't that right? Izz," Zidie turns his colourful cupcake face to Izz, grinning from ear to ear.

This feels normal. The interaction. The teasing friends. He could almost forget where he is. Where they all are. He has no idea what these men had done to get themselves thrown in here—he prays it's nothing terrible or malicious. But he can see himself becoming friends with them.

"My real name's Jasper," Izz offers. Rubbing a hand over the back of his neck, unsure how much of his personal life he's willing to share with these unknown inmates. "Jasper Marcelo. People call me Izz—it's a long story." A story he's not willing to share with these men. Not so soon anyway.

He returns a smile of his own to Zidie, leaving the explanation at that . . . Perhaps one day he may trust them enough with a snippet of information about his life outside of these walls? His family and friends. His failures . . . But not today—maybe not ever.

"Ugh. Well. Boring." Zidie pouts, flicking his hand dramatically in Izz's vague direction. "Don't spread that around. I'm happy my best friend has a weird name like me."

"Best friend?" Izz blinks in stunned shock at the phrase. He isn't sure how long you have to know someone to class them as a *best friend*, but he's sure it's longer than five seconds.

"Just go with it," Reni mutters, shifting to close the gap as the line drifts closer to the food serving bar. "He calls every newbie joining our group his best friend. He's like an overgrown puppy."

"Ay." Zidie protests. "I am not a puppy." He glares playfully at Reni, devilish smile in place. "If I'm anything, I'm a falcon. Swooping in to bring joy." His eyebrows dance mischievously to join his grin, the combination exaggerating his teasing tone.

"Falcons swoop in to kill," Izz adds offhandedly, rotating his head to take in the room for the umpteenth time. Mentally tallying the inmates constantly dribbling into the cafeteria.

How many more are in this cage?

A generous number of inmates are obviously part of gangs. Easy to distinguish from the other tables of regular men. A few clusters proudly displaying tattoos of a similar nature. One table is filled entirely with men sporting shaved heads—if the shaved head is a condition to join that particular gang, he will never be joining it. He's rather fond of his hair, thank you very much.

Zidie waggles his eyebrows in mock mystery, "I have many skills," he ominously informs Izz. Laughing moments later when Izz gives him a sceptical look.

They're at the front of the line before he realises it. Standing within the surprisingly delicious aroma of foods.

CAGED IN

His cellmate grabs a tray, slapping it down, before handing another tray back to Izz.

"Thanks." Izz accepts the tray—with its different-sized sections to hold things separate, like the foods' have vendettas and need to be segregated.

Reni nods at the gratitude, sliding his tray along to pick out foods. Izz mimics the tray slide motion, shuffling along after Reni.

The food does not resemble the nasty slop he'd pictured on multiple occasions during his hours at trial. Instead, he faces a selection of different soup choices. A rich orange pumpkin soup. A soft, clear, chicken noodle soup. A deep green coloured soup with floating green chunks, resembling broccoli—if the broccoli was frozen and mashed into a soup consistency. And there's a cheesy pasta dish, next to hunks of bread and different spreads. With small bottles of juice and water huddled together at the end of the row.

"What can I get ya, newbie?"

Izz glances at the towering inmate who addressed him. A beefy dude with hair buzzed into a short, to the scalp, style. Tattoos leaking from his head, over his jaw, down his neck, spilling out his sleeves to run down his arm. His face is clear of tattoos—other than a star above his eyebrow.

Izz peeks at the short blond inmate serving Reni, and notices he has the same star above the eyebrow.

A gang mark?

He clears his throat, turning his full attention to the server. "The pasta, water, and bread with butter, please." Choosing the pasta as a safe option.

He likes home-made pumpkin soup, that store bought crap tastes nothing like pumpkin. He isn't foolish enough to believe the prison buys fresh pumpkins to make their soup from scratch. It would be some sort of watered-down pumpkin-flavoured powder.

Gross.

The inmate serving Izz laughs. "Damn, so polite." He moves along to slap out the foods onto Izz's tray. "Wish the rest of these pricks had some damn manners."

Izz slides his tray along, following the server down to collect the food he had asked for. Politely smiling to his server, not sure how to answer the statement, or even if he should.

Don't piss off the hand that feeds you.

"Extra pasta, 'cause I like ya, kid," the server winks at Izz. And proceeds to bellow *'next'*—so loud Izz's ears cringe back into his skull—as the server makes his way back to the start of the food bar to serve the next inmate.

The four inmates serving meals are continuously shifting places to run up and down the serving bar, moving four inmates at a time through the process. Working like clockwork to get the meals distributed fast, the coordination is something that could only be acquired over years of practice. These are pros—

How long have they been here? to work together so efficiently. Moving as one, without the need to speak their actions, anticipating the others' movements before they're made.

Izz departs the area to follow Reni, who's waiting for him to finish collecting his meal. He trails behind his cellmate as they head over to a table near the back of the room,

CAGED IN

three rows down from the corridor entrance leading back to their cells.

4

Reni dumps his tray on the table which already has four inmates seated around it. They all look up at Reni's arrival, sending him friendly greetings—

The warm welcome drains away to a dull tolerance as everybody's eyes shift over to Izz—a synchronized movement, as if they rehearsed it—hitting him with the same intensity to shrink an elephant—

Did he forget to put his pants on? A swift glance down says no. So not a real-life naked walk through, like his stress dreams as a child—showing up at school naked. Wouldn't that be a shockingly memorable first impression. He's not sure he wants his first impression to be the pantless newbie.

Reni plants his ass on the bench, tucking his long legs under the table, gesturing for Izz to take a seat in front of him. Pulling Izz out of his irrational inward freak-out.

He complies, plopping down onto the hard metal bench, with the kitchen behind him—placing the vast majority of the room to his back. Everything is overwhelming, he'd prefer to ignore the room, and pretend he isn't surrounded

CAGED IN

by hundreds of inmates. He can see a few in his peripheral—as well as those at the table—but the rest are shielded from his sight. If he drowns out the constant noise, he can almost forget they're behind him.

Out of sight, out of mind.

Reni clears his throat, and begins the introductions. "Everyone, this is Izz. Izz this is Phelix." Flicking a thumb to the short-haired blond, at his side, with sleeve tattoos covering the inmate's hands and palms.

Phelix smiles, nodding at Izz. His golden curls an unnatural glossy gold, a pigmentation Izz has never seen in someone's hair. Delicate strings of gold, shaping his face in an almost movie star fashion. *Almost*, if they pulled a movie star out of a real-life drug cartel. He gives off the vibe of someone who's powerful without the need to show it off with brute force. The man who gives the orders from the background, disappearing those who don't follow those orders to his satisfaction.

"That's David—" Reni continues his point-and-name routine. Jabbing his finger at a sizable guy next to Phelix.

David wears a cluster of scripture tattoos on the sides of his face. The swirling text is too hard for Izz to make out the letterings . . . or read the script. It has the feeling of something Godly—purely based on the way its script resembles the old English text painted on parchments in church movie scenes.

It's saying something that all my references for judging 'bad guys' is based out of movies . . .

"He's Erik," Reni waves a hand at the inmate across from David.

Erik is the shortest at the table, skinny enough for his clothes to look baggy. Long brown hair cascading down to the small of his back. No tattoos, at least, none that Izz can see. He gives off a stoner-druggy vibe.

At least this time Izz can safely say he's not basing Erik's appearance out of movies. He has seen his fair share of druggies' around his family home . . . if you could call that run-down apartment a home.

"And that's Isco," Reni points out the last unknown inmate at their table.

The man occupying the space to Izz's left narrows his eyes at Izz, an inquisitive expression passing over his face which is littered with scars.

I wonder what happened . . . ?

A deep scar runs a curved path down Isco's chin, brushing against his throat, tearing through the previously unblemished skin. Two smaller scars slicing across his right eye, falling above and below the miraculously unscathed eye. A close call to losing the eye or being blinded. Three lengthy scars circling the right side of his neck, trailing under his ear and onto his collarbone to integrate with the tattoos peeking out from his collar.

If Phelix's vibe represents the cartel boss-man, than Isco's vibe screams hitman, readily able to do the boss's bidding.

Sucked into his little guess-the-crime game, his eyes shift down to Isco's hands. The need to confirm his theory of this inmate beating people to death is too strong for him to resist.

The hands attached to thick wrist on the intimidating inmate are what Izz expects. Roughened hands with boxy

CAGED IN

black letters engraved into each knuckle, matching the crude ink etched into the backs of both hands.

Isco is a man Izz knows is capable of murder. He knows it within his bones. Why? Because despite what people say, he's judging this book by its cover. And this book's cover terrifies him.

As if sensing his unease—or to mock him, who knows—Isco cracks his knuckles, snapping Izz's gaze away to his face, a smirk lifting his scarred cheeks.

Izz gulps, nervously digging into his food, he isn't intimidated often, but this man is daunting—okay, so he usually isn't intimidated. Except in here. Everything is new and strange, and all the people in here are unpredictable. Due to the fact that he has no clue why any of them are locked away. Has no idea who can be trusted and who can't.

Scooping the sticky mess of pasta into his mouth, he tastes the cheap cheese flavour. Sticking to his teeth and the roof of his mouth. Even with it fighting back he still enjoys the pasta. It's not as terrible as he was dreading the prison food to be.

Surveying the tables he can see, Izz studies the numerous clusters of inmates. Nothing beyond what he can observe without turning his head, trying not to be too obvious about his spying.

They're all outcasts—groups who are not part of the gangs. One table in particular has several inmates spread over it, alone, not interacting with one another.

Loners?

The inmate seated closest to him is sporting a black eye, busted lip and bruising down his arm, Izz can't see the other arm but is willing to bet he has more bruises under his clothes.

The bruised inmate's heavy-lidded eyes drag towards Izz, like he senses the gaze on him.

Izz darts his eyes away, not wanting to start anything. He doesn't know why they're covered in injuries, and has no intention to find out. For all he knows, the guy is a lunatic who gets into fights with anyone who so much as looks at him.

"We also got Sinj in The Hole," Zidie cuts in, dragging Izz's gaze over to him. "That's S-i-n-j not S-i-n-g-e even though they sound the same. Another weird name to join our midst. Ay, Izz." He squeezes into the space between Izz and Isco, unceremoniously shoving them to the sides.

Izz rolls his eyes at Cupcake. There are plenty of empty spaces on the bench for Zidie to plant his ass on, shoving between them is entirely unnecessary. Isco doesn't appear to care, unflinching, like the scarred inmate is accustomed to this type of behaviour.

An overgrown puppy. Is what comes to mind to describe Zidie. A giant, friendly, over-excited puppy who doesn't grasp the concept of personal space—

Colourful, intricately designed artwork flashes Izz, as Zidie's decorated arm rests on the table by his tray. A multi-coloured, full sleeve, of ocean creatures, swishing and swimming around each other to create a beautiful 3D picture. Whoever he went to, to get his work done, Izz wants their number. Their artwork is stunning.

"The Hole?" Izz questions, to double check his guess earlier was a correct assumption—when Reni mentioned

CAGED IN

it in their cell. It has to be some sort of solitary confinement—

"Solitary confinement," Reni answers for Zidie who's shoving food into his mouth. "But The Hole's what we call it."

Izz hums in understanding, snagging his small bottle to swish down the sticky cheesy pasta. He's not a fan of the room temperature flavourless liquid, but it's better than nothing.

I'm going to miss ice cold water . . .

Blake settles in next to Izz, laughing at something Reni said, Izz missed whatever it was. Others at the table are grinning and chuckling along with Reni, who throws back his head and lets out a deep rumbling laugh.

A flicker of movement seizes Izz's attention. Over Reni's shoulder, a subtle flash of red guides his eyes to a lone figure sitting at the furthest table. He can't make out who it is . . . the cafeteria's artificial fluorescent lighting is avoiding the inmate, curling away from the male, leaving him encased in shadow. As though it's too scared to touch—

Wait . . .

Izz sucks in a breath, it's that same inmate. The one who skipped the queue. With the spiked red and black mohawk. The one nobody objected to, for cutting the line. As if they are all scared . . .

His eyes eat up every detail of the mohawked male's face and body while he's shrouded in semi darkness in the corner of the room. Izz fails to perceive how both tables closest to the male are a barren empty wasteland. He's too busy studying the enticing male's frame.

He's so engrossed in his examination, he doesn't notice when the eyes of his obsession flick over. Not until their gazes' clash, the male's hard eyes boring into Izz's soul—

He swallows the lump forming in his throat, a hot flush slapping a red blush onto his cheeks. Heating up his body, a furnace inside his clothes on full blast. He's a schoolgirl, caught staring at the hottest guy in class. Blushing up a storm.

Whoa . . . He is hot as fuck.

Too entranced to pull his gaze away, Izz gives in to his impulses, allowing his eyes to roam . . .

The inmate has red tattoos, bleeding out from both sleeves, flowing down his forearms to pool at his elbows. Izz's unable to make out any details from this distance. But the rich red is easily seen, closely resembling blood . . . sliding and dripping down well-defined, toned arms.

He stares openly, fixated on the male—and the inmate stares right back.

Maybe I should introduce myself?

He doesn't know the etiquette in the prison cafeteria. Had he been at a bar—or somewhere else on the outside—he would have already approached the male—

An inmate scoots past their table, cutting off his view for a moment. Long enough to draw his concentration away from those intoxicating eyes. The reason for his fixation being broken so readily is the inmate's clothing. They aren't wearing grey like the vast majority are. This inmate, sideling past their table, is wearing blue.

Izz's thoughts rapidly change course, from his eye fucking, to a question that had crossed his mind upon arrival.

CAGED IN

Izz quizzically turns to Reni, "What's with the different coloured prison clothes?"

His cellmate misses the question, too busy slingshotting something off his spoon in a failed attempt to hit Erik who is sticking his tongue out at the former.

"Different colours for different meanings," Blake is the one to answer the question, tearing off a slice of his bread. Speaking around it as he chews.

"Like?" Izz enquires when Blake doesn't finish explaining.

Reni jumps in, an amused scowl firmly in place from his earlier antics with Erik, apparently on board with the whole conversation. "Blue is for inmates with medical problems, like oldies or epilepsy, seizure prone—or whatever—people. Purple is for I-Wing. Black is for lifers or those doing hard time—multiple repeats of long stints. Grey is for us normal folks, and orange is for the fresh meat, obviously." He gestures to Izz on the last part.

He does not like being referred to as fresh meat. A cow to the slaughter comes to mind. He lets the subject drop, it won't be soon enough to have his grey prison clothes. He hates the orange. Why do they dress the new inmates in orange? Making them stand out, like the guards want to put a target on the new arrival's backs—

A weird noise at Erik's end of the table has the whole table turning. A noise like a choked gasp of dread, or maybe anticipation—

The table falls silent, like a well-clogged machine, with all its parts seizing in a rehearsed stop—

Standing at the end. Right next to Erik. Is another inmate. And this inmate is massive with a hard-pressed face. Clipped short hair. Eyes narrowed and piercing, scrutinising everyone on the table. And he's covered in tattoos. Izz's starting to realise it's more shocking to see someone here without tattoos on display than to see men completely covered in ink.

"Erik," the newcomer flicks his chin to the side—indicating one of the twin flapping doors that leads out of the cafeteria—before the guy walks off, disappearing out the doors.

Izz raises a brow at the tension throughout the table after the inmate's departure. Watching as Erik's face drops, he stands and empties his tray in the trash bin, depositing it on top, and briskly following the departed inmate.

Izz must have been making a face, because Reni fills him in, "his dealer."

Oh, that explains why Erik's so skinny. Doesn't explain why he looked hollow and nervous before going off with his dealer. You would think an addict would be thrilled to see their dealer? Unless he owes money? Izz hopes he's going to be okay, and doesn't get beaten for late payments or something.

Letting out a breath, he pulls his eyes away from the door. The mohawked inmate in the corner is still watching him. And he finds he can't look away when their eyes lock once more. Drawn in by a strange allure. The male has an intense aura, a dark aura? Yet Izz doesn't hear any inner voices screaming warnings at him. He believes the inmate is trustworthy, even without knowing what they did to get thrown in here. Perhaps he should find out—

"Who's that?" Izz blurts abruptly to the table, before his common sense can stop him.

CAGED IN

When the group's hot gazes lock on him—fixated eyes heating his body into one of wary unease—he points his chin towards the red and black haired inmate—to indicate who he's addressing—at the unoccupied table. It's too late to pretend he hadn't said anything.

May as well embrace the chaos.

Reni jerks his head over his shoulder to take a gander at who Izz's referring to. His head yanks back around like he's burned, a grimace plastered on his face.

"Don't stare, man. Seriously," his cellmate bites off in a hushed, harsh whisper. "That's Sinn'ous."

Izz blinks at Reni. What's that supposed to mean? Should he know who that is? Is he famous or something? A singer?

"*THE* Sinn'ous." When Izz merely shrugs, Reni's exasperated voice adds, "the serial killer. He's killed, like, hundreds of people. They just can't prove it's *that guy*." Reni flicks a thumb towards the corner, careful to keep it concealed by his body so only those at their table can see the action. "Not officially, anyway. He's killed guards and inmates in here too. Stay as far away from him as possible, and don't frickin' look at him. Keep your damn eyes averted. Keep your whole body averted."

Izz checks the rest of the table occupants to ensure he isn't being punked. A messed-up prisoner fraternity pledge thing, or some kind of joke played on the newbie. The collective fear in their faces tells him everything he needs to know. Even Isco appears worried.

"And stick to large groups," Reni continues, laying out the rules in a freaked-out life and death tone. It's completely at odds to his fun-loving easy-going self. "Especially if he ever enters a room you're in. Make sure there are a dozen or more people around you. If you count only eleven, you sprint out of that room so fast the wind's impact will land you with black and blues, like you went up against a guard hell bent on beating you to death."

Izz swallows hard—and, because your mind has to look at a car crash—his eyes flick over to the inmate in question.

The serial killer—

Blake slaps him on the back of his head—Izz quickly snaps his attention to his tray, digging his spoon in. His appetite is gone, shrivelled up, along with his mellow this-prison-stay-shouldn't-be-too-bad mood. He uses the spoon to push his food around, playing with the leftover meal as a distraction.

. . . Well . . .

. . . Shit . . .

He's lucky he hadn't strolled over and clumsily introduced himself, and tried to flirt with the mohawked inmate . . .

A serial killer . . . ?

5

Izz's slapped in the face the moment he enters the shower room. The heavy steam assaulting his lungs. Thick and constricting, he wades through the smoggy sludge to get to the benches where they leave their clean clothes. With the amount of steam clogging the space, his clothes would be better off having a shower with him to stay dry.

Worse than the stream, is the pungent rank stench, its foul odour gagging him. A hundred times worse than anything he smelt back in school in the boys' locker room. He hadn't thought how prison would smell when he was being transported here. He fears his sense of smell will forever be tainted.

He sticks with his new friends. They seem to have taken him in with open arms. And he's glad for it. If he's to guess, having allies in prison is a good thing. Befriend as many as you can so you have less people to worry about attacking you. It's what he's planning to do anyway.

He's thankful he isn't alone the first time in the showers. He doesn't want to admit it, but he has been dreading this moment since he was found guilty. All the stories about what happens in prison showers have been close to mind, playing on repeat to frazzle his nerves. Being in this relatively large prison . . . friendship group? he feels somewhat protected.

He has a better understanding of the pack mentality now. It's comforting and safe. Better than going it alone, with no one to watch your back—or ass, in this case.

Pulling off his prison-issued clothes, he dumps them onto the ever-growing pile of dirty clothes from the rest of the group. He keeps the clean clothing at a safe distance, not wanting clean threads to be near the large pile of pungent fabric—

Izz yelps, stumbling forward as a towel cracks him on the ass. He's not sure which is louder, the towel's snap on his bare ass or his girlish noise.

"Don't drop the soap, new-*boy*," Zidie teases. Grinning madly while brandishing the towel like he's gearing up for a second whip.

"Piss off, or I'll throw it at you, *Cupcake*." Izz bites out with no real venom, raising his bar of soap. Grinning at Zidie, he shoves him away. He hates to admit it. But Zidie's nonchalant demeanour and joking nature is helping to ease his nerves.

He has no problem with his body, he's proud of his figure. Stripping naked with strangers isn't too bad. What he has a problem with is those strangers trying to get all touchy feely with him—all grabby, clawing hands. He can't close his eyes to wash his hair in a normal shower by himself without worrying about imaginary demons grabbing him. It's a weird thing but common. Maybe your

CAGED IN

body wants to remind you that you're naked and vulnerable?

But in here. Those grabby hands are a very likely outcome to closing your eyes. Or turning your back. Izz will create a mental note to shower with his back to the wall. It might expose his front, but better the front than the back.

His thoughts slowly drip away, as Erik joins them. The scrawny inmate shuffles in slowly, stiffly, as if he might have injured his leg—

Izz frowns at the bruising around the small inmate's neck. Was that there before? He can't recall. It must have been? It's a strange spattering of bruises, resembling a hand mark—

Izz swiftly turns when Erik begins removing his shirt. Not wanting to be caught staring at another inmate while they undress. He might be gay, and open about it on the outside, but that doesn't mean he's stupid. He knew damn well people get beaten and killed for that stuff. He isn't interested in testing whether or not the inmates in this prison are open minded.

Naked, and wanting to get this first shower over with, he follows along after Isco. Who's back is littered with ink, and scars, in a patterned way—

Scarification? That's what it's called, isn't it? When someone has skin removed to form pictures and designs, so it stands out as scars and not as ink like a regular tattoo.

It's unique. Intriguing. He's never seen someone with scarification done, he's only ever heard of it being done, and seen a few random pictures in tattoo shops.

Isco disappears behind a brick partition, and Izz follows along, ducking around the partition to join Isco and the rest of their group.

The showers are as expected. One big, roughly tiled room, with sandpaper gripping tiles—if you decided to start throwing hands, you would have a marginal amount of grip to stop you falling on your ass. Shower heads plugged into the walls in rows, wrapping around the room. Inmates are spread throughout, taking up their positions below numerous cascades of clear water. Making thorough use of the steaming showers to clean their bodies.

Good to know there will be hot water for his shower, he would become homicidal if the water only ran cold. . . Maybe that's why it doesn't. The . . . Warden?—or whoever the random person is running the place—might have figured out that keeping the murderous inmates happy with small luxuries will minimise the *kill-others* mood swings.

He sticks close to his . . . what? Friendship group? What do they call themselves again? . . . The Gang?

Izz sighs, this place is a world away from earth. The normal everyday lives on the outside are foreign—an entire planet of differences away, no longer accessible to him and these men. For one, on the outside, you don't have to shower with a room full of complete strangers. Trying your hardest to keep your eyes up and not look at anyone.

His peripheral vision is killing him.

Everywhere he turns, strangers' dangling bits are swinging all over the place. His body is too strung out with

CAGED IN

dread, and . . . fear—from the incident in the cafeteria—to relax enough to enjoy his shower.

In here, he's aware he can't judge people by the way they look. That . . . serial killer. . . looked like the nicest person he has ever met. Or . . . Maybe it's more that the male's handsome. Maybe his libido is getting a little carried away, telling him the hot guy is trustworthy.

Ha. Guess again.

He turns his own stream on, scrubbing the square of soap down his chest, rubbing it over his whole body. Keeping his back to the wall. He would rather people check out his package, than leave his ass vulnerable. He does not want to test out those prison shower stories people gossip about in the real world.

Which is why his grip on his soap is strangling, his knuckles white with the effort to hold onto the slippery sucker. If he drops this soap, it's living on the floor. No way is he picking that shit up. Maybe bending over in here is a sign you want some . . . fun—

Izz shudders. Yes, he likes men. Has always liked males. Ever since he can remember. But liking men is entirely different to being fine with allowing any random stranger to have a go at you. Especially when it's in a prison, and those random men could very well kill you.

Not that he has anything against escorts or whatever they call themselves nowadays. Hell, if you want random strangers, that's your business. He has no issues with it. To each their own. Personally, he just isn't interested. He wants to know someone first, before getting to the physical side of things. He wants someone he's attracted to, and who's attracted to him. A male who is easy to get along with and he can be himself around, without being ashamed or embarrassed.

He shoves his face into the shower's spray. Drowning his mind's ramblings. He needs to stop with his weird shower thoughts on hot guys and sex. Or he is liable to get hard, and that is something he doesn't want to do at this particular time. Naked—with a bunch of naked strangers.

He's almost finished scrubbing the suds out of his hair when the last of his group turns their shower head off and strolls over to the door.

Izz hurriedly rinses, like his life depends on it. Anxiety squeezes his heart at how alone he is. Vulnerable—without his friends next to him. Flight is his go to. He's not a strong fighter, and not willing to put himself into that position. On the first night. In this cage.

He practically flees the showers, scurrying out of the steaming room to get back to his friends—

Izz stops short in his hasty retreat when a solid mass steps out into his path. Effectively blocking the doorway. Another inmate entering the showers to scrub clean.

"Sorry. My fault." Izz takes the blame, even though it's not anyone's fault and he isn't entirely sure why he's apologising. It's not as if he ran into the other man.

Izz steps aside. Glancing up—

Only to freeze when he gets a gander at who's filling the door frame. He's patting his subconsciousness on the back for the quick apology now. Grateful for his ingrained manners.

It's the serial killer . . .

What's his name again?

Does the name matter?

CAGED IN

Serial killers don't make you say their name when they kill you, do they? Maybe it's a good thing his mind is blanking on it—or maybe that's bad, maybe it's disrespectful? Maybe the lapse in memory will get him killed—

Stop.

His mind needs to stop. Before he passes the fuck out with the amount of adrenaline pumping through his veins—

Where has all the oxygen gone? He can't breathe. He's choking in here. It's too small—is he claustrophobic? He never thought of himself as having any phobias.

You learn something new every day.

Izz swallows hard, his lips parting to try to suck in more air, to cool his lungs down, to—

He's going to have a panic attack. Or is he already in the clutches of a panic attack? He's never had a panic attack before. If he had to guess what one would look and feel like. This right here. Would be it.

The killer doesn't walk in. Doesn't say a word. Or appear to even be breathing. Maybe there really is an oxygen problem in here? And it's not just a problem in his head. But a physical one that also affects others.

Izz averts his eyes, glancing down—

Whoa. The same dripping bloody red ink is splattered down the insides of his thighs. Matching his arms—it hadn't been a result of the shadow concealing the patterns, there are no patterns, it's . . . blood . . . Whoever did the work knew what they were doing. It's absolutely life-like.

The black tattoo on the killer's abdominal muscles is well-crafted artwork too. An assortment of different animal skulls, held together by twisting, looping barbed wire. All interwoven into some kind of devil's mark. A cross of some type . . .

Leviathan cross? If Izz remembers the name correctly, from his dark-things obsession back in his earlier school years—

He's been staring too long, a few seconds is too long. Dead on the first day in prison is not how he wants to go out.

Shifting uncomfortably, cheeks burning red hot, his gaze roams to the killer's crutch. He quickly averts his eyes. This is definitely one of the times in life where he does not want to be mistaken for checking someone out. Even if he may have—somewhat—been doing just that, it's beside the point. He does not want to offend this particular inmate in the slightest way—

"Izz," Zidie bellows, from around the dividing partition separating the changing rooms and the showers. "What's taking ya so long, we wants' to go."

The bellowed words must have snapped the killer into motion. He strides off. His shoulders rolling in a predatory prowl. His footing sure and strong, his long strides shifting with coiled strength.

Izz stands there, shaken, and staring wide eyed at the doorway where the red and black haired inmate had been standing. His heart still stuttering wildly—the organ hadn't given out yet, so that's a bonus.

Yay for me.

Zidie's head pops out from behind the brick partition. An irritated expression taking over his cupcake face as he spots Izz standing there, "hurry up," he wines.

CAGED IN

Izz blinks back into reality. Glancing over his shoulder, but doesnt see who he's checking for. The killer must have been showering further in. He looks back to find Zidie is gone.

Taking a deep breath, he hurries over to retrieve his clothes and get dressed with the rest of The Gang who are fully clothed. Except Blake, the pale inmate is in the middle of pulling his shoes on, and still shirtless. The vampire lookalike has a nice build, with black tattoos marring the pale skin on his back. His chest completely clear of ink.

"You all good?" Blake shoots an enquiry over to Izz, pulling his slip shoes on—no laces for prisoners.

"Y-yeah," Izz clears his throat, slipping his shirt over his head. "Yeah. I'm good. Just lost in thought."

Blake hums, probably not buying it, but nods anyway.

Izz and Reni made it back to the cells shortly after their showers. Dropping off a few members of The Gang at their own cells along the way. Which's how Izz found out about their different *Wings*, and where their cells are.

His number is A-18910, and his cell is located in A-Wing. He discovered that he and Reni are the only ones in A-Wing. Isco, Erik and Zidie are located in B-Wing. David and Phelix had C-Wing. And Blake is in E-Wing. He isn't sure which block the guy in The Hole is from. But he can always ask or just read the number on the man's shirt when he gets out. However far away that might be.

E.P. WRITER

He was told D-Wing holds all the other activities. Self-help groups, classrooms—because you can study degrees in prison?—There are addict groups—he's sure they're not actually called that, but Zidie was explaining things, so he's not taking the man's word for it on the names.

The Med-Wing is located past D-Wing on the way to E-Wing. Like that's supposed to mean something to him? He can scarcely remember how to get to the showers, let alone where the various Wings are located.

Izz groans again as he shifts in the dark cell, trying to find a comfortable position on his bunk.

It's no use.

Everywhere he rolls—every position he tries—ends with the same results. Metal grinding against bone. It's a torture in and of itself. If being in a cage isn't punishment enough, this paper-thin mattress sure is. If he never has to see, touch, or associate with these mattresses again, he'd vow right here and now to never commit another crime.

He's not impressed with the prison's standards. With how they see fit to punish them in this way. He flops onto his stomach. It's the position with the least amount of pinching and digging.

Reni laughs, from his own bunk, apparently amused by Izz's discomfort.

He glares at the dark lumpy mound on his cellmate's bunk. Unsure if his displeasure is seen in the low lighting—either way, he gives it his all. "How can you lay there so damn still? These things are terrible."

"You get used to it," Reni murmurs, half asleep already.

Izz scoffs, wanting nothing more than to keep his cellmate awake all night to suffer alongside him. He knows

CAGED IN

it's petty and his cellmate doesn't deserve it—with how nice Reni has been to him and everything he's done to help him settle into this crappy life in a caged-in Hell—but his mind still races with the desire for another to feel his pain, so they can understand what he's going through—

Considering Reni was here first, his cellmate would already know the painful bedding situation. And he has lived it longer—long enough to apparently not care about it anymore. How long will Izz have to be here to become use to the torturous bed . . . ?

Nope.

No way. Not happening. He is never going to get use to this. Swishing his legs, he fights to will the mattress into submission. To fluff it up. To do anything.

Why must you be so uncooperative—

"So," Reni begins casually, "What did ya do?"

"Do?" Izz mutters, not paying Reni much mind as he flops like a dying fish on his metal frying pan.

"To get ya ass thrown in here?" Reni clarifies.

Izz curses under his breath, resigning his feeble attempts to sleep comfortably.

Are you allowed to ask about this? About how someone came to be an inmate? Or is that just in the movies where it's wrong to ask another prisoner that question? He doesn't know or care at this particular moment. Does it matter if Reni knows?

"I . . . acquired belongings that may not have been mine," Izz hedges. He only stole to provide for his family, he wasn't stealing out of greed. He doesn't want to be placed into the thieving category of those who do it for themselves with selfish intentions.

Reni laughs, a cheerful noise at odds with how depressed Izz feels. "Just say you're a thief, ay."

"I'm not admitting to anything." Izz leaves the rest unsaid. That he doesn't view what he did as being a bad person. Sure, it was wrong, he knows it was breaking the law. But he would do it a million times over to get the money they needed to save his sister's life. She had to have those meds, those operations, and everything else. And she never would have had her life-saving treatments without the money he contributed in a not-so-legal fashion. He has no regrets about stealing for her. His only regret was changing his MO, and, in turn, getting caught.

"Smart," Reni rearranges his body, facing Izz to make it easier for them to talk, "Well, it would be, if ya aren't already doing your time for it."

Izz lets out a dismissive noise, waving off Reni, even though the other can't really see him in the dark cell. He's not about to explain his life choices to someone he just met. Reni might have been nice to him so far but it doesn't mean he completely trusts him.

"What about you?" Izz isn't too sure he wants to know, but better he does. If Reni turns out to be some crazed lunatic, it will be better to know now, so he can prepare himself and not be caught unaware.

"Oh, I *acquired* cars that may not have belonged to me," Reni mocks Izz' response.

Izz puts on an accent to mimic his cellmate, and shoots back, "just say ya a thief."

It's silent for several seconds before they both burst out laughing, which earns them disgruntled colourful responses from the neighbouring cells—filled with more

CAGED IN

cursing than anything tangible, however, the meanings behind the words are crystal clear.

It takes Izz a long time to fall asleep. He lays awake, listening to Reni's soft snoring. And the not-so-subtle snoring from inmates in the surrounding cells—who snore like damn nuclear missiles going off. How does someone snore that loud and not wake themselves up? How have their cellmates not strangled them already? He does not condone murder. But, in this instance, he's willing to make an exception.

And they all got pissy at me for laughing.

He groans loudly, pulling his pillow out from under his head to smother his face with it. If he suffocates he won't have to listen to the noises in this stupid prison. A caged-in Hell-hole.

Won't have to worry about the crappy mattress either. It's a win-win situation.

Or perhaps not . . .

He wants to go home. Wants to be there for his mum. For his sister. He wants to go back to the way it was, before he started pickpocketing. Or back further to before his sister's cancer, and stay there, in that safe time and place. Before life became too real. Too cold and unruly.

Izz eventually drifts off, too exhausted to stay conscious a second longer.

6

By the time the prison bells rudely summon Izz into consciousness, his cellmate is already awake and ready for a new day. He can hear Reni pacing around, or maybe jogging on the spot? Izz's eyes are tightly screwed shut, and he harbours no plans to open them anytime soon.

He despises morning people—cheery, bright, happy, wide awake—morning people. He holds a slight jealous grudge towards them. He can't help it, it takes several hundred alarms every minute and an arsenal of willpower, to drag his butt out of bed. So, yes, he's resentful towards people who can spring out of bed one hundred percent awake on the first alarm. When he feels like a sleep deprived zombie.

Izz cracks an eye open, peeking through his lashes, to see his cellmate bouncing near the cell door. A trapped dog ready to be let out for its morning run.

Sighing dramatically, he rolls off his bed. Stumbling to his feet, to relieve himself in the microscopic prison toilet. You would think a metal toilet would cost more, wouldn't a plastic one be cheaper for the prison to buy? Although . . .

CAGED IN

plastic toilet lids break easily, no doubt an opportune weapon for a murderous inmate.

He lets loose a loud yawn, receiving a protesting jaw pop for his troubles. Rubbing a hand down his face to stimulate his mind for another *'fun'* day in this *'wonderful'* prison.

Cage is more like it.

Izz winces at his thoughts, they're saturated in sarcasm. Dripping with resentment. When one could argue he'd brought these circumstances upon himself—

Another shrill alarm sounds, the cell doors beeping open. Another day in Hell. Another day of punishment. Wonder what this day will bring his way?

"Be back. Gots' some people to see," his cellmate yells over his shoulder on the way out the door.

Izz grunts his reply. Letting Reni interpret the response any way he chooses. From *'yeah, I don't care,'* to, *'okay, no problem'*.

God, my back is aching.

Shuffling over to his bunk, he stiffly slumps onto the flat paper mattress, arching his back to crack some of the stiffness out. He's going to develop serious joint problems sleeping on this bunk in a matter of nights. How will he fare after months on the thing? He'll be walking around like a ninety-year-old crippled by arthritis by the end of the week.

Izz rearranges his slept-in clothes. Running his hands through his hair to flatten the unruly tangles into submission. He might need to get a hairbrush or comb, at some point—he's seriously lacking in the money department. Whatever money he had is with his family and it's going to stay that way. They need it more than he does.

How long until his meagre savings run dry? How long until his mum's the sole one making money for the two of them? How long until they can't pay the rent anymore—

He springs to his feet. If he stays in here with his mind eating away at him, he's liable to try that escape plan out the tiny window. See if his head truly is too big to fit out.

Izz steps free of his cell. Sauntering over to the railing. He peers at the floor below. There are so many inmates out already, interacting with each other, laughing and making a ruckus. They must be used to the early rising.

What time is it?

Early.

Early is what it is.

He yawns once again. Thumping his elbow onto the rails to lean his chin on his palm. Observing the inmates from above, not absorbing many details, allowing the chattering lull of voices to flow over him. Encasing him in a blanket of calm. He might fall asleep right here, can't be any worse than his bunk.

Izz locates Reni far beneath, leaning his ass back against a table, arms crossed, as he chats with a group of inmates Izz has not seen before.

Or perhaps he has but hadn't taken notice of them. After all, he's floating among an uncountable quantity of new faces. Trying to recognise everybody in less than a day is an impossible feat.

"Hey. You must be the new guy."

CAGED IN

Izz peeks at the voice, not bothering to remove his face from his palm. An inmate is leaning casually against the bars of the next cell. An amused smirk on their face.

The inmate's demeanour screams—sleazy and sketchy. With a terribly inked dragon tattoo—he believes it's a dragon, hard to tell with the back-alley quality of work—smack dab in the middle of a shirtless chest. The colours vomiting together in a swirl of mismatched slime.

"I guess so," Izz replies, to be polite. No need to make enemies if he can avoid it.

The inmate rolls off the bars, slinking over to the rails Izz's reclining on. Vomit tattoo and all, slithering too close. Way too close to be respectful of his personal space.

Izz straightens to his full height. His instincts flaring that this man harbours dishonourable intentions. So he backs off, leaving a considerably larger distance between them. Snarling at the man soundlessly, when the inmate again slithers up into his space.

"What's the hurry?" the inmate hisses, licking his dry lips. "We can hang in my cell. Have a little . . . *chat.*"

With the way the man's eyes glint, Izz has no doubts about what '*chat'* implies. And he has no interest in going anywhere with him.

"Nah, I'm good," Izz takes yet another step back.

What he wants is a few hours to wake up. A few hours of peace to laze around and try to forget about his stiff muscles. Instead, here he is. In a crappy situation he wants no part of.

It's too early in the morning to be dealing with this intrusion.

He takes another step back—

Colliding into a solid chest. Izz pitches forward, away from the inmate at his back. He hadn't been aware of anyone else approaching him. He's lucky the other inmate doesn't hold a weapon—he hopes the other inmate doesn't have a weapon. Glancing between the two men, he can't see any weapons, but that doesn't mean they aren't armed. The second inmate is twice Izz's size, a weapon would really only be a flex. The man's sheer size is weapon enough.

He opens his mouth to tell them to leave him alone. He's not interested. Doesn't want any trouble. But before he gets a word out, they back off, slinking away as fast as they slithered up.

Well, that was weird—

Reni is at the top of the metal stairs. Frown in place, he clearly saw the interaction taking place. Or at the very least, saw the two men standing close to Izz, before they scurried off, to who knows where.

"Ignore them," Reni states, strolling over to stand at Izz's side. "They're all talk. Got no spine in 'em." Reni rests a comforting hand on Izz's shoulder, directing Izz towards the stairs, "let's go eat. Shall we?"

An order? Phrased as a question? Is Reni more worried than he let on?

No . . . You're overthinking it.

Breakfast is basically the same as dinner. A long queue. Numerous voices mingling together fighting for dominance. Too many smells to separate food from body

CAGED IN

odour. Four inmates pacing up and down serving. Trays being lugged off to various tables.

On the menu today is bacon, cooked to a perfect crisp. A tray of scrambled eggs. Toast and various kinds of spreads in little containers. Small cartons of milk and juice boxes. Sausages. Some type of gooey sludge—oats?

Gross, oats are the worst.

He's served by the same beefy inmate, who gave him extra bacon, and commented on his politeness once more. He can't help it, he's always said thank you or please to people serving him. From clothing stores, to restaurants—on the rare occasion he went to a restaurant. He was taught to use manners, it's hardwired into him, he does it without conscious thought.

Izz tears into a bacon strip, slouching at the same table where he had his first meal. However this time he deliberately sits facing the kitchen. Studiously avoiding a certain back corner, at a certain barren table, to which a certain spikey-haired individual is present this morning. Not that he was looking when he walked over to The Gang's table. Of course he wasn't because that would be wrong.

It was merely a little glance. Does not count.

He knows he has no place to eye fuck a frickin' serial killer. Sure the male is handsome. But he *'is'* a killer. A murderer. A psychopath . . .

Izz will end up being a name in an article, if he's not careful. A name lost within an array of other names. A statistic in a list of kills for a famous serial killer. Forgotten except for a number people recite when talking about a serial killer.

Everyone knows the serial killers' name, no one remembers the victims' name. They become part of the number of kills the serial killer accomplished during their reign of terror.

He needs to focus on something less depressing. Less real. He doesn't want to know how many people in here have killed. He'd rather not think about it when he's living with them.

Izz digs his fork into the scrambled eggs, they don't taste that bad, a little bland, but overall not too bad. Orange juice to wash it down with—

He would love some pancakes. He usually drinks orange juice when he cooks pancakes, so his stomach automatically puts two-and-two together—his stomach is very disappointed it isn't getting pancakes with its orange juice. But the only other options were apple juice and milk. He didn't want apple juice and he hates plain milk. Flavoured milk is the only way he can drink it—he isn't sure the prison puts flavoured milk in their meal plan. He'll guess that they don't.

He isn't too fond of the processed orange juice either. He squeezed his own at home, when he cooked pancakes every Saturday as a treat for his little sister. She loves pancakes . . .

He's brought back from his memories when a hand ruffles through his hair. Blinking, he realises he was so engrossed in his memories, he'd missed when the table cleared off.

The Gang is lingering near the double doors by the kitchen, waiting patiently for Izz—while Reni is taking back his hand, an inquisitive expression on his face.

CAGED IN

"Ya coming? Or are you going to sit here all day staring off into nothingness?"

Izz smiles, pleased he hadn't imagined the friendships he'd formed among the group. Rising to his feet, he dumps his tray and joins the others. Walking as a group off to wherever. He has no idea where they're heading, but he doesn't care. It's not like they have many options, they're in a giant cage with little to nothing to look at. Everything is white bricks and long corridors. Corridors which twist, and turn, and weave throughout the prison buildings.

When they eventually arrive at their destination, he is officially lost. Absolutely no clue how to get back to the cafeteria, or his cell.

He can see a glassed-in room—a tiny prison store, with one inmate behind the bulletproof barrier. A guard stands close by, leaning back against the wall near the inmate, with a bored expression stamped on his features. Barred doors hang loose in front of the pair—like the shutters of an old house—indicating the store is open for purchases.

This must be the Commissary Store—do they call it a Commissary Store? or just Commissary?

There is a large variety of products lining the shelves. Snacks—chocolate bars, little bags of lollies and nuts, popcorn, protein bars. Beverages—a whole selection of ready-mix drinks, like coffee and hot chocolate, as well as bottled water, juice, bottled energy drinks. Foods—ramen noodles, soups, flavoured oatmeal, beef jerky, rice. Hygiene products—shampoos, soaps, toilet paper, toothbrushes. Electronics—MP3 players, headphones, batteries, book lights. There are even condiments like salt, pepper, garlic powder, taco seasoning. Clothing—shorts, socks, shoes, pyjamas, gloves. Stationary products—paper, envelopes, note pads.

And countless more items. The shelves are crammed full of products. He's stunned by the huge range of items, he had not expected such a vast selection in a prison store.

There are crayons too, the inmates must not be trusted with pens . . . Those would make some crude weapons. He'd feel pretty pathetic if he's killed by a pen—

Oh. No. Wait. There are tiny boxes of microscopic pencils. The crayons look easier to write with than those tiny little half pencils.

Izz waits in line with the rest of The Gang—he has no money to spend, everything he has is with his family—but it's not like he has anything better to do.

Besides, he enjoys hanging out with Zidie, the inmate might be a little over the top and loud, but he's a shining light of fun in the depressing dingy prison.

Izz likes the others too, Zidie is a little extra happiness he needs to keep himself grounded, so he doesn't spiral into dread and worry. His cellmate's constant talking is also giving his mind something to focus on.

Right now, Reni is in some heated debate with Erik over which ramen flavouring is the best, and which one should be burned and never spoken of again. Reni has his votes in the beef pile, and Erik is adamant that beef tastes like dog shit and the only good flavour is chicken.

Izz doesn't mind either flavour, he rarely ate packet noodles, but when he does he isn't fussed over what flavour they are—

CAGED IN

Izz involuntarily groans when his eyes land on the far corner of Commissary—quickly biting off the sound in his throat and glancing around, grateful no one heard him.

They have mattresses, available to buy.

Granted, they are the crappy paper thin ones he already has, but you could stack them on top of each other. They also cost three hundred dollars, how that tiny paper crap cost so much is a mystery. He can only dream. No way can he afford one, let alone the stack it will take to create a decently cushioned mattress—

Izz swivels his gaze from the offensive sight. Trying to keep his bitterness internal and not show anything to the inmates crowding the corridor.

His newly acquired friends are bunched at the window, handing over their prison numbers, to order all kinds of items.

Blake buys envelopes and paper—must be writing to someone on the outside? Izz wishes he could, he would love to write to his little sister. Let her know he's still thinking of her, and even if she can't see him each day, he's still there for her.

Isco fills his pockets with several protein bars, a chocolate bar, pretzels, nuts, beef jerky, chili powder, and a bottle of energy drink. The whole shopping list of foods disappearing into his prison clothes. How he managed to fit it all in his pockets is a mystery.

Zidie went for an unhealthy binge of practically every snack available. Collecting one of everything, as well as a pack of ramen.

"Not getting anything?" Zidie's over-excited face pops up in Izz's line of sight. So close, if Izz pursed his lips, he could kiss the boisterous inmate.

Does Zidie not grasp what personal space is?

"Not this time," Izz doesn't want to give Zidie the true reason for his lack of purchasing.

When Zidie opens his mouth to demand answers—answers Izz's not prepared to give—Izz speaks right over him, effectively cutting him off.

"So, Reni, what do we do in this place to keep from tearing out our hair in boredom?" Please let this be the end of Zidie's fact finding mission. He isn't in the mood to go into his money problems and the reasons behind them. His sister's illness isn't something he wants anyone in here to know.

Reni sidles up to Zidie's left, eating some kind of bar he bought, grinning around his mouth full of sugary treat.

"Well . . ." Reni muses. "You can play basketball—if one of the gangs isn't hogging the court. Or they have meetings you can attend, you know, for anger management and stuff like that. There's a church . . . Somewhere. Where you can pray—or sit there doing whatever Godly things you're supposed to do in a church. They also have the prison jobs after lunch, to kill a few hours before dinner. You could go to the library and check out books—"

"Wait. Prison job?" Izz interrupts. Flashing his palm in a stop motion, to physically slap a pause in Reni's sentence.

"Yeah. Haven't you got one yet?" Reni's brow raises as he glances over at Zidie, as if Zidie will fill him in on Izz's work status.

CAGED IN

"No." Izz moves over to the side to allow an inmate to squeeze past him, on their way down the corridor. "How do I do that? And what are the jobs?"

"There are loads of different jobs, there's—" The three of them walk away from Commissary, to lean against the wall further down the corridor, as more inmates try to push their way into line. "—the kitchen, gardening, laundry—I'm in laundry. Pretty much all of us are. Except Erik and Phelix, 'cause they're too good for that—"

Phelix spits profanities at Reni from his place at the Commissary window, giving Reni the bird over his shoulder as he finishes his order. Reni grins in response.

"They work in the library," Reni continues, unfazed. "Lazy fuckers. The rest of us actually *work.*"

"Yeah, 'cause cleaning peoples socks is difficult '*work*'," Erik snaps at Reni, using air-quotes on '*work*' to mock him. Mimicking Phelix with flashing the middle finger.

"You'd have to see the counsellors to get a job assignment," Izz flinches when Blake's voice emerges from the space right next to him.

I need to observe my surroundings better, so I know where people are.

Drawing in a deep breath to calm his nerves, Izz gives Blake his undivided attention. "Where do I find them?"

"We can drop you off at his office, on the way to E-Wing, I need to drop this stuff off at my cell anyway." Blake jostles the papers and chips in his hands which Izz hadn't seen.

So much for taking notice of his surroundings, that conviction lasted a good two seconds.

If I don't get it together, things could turn sour real fast.

"That would be helpful, thanks. This place is like a maze." A deadly maze, with criminals around every corner. Technically Izz's one of those criminals too, according to the law. But laws shouldn't stop you from getting help when you need it.

I didn't do it for myself.

He sighs, he would like a map to study so he can find his way around the maze of cages. He has a hunch asking a guard for a map of the prison would not work out so well. They'd probably add time for an '*attempted prison break*'— or something colourful like that—just to be assholes. Reminds him of the first guard who shoved him around, and fastened the cuffs excessively tight—

"You'll get used to it."

Izz blinks—like a stunned puppy—at Blake's response.

Did the vampire lookalike read his mind?

Blake smiles softly, obviously noticing Izz's confusion. "The prison. You'll get used to where everything is."

Ohhhhh . . .

He's relieved no one can read his mind, or he'd feel like more of an idiot than he already does. He's way too out of it. Actually thinking Blake read his mind. For someone who's a social butterfly, he sure is acting like a socially awkward recluse.

The sad smile Blake gives Izz says, '*it isn't something you want to get used to, but spend enough time here and it's inevitable*'.

Izz doesn't want to spend enough time in here to get used to it. However, he doesn't have a say in the matter. He is stuck here, until the day his sentence finishes.

7

Izz drifts behind as The Gang ambles their way down a corridor. The others are eating while engrossed in subject matters he can't engage in—without background information. Discussions of previous days in their prison life. Names of inmates or guards he doesn't recognise. Locations in prison he has no clue where to find. He's a little disgruntled at being left out, it is his second day here so he shouldn't feel frustrated with drifting on the outskirts . . . He is though . . .

Zidie tore off a hunk of his chocolate bar, presenting it to Izz in his outstretched hand, a chocolaty swirl of nuts that Izz eagerly accepts.

"Thanks," Izz nibbles it delicately, savouring the treat for as long as possible.

Anxiety at seeing a counsellor has his stomach participating in acrobatics and the chocolate chunks within it practising aerobics. He isn't sure why he's antsy, usually he doesn't squirm away from social interactions.

His mind and personality are frazzled in this place, he hopes he can regain his old self. . . . Eventually. Whoever this counsellor is, maybe they can help him on that front. To find himself again, and to cope with this new life he's been thrown into.

"So what job will you get? Huh? Huh?" Zidie energetically interrogates, circling Izz in a dizzying fashion, while spontaneously skipping, "You better pick laundry. Don't you dare ditch me for that stupid library."

Izz laughs, grabbing the overzealous inmate by the arm to halt his erratic movements. "I guess—"

Zidie grips Izz, tugging him into a bone-bending bear hug, shaking him back and forth like a dog with a chew toy, "Bye, bestie," Zidie gestures to the door next to them.

Oh, they arrived quicker than he'd expected.

"Don't disappoint me," Zidie throws out ominously, swinging an accusing finger towards Izz.

He rolls his eyes. That man is crazy. Yet Zid is no doubt going to make this cage bearable to live in. Somewhat acceptable to call it . . . home—

Ah, nope. That still sounds weird.

"Meet us out in the yard when you're done," Zidie bellows over his shoulder as he turns away.

Hesitating at the door with a plaque reading *'Counsellors Office'*, Izz's motionless. His anxiety is spiking, and his palms are clammy with sweat.

Come on Izz, pull yourself together. It can't be that bad. What's your problem?

He steels his shoulders, sucking in a deep breath, and raps his knuckles on the office door.

"Come in," a muffled voice drifts out from behind the wooden panels.

CAGED IN

Izz does as instructed. Pushing the door wide. Shuffling in. Clicking it shut behind him.

The office is small. White walls—as if he expects another colour in this bland prison. Tall cabinets stacked with books, a whole range in *Law* and many more in *Psychology*.

A large oak desk, with tree-trunk sized legs, housing an old style-computer, keyboard, mouse, a little cup of pens and notepads. A soft armchair in front of it for guests.

The man perched in the office chair behind the desk is exactly as he envisions a counsellor to be. Neatly cropped hair, smooth-rimmed glasses, tailored suit, and professional smile plastered in place. Smelling of tea tree oil and freshly cut grass.

"Take a seat." The counsellor murmurs, flicking a manicured hand at the armchair.

Izz settles in, nervously wiping his hands on his prison pants. He feels like he's being judged and scrutinised at the same time.

When did it get so hot in here?

"What can I do for you, inmate . . . A-18910," the counsellor speaks while squinting at Izz's uniform to read the prison number. "Let me just bring up your file."

The man swings his wheeled chair to the side, to tap at the ancient computer's keyboard, clicking and scrolling around on the screen.

"Jasper is fine," Izz tells the counsellor, his eyes darting around the room looking for something to occupy himself with while he waits. He can't see the computer's screen so he can't snoop on whatever the counsellor is searching in—other inmates' Criminal Records?

"Okay. Sure thing," the counsellor mutters, still focusing on his tapping and mouse clicking. "I swear this dinosaur computer is so slow I could manually find, and collect the files, from the filing room, a heck of a lot faster. And it's located on the other side of the prison."

Izz isn't sure what to say to the complaint. *'Alright'*. *'That's annoying'*. *'I feel sorry for you—'*

That last one definitely isn't it. Sure the man has a slow computer. So what. At least he gets to leave this place each day, and doesn't have to sleep in a tiny cell with a hundred other men snoring all night long.

"Finally," the counsellor exclaims. "Here we are. Jasper Marcelo, nineteen—oh, turning twenty in a few weeks, congrats." The counsellor reads from his computer screen. "Arrested for . . . Theft. Five-year prison sentence, three with good behaviour—It'll pass quicker than you think. No other arrests, first time in. All in all, not too bad." Steepling his fingers, the man closely examines Izz from his position across the desk. "Compared to the majority of other inmates I deal with, you're an easy one. So what can I do for you?"

Easy one?

What, like he's a new pigeon in a cage with other birds who've shown acts of aggressive behaviour—compared to his pliant nature?

One day he might end up among the watch list. If that dragon tattooed creep slithers his way back to Izz's cell. He will not roll over and take it, no matter if his record states he's non-threatening—or non-aggressive—or however they describe inmates who don't have murderous tendencies.

CAGED IN

Exhaling his irritation, he addresses the counsellor as politely as he can muster, "I was informed I have to see you about a prison job?"

"Oh. Yes. By whom?"

"Ah . . ." Is that really important? "A friend," Izz hedges. He's not sure where the counsellor is going with this line of questioning? Or why it's important who told him?

"Friend? Already." The counsellor leans forward, placing his elbows on the desk to rest his chin in his steepled hands.

Already . . . ?

The counsellor has a weird way of wording things, like he's belittling and inspecting Izz at the same time. Is it that hard to imagine Izz making friends the first day in prison? Is this an uncommon thing or something? Or is this counsellor full of accusations and scrutiny?

"He's more a friend of my cellmate, I've only just met him, so . . . yeah." Izz rubs the nape of his neck awkwardly, unsure why he feels the desire to explain—the counsellor's hard eyes boring into him might be part of the reason.

He squirms at the look that gets cast his way. Nervous doesn't even begin to describe how he's feeling about this conversation.

"I see . . . And your cellmate would be?"

Maybe Izz should leave and forget about the job? He can always buy wool from Commissary and take up knitting. Do they sell wool at Commissary? He couldn't afford it even if they do. He might have to resort to unravelling the threads in his shirt, use those to knit himself a hat or something—

Actually, he would rather gouge his eyes out with a spoon, instead of being caught knitting by another inmate. The no-eyes thing could work in his favour too, save him from the sight of the counsellor's heavy examining gaze and observant eyes.

"Reni," Izz tentatively replies.

"Reni . . ." The man taps his lips and glances into the far corner as if the answers are written on the ceiling's faded paint.

"I don't know his last name, or even if that's his real name. He said he was the guide for new inmates—"

"Ah. yes, yes, that would be Romos Casimiro. He's a lovely inmate, very well behaved. A good thing you have him as your cell buddy, there are a ton of unsavoury inmates in this prison who would make nightmarish cell buddies."

That is not helping his nerves. Isn't this guy supposed to be a counsellor here to help people? Not send them into panic attacks and have them leaving the office with more worries than they came in with.

And why call it buddies? Makes it sound like a little kids' camping trip—a boy scouts' mission—not an inescapable cage filled with hardened criminals.

"I—yes, I guess. I haven't really met many inmates yet." Well, there are those two creepy A-Wing locals—who left a bad taste in his mouth. He's in no hurry to bump into them anytime in the future.

There's also the serial killer, although, technically, Izz hasn't met him. Merely observed the inmate from a safe distance. Which gives him stalker vibes now that he puts it into perspective in his own mind. Why does he feel like

CAGED IN

the creeper in this instance? The male's a serial killer. Who wouldn't stare on their first day?

Besides, Izz was studying the male before he found out about the killing part—he'll choose to ignore the *whys* to that part of the story. He was not eye fucking a serial killer. Nope. He was studying a potential threat. That was all.

Even you don't believe that lie. Izz's inner voice mocks him.

"Perfectly understandable," the man's professional tone wafts into Izz's ears. "You've been here for what? Less than twenty-four hours?"

"Yeah." Has it truly been so little time? Izz feels a million years older than he did when he arrived. He's going to be a walking casket on his release day at this rate.

"Okay, so, about the job. Ah. You can't really pick. The system picks for you. Takes a day or two—usually—to work it out. I'll put your name into the programming thingy and presto magic-o, you'll get your assignment."

Izz sighs. He can't choose what he gets—he had to come here to get a job, but he can't choose it. And they put his name into the system themselves, to wait for a machine to hand them a result. Why didn't they automatically do this when he was being processed into prison in the first place? Instead of wasting all this time.

"Not to worry," the counsellor continues, "if it's something you hate, you can file paperwork to me for the Warden and see about getting moved. Although, it can take months to sort out. Warden's a busy man. And he has to approve all transfers. And a job transfer is low on the scale of importance. Sitting under—approval for cell transfers or Wing transfers, inmates moving in and out of solitary confinement, and a whole heap of other prison related drama I won't bore you with. It's simply easier to stay in the job you're assigned, grit your teeth, and muscle through—you're not here too long anyway. Unless, you're in fear of another inmate at your job stabbing you or harming you in some way. That usually jumps the transfers of jobs up in the Warden's to-do pile. Usually. If you happen to get stabbed, you're pulled out immediately."

Great, so if Izz hates the job, he has to endure it unless someone hates him more and shivs him.

Excellent. Izz rolls his eyes internally.

How is this man a counsellor? He's more of a doom and gloom giver. Handing out all the information—including every piece of bad information—even if you don't want it.

"So . . . Ah . . ." The counsellor contemplates. Tacking on questions after a short stretch of silence that Izz refuses to fill, "how are you finding it so far? No troubles?"

"Prison?" Izz questions, he doesn't particularly care what the counsellor means—

Izz wants to leave, will it be rude to get up and walk out? You can't be sent to The Hole for that, can you?

"Yes." The counsellor leans back in his chair, settling into a more comfortable position.

Izz's anxiety spikes at the movement, an indication this conversation is going to be longer than he first hoped.

"I haven't really seen much of the prison," Izz thinks of the two inmates outside his cell, they hadn't really done anything, except be creepy. He also isn't a snitch. "It hasn't been too gruelling so far. I've got a group that's been helping me out, my cellmate introduced me to them, they're the . . . people he hangs out with."

CAGED IN

He's not sure it'd be wise to call them *The Gang* in front of this counsellor, even if they aren't technically a true gang. At least . . . that's what Reni told him . . .

"Sounds like you're finding your place and fitting in nicely. It's good to find companions to keep you from going numb in this place. But just remember, it is prison so don't get too attached to people in here."

The man had been on a roll—nice and kind—then killed it with his salad of *crush-your-dreams-and-sharpen-your-fears*. Why can't the counsellor be more joyous? Dish out a bit of hope and ease your worries. Not stack onto them with more stuff to worry you to death after deflating your small balloons of light and hope in this colourless place.

"I know that," Izz grits out. It's increasingly hard not to lose patience and snap at the man.

Doesn't mean you have to bring it all up. I'm happy to live in a bubble, while I try to stay sane during my time in this cage. Thank you very much. Izz grumbles to himself.

"Very good. Okay, I'll add you into the system to get you that job assignment." The counsellor rapidly types into the keyboard. "Anything else happened? . . . Anything noteworthy? Anything got you worried?"

First inmate in here who caught my eye is a serial killer. Who was staring at me as I stared at him. Something I've been told I'm not supposed to do, or I will end up dead—

"No. Nothing." Izz elects to say instead. "I mean, the mattress sucks," Izz tacks on, chuckling nervously. "But, no, nothing."

"Good . . . Good . . . You can come by anytime if that changes, or you just have things you want to get off your chest."

I'd rather tell the metal non-mirror mirror in my cell, at least that won't lob more things at me to stress over.

"Thank you." Izz forces a polite smile.

"Okay, off you pop. I'll have a guard let you know when that job assignment comes through."

Izz nods, straightening to his full height, to leave the bad news counsellor and the rather comfortable chair to their own devices. Rushing to the door and his prison life waiting beyond it.

By the time Izz enters a familiar corridor leading to the cafeteria, he can hear the busy hustle and bustle of lunch being served and consumed. The discussion in the counsellor's office had taken longer than Izz initially anticipated. And his directionless wandering—throughout the prison, to find his way back to A-Wing, and in turn, the cafeteria—wasted even more time.

Izz pushes past the double doors—the same doors The Gang left from to go to Commissary—opening the way into the busy cafeteria. He must have arrived near the end of lunch, the cafeteria isn't its usual busy self, appearing rather empty. Many of the tables are bare and others only dusted with men finishing off their meals.

He spots the others with their own trays gathered around their usual table. At least they're all there, and he won't be stuck eating alone, with nothing to occupy his mind.

Izz joins the back of the queue. There aren't many inmates waiting to eat, he's at the food serving bar in no time. Sliding his tray along the wooden bar to collect

CAGED IN

what's left over to choose from. He doesn't have much of a selection, most of the holding trays now empty.

"Was wondering where you were at?" The usual beefy server enquires of Izz. "You almost missed lunch. How's your first day going?"

Izz always seems to be served by this specific inmate. Not sure if it's a coincidence or not? Probably a coincidence. He hasn't been to too many meals and there aren't many servers. Not compared to the amount of inmates they prep food for.

"Was here yesterday." He's tired of all the questions being thrown at him. He wants to sit and eat, and not answer any more questions today. It's only lunch, and he is already drained, his life force sucked dry.

"First official day," the server smiles, serving a large portion of lasagne and a bottle of water.

Izz's fighting his fatigue. Trying to keep his mind involved in the interaction is like staring at high beams—lots of effort to keep his eyes open, loads of pain shooting through his head with little to no outside information being retained, his whereabouts a foggy and blurry uncertainty.

"It's been alright. I guess. Beds are uncomfortable. Had to see the counsellor to get a job assignment."

"Explains why you looked so tired this morning. Takes a while to get used to sleeping here. And the counsellor is a real . . . nutcase."

"I'm not really a morning person anyway," Izz half-heartedly explains, dismissing the counsellor comment. He agrees but he's not about to bag-out the guy who sends reports to the Warden. He'd prefer not to piss off the one who could potentially sabotage his transfer paperwork if he wants to move jobs or anything. Best to avoid it, just in case.

"You want chocolate or vanilla cake?" The inmate serving enquires, his mood way too cheerful for Izz's liking—

Come to think of it, Izz doesn't know the inmate's name. Has never bothered to ask—he's too tired to care to ask now.

"Chocolate would be nice, thank you."

The server stacks two hefty slices of individually wrapped cake on the side of Izz's tray. He scrutinises the cakes, puzzled why this server is always so nice to him. He's certain the other inmates aren't getting two slices. Although . . . after his crappy start to the day, he isn't about to question this one kindness.

"Always got extra for those with manners," the beefy server smirks, leaning in closer to Izz to whisper, "don't go showing the others, they might get jealous."

At the table, Izz slumps down next to Blake. He opens his bottle, sipping the rehydrating water, enjoying the cool liquid running down his parched throat.

He can see the mohawked inmate in his peripheral vision. He can sense the killer's presence. A prey animal, aware it's being watched. He's proud of himself for not giving in to the urge to glance over. Instead he keeps his focus on the men at his own table. Which is why he spies his cellmate curiously raising a brow at his extra slice of cake. He's too muddled in his head from everything the

CAGED IN

counsellor said—and implied—wrecking his day, with its negative energy—to care enough to explain that the server thinks his manners are a nice change from the rest of the rude inmates and due to this, gives him extra food each meal.

He can't deal with anyone else shitting on his bubble today—he knows the server is most likely flirting with him. He knows he needs to let the beefy inmate down slowly. He knows the longer it goes on the worse it will be. He is not interested in pissing off the people who handle his food. Which is why he doesn't want to think about it. Why he's avoiding the thoughts and living in his little bubble. He wants to leave it to lie on its own, not poke at it until it starts throwing punches—

And now he's thinking about it. Destroying his own little safety bubble, and killing his lasagne with his fork in the process.

He inwardly sighs, forcing himself to set the fork aside before he has a new dish of mashed lasagne.

Take it one day at a time. One problem at a time. Deal with getting the Job assignment first, then deal with whatever comes next. Izz pep talks himself, not truly buying what his mind is trying to sell.

8

The Gang sneaks off to their jobs after they finish lunch. Izz remains at their table, unsure what to do with himself. Glancing around the room he observes the slow filtering of inmates off to their own assigned jobs, wherever those may be.

I could sit here until dinner?

Then again, that might get boring . . .

Maybe find the library Reni was talking about? Izz never liked sitting still to read novels. Perhaps that can be a new talent for him to learn in here. . .

No. No, that sounds torturous and dull.

He groans. Rubbing his face. When he drops his hands, his eyes lock on a certain male—an inmate he shouldn't be looking at—alone on the isolated table in the corner—

The killer's eyes shift over, meeting Izz's—

Yep, I'm not staying here.

Izz practically face plants it when his shoe catches on the bench in his hasty retreat to leave. Stumbling, he heads elsewhere, not to be caught in the vicinity of the serial killer. The one he's not supposed to be anywhere near.

CAGED IN

The one he keeps thinking about and staring at. It's like he wants to die. He should chain his wrist and cuff himself to the bed frame, and lie there for the serial killer to disembowel. He may as well, he's making it easy enough. Constantly sneaking glances at the inmate—not so unnoticed, if the way the male looked over at him is any indication.

He may be lining himself up as the perfect victim. Predators can sense weakness, can't they? Well, if they can, he's surely shown this dangerous killer how weak he is and how easy a target he would make.

He knows the double doors on the opposite side of the kitchen lead to the yard. You can see the grass beyond them, flashing every time someone exits or enters.

It's where he decides he will go, in the complete opposite direction of the serial killer.

He's going to check out the yard. See if it's as vast and unexpected as the selection of Commissary goods, or as flat and lifeless as the prison pillows.

Only one way to find out.

Slapping his palms on either side of the doors, Izz exits the cafeteria—movie actor style—throwing both doors wide—and instantly regrets it when one side slams into an inmate—

Who stands so close with their back to doors anyway? That's just asking to be hit.

Who throws open doors like they're a damn stunt double in a movie scene. Izz's inner voice snarks back at him.

"Fuck's your problem," the inmate growls, turning to glare ice into his veins.

Izz has two options. Hit the inmate with aggression or . . . Apologise? Grovel? Run? Maybe those three can be a one and done combo deal.

Fight or flight—

Or dismiss? He's choosing to go with dismissal. Play it off. Act indifferent.

"Nothing," Izz squares his shoulders and strides on, throwing his whole appearance into the persona of confidence—while moving swiftly to the small building across the way, to hide behind. It's close to the fence line, but not quite touching, so there should—in theory—be a gap between the two to hide in.

"I am filled with confidence," Izz mutters under his breath, optimistically lying to himself.

Izz skims the outskirts of the small compact shed-like structure which appears as if its purpose is to house the mower for the yard's lawn, and perhaps tools for the garden. He wonders what types of plants they grow here, fruits and vegetables? Or flowers? Both?

Izz rounds the corner, hoping to have some privacy to lay back in the surprisingly lush green grass and stare at the blue clear sky—

What he does not expect is to find an inmate—small and cute—leaning against the building's wall. He swallows hard as his mind comes to terms with what his eyes are identifying—

A guard, stepping away from an inmate—

The inmate who has their front squashed against the building, back bent, ass out, with pants bunched around the knees—

CAGED IN

A guard who is clearly tucking back in. And zipping up—and turning to leave—

Izz quickly ducks back behind the wall. To avoid being caught. Too late to run off, that will definitely make it obvious. So he casually sits back against the building. Sprawling out like he's innocently enjoying the sun, closing his eyes and trying to quieten his rapid heart rate—praying the guard can't hear it thumping in his chest.

He detects the guard sauntering closer, their strides faltering sloppily when they obviously become aware of Izz's presence. When Izz doesn't react—focusing on keeping his features schooled into indifference—the footfalls continue, disappearing off towards the yard.

He releases his breath, lungs deflating in a whooshing rush, cracking his eyes open—

"Not polite to stare."

Izz nearly dies. He's sure his heart exploded out of his chest and is now rolling a hasty retreat through the grass.

The cute inmate—who was being railed by a guard—is planted right in front of his outstretched legs, peering at him.

"Huh?" Is all Izz's mind can spit out. He tries to play dumb, to make a face like *what-are-you-on-about*. But he can feel his cheeks blushing bright red. He knows he's failing miserably with the whole innocent act.

Sure enough, the inmate rolls his eyes, sitting down slowly next to Izz. Adopting a similar position against the building's smooth exterior.

"Saw you watching, didn't anyone ever tell you that's rude?" The pretty inmate flutters his eyes at Izz, running them up and down Izz's frame.

'Watching' might be a stretch, *frozen-in-shock-for-a-split-second-that-felt-like-an-eternity* would describe it better.

Izz's mouth opens . . . and closes . . . he's entirely blanking on any responses to deny the accusation. He would make a terrible criminal—eh, well, one who has to lie for a living, and stay cool and collected under interrogation.

Guess that rules out spy work for me as a future career.

He decides to go with the truth, for the life of him he can't think of a lie to tell, the truth is all he has. "Not my fault you're doing . . . *That*," he defends, "out in the open," he adds exasperatedly.

"Was behind a building." The inmate dismisses it as if that makes it fine and dandy to be doing it in a public place.

Izz raises his brows at the cute inmate, willing his expression to portray his *you've-got-to-be-kidding-me* mindset.

The inmate laughs, a soft mellow sound, "you wanna share in my bounty?"

The cute inmate offers a thin white roll, nestled between delicate fingers.

" . . . that what I think it is?" Izz breathes out, eyes widening.

The inmate nods, placing the blunt between his plump lips. He lifts a battery from his pocket, proceeding to press a thin strip of . . . a gum wrapper? . . . between the two ends—a little flame sparks to life, licking into the air, dancing off the wrapper.

Wow, Izz had no idea you could make a lighter with those objects.

CAGED IN

"What's the catch?" Izz questions sceptically, as the inmate beside him leans into the flame to light the blunt's end. The warm scent in the air one he's familiar with—a happy reminder of home.

Between puffs, the man divulges, "you don't say shit . . . about what you saw . . . I share my blunt . . . with you . . . Deal?"

The delicate flame is snuffed out, the scorched wrapper's remains removed from the battery to float free, and the battery disappearing back into its pocket home.

". . . Deal." Izz will never snitch on anyone regardless, which is not something he'll willingly divulge to this cute inmate. Not when the revelation has the potential to screw up his chance to relax in this Hell-hole. And with the day he's had, he needs it. Badly.

Izz seizes the blunt when it's held out to him—brushing the man's fingertips as he pinches the tightly wound paper—dragging the smoke deep into his starving lungs. Holding it in, until his lungs are screaming with the strain—

He blows out a thick cloud of smoke, slumping back further against the wall. The buzzing tingle warming his veins, unlocking and loosening the kinks and knots. He hadn't been aware how much tension was within him. He's beyond grateful to have this opportunity to release it.

They talked for an extensively long time. Izz can't say he tracked the entire conversation, or that it didn't spin out into weird *life-values* and *shower-thoughts*. What he can remember is the cute inmate's name.

Vince.

Vince is in here for con artist things. He's apparently extremely skilled in manipulation and deception. Using the skill set to construct deals and garner protection in this hazardous cage.

The whole afternoon had disappeared in a flash, the bell sounding out, to inform them of dinner's arrival, too soon for his zonked-out mind to comprehend.

They say their goodbyes and part ways.

Izz glides off to find The Gang in the cafeteria and fetch some dinner. He's feeling the munchies coming on. His skin prickling and warm, like it's so hungry it's beginning to eat itself.

And Vince, disappears around the cafeteria building, heading off to—who knows where.

Izz hunches over his dinner, alone in his usual place. His back to the kitchen, his front facing the back corner. No clue where The Gang is, they may be still finishing their jobs?

His wacked-out mind keeps picking up imaginary signals, telling him he's being watched. He knows it's a delusional issue, brought on by whatever was in Vince's blunt—he's figuring out prison is a whole other world where he doesn't have the run-down of what is in the available substances. Who knows what may have been mixed with the blunt? He should have thought about it

CAGED IN

before it's already in his bloodstream. Too late for regrets on that front. As long as it doesn't kill him, he isn't too fussed—

Someone is definitely watching me. It can't all be a paranoid delusion.

Izz swivels his head around—bracing his hands against the table's surface when the sharp movement threatens to topple his rapidly-fading balance. His head is a million times heavier than humanly possible, straining his neck to keep it attached atop his body.

His eyes scan. Vision fluctuating in and out, like a camera's zoom on the fritz. The colours of prisoners' clothing are swirling together in blobs of grey and white mixed with blue and black from a few individual inmates—

There.

Across the path splitting the room—and the sea of churning colours—two vaguely familiar blurs catch his eye. They're seated at a table which is swishing and tossing like a cracked boat on a rough sea. He has to strain hard to force his eyes to comprehend why the blurred silhouettes are drawing him in.

He shudders when their sleazy mugs come into focus. It's those two scaly inmates from his Wing. The ones his cellmate said aren't a worry. They sure resemble a worry with how they're ogling him.

He scrunches his nose in distaste at how their squinting beady eyes bore into him. Like they're undressing him in their minds. Their leering gazes have him feeling dirty and unclean. He doesn't want to know how he'd react if he's forced to interact with them again. From the way they're grinning at him, he's going to be interacting with them again, it's enviable. Whether he wants to or not is irrelevant. He prays it's in the far, far off, distant future—

Izz sighs in relief—louder than he intended too, his mind still a groggy mess—when The Gang bursts in through the double doors. Flowing over to the dwindling line to collect their meals.

He's grateful for the distractions—and company—to pull his focus from the sleazy inmates. A concern he can easily shove to the back of his mind, now that he is not alone. He welcomes the distraction as The Gang trickles over to join him one by one, their food trays in hand. Slowly filling the places at their table.

Reni is a no-show, Izz's way too out of it to form the words to find out about his cellmate. He elects to stay silent and eat his dinner, he barely remembers picking out the foods on his tray. Some kind of meat and mashed potatoes, with a heaping side of cooked carrots that taste faintly like honey. He fancied the sweet orange vegetables over the rest of the meal.

What his rattled mind does pick up on—outside of the chattering voices that came to him as if in a foreign language—is Erik's weird antsy behaviour. The skinny inmate is squirming, drumming his fingers on the table, eyes rolling around to bounce off everything yet taking nothing in. Pupils dilated.

Izz scoffs to himself, guess he isn't the only one out of it tonight. Wonder what Erik's drug of choice is? The skinny inmate is way more out of it than Izz. Or at least, what he feels like he is. He doesn't think he's as far gone as Erik. But then again, he also feels like a crewman straddled over

CAGED IN

a wildly rocking table-ship. So presumably his judgement, currently, is not to be trusted.

The showers are uneventful. He has no serial killer to cut off his path. Reni and Erik are both no shows. The floor has a mind of its own and the only way to ensure it doesn't run off, is for him not to take his eyes off it.

So he spends his shower with wide eyes fixating on the tiles, trying not to blink, in fear of missing the tiles retreating and him falling into the black abyss.

Isco keeps giving him the side eye. He isn't sure what he did to deserve the judgemental gaze of the scarred inmate, but he isn't about to draw attention to it. He knows who will win in a fight between them, he will be picking his teeth off the floor. If he doesn't die before that. Or if his teeth don't fall through the wobbling churning sea of floor tiles. Perhaps the watery tiles will help him out in a fight? And swallow Isco down into their depths.

David gives him nothing to work with, eyes squinting at Izz every time he looks at the other inmate. He has heard the man talking with the others but so far the guy hasn't spoken a word to him. Or has he? Izz can't recall.

He loses his battle with blinking, pinching his dry eyes shut—blinking rapidly as his eyes fill with unshed tears.

Opening his eyes, he—

Is back in his cell. No longer vertical, but horizontal and staring at the low-cut ceiling of his little caged room— weird, his hips aren't digging into the metal beneath him.

Dragging his heavy head off his pillow, he slumps in a sitting position. Holding his head in his hands. Whatever he smoked is wearing off, leaving behind a sick nauseating feeling in its retreat.

"You doing better now?" Izz can hear the amusement in his cellmate's voice.

"I think so . . ." Izz mumbles. Lifting his head to find his cellmate in front of him, sitting on his own bunk across the way. When had Reni come in . . . ?

More importantly, when had I come back to the cell—

Izz's ass is cushioned, he can't feel the hard cold metal beneath. It's surreal. Like he's sitting on a real bed—

His mind is spinning with thoughts he can't keep a tight hold on. Switching and shifting, sliding away before racing back—

Perhaps the drugs haven't worn off as much as he presumed –

Izz jolts to his feet—closely resembling a weaving strand of grass, blowing about in the breeze—reefing back the blanket covering his mattress.

He finds his mattress—like he expected—what he hadn't expected, is the second mattress sitting on top of it.

Where did that come from . . . ?

His cellmate whistles low in his throat, "you giving it up already."

"Giving what up?" Izz analyses his cellmate's words, his drug-addled mind blanking on their meaning. Poking his finger at the second mattress to check it's really real.

Turning to face Reni when the man doesn't say anything further, he inspects the smug expression on the other man's mug—

CAGED IN

Izz's eyes widen as his mind clicks onto what Reni is implying. "Fuck off, I did not sell my ass for a bloody mattress." He grins at his cellmate's raised eyebrow, like the other man doesn't believe a word he just said.

Izz chooses to play a little. "I mean, I would have, if asked . . . but I didn't." He jokes, making his cellmate snort a laugh and punch Izz playfully.

"You may joke, newbie. But people have done worse for far less in this place—" Reni rubs his chin, pondering, his eyes scanning the second mattress. "Whoever this mattress fairy is, you might want to pray they're not the stalker type."

Izz's clueless where the mattress could have come from. Clearly it's from Commissary, but why? How . . . ? Who?

He remembers complaining to his cellmate about lying on the terrible metal slabs, but his cellmate is clearly shocked, so the man isn't responsible.

He told that weird counsellor guy? Didn't he? He doubts the depressive man would do this. And the cute junkie, Vince, smoked more than Izz did so they're out of the suspect pool.

Who does that leave? He can't recall anyone else—wait. He mentioned it to the beefy server, it was in vague passing, but he had mentioned it. Could the server have done this? But why? Those mattresses are extremely expensive—

Izz dismisses the thought.

No way would the server—who he has barely spoken to—buy him an expensive mattress. A little extra food is one thing, hundreds of dollars on a mattress is an entirely different story.

He should be worried, but he's extremely appreciative to whomever gifted the mattress to him. After all, he's not one to kick a gift horse in the mouth. If that is the saying?

"It's alright." Izz smirks at his cellmate. "They can stalk away, I know my ass is luscious." He waggles his ass at Reni, joking around light-heartedly.

Plopping back down onto his bunk, Izz groans at how it absorbs his weight, cushioning his ass and not hitting him with the bed's metal base. "Man, this feels like wonder bread. Heavenly. No more back pain for me."

Reni scoffs, laughing, "you've been here a day. Try years on these damn things, then you can complain about back pains."

Izz nestles in, tucking up into his blankets, loving that his hip bones don't grind into metal as he snuggles into a comfortable position on his side, facing his cellmate who's pegging him with an expression of fixated scrutiny.

"What?" Izz grits out at his cellmate, disturbed by how intense Reni has become.

"Be careful accepting gifts. They always come with a price."

Izz laughs, shrugging off Reni's worries. He closes his eyes longing to drift off into a well needed sleep. The lights are on, so the insides of his eyelids are a bright red. However, the cell door is closed which indicates the lights won't be on for much longer—if it's the same routine as last night.

He listens to a guard walking by the cell, clicking away at a little counting device. The Count guard last time carried a clipboard with a listing of the inmates for each

CAGED IN

cell, wonder if this guard has the same? Izz doesn't care enough to peel his eyes open to find out.

Lights out arrives nearly immediately after the guard finishes counting. The bright red he's inspecting behind his eyelids plunging into blackness.

He may have been a little weirded out by the appearance of the new mattress. But he isn't about to complain, and he is exhausted.

Drained and tired from the long day—and all the events that transpired throughout it—

Izz's annoyed by the image that crawls into his mind's eye—the cute stoner inmate shoved against a wall by a guard—it's burnt into his retinas now.

Yay for me. Izz cheers sarcastically.

He couldn't be more thankful when the dark abyss of sleep finally consumes him.

9

Izz's third day—or well—second and a half day. But he'll count his arrival half-day as the first day—possibly... He's too tired to figure it out. So he'll stick with it being day three in this caged-in Hell-hole.

His third day in prison.

Three down, hundreds more to go.

"You going to eat that?" Izz shakes his head at Zidie's enquiry, sliding his half-eaten tray of food across the table.

He's already bored with the prison routines. The alarms to tell him when it's time to eat. Unable to eat what or when he chooses. Only able to eat on the set schedule. He's sick of it, and it's only day three. How is he going to get through years in this place?

"How's your third day? You look rung out?" Blake's calming voice fills the space. The table turns their attention to Izz, as if they too are interested in his answer.

"Already want to kill the alarms, I miss sleeping in."

"Wow, I forgot that was a thing," Zidie lets his mouth fall open in shock, winking as Izz shoots him a glare.

CAGED IN

"He did get a new bed," Reni slips in, nudging Zidie's ribs and giving the other inmate a look.

"New bed?" Blake questions, frowning at Izz. His pale face an odd contrast—if the man didn't have black hair and blue eyes, Izz would swear he's an albino. His complexion is that pale.

"Someone gifted the newbie with a second mattress, and newbie here accepted the gift. Naive as he is," Reni informs the whole table, waving his spoon at Izz.

"And you just let him do it," Blake accuses, seething daggers in Reni's direction.

Izz blinks at them both. Arguing over his life like they're his parents or something. They need to lay off him and stop treating him like a fragile vase that's wandering too close to a shooting range. He's not that daft.

"I didn't let him do anything," Reni argues back at Blake, "I told him whoever the mattress fairy is, he's definitely a stalker."

Izz's not sure that's what Reni told him. It's close enough so he lets it slide. Let them bicker about the insignificant issues, so he can go back to staring off into nothing and feeling sorry for himself. Even though, technically, he did it to himself, he got himself thrown into this caged Hell-hole. No one else did it. He made choices. Bad choices. That led him to here and now. He may have had good intentions, did what he did for the right reasons, it doesn't take away from the facts. He broke the law. Now he has to suffer the consequences.

This sucks.

". . . you're supposed to be looking after him."

"I'm not his mother, lay off me. He's a grown ass man. If he wants to fuck random inmates for comfy living, that's his choice."

"You slept with someone for it?" Now Blake's venom is directed at Izz. A shocked exasperated expression taking over the pale vampire's entire being.

Izz does not appreciate being in the spotlight. Or that everyone keeps assuming he sold his ass for a frickin' mattress—

"No. I. Did. Not. If whoever left the thing was stupid enough to do it without arranging a deal beforehand, then they are going to be sorely disappointed when I tell them to piss off, I'm keeping the mattress, their claim to it became null-n-void the moment they left it on my bunk. It's mine now. They can screw off," Izz may have raised his voice to quite a degree in his anger, but it is valid and he is not apologising for it.

Everyone at the table gawks at him. Zidie—trying to suppress a grin. Reni—blinking in shock at the outburst. Isco—displaying no sign of caring. Phelix—stunned bewilderment. David's face is a tight knot, his lips thinned out, like he's irritated—with what? Izz couldn't tell. Erik . . . holds an understanding, sad, expression . . .

Erik's expression makes Izz anxious, so he spuns back to face the rest of the table. The pale vampire is the only one presenting a slightly apologetic face for the crap they were saying about him.

Izz exhales, pressing his fingertips into his eyes, irritated with everything. He's already on the edge of completely losing it. And the day has barely begun.

CAGED IN

Everyone at the table resumes eating in silence. No one wanting to poke the proverbial bear sitting with them. Everyone solely focusing on their own meals.

Great, now I feel like the asshole.

Blake's clearly worried and trying to look out for him, and he took the guy's head off for it. Even if Blake was being slightly overbearing and rubbing him the wrong way by making out he can't take care of himself. He has to admit, it's somewhat correct, he is a terrible fighter and would have trouble keeping himself safe.

Is it that obvious?

Izz pulls his fingers away from their assault on his eyeballs. Little white and black flecks sparking over his vision in protest to their rough treatment. Even with his sight on the fritz, he can still see the serial killer across the room. See the way the killer is studying him.

He's caught in a tangled web, unable to turn away from the predator's gaze, even if he wanted to—

A barely visible half smirk lifts the edge of the killer's lips, it's gone in a flash, so fast Izz's convinced he imagined it.

Izz finds himself in a small room—compared to A-Wing and the cafeteria, this room is tiny. One door entry. A small television set, boxy and old, is mounted on the wall in the far corner. To its left is an ancient microwave sitting on a shelf that is likewise mounted into the wall.

Several tables are scattered around the room—the first ones he has seen not attached to the ground. The chairs are likewise free standing and horribly uncomfortable.

The cushioned armchairs encircling the television are appealing to him, however those are occupied by multiple inmates. Including one inmate reclining back in the chair—eyes not focused on the screen—as another inmate straddles his lap, very obviously with his hands down the reclining inmate's pants and face tucked into the other's neck.

Izz rearranges his position in his chair as his pants became increasingly tight. He can't help it, it's been a while for him, and those two are rubbing it out practically in the middle of the room. The guards are none the wiser, leaning back in the corner, in their own little world, laughing and talking, ignoring the inmates. Apparently they don't give a shit about inmates having sex out in the middle of the damn room.

The guards in this cage are dreadful. Why do they bother hiring them? The inmates would fare better if they were left to fend for themselves.

"You're up, Izz," Reni slaps a palm down on the table to get Izz's attention.

He pulls his distracted mind back into the game, studying the cards fanned out in his hands. They aren't playing for any valuables or cash which he appreciates, as he has nothing to bet with. No way is he putting his second mattress into the pile, and apart from that he only has his clothes which he doesn't want to risk losing.

"This room's pretty small, how do they choose who gets to come here or not." Izz mulls out loud, picking out a card to throw onto the pile.

"There are seven like this," Reni begins to explain, "Although, one's limited to I-Wing, so six rooms for the

CAGED IN

rest of us. They're supposed to be allocated to each Wing, but this one, in B-Wing, is the only one not taken by a gang. The rest are owned and you invite trouble onto yourself if you venture into any of them. This room is for the rest of us non-gang worthy inmates. Yay for us, hey."

So gangs in prison really do take over and form territories. A good titbit of information to file away for later use. He doesn't want to encroach on a powerful drug gang's patch. He has a sense it would end painfully for him.

"I-Wing? I haven't seen anyone with 'I' in their prison ID." Izz has read a lot of ID numbers, purely because they're right there in large lettering on the front of everyone's shirts. Kind of hard to miss. Similar to the guards who have a three number ID on their uniforms.

"That's 'cause it's for the Psych-Wing rejects," Zidie cuts in, and Reni raps the back of his head. He laughs as he shoves Reni, sticking his tongue out.

"I-Wing is allocated to inmates who get released from the Psych-Wing," Reni corrects, sending Zidie a look. "To integrate them into the general population, it's only small, holds 'bout thirty inmates, if their cells are doubles like the rest of us. Those inmates wear purple. There are none at the moment. The Wings for Gen-Pop are A, B, C, E, G, and H. Stay away from H-Wing, that place is run by a nasty individual you don't want to meet. Sinj got lobbed into H-Wing although he has an . . . understanding with the boss man, so he's safe as chips. The rest of us steer clear." Reni throws down his next card, sifting through what he has left.

An understanding? Wonder what that implies. Is Sinj a drug runner for them or something?

Izz wants to ask, and at the same time he finds it safer to keep his mouth shut and ponder it internally. He doesn't really need to know, it's his curiosity that wants the answers. Won't affect him not to know, selectively oblivious to everything drug related is the way to go. If he doesn't want to create enemies, which he definitely does not want.

"M-Wing, we call Med-Wing, which as you can probably guess, holds the medical rooms, doctors and all that needley stuff—hate needles, they give me the heebie-jeebies," Reni shudders, exaggerating the movements, to demonstrate his dislike. "F-Wing is the Psych-Wing, J-Wing is The Hole, D-Wing you already know—counsellors and self-help whichever. K-Wing has everything visitation related, Warden's office and guards' Break-Room and lockers—"

"Hence why the guards' presence is thick in K-Wing," Zidie tapes on. Widening his eyes at Izz, his grin obliterating his pretend fearful expression.

Izz grins at Zidie, rubbing a hand over his lips to hide his reaction to his outgoing, self-proclaimed *'best friend'*. He's not protesting against it, he's stuck here for years, having a best friend in this cage will help keep the time from dragging out for an eternity.

"Commissary is next to C-Wing, as you've seen. L-Wing holds the workshops. The phones are outside. . ." Reni plays his next hand, humming in thought as he makes his move. "That about covers it. The cafeteria's easy as we practically live next door to it, and the kitchen is attached to it—obviously."

CAGED IN

"The library is in E-Wing and the laundry room is near G-Wing. Church is on the other side of H-Wing;" Blake adds, as everyone waits for Zidie to decide which card he will play.

Reni slaps his cards face down, slumping back in his chair, already sick of waiting for Zid to pick a card. "Hence why none of us go to the church," Reni adds on, "and I have no idea what the place looks like, or if it actually exists, and isn't some made-up story."

Zidie finally throws down a card, knocking over the pile which spills over the table. "Who would bother creating a fake church story?"

Blake sighs when Zidie leaves the mess of cards where they fell. Scattered, forgotten soldiers, left out to fend for themselves. Blake sets his hand face down on the table, to gather the soldiers and reunite them in an orderly pile.

"I don't know—" Reni snaps at Zidie. Glowering at the man who keeps interrupting his story with all his unhelpful comments.

"I'm never going to remember all that," Izz mutters, diffusing the verbal lashing the other two are about to break into. He checks over his cards, and with a resigned sigh, throws them down and forfeits his hand.

"You will," Isco's deep voice rumbles over Izz's skin.

The soft chuckle leaving Isco's throat has Izz's hairs standing on end. He doesn't know why Isco creeps him out. Can't put his finger on it, his instincts tell him to be wary—he has no idea what they know and aren't telling him. He chooses to take their word for it and watch his back around the scarred inmate.

Zidie follows Izz's example—only with a more dramatic flair—flinging his cards away in disgust. Leaving Blake and Isco as the remaining two to finish this round.

"Why can't we play for contraband? I could do with some more snacks?" Zidie blurts out—or more accurately—bellows as loud as a freight train.

Izz shoots his eyes to the two guards, worried they heard—if they did, they give no indication they're going to do anything about it. Leaning back, chatting amongst themselves, with not a care in the world about the room full of criminals they are supposed to be baby-sitting.

"Because—" Blake studies Isco as he plays his next move, looking for telling signs in the other's stone-cold expression. "—you always bet big and lose bigger."

"I do not." Zidie bellows louder, drawing attention from a few inmates.

Reni leans back in his chair to peek at Blake's cards, the pale inmate turning his cards away from Izz's nosy cellmate. "That's why you have a unicorn tattoo on your ass, or did you forget about that?" Blake drawls, glaring at Reni who's attempting to view his cards again.

"I just so happen to love Mister Zombie-Uni," Zidie slaps a hand on Izz's back, grinning right in Izz's face.

"You seriously named it that?" Blake blinks at Zidie in shock. Like he can see Zid doing a lot of weird things but this tops them all by far.

Isco scoffs, throwing out another card at which Blake scowls. Blake isn't too good with his poker face unlike Isco who has a solid composure you could cut diamonds with.

"Yup." Zidie pops the 'p' loudly, interlocking his fingers behind his head to rock back in his chair smugly, revelling

CAGED IN

in his own self-satisfaction. "Z-Uni for short. Or *fluffy* if I'm feeling cute."

Multiple groans from everyone around the table. The painful noise travelling throughout the room.

Izz giggles—choking the sound off before anyone else can hear it—would have been extremely embarrassing if anyone heard.

"Who bet you to get the ink?" Izz ponders, curious about his friend's lost game.

"I deeply regret it," Isco speaks in a flat voice, giving no actual emotions, regret or otherwise.

Zidie lets out a burst of laughter, sticking his tongue out at the scarred inmate.

Izz laughs tentatively—but cuts off short, not comfortable enough around Isco to know if he's allowed to laugh at the other.

They file into the cafeteria, clumping in a group at the back of the queue. Izz's lighter than he had been for breakfast, his worries slipping away in their bantering over hours of card games. He never won a game but enjoyed himself, nonetheless.

"Inmate A-18910. Counsellor wants to see you."

The guard who addresses him is young. Can't be older than twenty-one, surely. Giving off a harsh *don't-fuck-with-me* vibe. A real y*ou'll-end-up-eating-out-of-a-straw-in-a-hospital-if-you-try-it* mentality.

Izz trails along behind the guard meekly. Back to the see the dreaded counsellor, and kill the light happy mood he had newly acquired in this depressing cage.

"*Yay,*" Izz mutters sarcastically under his breath.

The room hasn't changed. White walls encroaching on Izz. The counsellor in his office throne with eyes that judge. The lingering smell of cut grass and tea tree oil. The comfortable chair in front of the desk as soft as the first time Izz graced it with his ass—

How many asses have sat in this chair before him? How many of them did the counsellor actually help? He's thinking less than five percent, if he's being generous with the percentage.

"Hello. Jasper, wasn't it," the counsellor asks without actually asking. They both know he knew, so why put on the charade?

"Yes," Izz answers the non-question anyway.

He still hates this counsellor. Now that he knows the man's a consumer of life's joy, he can see the sketchy aura surrounding the counsellor. It's obvious now that he knows it's there.

"So, how's it going? Still settling in?" The counsellor steeples his fingers over the desk, the same way he sat last time Izz was here.

"Fine," Izz avoids looking at the counsellor by eyeing the pens nestled in their little cup home on the desk. The same unhappy conviction surrounding him as it had on the first visit. "Thank you," he tacks on, not even remotely

CAGED IN

meaning the polite phrase. He's merely being nice, to not piss off the man in charge of the transfer paperwork.

"Okay, so. Your job assignment has come in. And I'm happy to inform you that you're working in the kitchen. Starting tomorrow—the paperwork is being finalised and all that jazz."

Izz will never get used to how this counsellor talks. Dressing all professional, and yet talking like a high schooler.

Why didn't the counsellor tell the guard who collected Izz and escorted him here? Would have saved everyone this unnecessary hassle.

"Okay. Is that it?" Izz dismisses.

He wants to leave. He trusts the inmates caged in with him more than he does this counsellor. And that's saying something, considering his run-in with dragon-ink-vomit dude. And that this prison holds at least one serial killer.

Or so Izz has been told. He's not sure he's completely on board with believing the mohawked inmate is a serial killer. Perhaps it's more wishful hope than actual truth.

"Yes, yes. That's it. You'll start tomorrow. Guards will collect you from your cell for breakfast."

Izz springs to his feet, hastily launching himself towards the door. Not wanting to stick around a second longer and give the counsellor an excuse to question him about other things.

What a waste of time.

He's not sure he wants the kitchen job. He has no cooking experience. It took him dozens of tries to get simple pancakes right. He has no illusions about how long it will take him to learn how to cook actual meals.

E.P. WRITER

He hopes they're fine with a novice in their kitchen. And don't hate him for becoming part of their cooking group. After all, it isn't his choice. Not much in this cage is his choice. He's beginning to understand the full extent of what had been stripped away from him—his freedom isn't the only thing he lost. He lost any power he has over himself, any control—he's nothing but a number, a criminal in the *justice system*—if you could even call it a *justice system*.

When Izz enters the corridor, there is no sign of the intimidating young guard—guess he's on his own navigating back to the cafeteria. Unfortunately, he's beginning to get the hang of where things are located.

Izz finds the cafeteria quickly this time, with only one wrong turn which he had to backtrack.

Chatting with the beefy server guy like always, a routine with which he's now familiar. The server's nice, nicer than other inmates Izz has interacted with. He's convinced it's not a coincidence the same inmate serves him at every meal. He holds no complaints on his end, the server always gives him a little extra food.

He sits his butt on his usual bench, at his usual table. It's his place and has absolutely nothing to do with how it faces directly towards where the mysterious killer usually resides at the back table—half hidden in shadow. The killer occupies the same place every meal—except for this one where the killer's table is unfamiliarly empty.

CAGED IN

He isn't going to admit he's disappointed to discover the inmate is not sitting in their usual domain. The killer's territory is empty and cold, as if no warmth has graced its presence this meal. Not that the usual presence houses any of the warm and fuzzies.

I don't think I've seen the killer smile once . . .

What would it look like? Izz's sure his smile would be warm and kind.

He's not sure why he's thinking about it or needs to know what the male's smile resembles—

Maybe the killer has a facial muscle disease and can't smile?

Wow, your thoughts are a weird place to be.

Izz pushes his thoughts aside and resumes studying the empty back corner. Willing the killer to appear in the shadows. To give his mind something to focus on and occupy itself with. To stop thinking about what the male's smile may or may not look like.

Why is the killer running late?

Not eating?

Killing someone in the *Cleaning Supplies* closet?

Izz scoffs, disappointed in himself for showing he cares where the killer may be. It's not his place and there is a good reason for it—because—*Hello*—the male *'is'* a serial killer. Not some crush he has any right to gawk at.

Izz reprimands his own mind, digging into his food. Telling his thoughts to concentrate on other issues, not the serial killer criminal he's sharing a cage with—

Reni and Zidie snap into action when they both notice Izz has returned. Over-excited and jumping down his throat on what job assignment he was handed.

"Kitchen," Izz answers, unimpressed.

Watching both their faces light up in surprise. Like they were both certain he would be put in the laundry room with the rest of The Gang. How they could be certain on that, he has no idea.

Reni rubs his chin, a frown creasing his eyebrows. "Weird. Counsellor usually does the *'random'* pick, by looking at who you hang out with. That's why it can sometimes take a while. They have to see who you're in with. If you have gang tats, you usually get the job assignment almost instantaneously."

Zidie nods along with Reni's contemplations—a cupcake tattooed, bobble headed criminal doll, bobbing along a bumpy track. The train of thought moving from Reni to Zidie like they're connected by one mind's eye.

"Keeps groups together, minimises fighting during the work periods," Blake inserts into the explanation, becoming part of the conversation.

Izz doesn't mind. He's beginning to form a bond with the vampire, like that of an older brother or favourite cousin.

"The only ones who work the kitchens are The StaZos. I'm sure you noticed the star ink on their faces?" Reni points to his brow, with Zidie mimicking right along with him. "Considering you hang with us, you should have been put in the laundry. It's . . ." Reni's voice trails off, a distant expression appearing on his face.

" . . . It's what?" A knot is forming in Izz's stomach from the look on Reni's face—a dawning understanding and an expression of dread taking over his cellmate's features. And the puzzlement on Zidie's face isn't helping the knot untangle.

CAGED IN

"What?" Izz isn't sure he wants to hear the answer.

" . . . almost like someone wanted you there," Reni finishes ominously.

Izz scoffs at the answer. His stomach unknotting in an instant. Trust his cellmate to make a big deal out of nothing, throwing a conspiracy theory into the mix. "Well dah. They wouldn't put me in a job with no available space, of course someone wanted . . . me . . . there . . ." Izz trails off when Reni's expression grows substantially more serious.

Izz frowns at Reni. *Maybe he means an inmate wants me there?*

But why . . .

An image flashes into his frontal lobe—the beefy server who always hands him food. Is always so nice to him and giving him extra—

His mind races away from that train of thought as if a bomb went off and disintegrated it—the killer has appeared by the doors. Striding in like he owns the place and isn't afraid to kill to keep the entire prison as his territory. Like the rest of the inmates are as insignificant to him as ants. A predator who fears no others.

The killer reclines in his claimed eating area. Reigning over the non-worthy animals eating around him. His tray is empty of any food, like he isn't hungry. Although he came here, and collected a tray. So maybe it's more the food being served today isn't to his satisfaction or he dislikes the items available?

Why else would he come to the cafeteria if it isn't to eat?

Why stay in the cafeteria, if you're not going to eat anything?

Why is he frustrated about it? Who cares. It's not like any of them have many places to be in this cage. He shouldn't even be taking note of the killer's whereabouts, or actions. Let alone being annoyed by the killer not eating, like that's his concern—it is none of his business.

Izz jots it down as morbid curiosity, and leaves it at that. He does not want to dig into why he's noticing changes in the killer's routine. He'll call it a prey response to the predator in the vicinity. Not a human response to his libido's call—

Izz's heart stops when the killer's cold gaze lands directly on him, and doesn't shift away.

10

Izz chooses to relax in his cell during his downtime while The Gang are working their prison-assigned jobs. He'll have to do that tomorrow. Something he is not looking forward to. Not only is he stuck in this cage, but he has to go to work too. Talk about being screwed over twice.

It might not be all bad, he supposes. He's sure he can make friends in the kitchens, he already has one server who likes him. He's sure the others will be fine once they get to know him.

He's not too keen on them being part of a gang—an actual *gang*. On the outside he'd never met a gang, let alone cooked with one. Now, inside these walls, he's seen too many gangs to count, and he's expected to cook with one. He could encounter hostility or he could encounter kindness. He's leaning more towards the former, he's sure gang members are not too pleased with outsiders hanging around on their turf.

His biggest worry is if they try to recruit him—do they call it recruiting? Sounds more like a military term than a gang one. And no, he will not be asking them what they call it. He'll not say anything even remotely related to gangs or joining or anything in between. He's already in prison, he doesn't need to be in a gang on top of that.

And when he says *no*? What will happen to him? Will they accept *'no'* for an answer? Or will he be killed—

Dropping his increasingly troubling thoughts—not what he needs to be working himself up about. Best to let events play out and not imagine scenarios that have not transpired and may never come to pass.

Yawning until his jaw spasms and cracks, Izz settles back against his soft bunk. The alarm for dinner should rouse him, he doesn't see an issue in catching some shut eye, while the inmates are off working. Seems safe enough, and not a disaster to end with him alone and defenceless getting shivved . . . He hopes.

Tucking in, he curls into the fetal position. Pulling the thin blanket over his head to block out the majority of the prison's invading lights. Drifting off into a peaceful sleep.

The blissful respite had been God sent. Izz feels refreshed and revived. Ready to kick this prison life in the butt. He's not sure why violent thoughts are necessary, but he isn't questioning his eager, energetic mood. It's better than his down and depressed mood ever since he walked into prison.

He hadn't realised how bad it'd been, how much weight had been slumped over his shoulders. Now that its lifted, he feels a million times lighter.

It's a euphoric feeling.

CAGED IN

Grinning to himself—like a lunatic—he tries, and fails, not to skip down the metal steps. Swinging off the railing to jump the last couple, plopping to the first level's concrete flooring. Ignoring the snide comments aimed his way by passing inmates.

Dinner time.

Wonder what they have on the prison menu tonight. The food has been surprisingly diverse, a huge variety of ever-changing assortments to pick from. He hasn't attended many meals, those he had were all different. He's cheerfully optimistic it's the case for all the meals. So no one gets bored by the food. You know the saying, *'boredom leads to fighting'*—

Is that a saying? Or something his mum made up? It's true either way.

Izz extends his arm to trail his fingertips along the rough bricks as he makes his way down the corridor. The lumpy paint job exaggerating the defects in the bricks texture. The paint may have smoothed it out, taking away the gritty brick texture, but it did little to smooth out the lumps and divots. A slippery slide for his fingers to trace over.

"Well looky here, boys. We gots' ourselves a little lost birdy."

Izz wheels around, to find he is no longer alone in the corridor. Four inmates have ambled in after him—looking smug and self-satisfied.

The leader in front is the one who spoke, Izz assumes he's the leader by the way he holds himself. Sure, confident, commanding. And very, very, bald. His lackeys are likewise as bald as a baboon's ass.

They have to be part of that gang Izz noticed on his first day. The whole table that was filled with shiny hairless heads. The one gang he will never join—not that he's going to be joining any gangs. This one though. No frickin' way is he shaving his head for a prison gang.

Heck no.

Should I say something? Will it help the situation or make it worse?

"Um, can I help you?" Izz questions, he figures ignoring them will be rude and would garner a worse reaction then acknowledging them.

All four laugh.

Not a nice, happy, joyous laugh. No. Rather it's a mocking, distrustful, sarcastic laugh.

They remind him of cats. Flitting in, mock striking, assessing their cornered plaything. A poor mouse trapped in the clutches of a group of feral felines—

Definitely not a hot idea referring to himself as a mouse. Or plaything for that matter.

"You're walking on my turf," the leader one snarls, confirming he's the leader. Wouldn't be his *'turf'* if he isn't.

"Sorry. I didn't know that."

Pretty sure you're lying on that front. This is the main corridor to the cafeteria, hardly likely any gang would own it. Not with every gang needing to use it to get to the cafeteria.

He leaves his inner ramblings unsaid. No need to provoke these inmates any more than necessary. He doesn't need to give them an excuse to become pissed off.

"I was walking to the cafeteria. I'll go straight there and get out of your hair." Pun intended, mockery meant to be included, even though Izz keeps his voice low and

CAGED IN

respectful. He still doesn't like these inmates with their swagger and *I-own-this-place* persona.

He backs away slowly, keeping his eyes on the four men. Edging closer to the cafeteria and its relative safety. He doubts these inmates would have a go at him in the open cafeteria in front of hundreds of witnesses and a dozen, or so, guards.

He has countless off shooting corridors he could run down, but only the doors at the end will lead him straight into the arms of witnesses. The cafeteria is his safest bet. He doesn't know the prison's layout enough to gamble with which other corridor could potentially lead to safety.

"I think you should stay. Let us show you where you *can* and *can't* go. Give you a *tour*," the bald leader sneers, glancing back at his lackeys like he's scared they left and he isn't man enough to take on anyone in a fair, one on one, fight.

"Already had one of those," Izz fires back, backing away faster to get out of here and into the safety of the cafeteria and its crowded interior—

The leader swivels two fingers. A small movement Izz would have missed if he hadn't been focusing intensely on the man. Two of his lackeys surge forward, right at Izz.

He back-pedals fast, catching himself on the wall as he spins around, digging his heels in, he guns for the exit. For the cafeteria behind it. He makes it several steps before a thick arm snaps around his middle. Popping him off his feet and hauling him back the way he'd come.

Flight failed.

Trapped. With only one option now—

His back becomes acquainted with the floor, the harsh landing expelling air from his lungs in an explosive rush—

Izz swings his head to the side dodging his attacker's fist by a fraction of an inch. Hearing the solid thud as meaty flesh hits the concrete by his ear—

He tucks both feet in, kicking out with all the force he can muster—

He hits a solid chest with both feet planted, sending his attacker sprawling backwards. He's never been in a hand-to-hand fight—or any fight for that matter—but he knows he has to get up.

Being on the floor—with three men standing threateningly above him, and one other who is no doubt getting their footing back under them this very second—is not a hot idea.

Rolling to his side, Izz pushes himself onto his hands and knees, ready to spring to his feet and defend himself—

He doesn't achieve his goal. What he does accomplish is opening his stomach up—leaving his organs exposed—to cop the full brunt of the prison-issued shoe that lands the blow.

Insides screaming and convulsing, he curls around his middle to protect himself from further harm. Coughing out what little breath he managed to suck in after his back slammed into the floor—

The next kick is aimed at his head—he has enough presence of mind to raise his arm to block it—effectively punching himself in the face when his weak block fails to stop the kick's follow through. His head snapping back, off balancing him and sending him sprawling onto the concrete floor.

CAGED IN

On his back once more. Vulnerable to the men above him, who are hell-bent on causing him grievous injuries.

He can taste metal—a metallic warmth—he's split something in his mouth, the taste is foul, causing him to gag, coughing out as much as he can—

A savage stomp lands on his ribs, the pain is immediate and sharp, sending a tidal wave of agony through his whole body.

Curling into a ball—as the assaulting leg rises above him—he tries his best to shield his body from the blow he knows is coming. The blow that will cause more excruciating pain. His body is already screaming in agony. It isn't going to appreciate another bone-stomping hit.

My first fight, and I'm going to die—

The inmate with the death stomp lined up to crush his ribs—flies off out of sight. A quick flick of an invisible giant's hand sends the inmate into the air and crashing onto the floor.

How is that possible . . . ?

A blur of multi-coloured ocean creatures' swishes past his line of sight—

Izz coughs, spitting up warm liquid. He reaches for his face with a shaky hand, swiping at the rapidly-cooling fluid over his chin. Pulling his hand back, he looks down at the dark red coating his fingers, sliding through the cracks to drip . . .

Drip . . .

Drip . . .

Splattering on the concrete floor next to his rapidly bruising body, forming a little puddle of crimson.

He groans, curling in on himself, trying to release the pain from his body. A burning sharp agony that doesn't want to subside, adamant on letting him know it's there.

Three days in, and I'm dying in the corridor.

Izz can hear yelling, cursing above him, the sounds of flesh hitting flesh. Going by the rising noise level, more inmates have gathered in the small space to watch, or participate, he isn't sure which.

Sucking in a deep breath to ground himself—wheezing when the movement ignites pain in his ribs—he uses the wall to sit up, slumping over the bricks to hold himself steady. Blinking rapidly to clear the throbbing in his head and the pains' haze from his vision, he leans his head against the wall. The pungent smell of his own blood burning his sinuses.

The change from horizontal to vertical brings Izz's line of sight to the fighting above him. To the two other inmates who joined the fight. Who saved his life.

Reni and Zidie. They're drawing the attention off Izz and taking the gang members on in full force. A powerful team working together to kick ass.

Reni's crouched over a downed inmate, his fists raining down while they try to shield their face from the brutal impacts. Izz sees a different Reni, his face twisted in rage, teeth bared and eyes flaming.

Who knew Reni cared so much about me.

Another of the bald gang members is sprawled on the concrete floor, either dead or unconscious. Izz can't tell, the inmate isn't moving, but they may have been breathing shallowly? Hopefully.

CAGED IN

He doesn't know what to feel if he's looking at someone dead in front of him. Sickened? Relieved they won't come after him again?

Sickened. I am not relieved about their death. That is not who I am. It's not who I ever want to be.

On the other side of the *not-dead* man, Zidie is bouncing on the balls of his feet, squaring off against two bald men. He's throwing punches and kicks, blocking blows and returning them in kind. He's agile and quick, able to outmanoeuvre the gang members who are relying on brute strength and little to no skills—

A blaring siren sounds out, thundering down the corridor, bouncing off the brick walls to echo louder. Izz covers his ears, trying to block out the screeching. Jumping to his feet, as if it will help his ears. It sure doesn't help his battered body. Instead, it awakens injuries he hadn't felt before. Perhaps the adrenaline is wearing off? Or the swelling and soreness is too advanced to ignore.

How much damage have I endured—

The guards' stream in—pushing and shoving the onlooking inmates to the side—cuffs in hand. They make quick work securing the inmates involved in the fight, handcuffs clicking on wrists in well-practiced precision.

He's surprised when he isn't also cuffed. He receives nothing more than a side-eye from a guard before the man's eyes dart over Izz's shoulder and he walks on to help his thugs-in-uniform drag off inmates.

Izz watches in stunned shock as Reni and Zidie are hauled away, along with three of the four gang members. And an inmate he doesn't recognise who's swearing and trying to kick every guard in sight.

E.P. WRITER

Going to The Hole?

The unconscious inmate is hefted between two guards and dragged over the floor, his feet flopping as he hangs limp between them. Perhaps heading to Med-Wing? If Izz's to guess. Or the morgue.

Does the prison have a morgue?—

He doesn't want to know.

The spectators disperse, now that the excitement is over, drifting off to the cafeteria to resume eating. Izz's appetite has disappeared, he turns and limps off to the showers to wash the blood off his face. Holding his ribs protectively.

Halfway to the showers, he remembers he has a sink in his cell—he could have washed there. He considers turning around and going back, but he's already this far so he sticks with it. Only a few more turns to the showers—

Voices drift over from around the next corner. They're voices he recognises from The Gang. Izz drops his head, his shoulders slumping, shame rolling over him. Covered in blood, hating himself for Reni and Zidie now stuck in The Hole. All because of him, because they had to step in to save him.

He falters at the periphery of the bend in the corridor, the hushed snippets of conversation giving him pause. He peeks his head around the corner, leaving his body hidden by the wall so he doesn't draw attention to himself. Overhearing the tense conversation between Isco, Phelix and David. Who are facing away from him, slowly strolling down the corridor, heading in the direction of the showers.

Would have been embarrassing if they'd been right near the corner facing him. With his head popping out all

CAGED IN

'hello'—he probably would have squealed to add insult to his obvious spying.

David's voice carries back to Izz strong and sure, "we can't keep protecting him, or we will all be targets or in The Hole. And I for-one, am not going back to The Hole for anyone. Especially not someone who can't fight to save his life," David grumbles, anger lacing his words. "He's attracting attention. Pissing off gangs—gangs who we don't need to be drawing attention from. It's going to get us killed. Protecting him. Is it really worth it?"

Izz's stunned, to say the least. He's never heard David speak so much, and he never would have guessed the man harboured so much anger towards him. He thought David was merely shy or didn't like talking much.

Never would have guessed it's due to him hating me.

Isco? Sure, Izz can see the man hating everyone—he still gets jumpy around the other and he has no idea why. And as for Phelix? Izz's learnt he's the pacifist, the background man who doesn't involve himself in any drama. The glue no one notices keeping The Gang in check.

Izz turns away, not interested in listening to Isco's reply, limping back to his cell. Maybe they aren't his friends. He can't say he blames them. He's known them for ten seconds, can he blame them for not wanting to die for him. He doesn't want anyone to die for him.

But what is he supposed to do? He didn't ask to get attacked, he didn't ask Reni or Zidie to step in. Of course, he's beyond grateful they did. But he never asked for it.

He doesn't understand why the gangs are pissed off at his group because of him. What did he do? He hasn't talked to any of the gangs, he's kept to himself and only hung around with The Gang. Sure he spoke to the server but he's only being polite. That gang can't possibly be the one David's talking about, can it? The server is always nice to him, always pleasant and chivalrous towards him.

He knows it isn't the bald gang members, he's never once spoken to them. And he has no idea why they picked a fight with him. Bored? Or something else? He can't think of anything else, so boredom must be it—bullies looking for their fucked-up idea of fun, someone to poke at and occupy their time with.

Izz stretches out on his bunk with a grunt. Too exhausted to wash his face, the blood already dry and cracking, itchy and flaking off.

His body hurts. He wants to sleep. He'll deal with the blood in the morning.

His stiff legs are doing a marvellous job of impersonating jelly—it's impossible for him to stand any longer. He isn't interested in face planting the floor by attempting to wash his blood off. He doesn't need to add to his injuries when his legs inevitably give out on him. With his luck he'll split his head open on the sink on his way to the floor, and bleed out alone in his tiny cell.

Stretching out slowly over his bed, he groans as his muscles twist and pinch him under his skin. The double mattress pile may keep him off the metal bed frame, but it does little to cushion his bruises. The aching twinges surging involuntarily through his limbs. His bones ache— how do bones ache?

I wish I had something to kill the pain.

Sleep claims him quickly—had he not been in so much pain he might have considered sleeping a bad idea. If he

CAGED IN

has a concussion, sleep is a terrible idea. He'd heard that sleeping is a no go for concussions. His mind—and body—have other plans, slipping him under the black veil of a deep, dreamless abyss, before he has the sense to stop it.

11

He isn't impressed.

Pulled out of bed by a guard and told he has ten minutes to be ready and down in the kitchen to start his shift.

That was about ten minutes ago and he's still in his cell hovering over the sink.

Izz has been in a go-slow kind of mood since the guard left. His attitude is likewise slow and grumpy. He's a zombie—he has the same brain function as one. His body is stiff, sluggish, and he groans in pain with each step—a zombie.

It's so early he has to squint in the darkness to navigate his box of a cell. No light coming through the tiny window. The sun is sleeping comfortably behind the soft blanketing hills, marshmallowed in their fluffy embrace—unlike Izz. Who is out in the cold, with a headache to rival the dead.

What time is it—

Izz squints at his little cupboard, at the dark shapes on its surface. He hadn't put anything on top of it, so what is . . .

Shuffling closer, he grunts his way over to inspect the foreign objects. It's medical supplies. Bandages, tapes,

CAGED IN

some type of disinfectant wipe. He sifts through the little assortment of first aid gear—

Pills. There are two little pills wrapped in a square of plastic. Tiny little white pills. No label. No name. No description. Just pills.

He knows he shouldn't take them. He really shouldn't. But he's racked with aches and random muscle spasms threatening to drop his ass to the floor—and it's killing the possibility of rational thinking.

He gathers the pills with trembling fingers, plopping them into his mouth. Swallowing them dry is a no go. He has to hold the tiny dissolving drugs on his tongue as he wobbles back over to the sink. Using his hand to scoop water into his awaiting mouth, swallowing it down and taking the pills with it.

At this point he is okay with whatever effects present themselves. He'd take anything as long as it took away the excruciating tenderness. He didn't start the fight. He didn't cause it. But it doesn't matter. He is still the one who'd been viciously beaten.

He isn't a fighter. He'd been lucky Reni and Zid were nearby to come to his rescue. He'd tried his best to lay low, to settle into his new life in this Hell-hole.

He'd failed spectacularly.

Please let these pills kill the pain, and not me.

It requires some deep soul searching and concentrated conviction to get his legs with the program, to shuffle his ass down the corridor. His legs still insist that Izz should be lying in bed asleep. He has to agree with them. Smart legs. The rest of his body is on a similar track, unhurried and dragging. He can't remember the last time he was awake to start his day before the sun.

Slinking past the empty cafeteria feels surreal and slightly haunted. His mind running wild with thoughts of imaginary creatures watching him from the dark corners of the shadow-filled room. It's creeping him out. His heart pumping rapidly to wake up his body with microbursts of adrenaline sparking through his bloodstream. Tiny shots of caffeine to energise his brain and body into the land of the coherent.

Shaking off the creepy vibes, Izz sucks in a deep breath to centre himself, before pushing past the doors to enter the kitchen—it's strange being on the other side of the food serving bar—rounding the partition, he walks in on a whole flurry of activities.

Inmates rushing all over the place. Meals being cooked, the air swirling with multiple scents. Trays being stacked, pots and pans and utensils clanging loudly.

The organised chaos is daunting from the outside. And that's what he feels like. An outsider. From what happened to his cellmate and self-appointed best friend, and the conversation he overheard between three other members of The Gang—the ones he thought he was on okay terms with—his essence is rather drained.

"You made it."

Izz twists in the direction of the familiar voice, heart skipping and catching in his throat. The painkillers—he hopes they're painkillers—are doing their job. His body is

CAGED IN

numbing out. Allowing him to move without gasping and curling over in agony.

The beefy server is approaching Izz with a grin, "heard about what happened, wasn't sure if you'd be in The Hole or not. Glad to see you are not."

". . . Yeah. Thanks . . . I guess." Izz mutters, wincing at the thought of the others being punished in his place. Not that he started the fight, he was the target for an unknown reason. Reni and Zidie were only trying to help him. They don't deserve The Hole as a punishment.

The server loops an arm over Izz's shoulders, he doesn't have the heart to shove the inmate away. He kind of needs some human contact right now, to get him out of his head and away from the guilt eating at him.

"I don't think we've been formally introduced, after all this time. I'm Levis." The server waves his arm in an arch, indicating the whole kitchen, "I run this place, and these sorry losers you see, they're the cogs that keep this shit running moderately well. I'm sure they'll introduce themselves later on, or not, who cares, they're not really important. The only one you got to listen to around here is me."

"Alright."

Izz counts fourteen others in the kitchen, working around multiple benches, busy with various tasks. All the inmates have the same tattoo above their eyebrow like Levis. So they must be part of the same gang.

Great. I was hoping they weren't all gang affiliated.

"Today I'll start you off slow." Levis informs Izz, leading Izz over to the side, towards the serving trays in the food bar. "I'll have you on cleaning for today, to get a feel for where everything is and how things are set out and the routine."

He's in no way thrilled to be stuck on cleaning duty. He'd rather try—and fail, several dozen times—at the cooking aspect of this job. Not the cleaning. He does not want to be stuck as a dishwasher, it's bad enough he's stuck in prison. Now he has to do chores?

Reni's words filter down to Izz, their conversation on why he would have been shoved into the kitchen and not with them in the laundry.

As the inmates in the kitchen are in the same gang, it's likely he's chosen as the designated cleaner. Why wouldn't they bring in an outsider to do the labour for them. So no one in their gang has to do it. And it appears he drew the short straw on the cleaning job.

Levis removes his arm from Izz, but doesn't step back, "Under there—" Levis points at the closed cupboards under the food bar. "—you'll find the cleaning gear for the bench tops and trays."

Izz nods his understanding. He's not thrilled with this job assignment. Had he been in the laundry at least he would have Zidie to keep him occupied and make the hours bearable . . .

Except Zidie wouldn't, would he? He isn't in the laundry room. He's in The Hole. Probably lying in the middle of the tiny box cell, twiddling his thumbs, bored out of his mind.

Because of me. It's my fault.

When Levis flicks his hand towards the cupboards, Izz's face flushes a little.

Right, he's supposed to get the stuff out.

CAGED IN

Bending down he pulls the doors open, grabbing out a spray bottle and wipes. Angling it towards Levis for inspection to ensure he picked the correct products.

Izz frowns at Levis, he's sure the man had been staring at his ass. But he can't be sure where Levis's eye level was at.

He brushes the thought off, chocking it up to a paranoia thing. He's agitated over being attacked, that's what it is. Levis had not been staring at his ass. No way.

"Wipe down the countertops, and all the trays. To prep it for when the food comes out. I've got some other things to handle, come find me when you've finished, and I'll show you where to load the dishes and trays for cleaning."

And that's how Izz gets stuck scrubbing down the food serving bar. Cleaning the areas where the trays will sit with the breakfast selection. Wiping the bench top inmates slide their trays along to collect food. Scrubbing it down nice and clean.

A lifetime passes before he finishes, the place looking shiny and sparkling new. Ready to go.

A spark of pride enters his chest over the job he did, he's never wiped down a large bench before, or the other things he had to clean. He's a cleaning pro now.

Strolling into the depths of the kitchen, Izz wanders around, trying—and failing—to locate Levis. He swears he's searched the entire kitchen twice and he can see no sign of the kitchen boss anywhere.

"Excuse me," Izz asks one of the inmates flipping the cages of bacon to drain off the oil, "do you know where Levis is?"

"He went around back, to check supplies for lunch," the guy points to a small flapping door.

Izz slowly pushes the doors wide—a huge walk-in pantry greets him. Stacked with a large selection of bulk food supplies. Barrels of flour as tall as him. Shelves stuffed with more potatoes and onions than he has seen in his lifetime. Other shelves holding salt, pasta, rice—bags and bags of it.

Damn, this has to be a hefty food bill.

Izz locates the server in the third aisle of shelves. Levis is sifting through a barrel of something . . .

He spies items he knows are definitely not prison issued.

Contraband.

Levis doesn't appear to have heard Izz come in. The man is hunched over counting products, maybe fixing up orders or other contraband type activities.

Ducking back around to the other aisle, he sneaks off, tiptoeing further away to avoid being discovered. He doesn't want to be associated—by the guards—with contraband distribution. Or worse—getting caught by the shady kitchen boss, spying on secretive prison business.

"Levis, you in here? I finished the cleaning," Izz's voice carries through the entire pantry. He positions himself next to the doors and pretends he hadn't walked in and seen what he had.

"Yep, give us a sec' I'll be right with you," Levis's voice drifts back to Izz, along with the clatter of a barrel closing tight.

"Alright," Izz loiters on the periphery of the pantry, waiting for the kitchen *Boss*—and apparently, contraband distributor—to come out.

CAGED IN

"Terrific," Izz mutters sarcastically to himself.

He prays this incident doesn't go south, prays the guards don't find out and add more time onto his sentence. When he has nothing to do with the contraband, he was given this job by the counsellor. He has no say in what the other inmates in here have been doing—and will no doubt continue doing.

Come to think of it, the knowledge may be useful. Good to know who to approach for things like weed. If Levis distributes weed—and Izz has money to buy it. And he is willing to risk dealing with a mob boss—or gang, or whatever they call themselves—to get illegal contraband inside a prison. And if he is willing to take the risk of potentially getting caught in the process.

Seems like more risks than it's worth.

He is not enjoying washing up. The dishes are endless. Packing the dishwasher is boring and gruelling—even with four machines available to use, it still takes forever. And the pills are wearing off, his aches and pains returning to him with a vengeance. Punishing him for making them disappear.

Levis had shown Izz how to pack the machines, where the soaps and scrubbing brushes are located. Where the dials had to be set. And where to put everything once it's cleaned and dried.

Izz sighs as he slams the last dishwasher shut, clicking its little digital buttons to start the wash and rinse routine.

This particular machine is the newest model out of the four washers, it's way easier to use than the rest of them.

He's the last in the kitchen. The other inmates—who cooked and prepared the meal—have finished their work and left to eat. The servers are the only ones hanging around the front of the kitchen, past the divider, out of sight. He can't see them and they can't see him. Which he takes full advantage of, leaning back against a machine to take a break, with no one around to notice him slacking off. It's not like he actually has anything to do. Not until the loads are finished and he can pack everything away.

Am I going to be the cleaning boy now?

Is this what Reni meant? When his cellmate said someone wanted him here?

He would hate to be stuck in this kitchen job, for the sole purpose of cleaning. He doesn't know how to cook but that doesn't mean he wanted to do dishes for the rest of his long prison stay. He has plenty of time to learn how to cook—

Approaching footfalls have Izz spinning to face the machines, and pretend like he's very busy doing . . . something.

"How's everything going?" Levis's heavy strides rounds the corner, "I remember you like the bacon. Made you a tray."

Izz turns to find Levis holding out a tray containing his usual breakfast choices. Well, *'usual'* for the couple of times he's had it prior to today. He hasn't been here long enough to have an actual meal preference.

CAGED IN

"Thanks, I'm starving. I don't think I've cleaned this much in a year, let alone a single meal." Izz laughs nervously, accepting the tray from Levis's grasp.

He places the tray down on one of the clean bench tops. Eating slowly—while hunched over the bench—as the bacon grease stings the split inside his mouth.

"You'll be on cooking for lunch. Get here early so I can run you through where everything goes."

Izz nearly chokes on his mouthful of bacon at the server's words. Turning his stunned face to Levis, he watches the man break into a slow grin.

"What? You think I was going to keep you on cleaning indefinitely?" Levis's voice is laced with amusement.

"Well . . . yeah," Izz splutters sheepishly, rubbing the back of his neck. "Figured because I'm new, and . . . well, not part of your . . ." He isn't sure if they go by gang, or mob? He tapped above his own eyebrow to indicate what he's referring to. He doesn't want to call Levis by the wrong term and accidentally offend the man.

Levis doesn't answer, he just smirks. Leaning back on one of the kitchen benches, indicating with his chin to Izz's tray.

He digs back into his meal. It tastes amazing, he's starving from the huffing and heaving of multiple kitchen equipment into the washers. Probably part of the reason why the food tastes so good, his stomach is completely empty and he's desperate to fill it.

He can sense Levis watching him. He chooses to ignore it. Continuing to eat his food hastily muscling through the stinging burn—he's alone with an inmate who he doesn't know, who runs a gang, and is into shady business—he'd like to leave as soon as possible, to be on the safe side.

"So," Izz talks over his insistent worries, "do we have to cook every meal, every day? No holidays in prison?"

"No. Other inmates who don't work in the kitchen, work one shift a day, and have Sundays off—unless they're cleared by Medical for more days off." Levis explains. "We—inmates who work the kitchen—work three shifts in one day for the week, so we have the second week off. A week on, a week off."

Well, that's a bonus Izz supposes. He's not sure he could survive prepping for three meals indefinitely. He'd be a walking zombie in no time. Especially having to wake up so early. A week off will be excellent. If he can find things to do. He's going to get bored real fast if he doesn't find something to kill his down time.

Izz went back to his cell after breakfast, finding a pair of white pills plastic wrapped on his pillow. He takes them without a second thought, the first lot hadn't killed him, this lot should be fine.

Sitting tentatively on his bunk, he waits for the pills to kick in and kill the pain. He'll stay in his cell until lunch, he is not in the mood to deal with The Gang. He can't pretend as if he hadn't heard what David said. Pretend like it's fine. They're probably thrilled to be rid of him and all his, *'attracting attention', 'pissing off gangs', 'can't protect himself to save his life'*.

CAGED IN

He's an outsider in this world. He has no idea how to act in this place, how to carry himself, how to pick friends—can you even be friends in prison? Or is everyone in here using everyone else—

No. That can't be it. Or Zidie and Reni wouldn't have stepped in to help him. They would have left Izz to deal with his own fate. That fate would have been death, no doubt about it.

Izz mulls over his thoughts. Drawn into the inner ramblings of his mind. Trying to link puzzle pieces together and map out his plans to survive this cage. To make it out—if not in one piece, then at the very least—alive.

He's so caught up in his own thoughts that he's shocked when a guard stops by to tell him to report to the kitchens for lunch prep. He hadn't realised he'd been sitting in his cell so long.

He's slightly wary about going back. Levis was throwing off weird vibes. His senses kept twitching around the man, like they knew something was off, something he can't yet figure out. Maybe it's uncertainty?—unease?—linked to working so close to gang members.

Izz darts down the corridor, moving swiftly to avoid any more unpleasant run-ins. He does not want a repeat of the attack. The pain meds he'd found left in his cell had helped, but he doesn't need more bruises on top of bruises. He'd like to have enough time to heal, without adding to the collection.

Shoving past the kitchen doors, he takes a moment to catch his breath, he's sure the kitchen has moved further away, he can't be this unfit. His lungs expand in their struggle to draw in much needed oxygen, inflating around a small flutter in his chest at avoiding having his face stomped in on his brisk walk here.

The little things to celebrate in life. Go me. Izz's inner cheerleader flips its pom-poms to his success.

Scrunching his face he steps past the partition into the kitchen, disgusted in himself for thinking he has an inner cheerleader doing anything, let alone cheering him on for *not* getting beaten up.

Again.

This place is already getting to him, driving him into insanity. Maybe they have a spare bed in the Psych-Wing he can use. He's arguing with himself about cheerleaders dancing in his head, he's well on his way to joining the crazy train—he might find himself running it, if he's not careful.

"You're in charge of these pots. Stirring them to prevent it sticking and burning. No one wants burnt mashed potatoes." Levis hovers over Izz's back, breathing down Izz's neck like an over-zealous teacher waiting for the student to screw up so they can reprimand them. Before walking off to yell orders at other inmates.

Izz grabs the giant ass wooden spoon—he's sure this was a broom before the guards attached a spoon end to it. They can't possibly make wooden spoons this big? It's almost as tall as him.

It's surprisingly easy to stir. He thought the bulk amount of mash would gunk together, resulting in an immovable mess of boiling sludge. What he got, is a mixture easily parting to allow the spoon to slide through it like soft butter.

CAGED IN

It's relaxing. Stirring the smooth cooking potatoes. Pulling him into a lulled zone of peace. A zone of calm encasing him. Who knew stirring a giant pot of simmering mash would turn out to be so relaxing—

Izz's rudely dragged out of his trance when a hand runs down his back, rubbing over his ass—

He stiffens, swivelling to identify who's touching him. Coming face to face with Levis occupying the space right behind him.

Levis is inspecting the pots, hands in his pockets, no acknowledgement whatsoever written on his smooth face.

Had Levis only bumped into him by accident?

Was I imagining it as a hand? It had been a quick motion, perhaps I'm jumping to conclusions?

Izz frowns, resuming his assigned task. He does shuffle a step to the side, to place Levis in his line of sight. In case he hadn't imagined it, in case it is more than another inmate brushing against him unintentionally in a cramped room. The kitchen is very small, considering how many fully-grown men are lumped in together.

He moves on to the next pot to give it his attention. He's somewhat nervous to take his eyes off the mashed potatoes, afraid of burning his first meal. And in consequence, wrecking his chances at being given any other cooking tasks. He does not want to go back to washing dishes. One shift is enough cleaning to last him a lifetime.

He narrows his eyes at the white mass in the next pot, his sixth sense alerting him to Levis repositioning closer.

Why is Levis moving closer?

He moves to the next pot, and sure enough, Levis follows Izz there. What is up with him today? Why is he acting so creepy? He isn't always like this, is he?

Izz thought Levis was nice. Normal. Respectful and maybe becoming a friend. He is second guessing himself now—

No. No, Levis has always been nice. Never weird. Izz had talked to him on many occasions. He'd not sensed anything amiss, not like he did with the vomit-dragon tattoo guy. Or the bald gang members. Surely he hasn't misjudged Levis so spectacularly?

Maybe the server is merely passionate about his food, checking that it's cooked to perfection. The meals Izz has eaten so far were of great quality, and Levis does run the kitchen. Therefore the man must be doing something right, right?

So . . . why is his skin crawling at Levis's close proximity? It feels like more than the kitchen boss teaching him the ropes to food prep. More than the normal level of attention.

His body tenses when a solid chest comes to rest against his back. His spine locking in place, he finds himself unable to move.

"I can protect you," Levis whispers, the clogging warmth of his too-hot breath filling Izz's sinuses. "Stop those other pieces of shit from coming anywhere near you. When you're mine, you won't have to worry about anyone."

When I'm what? What is Levis talking about?

He is not interested in . . . *belonging* . . . to anyone. Is Levis on drugs or something? Why would Izz sell his soul for anything. The vibe radiating out of Levis is telling him

CAGED IN

he's not talking about a friendship, the man is insinuating something far worse. Along the lines of selling his body for protection.

He stumbles away from Levis. He knows his face is displaying his utter disgust with this conversation. His upper lip twisting in his distaste for Levis's proposition.

Levis doesn't take the hint. Instead, the man invades Izz's personal space some more. Before he's able to protest, Levis grabs his ass. Caging him in against the kitchen bench, its hard surface digging into his spine.

Izz panics. Eyes widening, he frantically searches the kitchen. Praying he's not alone, that what is happening isn't truly happening.

The handful of inmates scattered throughout the kitchen space—finishing their prep work—are pretending not to notice. They turn their backs or avert their eyes, blatantly ignoring what Levis is doing.

I'm all alone against this creep.

How can they do this? How can anyone turn their backs on something like this? What is *wrong* with them?

"Come on, Sugar. You been flaunting it around for days. Teasing me," Levis's hand gropes Izz's ass, grinding his hips into Izz, "after all I've done for you. I think it's time you start reciprocating."

After all he's done?

What has Levis done? Given him a little extra food. Nothing that would even remotely come close to allowing the man to feel him up without his permission.

"S-seriously, back off," Izz warns, but his voice is not as strong or forceful as he intended it to be.

E.P. WRITER

Why is this happening to me? Why can't people just leave me alone?

When he receives no reaction, he tries a different approach. Praying it will save him, "I'm trying to cook the potatoes, do you want them to burn? Back off."

Levis lets loose a huffed laugh, stepping out of Izz's space, "we'll finish this after lunch. Think about my offer."

Izz practically sprints out of the kitchen as soon as the meals are brought out for serving. Not sticking around to clean or top up the serving trays when the food runs low. He's gone before the pots he's in charge of stop sizzling.

He is not sorry about ditching out, not apologetic in the slightest. None of the others did shit. Every one of them pretended not to notice him being molested by that creep. They are as bad as the one who groped him. They stood by and said nothing—did nothing—when it was happening.

Back at his cell, Izz repeatedly thumps his head into his pillow. Crying out at how unfair everything is in this Hell-hole.

He doesn't want it. He doesn't want to be with anyone for protection. He isn't into Levis in that way. Doesn't find him even remotely attractive.

Levis is not Izz's type. Not even close. The man is foul. A revolting molester.

Why do they keep targeting me?

Despite the noise from various inmates crowding his Wing, he eventually cries himself to sleep. His dreams are

CAGED IN

filled with crazed nightmares. Hands reaching out for him in the darkness. Laughing sinister faces surround him as he runs. Trying to escape the grabbing hands—

A shrill alarm offers a lifeline to pull Izz free of his nightmares. Free of the reaching hands.

The alarm is the calling card for dinner—he must have missed dinner prep? And he is pleased by it. He wouldn't have gone either way. But now he doesn't have to sit in his cell worrying about a guard coming to collect him for food prep. He's not sure he could have stayed sane with that level of anxiety breathing down on him.

He picks up the new wrap of pills off his cupboard—where do they keep coming from?

He uses the cell's sink, swallowing the meds. Stripping out of his sweat soaked clothes he washes his body as best he can—water running down his sides to drip onto the floor, forming a puddle around his bare feet.

He ignores the water, which will dry during the night—or not, he doesn't care either way. Perhaps it will form mould and he'll have to be escorted to Med-Wing for mould inhalation. He'd have some days in a private room without any worries of inmates jumping him in the corridors. Or in the kitchen. Or outside his cell. He'd have a medical clearance to keep him out of the kitchen, and away from the *gang* boss.

Does mould grow overnight?

He hopes so. He's dreading going back. He knows it's inevitable. He has to work in the kitchen, he'll be dragged in by a guard and forced to stay there. Levis will have another opportunity to touch him. And none of the other inmates will help him.

E.P.WRITER

He plops down on his mattress, shaking off his feet to air dry them. Water flicking over the cell—it doesn't work, just wets more things.

Whatever.

Izz stuffs himself into a burrito of blankets, tucking himself into the fake protective shield. The thin fabric moulding to his body. Tightening over him, protecting him so nothing bad can harm him. A cocooned embrace to hug him to sleep.

With a huff he worms his cocoon over to the beds edge, so he can reach his cupboard without the need to stand. Hanging over the edge to collect a new set of prison clothes. He may have the cell to himself for the night but that doesn't mean he trusts this Hell-hole enough to sleep naked in it.

For all he knows the guards may not even lock the doors correctly. He's never tried to open them once they close. How does he know they don't just shut, beep, and stay unlocked?

You're paranoid. Izz's inner voice whispers, and he finds himself cursing at it as he wrestles his clothes on inside his blanket cocoon.

12

Breakfast hits all too soon the next day. Izz couldn't avoid it because the guard marched into his cell and told him he can either get up on his own, or be dragged out to prep breakfast, and then go to *solitary confinement*—they don't call it The Hole, guess the guards' are too *cool* to speak prisoner.

Izz informed the guard he'd choose the former and be at breakfast prep. Even when he was nearly overwhelmed with the urge to blab, he knew it would do him no good. The guards' don't care—

Which is how he ended up in his current position— hiding out alone in the dark of the showers. Uncanny doesn't even begin to describe the place. He thought he felt wary in the showers when it was open for the inmates to use. That pales in comparison to the trembles racking his body with nervous anxiety while alone, with little more than a square of light by the door to navigate his surroundings.

E.P.WRITER

It is way worse in the dark. As if he's the star of a horror film, about to be dragged back into the shadows and murdered in the dark dingy cold room.

He does not relish the idea of his death certificate reading the cause of death as a prison shower shanking—shivving?

He thinks he's been sitting on the cold tiles for the better part of an hour. His ass numbed out a while ago, he no longer has feeling in that part of his body. He'd like it to have been an hour, but knowing his luck in this prison so far, it's likely to be more like ten minutes. Wishful thinking has him hoping it's the former.

So far so good.

No guards have come in looking for him. No alarms have gone off indicating his disappearance has been noticed. Things are starting to look up. If he can hang out here until the breakfast siren sounds—when the rest of the prison becomes alive with activity—he'll be in the clear, at least for breakfast prep. He has no idea how he's going to avoid lunch and dinner. But he has to try.

He's in no hurry to go anywhere near Levis any time soon. He intends to avoid that particular inmate like the man has a contagious disease—Levis gives off the aura of *being* a contagious disease, let alone carrying one.

Izz jumps when the sirens chirp, echoing off the tiled walls. Marking the beginnings of a new day and the start of another meal. One he has successfully avoided prepping

CAGED IN

for. Avoiding the kitchen boss for another shift. He hopes he can do so for the whole day.

A new day in Hell.

During the tedious time he hid in the showers, he had planned to go to breakfast and sit with The Gang. To occupy his mind at least. However, he quickly dismisses the idea. Levis will be there, demanding an answer as to why he wasn't at breakfast prep.

He can't very well say he overslept and missed it. They both know the guards collect the kitchen inmates for morning prep. There is no way to sleep in and miss it.

He feels like a criminal—scratch that—he feels like a tiny mouse in a criminal's house trying to avoid the gigantic cat that wants to toy with him before it consumes him.

He's grateful when he manages to avoid any and all guards. Making his way back to his cell without being dragged in for breakfast cleaning and thrown in The Hole.

He's becoming paranoid, frightened out of his wits that Levis is lurking around every corner, ready to pounce on him. He's seriously considering The Hole as a good alternative instead of this consuming anxiety eating away at him—

Speaking of eating, he's starving. He hasn't eaten since . . . breakfast yesterday? It's all piling on top of him—the stress, the mentally draining breakdown in his cell last night, his restless sleep. His body is gnawing at itself. And he can't do anything about it. He's not going into the cafeteria. He can't. He's stuck. He has no idea what he's supposed to do.

If only Reni were here, his cellmate would have answers. Reni would no doubt sneak food out of the cafeteria for him. He'd even take Zidie's childish thought processes over his lack of ideas.

He requires food, and soon. He's not going to be able to go on like this for much longer. Not without his stomach eating itself. Or without what little muscle he has withering away to nothing.

Tripping into his cell he makes his way to the sink. Splashing cold water over his face may help his mind spit out some ideas. He'll waterboard the answers out of his head, see what magical plans his brain will cough out under duress—

A metallic glimmer catches his eye on his way past his bunk. Backtracking, he squints at the shine peeking out from under his pillow. He rocks back and forward in his flat prison-issued shoes, nervously reaching out to grasp his pillow, lifting it to reveal what's hidden beneath—

If this was a horror film, I'd be yelling at the screen, telling the idiot not to look under the pillow.

What's revealed is not a murderer's axe under his pillow—that last part has a real possibility of happening, given where he is. No. What's revealed is a bag of potato chips, beef jerky and a chocolate bar . . .

Izz positively gapes.

Where did it come from . . .

He glances around. Like the furniture will fill him in on where the food appeared from, on who brought it here and why?

Reni is in The Hole. Same as Zidie. Izz has been avoiding the rest of The Gang after what he overheard.

Maybe Blake? Although Blake doesn't seem like he would do this—actually he has always been nice, and he

CAGED IN

gave off caring brotherly vibes. It must have been him? Izz feels terrible for ditching them now. Especially if Blake had been the one to drop the food off. But what if it wasn't him?

Pursing his lips, he leans out the cell door, grasping the bars on either side to hold his balance in his lean-and-spy. Head tilting in both directions to check out each side of the second-floor platform.

Absolutely no one can be seen anywhere. No talking. No footfall. Only silence greets him.

Ducking back into his cell, he contemplates the food. His stomach growling, demanding he quit stalling and start binging.

He shrugs, what could be the harm in it?

Ripping into the plastic wrapping of the jerky first, he shoves a hand in, grabbing out the meaty treats. Eating the dried slices of goodness so fast he barely tastes it. His body telling him it hasn't eaten in days, his stomach continuing to growl and churn as he feeds it. Like it's angry at him for starving it for so long. At least his stomach's no longer trying to cannibalise itself, so that's a bonus.

Izz tries his best to avoid lunch. Tries to hide out in the yard but a guard finds him. He tries to argue he's unwell, and therefore not fit to be preparing meals for others, and doesn't want to make anyone else sick. The guard's response is that they don't care, informing Izz that he'll be thrown in solitary confinement if he doesn't move it. In the end, Izz's lugged back inside by the guard who waits at the door until he walks into the kitchen.

Izz would choose option two and gratefully go to The Hole. If he didn't still have to prep lunch before being thrown in there. He wanted to go to The Hole in order to avoid the kitchen. Not as a punishment on top of going to the kitchen.

"Where were you for dinner prep yesterday, and breakfast this morning?"

Izz closes his eyes to the familiar voice sleazing up behind him, the voice he dreads hearing.

Why couldn't Levis have been sick—literally anywhere else other than here. Izz cautiously turns, facing the beefy man, whose arms are crossed over a wide chest. Inspecting him like a disapproving boss who can't figure out why their employee is skipping work.

I'm sure if you think on that one real hard, you'll figure out why I wasn't here. Izz rants angrily in his head. Too nervous to speak any of it out loud.

"Sorry, I wasn't feeling the best," Izz mutters. Wishing he could disappear, "I'm still not feeling well but the guard didn't give me a choice, I had to come here."

Izz flinches when Levis reaches out. Not sure what to expect but completely taken off guard when the server touches his forehead. Like someone would do to a sick child. It's strange. Leaving him standing there like a stunned fish.

"You do feel a little warm," Levis informs Izz, letting his fingertips linger on Izz's skin before dropping his hand away. Not stepping back to give Izz room to breathe. "I'll keep you on light duties today, Sugar. You can do a run down on what we have for the dinner supplies, make sure it's in order for meal prep."

CAGED IN

Levis ambles off to yell at a few inmates about stirring their pots correctly—something along the lines of smelling burning, and not letting it stick to the bottom.

He zones out, allowing the yelling to waft to the back of his mind—or rather, the boss screaming at other inmates while they bow their heads in shame. Either way, Izz lets it sift out of his immediate consideration to become a background noise he ignores.

Collecting the clipboard hanging on the wall outside the pantry room's door, he reads down the list of items required for dinner prep. There are a lot of products on the list. All in bulk quantities.

This is going to take a while.

He's still counting and ticking off the list as the sounds of lunch wrapping up reach his ears—

Panic seeps into his bones, his heart rabbiting as his ears strain at the voices outside the pantry. Listening for one voice in particular...

Izz can't hear Levis in the kitchen, he takes the opportunity to make good his escape. Fumbling the clipboard back into its holder. Swiftly rushing out of the kitchen.

Darting through the double doors at the kitchen's exit, he'll have to take the long way back to his cell. It'll be worth the extra exercise to avoid being spotted by Levis who is serving the last few inmates standing at the food bar.

E.P. WRITER

He's sure someone's following him back to his cell. Checking over his shoulder every ten seconds, his paranoid mind expects to see Levis around every corner or standing right behind him.

He's more jumpy than he has ever been in this cage. And he's more alone than he has ever been. With Reni and Zidie in The Hole, he is left to fend for himself in the carnivorous general population.

He sighs with relief when he reaches his cell. Rushing into the barred room like the place is his own personal prison. His protective bubble where no bad can ever breach its threshold.

He's too depressed, and anxious to worry when he finds more snacks on his bunk. A packet of chips, and some other food items which are extremely appealing to his starving stomach.

He kicks out his fearful thoughts. The who, why and how questions surrounding the food are not welcome. He can worry about it later. Right now, he's hungry and this is edible. He will take it and enjoy it. Without thinking about who put it here and why. He doesn't want to think about the consequences for him to accept the snacks. He will forget his fears and drown his stresses in the sugar-filled snacks he's been gifted.

Let the worries wash over you, Izz. You can stress over the consequences at a later date. His inner voice instructs.

13

Izz walks to the kitchen of his own free will, not out of any sense of duty or obligation. No. It was due to a guard spotting him, he had watched the expression on the guard's face tighten to one of annoyance. He had hoped the guard didn't know he was supposed to be in the kitchen. The way the guard's expression shifted, flattening out into a snarl informed Izz that this guard knew exactly where he was supposed to be. He had turned tail and made his way to the kitchen, much to his displeasure, and the guard's delight.

The cooking is already finishing, the last of the meals dished out into serving trays. He's thrilled to discover the prep work is completed. Levis is always serving, which means Izz can hide in the back rooms of the kitchen, avoiding the dirty pervert boss until he's sure he can sneak off without a guard catching him.

"Hey, Sugar, where'd you duck off to after lunch?"

He's never so lucky. This cage is cursed, and he has the worst luck. The one inmate in this place he had been praying to avoid walks out from behind the shelves.

"You know you can't get away with not helping in the clean-up," Levis smirks, leaning casually into Izz's personal space. "But I'm willing to let you off with a warning if you . . . apologise to me . . . very . . . very . . . nicely."

Levis's hand slides over Izz's ass, fingers brushing under his shirt. Brushing the skin of his stomach. He grits his teeth, about to erupt and do something he has never done before.

Punch a person in the face.

He's a virgin when it comes to punching people. With everything that's happened to him in this Hell-hole, he's impressed with himself for not losing it and lashing out sooner.

His hands squeeze shut, tightening, ready to swing his fists at the perv's face. Tensing, he plants his feet, shifting to swing—

The dinner bell rings—snapping Izz out of his bravado, and sapping his courage like a deflating balloon— informing them dinner is now commencing and serving is due to take place.

Ha. Saved by the bell. Never thought that would be something I ever said.

"You're on serving today, Sugar," Levis grabs Izz's shoulder, guiding Izz towards the front of the kitchen.

Levis's unwelcome touch has his skin crawling, a gritty charcoal taste coating his mouth. His body's negative reaction to this man is so intense it's manifesting itself into a physical form which can be felt and tasted.

Why does Levis insist on calling him Sugar? It's gross, demeaning and flat-out weird. He is not some product to

CAGED IN

be consumed by whoever wants it, without any say in who consumes it.

Begrudgingly, Izz stomps over to the serving bar, allowing himself to be guided by the kitchen boss. Hating every second of the close contact between them. Not wanting to cause a scene or garner attention, he keeps his displeasure to himself. Too many inmates out here, he doesn't want them catching on to how freaked out he is.

He's relieved when Levis leaves him alone to serve, disappearing back into the kitchen. He tries his best to move through quickly. To give the inmates their meals fast and not hold up the line. It still takes him a dozen or so inmates before he gathers his wits and finds his rhythm.

By the seventh dozen inmate, he is a pro. He is also figuring out that he hates serving people. It's gruelling work. Slow and monotonous.

He's sick of repeating the same sentences over and over. What's on today's menu, do they want this or that, yes this has that in it, no there is none of that available or in any of the dishes.

It's repetitive, tedious work. And hot. It's hot as Hell back here with all the food. Like the kitchen's heat is an invading parasite hell bent on making his life as miserable as possible. It would be so much better if the inmates served themselves.

Why can't they serve themselves?

He's marching back to the start to begin the next order. The umpteenth time running through the same routine—

The change in atmosphere is nearly instantaneous. A dark glacial torrent hitting Izz from the other inmates. A solid mass of frozen terror. He surveys his surroundings, dread filling his lungs, constricting his chest. The next inmates in the queue shuffled back quickly, opening a large space in front of the serving bar.

The next male to step up—skipping the line—is HIM. Red and black mohawk spiked hair, in its signature presentation. Sharp eyes cutting through everyone, missing nothing. Thick legs corded with muscles devouring the distance to the bar. The killer moving with deathly purpose across the vacated space.

Striding straight towards Izz.

Why do I have to be the unlucky one in charge of serving the next inmate?

The entire room washes away, drowned out as Izz stares with wide eyes at the serial killer approaching him. The killer who is right there. Right in front of him, and getting closer . . .

He swallows hard, his eyes drawn to the killer's face. With only a serving bar separating them. A bar he wishes was bigger, with safety glass separating him from the room beyond.

The killer stops in front of Izz, close enough to see the flecks of colour in the male's irises, an onyx black with little flecks of chocolate brown. A multitude of dark colours framed by thick lashes. At a distance, the killer's eyes appeared jet black. But this close . . . Izz can see the flecks interwoven within the black.

He drags his eyes downwards, to the tattoos covering the killers arms. Dripping down to pool in the crook of his elbows. Blood droplets escaping from a blood splatter peeking out under short sleeves.

Wonder what made him get that design—

CAGED IN

Oh, right. Serial killer. Dah.

The killer reaches for a tray, flashing a wrist inked by a black triple six tattoo, at the suicide point. If it's called that? It's apt to call it that, considering the killer's arms are covered with lifelike blood. The three thick black letters standing out from the deep red rivers flowing over his upper arms.

Devil worship? Or a random design he just happened to like the look of?

The male is a serial killer—supposedly—Izz would place his money on the tattoo being a worship one and not an *it'll-look-cool* type thing.

"I'll take the potato, and whatever pasta you think tastes the best," the killer's voice is deep, commanding . . . domineering—

Izz clears his throat. Trying to gag his mind as his emotions rise inside him, hot and heavy—

You're gawking. Like a fool—a fool with a death wish.

He doesn't have a death wish. Although from an outsider's perspective it would appear as though he does. With the way he's staring and not moving—

Pull yourself together man. Izz inwardly scolds.

"Yes, sure thing, I can do that. That'll be fine."

You're rambling. Izz's inner voice pipes up. It would be more helpful if his inner voice told him what to say to the dangerous male in front of him, so he doesn't say the wrong thing and piss off a serial killer.

His hands are trembling, he tries his best to corral them into cooperation, failing miserably. Doing his best to ignore the tremors, to pretend his hands aren't shaking leaves caught in a hurricane. He scoops out a hefty heaping of mash. Carefully placing it down on the tray. He isn't sure how much the killer is expecting to be given . . .

Not wanting to be stingy Izz gathers another mound of mashed potatoes. Best safe than sorry. Especially when it comes to dangerous inmates. Who may or may not be capable of murdering you in your sleep.

He slides over to the pasta dishes. Inspecting the different selections of pasta as if it were his first time seeing them. Not as if he'd spent the last . . . hour? serving countless inmates.

He has no clue which ones taste any good. He's never eaten any of them. He didn't help cook them, he has no idea what's actually in any of them. Has no idea if the ingredients were measured correctly, if the flavours are to perfection or salty as shit. It could be a wonderful meal or it could be a disgusting sticky mess.

Shit.

He is in the whole tell-the-truth faze, isn't he? It hasn't really kept him out of trouble so far. Though faking it would end badly if the pasta he picks turns out to be a rubbery sludge and not the *best pasta choice.*

"I actually don't know what's good. I've never eaten any of these." Izz's going with the truth, and hoping it doesn't turn around to bite him in the ass.

It would be worse to lie to the killer.

"I'm new here—" Izz gestures to his orange shirt, like that isn't obvious without pointing it out. "—I haven't tried all the foods the prison cooks."

And I hope to not be in the kitchen long enough to learn how each meal is made.

"Whichever you think would be best."

CAGED IN

The killer's eyes bore into Izz's soul. Surprisingly though, he doesn't feel afraid. He feels as if the killer is silently checking if he's okay. Which is weird. He has to be imagining it . . . ?

Maybe he is as pale as he feels and the killer is expecting him to pass out into the pasta. That would be an embarrassing incident he would never live down. He'd take himself to The Hole indefinitely so he wouldn't have to look the killer in the eyes ever again.

"Alright . . . But if it tastes like shit, just letting you know, I warned you. I also didn't cook it, so there's that too."

Izz hears a sharp intake of breath down from him—guess that server was part of the pasta cooking team. He has to say, he is not sorry for throwing any of them under the bus. None of them did shit when Levis was putting his disgusting hands all over him. The multiple times that asshole has done it.

Screw them.

He flicks his eyes over to the inmate beside him—who had made the small distressed noise. One of those who deliberately turned away when he was being groped.

He sends the inmate a smirked *paybacks-a-bitch* and is deeply satisfied when the other man pales somewhat. He has to bite his lip to stop the laugh from escaping his throat.

He decides on the Bolognese type pasta—it's the one he would go with, the nicest looking of the dishes—and delicately places it down on the killer's tray. Extra careful not to splash a drop of food anywhere out of its little section. He does not want to flick pasta sauce off the tray in fear of hitting the killer.

How did Izz die? Well he flicked Bolognese sauce on a serial killer.

Izz bites his cheek to suppress the laugh he almost let loose. He is not yet a crazy person. He has to hold his composure as long as possible. Laughing at his own mind's ramblings is not a good look on a sane person. Not when you want to stay out of the Psych-Wing.

"Would you like a drink or cookie?"

Okay, offering a cookie to a serial killer is laughable. And nothing Izz ever thought he would do in his lifetime, but here he is. Offering a cookie to a killer. Oh, how his life has changed drastically.

"Chocolate. And a water."

Again with that deep voice, sending sparks through Izz's body. He is so out of whack he can't determine what the sensations means.

It has to be a fear response. Right?

"Perfect," Izz cringes as soon as the word leaves his lips, spinning away swiftly to prevent the killer from glimpsing the involuntary shift in his expression.

Perfect? Seriously? That's your reply? Moron.

He wanders over to the end of the food bar to collect the cookies and drink. He picks out three chocolate chip cookies for the killer, because why not? No one's going to say anything. And he's going to be running off straight after he finishes serving, so he's not going to be needing any with his meal. A meal he won't be having, not when it potentially risks him running into Levis.

The killer nods at Izz, before prowling off to the far back corner to consume the meal. Izz has to force his eyes away

CAGED IN

or he'll be frozen in place, gawking at the killer instead of continuing to serve meals.

He accepts the killer's nod as a thank you. And the lack of a knife in his face, as a sign he had done well with his newly acquired serving skills.

Struggling to suppress a grin, Izz drifts back to the queue once more, floating over to serve the next person. A cloud of content cushioning his steps.

All things considered, he thinks that interaction went pretty smoothly—

Izz scoffs. Mentally scolding himself for trying to act cool and impress the male. He is a serial killer, for Christ's sake.

Why does he become starry-eyed around the dangerous mohawked inmate?

Serving is finishing, the inmates already dispersing from the cafeteria to go off and do their prison life things. He is handing over a bottle of apple juice to his last '*customer*', the last two in line are being taken care of by other servers.

Finished with the tedious task of serving, Izz collects two empty trays and lugs them back into the kitchen for whichever inmate is in charge of washing up today. He can't see their face as they're already bent over scrubbing away at one of the giant cooking pots, leaning bodily inside to reach the bottom. Not that he would have known who it is anyway. He doesn't know anyone's name in here except for Levis. He doesn't want to learn any of their names, and he sure as hell doesn't want to be anywhere near the one he does know.

Clanking the trays down, he back peddles through the kitchen to ensure he doesn't run into Levis. The one inmate in here he truly wants to avoid. The rest sat back and didn't help him, but at least they don't grab at him.

He groans when the inmate he detests steps out from behind one of the cooking benches. Effectively blocking Izz's path to the exit.

Life is never simple, not in this cage.

The only inmates loitering within the kitchen are the pot scrubber in the back and the two out front finishing serving, the rest are long gone. The cafeteria is near empty, not that any of those inmates can see all the way back here.

Izz's alone against the creep who thinks he's entitled to feel people up without permission. All based on a delusion that someone being nice to you means they want you to touch them. That giving the person extra food in meals means you have the right to touch them.

What is wrong with this man—

Wait . . .

Extra food . . .

What was it Levis said . . . *'after all I've done for you. I think it's time you start reciprocating'*.

'All I've done'.

All he's done.

No.

No no no. The food. The food left in his cell. Was it Levis's doing? The mattress too?

It has to be. And like a fool, Izz had taken it, eaten it, slept on it. He can't pay back the money. He hadn't asked for it. And he wouldn't have been starving if he'd been able to

CAGED IN

eat the prison meals like everyone else. And not have a creep in his face wanting—no, demanding, Izz pay everything back.

What else could it mean? It has to be that. Levis can't possibly only be referring to the little bit of extra food at mealtimes. Levis can't be so deluded as to think giving an inmate a bit of extra food entitled him to sexual favours?

Then again, you shouldn't think a mattress and snacks left in a cell entitles you to whatever you want from a person either. If you voluntarily give someone a gift, you aren't entitled to receive whatever you want as compensation.

And to think, Izz used to believe Levis was nice. How naive he'd been . . .

"You thought about my offer?" Levis grins, squishing into Izz's personal space.

"No. Thank you. I'm fine." Izz sidesteps in an attempt to weave past the kitchen boss—

Things go south, real fast. Before Izz can raise a hand in his defence, he is grabbed and manhandled backwards. His back hitting the pantry doors as he's shoved right through them.

Out of sight.

Utterly alone.

Not that anyone in the kitchen has shown any sign they will do anything to help. Even if they were all huddled inside the pantry, they wouldn't raise a hand to help him.

"Let me go. I'm done with this place," Izz yells at Levis's face, thrashing in the tight grip squeezing his upper arms. "I'm leaving this shitty job, and I don't care if it lands me in The Hole for the rest of my stay."

Okay, so he's bluffing. He does not want to be stuck in a room alone for years, but at this particular moment he is too pissed off to care.

"I said. LET. GO." Izz bellows, throwing all his strength into his attempt to dislodge Levis's hold.

"Nah, Sugar. I'm not going to do that," Levis's calm voice holds no indication he is straining to restrain Izz.

His back hits one of the huge barrels—containing flour or perhaps rice—

He's aware his mind is trying to distract him, it doesn't matter what is contained within the barrels, only that his mind can channel that thought to draw him out of the situation he is being forced into.

This freak is touching, touching what he was not given permission to touch and is not backing down.

Fight or flight.

He's trapped, he can't run. He's stuck between a creep and a heavy immovable barrel.

Defence. Defence it is. But how is he going to defend himself? He's overpowered, the perv's packing twice—if not more—muscle mass than Izz could ever dream of possessing.

His scrawny ass is going to lose this fight. He can't afford to lose. Not with what the stakes are. This inmate isn't going to kill him, they're going to do something far worse—

The world spins. Izz's vision swirling as he's repositioned. Shoved belly first over the barrel. A large disgusting hand pinning the back of his neck. Holding him down with little effort on Levis's part. The man isn't even

CAGED IN

breathing heavily. It makes Izz's skin crawl—all he wants to do is run to the shower and scrub his skin raw.

Frantically trying to pull away, his breathing increasing to erratic hyperventilating gasps. Levis's grasp is too powerful, he is terrified and weak, his feeble attempts are getting him nowhere. All he manages to do is scratch his knees on the barrel's rough exterior.

His legs are shaking, his palms sweating, he cannot believe this thing is happening to him. He'd never in a thousand years thought it would ever happen to him—

This is something that happened to women. To women in horror stories people don't want to think too closely about, too horrific for anyone to believe it could happen to them.

Izz hisses when Levis's other hand drops down between him and the barrel, gripping his waistband and tugging down the only form of protective barrier between him and his attacker.

He's too stunned to cry out. Too shocked to think clearly. His brain screaming full blast at him but he can't understand what he is supposed to do to save himself. The hand clutching his neck is iron hard, rooted in place. Digging into his flesh.

"Let go," Izz breathes out, trying to portray strength. To demand he be taken seriously. His voice is barely above a whispered plea, "you don't have to do this."

He wants to say *'please'*. To beg. A little voice inside tells him it's a bad idea. If this creep is willing to force someone, him begging them to stop would result in turning them on. Wouldn't it?

Izz blinks rapidly, he can't cry. He won't give this monster the satisfaction. Blinking to clear his vision, clears his sight to the crumbs scattering the lid by his face. Little grains, safe from harm. He'd give anything to be a crumb. To disappear into the barrel and never return.

"I don't, but I want to," Levis mocks.

The dank stench wafting off Levis is making Izz nauseous. He wants to vomit. But he's terrified at the anger it will provoke. Will he die? If he pukes, will Levis beat him to death?

"If you'd taken my offer this could have gone a less painful route."

The sneered remark sends shivers down Izz's spine, tears pricking his eyes, threatening to break free. He's going to be one of those horror stories. One no-one completely takes in, too afraid of the pain it would cause—

A clattered noise from beyond the pantry doors draws his attacker's attention. A jingling noise following soon after. He can't concentrate on the sound long enough to figure out what it is. He's heard it before, he knows it's familiar—

Izz's pants are yanked back up. And he's released from the crushing hold—

The pantry door clanks open—with so much force it bounces back off the wall to fly at the person that assaulted it—

Caught in an outstretched hand, of one very pissed-off guard—

The noise had been his keys—the keys every guard carries on their belt—

CAGED IN

"We having a picnic in here or what?" The guard demands, his voice cracking off the pantry walls. "Get the fuck out and back to your cells."

Izz doesn't hesitate for a second. Scrambling out. Placing as much distance as he can between himself and Levis.

Stumbling out past the food bar, he steps free into the cafeteria—

Stopping dead halfway to the corridor that leads to his Wing—

The black and red mohawked serial killer is leaning back against the cafeteria wall, consumed by shadows. A dark menacing presence.

Why is he here? What . . .

Izz throws a look over his shoulder, watching Levis storm out the side door, the double doors flapping wide. The kitchen boss didn't notice the serial killer lurking in the cafeteria's depths. A shark in dark waters.

Izz pulls his gaze back—

Only to find an empty space. The killer is gone. No trace he'd been there. No sounds of his departure.

Is the killer the reason the guard came in? Or pure coincidence?

"Get moving, inmate," the guard's voice doesn't seem as angry this time. More tired and exhausted.

Izz studies the empty shadows one last time, as though he'll find the answers he seeks if he stares long enough. He has so many unanswered questions . . .

"Thank you," Izz breathes out under his breath. Not sure if he's thanking the guard or the serial killer. Perhaps a little of both.

14

Izz sprints to his cell in a hunger-filled blur. Weaving around inmates. His ravenous stomach growling demands to be filled.

He discovers more snacks waiting for him in his bunk. Nestled among the messy sheets he hadn't tucked back in.

He can't get Levis's words out of his head. Like the power-saving mode on an old computer screen, they bounce from one corner of his mind to the next in a hypnotising rhythm, dancing across the screen of his mind.

'After all I've done for you'.

Around and around. Circling and changing. Restless thoughts, colliding with other unanswerable questions—

Izz rushes to the toilet, grasping the sides just in time for his stomach's evac'. Little more than bile forcing its way out. No food in his stomach to expel.

Squatting by the toilet, with his stomach's growls increasing in volume, he hangs his head over his arm, closes his eyes, and weeps.

CAGED IN

He lets his emotions loose—the emotions which have been hidden by surges of adrenaline. Free to explode out his chest as he cries silently in his cell—alone and scared, slumped over a prison toilet bowl.

This isn't fair. No one should have to go through this. Why is this cage so cruel?

Why do they have to target me?

Gathering a minuscule of composure, Izz shakily gets to his feet, his knees wobbling. Biting his lip through the pins and needles, he washes his face in the sink. Hitting the flusher on the toilet, as water drips off his chin to wet his shirt collar.

Gritting his teeth at the onslaught of agony riding up his calves as the feeling comes back to his legs. His body's way of cursing him for his mistreatment, for leaving it curled up on the cold floor.

His stomach is a hollow pit. Empty and sad. He refuses to fill it. The only food he has are the snacks that creep left him. He may be many things but he isn't stupid. He is not going to risk more repercussions for accepting food from Levis.

It had to have come from Levis?

Izz crawls onto his bunk, too exhausted and mentally drained to reach over and pull the thin sheet over his body. He can't even pluck up the energy to kick his shoes off. His eyes heavy and swollen, his throat raw and aching. His will is frazzled and his essence numb.

With his adrenaline dropping. He doesn't so much fall asleep as pass out cold.

E.P. WRITER

When Izz had woken, he was surprised a guard had not come to collect him for the morning meal prep. Instead, it wasn't until the cell doors opened for the whole of A-Wing that a guard rocked up to inform Izz he was to go to the counsellor's office.

That's how he found himself here. Seated once again in the cushioned chair. Looking over the oak desk at a furious counsellor.

"So, you've been moved into laundry," the counsellor grumbles. Biting off his words as if they offend his very soul to say them.

"Really?" Izz can't restrain his excitement, even in the face of an infuriated counsellor.

Leaning forward in his chair in case he isn't hearing correctly. He never considered he'd be delighted to do the laundry. Then again, he's been put through a lot of things in this cage he never thought would happen to him. And he's only been in this Hell-hole for . . . What? Six days . . . ?

Too much has happened in too little time. His mind is going to snap. He can feel it straining to hold on to his sanity. This place is going to break him.

Only if you let it. A small comforting voice whispers to him.

"Thank you," Izz grins. Throwing away the crap from the past, already optimistic about his new job assignment.

"You could have come to me with the paperwork—" The counsellor's angry voice does little to quell Izz's joy in

CAGED IN

getting out of that vile kitchen. "—not gone to the Warden. Going around me. Now I've got the Warden all over me. I thought I was pretty nice to you. Now you go and do this."

Do what?

Izz didn't do anything. What is this counsellor going on about? Who went to the Warden to get him moved? He sure didn't. Wouldn't even know how to find the Warden in the first place.

This counsellor guy is insane.

"May I leave?" Izz glances over his shoulder to check that he has a clear path straight to the door—

It's clear, no unexpected roadblocks have popped up in the few minutes since he entered the office.

Refocusing back on the counsellor, Izz discovers the man glaring at him. He smiles in a way he hopes comes off as sincere and not mockery. Several long moments of glaring later, the counsellor waves a hand towards the door.

He doesn't stick around to make sure he interpreted the dismissal correctly. He springs out of his chair like the room is on fire. Diving for the door as if the last drops of water in the world are on the other side. Practically slamming the door in his hasty exit.

Out in the corridor, he leans back against the door. Catching his breath, and composing himself.

What a weird guy.

Why is the counsellor so angry? It's not like the man is being felt up in the kitchen by a gang member, while the rest of the inmates pretend not to notice. He's sitting there, making it about himself. Like he has a right to get pissy at Izz for being moved to another job.

E.P.WRITER

Someone else has apparently gone to the Warden on Izz's behalf and requested he be moved. If he can believe a word that counsellor spouts. And at the current time, he believes the man as far as he can throw him. Which is not far.

What an entitled jerk.

When Izz returns to his cell after his brief talk with the counsellor, there's more food. More snacks stacked on his pillow. A nice neat pile demanding attention, but there's something else that has him stopping dead in the cell's doorway. It's a pleasant surprise, one he's equally ecstatic and uneasy to discover.

Dull-faced and exhausted, his cellmate is sitting on the opposite bunk.

"Hey," Izz greets Reni, delighted to see his cellmate out of The Hole—speaking of which, "how'd you get out of The Hole so soon? Didn't I hear it was going to be two weeks or something?"

He could have sworn he heard a conversation when Reni and Zidie were being dragged away. Inmates whispering to each other how unlucky they were, how they'd be stuck in The Hole for weeks for being involved in a gang fight.

"Good behaviour," Reni mutters dryly. Which tells Izz absolutely nothing.

Did his cellmate break out of The Hole? Is that possible to do?

He's letting his movie imagination run wild. In real life, no way could someone break out of The Hole without the guards noticing.

"So what's that?" Reni enquires. His eyes gluing to the snacks lying on Izz's pillow.

CAGED IN

Izz blinks out of his puzzled state of mind—it would take a James Bond movie scene to explain Reni's return—following Reni's line of sight to check out what he's referring to.

He isn't sure if Reni is only now noticing the pile on the pillow. Or if he had seen it ages ago and couldn't hold the question in any longer.

Izz scrambles to gather all the snacks into his arms, rushing them over to his cupboard. Stuffing them out of sight behind his spare towel. As much out of Reni's line of sight and questioning, as it is out of temptation for Izz. He doesn't want to talk about it, and he isn't entirely sure who's leaving the treats. If it is Levis, he doesn't want to discuss it with his cellmate. He would prefer Reni doesn't know what has been happening in the kitchen.

"Nothing," Izz hastily dismisses, stuffing the last of the packets into their hiding place. As though his rushed grab and hide isn't suspicious in the slightest.

Smooth Izz, real inconspicuous.

Reni gives Izz a look which he decides to misinterpret. "So . . . thank you. For . . . you know, stepping in." Izz rubs the back of his neck, having to admit he needed someone to defend him, made him feel like he's some kind of weakling.

He knew he wouldn't have come out of that fight alive without the intervention of his cellmate . . . His friend. And of course Zidie, who can forget about his best friend, he is more than fine referring to Zidie as such. It would be strange not calling the two of them friends, after they jumped in to save his life. A very best-friend thing to do.

"Nah," Reni waves a hand dismissively. Like it's no big deal, and he has no idea why Izz's making a fuss over it. "Don't mention it, it's what any friend would do. I have to go to an anger management class now—and don't change the subject. Who's leaving you food? Or did ya magically get money in the last couple of days?"

His out of sight, out of mind logic hadn't worked. If only it had. He doesn't want to go into all the details, to try and explain his situation to his friend.

Izz sighs, knowing Reni won't drop the subject until he hears some information, "I don't really know, though I have my suspicions. It's not important. Forget it."

I'm terrified Levis is going to trap me and no one will be there to help me . . .

He bites his tongue to hold back what he really wants to say. He can't tell his cellmate what's really going on. What if Reni looks at him differently? Or worse, stops talking to him. He can't lose one of the only people in here who he can talk to.

Izz mimics Reni's dismissive hand gesture, dropping the subject and hoping his friend will let it slide. "I'm glad you're back. Missed your energetic butt being around to keep me occupied in this boring cell."

Reni grins, his chest inflating with importance at his presence being missed, "I knew ya loved me."

Izz snorts a barked laugh, shoving Reni playfully in the shoulder, earning a chuckle from his friend.

CAGED IN

Reni convinces Izz to go to breakfast with him. It doesn't take much persuading, his stomach is beyond empty.

Having Reni around gives Izz back some of his strength. It's also a bonus to have his cellmate nearby when they're being served, it keeps Levis's trap shut, no lewd comments or inappropriateness. Granted, the kitchen boss is hostile and glaring at Izz, and barely speaks more than a few words to him, for which he is grateful.

For the first time he is not being polite to someone serving him food. There is no *'thank you'* or *'please'* or *'I would like'*. Nothing remotely polite leaves his lips, it's all *'I want that'* and *'give me some of those'*. He throws in a sarcastic *'cheers'* at the end, in a mocking thank you. Meeting Levis's hostility glare for glare.

He is filled with bravado with Reni standing right next to him, backing him up. There to protect and defend him if things turn sour. Not that his cellmate knows about any of it.

Izz finds himself understanding why people play up and act tough in gangs. The back-up reinforces arrogance in you. Inflates your ego to the point where you think you can take on anyone. A whole group of tough-acting people like that is a dangerous combination. It feels great though, the feeling of power, however artificial it may be.

For the first time since the fight, Izz sits at the table with the rest of The Gang. He's on edge, knowing at least three inmates at this table have been talking crap about him behind his back.

"Yo, Reni, what happened in The Hole? We heard rumours about the guys you got thrown down there with.

Care to share the details?" Erik peers past Isco's massive bulk, wide eyes blinking at Reni—pleading for gossip.

"I don't know," Reni shrugs, digging into his food. He looks like he wants to avoid the question altogether.

Izz's interest peaks, he hadn't heard about anything happening in The Hole, but he has mostly been keeping to himself these past however many days—it feels like months since the fight.

What is Erik talking about? What happened in The Hole?

"Come on Reni, spill," Blake chimes in.

Izz leans in closer, so he doesn't miss a single detail. Prison gossip is the only real form of entertainment in this cage. Some inmates would argue a good fight is better entertainment, but it's not his thing to watch some poor sap be beaten to death and place bets on it. With his luck, he would be the poor sap.

"Alright. Alright." Reni throws his spoon down, shoving his tray away, as if he's lost his appetite due to the direction of the conversation, "they're all dead."

When Reni doesn't elaborate, Erik scoffs, "come on, man. You have to give us more than that. We already know that part."

Izz sure didn't know it. How is it possible they're all dead? The one who had been on the floor—who was carried away by guards presumably to Med-Wing—could have died, if he hadn't already been dead. But the rest of them . . .

Reni scrubs at his face, the irritation he feels showing in the tense lines of his shoulders. He's usually so open about everything that it is next to impossible to get him to shut

CAGED IN

up. His silence made Izz very uneasy, he's acting completely out of character.

"They were all locked in cells—" Reni begins, his soft voice barely loud enough to carry over the thunderous volume of the busy cafeteria, "—single windowless cells, down in The Hole. No guards came in or left, no new inmates were thrown in. Nothing. But that first night in . . . by morning . . . they were all dead—killed—inside their locked cells. Not a sound was heard from any of them." Reni's eyes dart and flicker over the room, which has Izz subconsciously doing the same. On alert, checking their surroundings. "I couldn't sleep, The Hole always gives me the creeps. And I heard absolutely nothing. No one walked up that corridor. Nobody left. I heard no doors clanging open. Nothing."

"So, what?" Erik pipes in sceptically, "they killed themselves? All three of them?"

"—and that's not all of it," Reni ignores Erik's comment, "the one who went to Med-Wing. He didn't wake up the next morning either."

"He looked like death when they dragged him out," Isco states dryly, shovelling in the last of his breakfast, casting his spoon off to the side.

The rest of the table have forgotten their own breakfast or, like Izz, are too grossed out by Reni's story to continue eating. He wonders whether these hard men around the table are still capable of being grossed out by anything that happens in this cage? They hold themselves like they've been through Hell and back—tough and unflinching.

Except Reni whose stricken features betrayed his confusion and terror.

"No," Reni spits out at Isco, "I mean, his throat was slit. I don't know if that was before or after the rest of them were killed. But Med-Wing is locked down tighter than The Hole."

"Whoa," Erik utters, his scepticism wavering, "so how'd the ones in The Hole die?"

"Their throats were slit." Reni leans into The Gang, dropping his voice lower to whisper, "there was so much blood, it seeped out from under the solid doors. That's how the guards figured out something was wrong."

"Who did it? Or did they have a suicide pact?" Erik leans in further, entranced by Reni's story and hanging onto every word.

Reni smirks, eating up the attention Erik and the rest of The Gang are directing at him. "No. I heard the doctors talking in The Hole, there were stab wounds in them, the wounds were done *post-mortem*. And I've watched enough TV on the outside to know that means *after death*."

"Does it?" Erik ponders and peers at Blake to see if the other can confirm. He receives a shrug in response.

"Sure it does. Who would willingly stab themselves multiple times, for a suicide, then slit their own throat." Reni slaps the table, leaning forward. "I'm telling you it was the SC-Ghost."

Wait? What?

Reni's revelation is met with loud groans and exasperated dismissals. Everyone complaining over the top of each other in a mash of the English language.

"Are you kidding me—"

"You made up the whole story, didn't ya—"

"Was anyone even stabbed—"

CAGED IN

Who's the SC-Ghost? Is there another serial killer in this cage? That's all he needs, more serial killers living right next to him. Eating in the same space, showering in the same room, sleeping within the same vicinity.

"Who's the SC-Ghost?" Izz blurts, he had meant to keep the question to himself. Too late now, it's out absorbing airtime.

Reni turns wild eyes on Izz, "the Solitary Confinement Ghost. It's the ghost of an inmate who was killed down there years ago. It haunts the place."

He isn't sure what to say. Does his cellmate really believe this? He is relieved it's only one of Reni's dramatic stories and not an actual person who could kill him—

Well, whoever did do it is still in here, so maybe he's jumping the gun on the relief train. Thinking he's safe and relaxing his guard. That's when everyone gets killed in horror movies. A sigh of relief, then bam, out jumps the serial killer and you're done for—

"Ren, you got to stop spreading ghost stories," Blake chuckles, straightening up as he loses interest in Reni's ghost tale.

"What? How else do ya explain it?" Reni pouts at The Gang, crossing his arms over his chest.

"The guards did it," Isco states flatly.

The only obvious answer to the mystery. Who else could kill multiple inmates while they're locked in individual cells. Alone, with no bars for any inmates to stab them through. The guards have the keys.

"Boring. You wanted me to tell the story. And this is it. The SC-Ghost killed them," Reni concludes, not accepting anyone else's logic. His story set in stone in his own mind, and he is not budging from it.

"And what? It floated up to Med-Wing to kill the man there. Why not kill you as well?" Isco points out, garnering a furious glare from Reni.

"Get out of here with your buzz killing. It has no place at this table with my ghost stories," Reni scowls at Isco who smirks in reaction to the hostility. "The SC-Ghost had to be one of their victims who came back to take revenge. That's why I wasn't a target."

"Thought you said the ghost never left," Isco's smirk widens. He's enjoying poking fun at Reni and watching his annoyance grow.

"Whatever, man. It stuck around all this time waiting for the perfect opportunity to strike."

Isco isn't finished debunking the story, "so it haunted The Hole for years, waiting for them to be thrown in there at the same time. Only to leave, and kill one in Med-Wing, that same night. Could have killed them in their cells years ago and been done with it."

"He has a point," Phelix chimes in, shrugging his shoulders.

"Boring," Reni groans, shooting Isco and Phelix his middle finger. "Maybe the SC-Ghost wanted to intimidate and haunt them first—"

Isco raises a brow, "From the Hole—"

"Shhhtt. No more from you," Reni slaps his fingers over Isco's mouth, hushing the scarred man from saying another word, "you're killing my perfectly flawless story."

Isco chuckles, shoving Reni's hand aside, grinning wildly. A gun that sends shivers down Izz's spine and has

CAGED IN

the hairs on the back of his neck standing on end. He hasn't figured out why Isco puts him on edge. His fight or flight receptors always perk up and whisper whenever Isco's close.

What crimes did Isco commit to be thrown in this cage?

Izz redirects his focus from Isco back to his cellmate before his mind crumbles into a powder of worry. "So what really happened to them?"

He's leaning more towards Isco's analysis. The guards had done it. But why? Were they paid by another gang to murder them? Or did they do it just because they could? Because they would get away with it? Because society won't care or look too closely at a few dead inmates?

"Don't know," Reni shifts like a switch flicked over to a new line of fact sharing, "probably a hit from another gang or something. Who cares. Good riddance, I say." Reni verbally waves off Izz's concerns, and confirms Izz's suspicions in one statement.

So it had been a hit. But why—

Never mind, it would have something to do with drugs or turf wars, no doubt. Nothing Izz wants to be involved in. He'd prefer to stay as far away from the gang dealings as possible. Adding more time onto his sentence is not his goal. He wants to get out of this Hell-hole sooner rather than later.

"It was the SC-Ghost," Reni grins—winking at Izz—when Isco gives him an exasperated look.

Izz bites his lip, suppressing a smile—

"Wait."—he can't believe it took him this long—"What about Zidie? He didn't get kill—"

"Nah. Nothing can kill that unkillable fucker," Reni mutters, sliding his tray back over, reconsidering his decision not to eat.

Izz breathes a sigh of relief, he's not sure he could live with the guilt of being responsible for the murder of his best friend. Zidie never would have been in The Hole—to end up in the crosshairs of a hit—if Izz hadn't been losing the fight and Zidie hadn't stepped in to save his life.

Those other inmates wouldn't have been there either, if it hadn't been for you—

No, that wasn't his fault. If a hit was out on them, those inmates would have been killed either way. And he hadn't done anything to deserve them attacking him. He'd been walking to the cafeteria, minding his own business. They attacked him, and he can't say he feels sorry for what happened to them. He never wanted them to die, but he isn't sad they have.

15

It's over a week since Reni returned from The Hole and Izz's no closer to figuring out who's leaving him gifts. He ruled out Levis as he served Izz every meal and always raised the topic of the extra food from meals. He never fails to offer other items if Izz will come out the back of the kitchen to collect them.

Which always disgusts Izz and leaves a bad taste in his mouth. He remains silent and doesn't engage Levis, not even looking at him. Ignore the problem, he figures, and eventually it will go away.

Or fester and grow to an even bigger problem. His inner voice points out.

Screw the kitchen boss, and the fake leverage to get into his pants. The freak is trying to manipulate him and give him extra things to push him into *owing* something.

Izz rolls onto his side, peering out into the dark cell. His bunk's way more comfortable now that he has two mattresses to lie on. With the ever-present question of *who-done-it—*

E.P. WRITER

His inner monologue doesn't contain a whole lot of sense. His mind and body are so exhausted he can't line up his thoughts. His new laundry job is draining and labour intensive. Muscles he didn't know he had are aching something fierce.

He does have one upside to his days, kind of. He's receiving gifts each day, usually in the form of chocolates or beef jerky. He has seen the price tag of the latter in Commissary and it's not a cheap product. Whoever is leaving him the snacks does not lack funds.

To those on the outside, these gifts would be insignificant and hardly worth mentioning. But when you are on the inside, it is a massive deal. Being able to enjoy chocolate is no longer something you can simply go to the store and buy for a few dollars. It costs three times more to buy it in this cage, and the money you earn in the prison jobs is less than a dollar an hour. There is no cushy thirty dollars an hour job on the inside, no freedom to go to the shop whenever you want. Commissary is open four days a week for a few hours at a time. Usually for the duration between breakfast and lunch, but it's unpredictable.

Izz digs into the snacks and doesn't regret it for a second—okay, so maybe there are times he worries over what the gifts mean and what will happen if he keeps accepting them. But then he would spot Reni and remember the fight—he is in over his head in this cage already. He has been targeted and treated like garbage by most inmates—Levis for one. So why not enjoy the gifts in the meantime? If the gift giver wants to hurt him, he's sure they'd find an excuse to do so either way.

CAGED IN

And he is drowning in food. He has his own hoarded collection stashed away in his cupboard. He's running out of room and will have to figure out where to put it when it reaches overflow levels.

Maybe I can leave a note on my bed to tell whoever is leaving the gifts that I have no more space to keep any more—

"Or maybe I can just eat more," Izz chuckles to himself in the darkness, a crazy person whispering in the lightless cell.

The prison lights have yet to blast into life for the start of a new day. Izz's inner alarm clock woke him slightly earlier than the automatic time the cell doors open. His cellmate is still out cold in the other bunk, quietly snoring away.

Another day in Hell.

He's tucking into his breakfast when the two side doors clanked open, allowing two inmates to walk in late for the party. He wouldn't have taken notice if the second inmate hadn't been one he's thrilled to see—

Zidie is out of The Hole. Accompanying an inmate Izz does not recognise. They both bypass the food line, gunning straight for The Gang's table. A massive grin plastered on Zidie's face.

"We're back," Zidie's sing-a-song tone is music to Izz's ears.

He's delighted to see Zidie out—the guilt is still there, but less so with his best friend no longer stuck in The Hole. Which was his fault—

He winces, refocusing on his food. Will Zidie still want to be his friend? Or did that ship sail when Zidie spent all those weeks stuck in a dank cell all alone?

Zidie throws an arm over Izz, planting his ass down beside him. "Hey bestie. How are you?"

Zidie pinches Izz's face between two fingers to turn his face side to side, looking for any marks?

"You don't look like you took a beating," Zidie informs Izz.

Izz takes his head back, sticking his tongue out at the other. "Ha. Ha. Very funny. I was doing just fine in the fight. Definitely winning."

"Uh huh, right," Zidie raises an eyebrow at Izz, "so you weren't on the floor about to become chow."

Izz snorts dismissively at Zidie, "no. No way. Not at all. That time alone in The Hole has you hallucinating what happened."

Zidie laughs, "sure I did. You keep telling yourself that if it makes you feel brave."

"I don't need an ego boost, I already know I have mad fighting skills—"

A scoffing noise catches Izz's attention, bringing his face around to the new inmate. "*Mad fighting skills . . .* Anyone who has to say that has zero fighting *anything*."

For the first time Izz scans the new arrival. The man is handsome, in a savage tough guy kind of way. Hazel eyes, the perfect shade to link nicely with his messy dyed-red hair, ruggedly cut into scruffy layers. Its length disappearing behind his back, peeking out to kiss his elbows. The hair style fits the man's perfectly symmetrical features. Hands encased in a black splatter ink tattoo

CAGED IN

design which speckles into sleeves, mixing and mingling with golds and reds. A whole array of different images merged together to make two incredible sleeves.

Unique.

He could study the tattoo designs for hours and still find something new in the network of art. All the details that went into the piece must have taken days.

"Hey, I'm Sinj. And you must be Izz." Sinj lifts his chin in a half nod of greeting.

Izz blinks at Sinj. How does the man know his name? The man is a walking talking art gallery on a model's body, and apparently he's a mind-reader as well?

Goes perfectly with the pale vamp in The Gang. Izz's inner voice mutters inside his head.

He shakes his head to clear it out. Hopefully, he can rattle the loose wires back into place, get things working properly again. The tactic always worked on the television remote, so why not on his brain wires too.

He can't help the speechless mute he has become. He's never met this inmate before and they know things about him. His luck hasn't been the greatest in here, another inmate knowing his name is worrying. He doesn't want another Levis sniffing around him.

Izz must have stayed quiet for too long, as Sinj offers up an explanation, "Zid wouldn't shut up about his new *best friend,* with a weird name like him, and blah, blah, blah—the entire time we were stuck in The Hole."

"Oh. . ." Is the only thing Izz can think of. His mind's racing over mixed feelings with Zidie's return—unsure if Zidie will be angry at him or forgive him.

Zidie is still calling him *'his best friend'*, so it stands to reason Cupcake isn't completely filled with hate towards him?

Sinj is an easy-going guy. Someone Izz could find himself becoming fast friends with. The red-head has a level of high energy and happy vibes to rival Zidie.

Izz joins the rest of The Gang as they wander down the corridors. He's going back to his cell to use the toilet. Surrounded by The Gang, well protected and at ease. For the first time in a long time, he is at peace. A part of the group. Not a shunned outsider. He hasn't looked at or spoken to David since the fight and the overheard conversation—but it's not like they'd ever spoken before that. But now . . . yeah. He's not doing it. He is not going to pretend that David isn't an asshole. And he definitely isn't going to be the guy's friend.

". . . you're a paid companion, it's not like they actually like you hanging around, they only like what you can do."

Izz zones back into the conversation, unsure what Erik is talking about . . . *Paid companion?* Who?

"You're just jealous I have skills and can walk into whoever's turf I want to." Sinj cracks his knuckles, blowing a kiss towards Erik.

The red-heads reply does nothing to fill Izz in, he's still confused. Who's paying who? And for what? Is it a drug thing?

CAGED IN

He can't stand it, he has to ask, and Sinj is a stand-up guy—at least in the few hours since they met. He won't mind Izz nosing into their conversation?

"Paid companion?"

Sinj smirks, bouncing his eyebrows at Izz—

It doesn't so much dawn on him as slap him in the face with its reality check. He can feel his face literally erupting in heat, his blush hitting him so fast it's liable to melt his face off. All the blood in his body must be in his face by now.

Sinj is an escort.

Hooker? Whore? He isn't sure what they like to be called, or what will offend. He doesn't have a problem with it, to each their own. He's just never met one, let alone a guy one. In prison . . .

Everyone around Izz burst into hysterical laughter. His blush deepening by the second. How is his body still able to find blood to push into his face, without him having a heart attack, or passing out? He's sure his neck is flushed right along with the rest of him.

This is so embarrassing. I feel like a blushing virgin.

"*I have wicked mad skills,*" Sinj uses Izz's words, mocking Izz's voice from the previous conversation with Zidie.

Glad to see I amuse people. Izz tries to be annoyed about it. But he can't help but feel joyous that he's settling in with The Gang. Enough for them to be playfully teasing him—

Sinj destroys Izz's composure completely—sticking his tongue out, and flicking it between two fingers—

Izz trips on nothing, stumbling a few steps before catching himself. Nearly face planting the prison floor.

Sinj has a split tongue—

It's literally split down the middle. A snake's forked tongue. Two separate pink-muscled pieces of flesh where there should only be one.

"How . . ." Izz squeaks, his eyes as wide as saucers.

"What? Never seen body mods' before," Sinj grins, enjoying every second of Izz's shock.

"You did that to yourself?"

He's going to puke.

How could Sinj—

To slice it—

Okay, yup. He is going to throw up on the prison's uneven concrete floor—

How much would that have hurt? To do that to your own tongue—

"We'll, technically, a tattoo artist I know did it. He dabbles in the extreme mod' stuff. The tongue is numbed and all that jazz, you don't feel a thing."

Izz sags in relief—or his body gives out on him. Either way, he leans against the wall like it's a lifeline.

Now that he's recovered from his initial shock—and he knows it's not some in-the-bathroom-over-the-sink-with-a-razor-blade type thing—it's actually kind of cool.

Different, but not all bad. It matches Sinj's qualities quite nicely—

Izz gets it—what Sinj meant when he said Erik's jealous. A split tongue would feel amazing and completely different from anyone else in here, for . . . Umm . . . *paid companionship* . . .

Wonder how much he charges?—

No you most definitely do not. Come on Izz. Pull yourself together, man—

CAGED IN

"Be careful with that one, he's crazy," Erik nudges Izz's ribs with his elbow, "bit a dude's dick off once."

"Really," Izz breathes out, eyes glued on Sinj to wait for his reply.

A confirmation he's not sure he wants to hear.

Sinj grins wickedly. Causing chills to run up and down Izz's spine. He wants to check his own parts are intact as a phantom pain invades his own dick at the thought of being the victim of such extreme violence.

"I told the prick *'no'*. He should have listened," Sinj grins wider, laughing ominously.

The queasiness returns, his throat muscles working overtime to depress his gag reflex. His last meal threatening to make an unwelcome appearance.

Reni shakes his head, mouthing to Izz that it isn't a true story. Leaning in to whisper for only Izz's ears to hear, "he might be crazy, but he's never done that . . ." When Reni leans back, Izz hears him say under his breath, "at least . . . not that we know of."

Not reassuring in the slightest. In fact it has him thinking, it might just be true—

Izz sighs as they stop near the stairs leading to his and Reni's shared cell. Breaking away from The Gang to clomp up the metal steps. He's glad to leave the conversation behind, to pretend it never took place. He doesn't need more fuel for his nightmares. He's already struggling to sleep with the creep from the kitchen and the vomit-dragon tattoo creep who lives in the same Wing.

This cage's filled with too many creeps for his liking.

More chocolates. Izz discovers the sweets on his bunk, half tucked under his pillow. He leaves them where they are, and uses the toilet. He isn't sure he has room left in his cupboard. Where else can he stash them?

Once he finishes relieving his bladder, he strolls back to his bunk to collect the chocolates to stuff into his overfilled cupboard. A squirrel storing its nuts for the harsh winter months when food is scarce—

Tucked out of the way—under his pillow—is a neat little roll. A thin roll of tiny paper—

Izz scoops up the joint so fast he almost whiplashes himself. Cradling the precious bundle in his palms.

This is the best gift yet.

Izz squeals in his head like a girl, giddy to try it and take his mind far away from this overcrowded cage he's forced to live in. With people he is forced to live next to.

Reluctantly, he sets the joint to the side, nestled on his pillow. He can't smoke it now, it isn't safe, he'd be caught by a guard. Either while smoking it, or because his cell will stink of it.

Choosing one of the chocolate bars, Izz rips into it. Munching on the chocolate to keep his mind off the joint he desperately wants to light up—he has no lighter for one, and two, he needs somewhere private to smoke.

How is he going to find something to light it with? Will he have to rock-and-stick-it like a caveman—

Reni appears in the cell's entrance, a frown scrunching his normally relaxed features.

Izz breaks off some chocolate to hand over.

"Nah, man, I'm good."

He shrugs, stuffing the piece into his own mouth. His cellmate is still frowning at him weirdly . . .

CAGED IN

"What? You're killing my chocolate bliss," Izz grumbles, devouring the last morsel. Ready to find another to eat.

"You might want to stop accepting these . . . *gifts*. You have no idea who they're from. And things in here don't come for free. There are prices attached to everything. Prices you may not want to owe people."

Reni folds his arms over his chest, the way he does when he's displeased. Like it's a protective barrier between him and whatever is threatening him mentally or emotionally. During a physical threat Izz had seen how Reni reacted, and it is in a defensive attack, not a cowardly timid retreat.

He isn't sure what the big deal is. "It's only chocolate. Lighten up."

Izz watches his cellmate's face change from an annoyed frown to intense rage—

"Where did you get that?" Reni jabs an accusing finger at Izz's bed, "do not tell me it was left under your pillow."

Izz doesn't need to look at where his cellmate's eyes are glued. He already knows. He'd stupidly left the joint out in the open. Foolish mistake. And after he'd been worrying where to smoke it so no one caught him—he leaves it lying around where anyone walking past could have spotted it.

Reni curses, dropping his arms down by his sides, "seriously, man. You are digging your grave deeper."

"How? It's been days and days." Izz gestures around the room, like that's supposed to mean something—what?—he has no idea, maybe that he's still here in one piece and not dead? "Nothing has happened. You're just jealous I have a secret admirer."

Yes, he's aware how stupid he sounds. But it is the only defence he can think of. And it absolutely sucks. He's hopeless at handling these new situations he keeps finding himself in.

He needs to stop shorting out, like a defective fuse, and start defending himself. Especially if another attack like the one in the kitchen takes place—he can't avoid Levis forever. And his body would not cooperate, all it did was waste energy being scared and shaking uncontrollably. It doesn't help him, and he would have been raped if that guard hadn't stepped in.

"These gifts are getting bigger," Reni mutters, closing his eyes and rubbing the bridge of his nose in irritation.

Izz picks up the joint, raising a brow at the small roll. It's tiny compared to the chocolate bars, and other snack items.

"I'm talking about in value," Reni snaps, as if he too can read minds like Sinj.

It's freaky the way Sinj reads Izz's body language and knows what he's about to say before he says it—and Sinj has only been around him for what? An hour? Two hours?

Why can everyone read him like a book? Are his emotions that obvious?

Shit . . .

Reni has a point. The gifts are going higher in the price range. He's now receiving—well, according to his cellmate's claims—drugs.

He curses under his breath. Tucking the joint out of sight into the pocket of his prison-issue pants.

Out-of-sight out-of-mind.

He can live in denial a little longer. No point worrying about make-believe scenarios that have not come to pass. And may never happen.

CAGED IN

Over the past weeks, nothing dreadful has happened to him as a result of taking and enjoying the gifts. He should be safe, shouldn't he?

16

Izz walks to the showers, halfway through breakfast, as today is the day Reni and Zidie have to attend their anger management meeting during the meal. He's not sure why the group runs at different times on different days. But its schedule is all over the place. Most often it's held during the work periods, or the break before lunch. Though recently it's been getting more and more out of whack and starting at very inconvenient times. For instance, halfway through a meal.

He finished his food when they both left and wasn't interested in staying at the table with only Erik and David. He wasn't sure where the rest of The Gang were. And he was not going to ask, and risk it sounding like he was talking to David—yes, he knows it sounds petty, as if he still holds a grudge. Which he doesn't.

. . . Okay, maybe he holds a little bit of a grudge.

But whatever, the other inmate deserves it—

He's counting down the days until Reni and Zidie don't have to go to that stupid, pointless meeting. He hates being alone with his thoughts.

CAGED IN

A few more weeks and those meetings will be over. Reni and Zidie will be signed off and free to go about their normal prison routines.

He would have stuck with Sinj, but he has no idea where to even begin looking for the red-head. Sinj could be anywhere in this prison. Including H-Wing, and The Gang had specifically told him not to go near H-Wing. He is not about to risk it and go investigating anywhere close by there. Knowing his luck he'd end up pissing off some mob boss and getting shivved.

He strips down in the shower room, leaving his clothes out on the benches. It's bizarre, coming here alone. He's only ever been here with someone else from The Gang. Never alone like this. He'd washed in his cell for the few days Reni had been absent.

Izz picked this time specifically, because he knows he won't have to worry about the showers being overcrowded with other inmates. Practically everyone is in the cafeteria. He'd also chosen this time as Levis will be in the kitchen and he won't have to worry about running into the creep in here.

He selects a shower head out of the way, close to the back corner to avoid the couple of men who were under their own sprays throughout the room. They are loners, minding their own business like he's doing—

Speak of the devil—isn't that the saying? Speak of the devil and the devil will appear?—he never should have thought the name. It's almost as if he summoned the other man.

Levis.

E.P. WRITER

It has to be Levis. While he's vulnerable, standing naked and alone in the shower room. The beefy server has to choose now to come to the showers—

Wait. Why is Levis here and not serving breakfast?

Izz swallows involuntarily, the lump in his throat growing and threatening to cut off his air supply. Why does his luck always have to be bad. Ever since he landed in this prison everything has been against him. Anything he thinks might be sweet, twists into a sour mess before he has the chance to savour the sweetness.

Levis saunters in, like he owns the whole room. Just like he does patrolling the kitchen—immensely up himself with an over-inflated ego. An ego that Izz's dying to knock down a few pegs—

Perhaps dying isn't the best term to use . . .

The beefy creep marches forward, a gloating grin plastered on his face. Gross naked body on full display—

Something to haunt Izz's nightmares. If he makes it out of this encounter alive—

The creep's smile vanishes, his mouth twisting, eyes narrowing as he comes to an abrupt stop. He stares at Izz, his expression twisting into one of extreme annoyance and frustration.

Surprisingly, Levis turns sharply on his heels and storms off to the other side of the shower room. As far away from Izz as physically possible while still able to use one of the showers.

Strange—

The shower next to Izz flares to life with a swirling rush of water. His heart rate sky-rocketing an electric charge

CAGED IN

through his body—swivelling, he faces off at the newcomer, his stomach dropping out into an empty pit—

Losing his footing Izz slaps his palm on the tiled wall to catch himself, so he doesn't face plant the tiled floor—so many tiles in this room—

This shower alone idea is the stupidest thing he's done since he's been in prison. Why did he choose to come here alone again?

'Cause I'm an idiot.

The red and black mohawked male—basking in the warm water cascading down his broad shoulder blades and over his thickly muscled back—is the serial killer Izz has been telling himself to stay away from.

And here he is, showering right next to the killer—and for the longest few seconds he's transfixed on the male's naked body—

Izz clears his throat, abruptly swivelling away to face the shower wall. His peripheral vision doesn't help him, he can still see the details he's trying desperately to avoid . . .

The killer doesn't speak, or do anything threatening. No shivs are uncovered from hidey-holes. He doesn't attempt to look at or interact with Izz. He utterly ignores Izz—who's surreptitiously trying not to peek at him. He goes about washing his own body, scrubbing the soap down coiled muscles—

Muscles that helped in killing people—

Izz rushes his rinse job, trying to slosh the soap off as quickly as possible. To leave, to get out and away from the dangerous male beside him.

Why is the killer here? Why is he insisting on standing right next to Izz. Is this the killer's usual place?

Does that mean Izz's in the wrong? Is he going to be killed for showering in the killer's space?

He hopes it's not what his family finds on his death record. *Killed for using a serial killer's spot in the showers.* Is not what he wants his life to come down to.

The killer is always in the cafeteria during the breakfast meal. So why is he here now? Is breakfast over? Or did Levis and the killer both skip it to come here?

Is it a coincidence?

This day has only just begun and his mind is already filled with far too many questions, and far too few answers. He feels as if he's going to self-combust due to the amount of pressure building in his head.

The killer shifts, and Izz dies—

Maybe he's a tad dramatic, but it sure feels like his heart gives out. Its beating is so fast it's one long thud with no ending in sight.

He can see the killer's gaze lock on him. His skin pricking with awareness at the killer's sharp eyes running up and down his form—

The intensity of the killer's inspection is constricting Izz's throat. His nervous system firing up and running rampant to such a degree it manifests into a physical reaction in his body. A sheen of sweat trickling over every orifice, noticeable even under the shower's warm spray. The water stinging his sensitive skin, almost as if the killer's eyes are tenderising his flesh and making it hypersensitive. Increasing his awareness to how utterly naked he is. He'd be self-conscious if he wasn't so terrified.

CAGED IN

Izz can't hold his tongue a second longer. Letting his unease escape in a torrent of scrambled words, "I'm n-not interested in d-doing anything with y-you."

The killer's fixation remains on Izz. No apology for the obvious ogling he's doing. No explanation. Nothing but silence.

Izz tacks on nervously, "I don't w-want it, I don't want you to t-touch m-me," he stutters, showing this dangerous male how panicked he is. His inner prey animal screaming at him for revealing his weak and helpless state.

The killer smiles softly—a soft, warm, friendly, smile. Stunning Izz in its unexpectedness. He was fully prepared to have the killer let out a mocking laugh and smirk at him before slitting his throat. He did not expect a warm smile. This soft expression, the closest Izz has seen the male come to a smile—not that he has been constantly studying the other. Nope. Of course not. All those times he sat in the cafeteria facing the corner where the killer sat, they were all coincidences—

You lie to yourself too much.

"Relax," the killer's deeply resonant voice rumbles over the sounds of the shower's spray, echoing off the surfaces around them, "I've done a lot of . . . questionable things . . . but I've never raped anyone, and I don't intend to change."

Izz's, in equal parts, shocked the killer respects his wishes and astounded the killers being genuinely nice.

No one else in this cage has done so, not without underlying intentions. And he isn't including Reni or Zidie. He is thinking of the other inmates in this Hell-hole. They have demanded and taken even when Izz says no—

E.P. WRITER

Is the killer being truthful? Or is it all lies, to lull him into a false sense of security, before striking? Would he find himself bleeding out in some forgotten back room of the prison?

Izz's aware he's staring at the killer, with round wide eyes. But he can't stop himself. He's too stunned to move. To react. To think of anything to say . . .

His mind searching desperately for something to snap him out of his frozen state. He finds himself drawn to how the killer washes, like a normal person. But what did he expect? For a serial killer to wash themselves the *serial killer way*?

Several more moments of Izz frozen under the water's embrace pass, his flesh starting to prune. He's been under the water for far too long.

The killer breaks the silence, without looking over at Izz. "You can enjoy your gifts. You don't have to keep hoarding them. No strings attached."

Wait? What?—

The killer hums softly, rotating to face Izz, giving him a full view of his front, "I find you . . . intriguing. I enjoy giving you things even if I get nothing in return."

Izz has to force his eyes away from the killer's body and look the male in the eyes—those same black irises flecked with golden browns, intensely watching, waiting.

"That—" Izz clears his throat. "T-those were from you . . "

He's not sure which is worse. Levis—who got handsy-feely into Izz's personal space without consent. Or this serial killer inmate who's murdered hundreds of people—according to Reni.

CAGED IN

"Who else would they be from," the killer's eyes bore into Izz, a question without it being a question, with the expectation of an answer.

Izz feels small. Shrink-wrapped into a tiny helpless form. He's shorter and skinnier than the killer, physically weaker. His fighting skills are questionable. He wouldn't stand a chance going toe to toe with the male. His entire body is insignificantly powerless.

"Ahhhh," Izz can't think of a single word to say in his defence—he's unsure why he needs a defence . . .

I can't think with his gaze on me.

Unconsciously Izz's eyes flick over to Levis on the other side of the room—who is still glaring daggers at him. Seething on the far side of the tiled expanse. It's a brisk flick of the eyes to and from. Yet it's enough for the killer to catch it and know his meaning. The air changing around Izz, stirring, constricting, cooling. As if the killer's anger is manifesting itself so intensely the air is affected by it—

A cold deathly growl rumbles over to Izz, as the killer faces the wall, "he won't bother you ever again."

Despite his instincts going haywire, Izz finds himself relaxing at the statement. He's not sure he should. But his instincts are informing him this male is trustworthy. Half his instincts are screaming and flashing warnings at how dangerous the killer is, but at the same time, the other half are relaxing and fighting the agitated fear receptors. Trying to tell his mind to '*calm down, there's nothing to fear*'.

So which half of his instincts does he trust? Which half *can* he trust?

Izz's aware that he's probably delusional. But screw it. He'll keep his delusions. Better than acknowledging the thought wedged in the back of his mind that this serial killer has attached himself to Izz to make him the next victim—

A flash of red at the small of the killer's back draws his eyes. The tattoo inked in smooth skin has a word written in red ink, but it's on a sharp angle and all he can read is the ending O U S . . . What does it spell? The middle of the word is consumed in a large blood splatter. The red letters running through the blood-ink puddle fade into open skin, so you can see the writing through the blood. A finger drawn through wet blood in a killer's written message—

Izz curses himself for falling for a predator's charms. Smacking the shower off he storms out of the room. He keeps his eyes locked on the exit and doesn't turn back to look at anyone. He prays no one follows him out. He wants to dress and get back to his cell to process what just happened before his mind spirals out of control.

Izz's too antsy to think straight. This stuff he's been gifted . . . it's from a serial killer. A serial killer, who for some unknown reason, has formed a kind of attachment to him—

Scratch that, if Izz thought about it, he can think of the reason why—

He doesn't want to end up the next victim, so he's refusing to give voice to those assumptions. Leaving them to rot and fester in the back of his mind.

He decides his nerves will be soothed by a sugar binge. A sugar rush will fill his belly and take his mind far away

CAGED IN

from his anxiety. Chocolate helps with anxiety—he read it somewhere, at least he thinks he did.

Kneeling on the floor at the head of his bunk, he sifts through the large selection of snacks in his cupboard. Throwing the chocolate bars and pop tarts and a bag of potato chips onto his bunk. He'll have a party—a party of one—to ease his nerves.

He's sitting on his bunk—pale as a sheet—in a nest of food wrappers—when Reni arrives close to the time the lunch bell is scheduled to ring. His cellmate must be here to collect him for lunch. From the look on Reni's face, Izz's inner turmoil and worries are written all over him.

"You okay, man?" Reni approaches, frowning as he sits on his own bed, directly in front of Izz. "You don't look too good. You need me to get a nurse? Or something?"

He isn't sure how to respond. Is he okay? He's not sure . . . Yes? . . . No? . . . Quite possibly . . . ? Not in the slightest . . . ?

Perhaps it will be better not to answer. He casts his eyes down to the wrapper mess surrounding his legs. His cellmate doesn't deserve to be lied to, or ignored. Reni deserves to be told the truth. It's the least Izz owes him for everything his friend has done for him.

". . . I . . . I f-found out who the g-gifts are coming from." Is that really his voice? He sounds timid and weak. Sounds utterly unlike his usual self. He sounds . . . vulnerable.

Reni remains silent, his gaze boring into Izz. Waiting for information. For an answer. An acknowledgement to the enquiry. Or for Izz to faint. To pass out cold.

His friend always knows what he needs. Senses where Izz's heads at. Why did he have to meet Reni in here? He could have done with this type of friendship on the outside. Maybe then he wouldn't be locked in this cage. Rotting away with criminals who enjoy tormenting him.

"... I ..." Izz curses, clearing his throat. He manhandles his fear to the side, pushing through it to let his words out, "I should have listened to you. What am I supposed to do now? How am I supposed to pay him back? I have no money. I can't give it back. And he—he—" Izz breaks off, running out of steam. Dropping his head into his palms, he tightens his muscles, trying to quell the urge to shake.

Why does your body shake when you're scared? He's sure there's some sort of scientific mumbo-jumbo to explain it—

"What's he want." Not a question. Reni already assuming he knows the answer.

"I don't know. I don't . . ." Izz trails off. Taking a deep breath to steady himself for what he has to say next. He knows he has to tell Reni everything. How else will his friend be able to help him if he doesn't know everything . . .

Biting back a sob, Izz slowly lets the story pass his lips. His dry throat is having a hard time allowing the words to come out clearly. He starts from the beginning. The creepy server guy. What the server demanded. What the creep tried to do. To the moment when Levis walked into the showers and turned away. The serial killer materialising out of nowhere right beside him. To the killer informing Izz that he was the one who left the gifts. Left the gifts for Izz to enjoy, no strings attached.

Reni remains quiet throughout the whole story, nodding slowly in places. But other than that, his friend keeps silent—eyes wide and unblinking, listening intently.

CAGED IN

A lifetime passes after Izz finishes his story. A lifetime filled with him stressing over how his friend will react. If his friend will abandon him. Or turn on him like David, saying that he is the problem and David was right all along. Or worse, go after the serial killer, like the last time Izz was in trouble. Only this fight wouldn't end with his friend in The Hole . . .

He wouldn't be able to live with himself if he got Reni killed. Not over this crazy situation. Not over him. Reni never deserved any of it—why did he think it was a good idea to unburden himself on his friend?

"Shit," Reni finally releases the breath he's been holding onto. His eyes blown wide.

"Really?" Izz sputters. "That's all you've got? What the hell am I supposed to do?" Great. Now Izz's yelling at his friend.

Way to go. Yell at one of the only friends you have in this cage of hundreds. Drive away the inmate who cares about your survival.

Izz rubs frantically at his hair, as if it might stimulate his brain into blurting out a solution to his problems. He isn't coming up with any viable plans, and it doesn't appear as though Reni is having any less trouble in the planning department.

"I—ah . . ." Reni opens and shuts his mouth a few times. Closing it for good when he can't find anything to say.

"Great. Just . . . great." Izz throws his hands in the air.

I'm screwed. I'm so fucking dead.

17

Izz stuffs his pockets with various chocolate bars before following Reni out into the prison to go to the early morning meal. A routine he's become used to—the early breakfast, not the chocolate community filling his pockets. The sugary treats he's bringing outside the cell will be a new experience for him. He usually keeps his depression-slash-anxiety eating—ironically—locked up behind cell doors.

He skips the line, forgoing the somewhat nutritious meal, in favour of his sugar-filled pants. He's having himself a healthy breakfast today, chocolate comes from a plant so he's practically eating fruit bars.

He doesn't even try to convince himself he isn't scanning the room for the killer who hasn't yet taken the usual place in the shadowed back corner. He and Reni are arriving late, breakfast had started . . . 'bout half an hour ago? The killer is usually always early, he should have arrived by now.

Where is the killer?

CAGED IN

He's worried and relieved at the same time. Relieved he won't have to pretend not to watch the male through the entire meal. Worried he doesn't know what the killer is doing, worried that the killer had been freed, or moved prisons or been thrown in The Hole, or—

Izz groans, loud enough for The Gang to hear and look his way. He plants his ass in his usual place—pretending he didn't utter a sound—the hard seat already driving an ache deep into his muscles. Why can't they put cushions on the chairs or something? Every time he sits he feels like he's going to take a metal splinter up his ass.

He worms his fingers into his tightly stuffed pocket to retrieve his *fruit bar*. Squeezing the little *health bar* open to eagerly consume its contents. Biting off half the bar in one chomp—the caramel chocolate sludge sticking on the roof of his mouth. His tongue working overtime to try to dislodge the uncooperative goo.

"How are you still eating them? Why are you still taking the bribes he gives you?"

He'd been so focused on his sticky task he failed to notice Reni sitting down with his full tray, right beside him. Reni's regular spot is normally in front of him, not this *beside-thing* the other has going on today. It threw his composure off.

First, the killer hasn't shown up, now Reni is sitting in a different place. Is it because he changed the routine by bringing chocolates to breakfast? A weird karma revenge scheme?

Is that how karma works? Probably not.

"They aren't *bribes*." Izz feels the need to clarify. "And besides, *He* said there are no strings attached. What were his words . . ."

Izz bites off the last of his bar, thinking back to the shower room. "Oh, yeah, it was—" Izz plays down his voice, deepening it to try to mimic the killer—failing miserably, "I've done a lot of bad crap, but I've never raped anyone. I find you *intriguing*."

Sceptical, his cellmate pulls a face at him, "he said '*crap*'?"

Izz playfully punches his friend's arm. "Alright, so maybe not those exact words but you get the point."

Under his breath, Reni mutters something about Izz having a death wish.

Izz laughs, opening another bar and brushing off his cellmate's worries. He has worries, sure, but he's avoiding thinking about them. Maybe they won't become tangible? If he permits Reni's words to sink in, he's afraid his own stewing concerns will gain a foothold in his frontal lobe—

The prison's blaring alarm blasts through the cafeteria rattling Izz's fears free. Building up their momentum—he quickly stomps them down before he begins to freak out that something has happened to the killer. Which he shouldn't be doing, those thoughts should not be crossing his mind.

He drops the half-eaten bar in favour of blocking his ears with both hands. Sealing his palms tight enough over his ears that they're liable to embed into his skin.

"What's that?" Izz bellows over the shrill noise, unsure if anyone can hear him. He can scarcely hear himself.

CAGED IN

"Lockdown," Reni yells back, grabbing Izz's arm to drag him to his feet.

Izz lurches along as he's half dragged towards the exit, the other inmates in the cafeteria are rushing out right alongside him. The trays and food are left behind on the tables—the large mess a calling card for the chaotic scramble back to their cells.

And there's not a moment to spare—the barred cell door slamming shut behind Izz's uncoordinated fall into his cell. He exhales a sharp hissing breath as his knees hit the hard cold floor.

A crushing anxiety is overwhelming him. His leg twitching and his foot nervously tapping. His elbows digging into his knees and his chin bouncing up and down like a wild animal in his palms.

To say he is freaking out is an understatement. He's skirting the edges of a severe panic attack, a hair's breadth away from losing it completely and falling off the edge. His mind racing over what could have happened.

The serial killer not showing up in the cafeteria . . .

The alarm going off . . .

Reni had mentioned something about the alarm meaning an inmate has been grievously injured or killed—

Is the serial killer dead . . . ?

They are released at the lunch bell. He's sure it's because the guards don't want to feed the entire prison individually in their cells. The time locked up passing too fast and not fast enough for Izz to get his answers. He can't remember if he talked to Reni during their forced lockdown. His mind is a muddled mess, his thoughts all over the place. Returning again and again to the same questions.

Who died?

Who was killed? And why?

Dread consumes his thoughts. Somehow he knows the unknown incident has something to do with him. He cannot shake the feeling of impending doom. He feels hollowed out as if he's nothing but a shell—a pitifully weak and cowardly shell. His subconscious knows, he wishes it would do the decent thing and fill him in on the details. And not leave him hanging with no answers.

Izz trudges over to The Gang's table, he's not even going to pretend he's hungry. He can't stomach a morsel—his digestive tract churning and twisting.

As Izz takes a seat at the table, the first thing he hears is Erik speaking low, ". . . B-Wing was abuzz with chatter. That kitchen boss dude was killed, brutally too, his—"

Izz zones out of the morbid explanation Erik is about to go into, his concentration distracted by the male lowering himself into his usual place at the table in the far corner—

The male's eyes lock right onto Izz's. Like he was expecting Izz to look his way.

Izz tries to read the killer's mind, scanning over the features he can make out in the shadows. Hoping something, some small tic, will tell him what he needs to know—

CAGED IN

The serial killer—the one Reni had warned him to stay as far away from as possible—dips his chin slightly. His eyes locked on Izz . . .

His sinking heart plummets into a full-blown Atlantic Sea. His instincts had been warning him. Had known a horrendous crime was carried out.

It happened because of him . . .

The killer really did it. He killed Levis. . . for me . . .

How. . .

Oh God.

This can't be happening.

Izz is responsible for a man's death. It's his fault—

No, it was Levis's fault. That asshole never should have done the things he did. Never should have touched Izz when he told Levis that he wasn't interested. And it was the killer who did the deed. Izz never asked, nor would he have ever asked.

This death is on the serial killer, not me—

"You have visitors, A-18910."

Izz jerks his head to the side to see a guard standing at the end of the table, blue eyes squared on Izz in a stern no arguments kind of way.

Visitors?

Izz trails along behind the guard, trying not to get too excited. He doesn't want to build his hopes, only to discover it isn't his mum and little sister.

It's easier said than done. By the time he finds himself outside the visitation room, he is practically jumping out of his skin.

"No touching," the guard barks before shoving Izz through the door. Izz has to hold out his hand to stop his face from crashing into the door. Even the guard's rough treatment doesn't dampen his eagerness.

The guard strides off to stand with the other guards, talking about whatever—probably ways to torture the inmates.

Izz grins at the sight of his family seated at one of the small plastic tables scattered through the room. Other inmates are here too, with their own visitors. But none of them matter, there are only two people in this whole room he cares about. And they're both smiling at him, even before he weaves his way around tables to get to them.

Izz's sister jumps up to grab at him, and he wraps his arms around her. Which earns him a reprimand from a guard, and a '*point*'—whatever the hell that means—he'll ask Reni later. It was worth it, he wouldn't have taken it back for the world.

"I love you, brother," Lucia snivels, wiping at her red teary eyes. Her wavy brown hair sticking out at random angles, like she was so excited to come here she forgot to brush it. Or there was a tornado outside she had to battle through to reach the prison visitation door.

"I love you too, little sis," Izz pats her head, stepping back before he pisses off the guards' more than he already has.

The plastic chairs are comfortable, compared to the cafeteria seats, and that is saying something, considering these chairs are hard as rock with zero support for your ass bones. By the time he's freed, he's not going to remember what a normal chair feels like.

CAGED IN

"What's it like in here?" Luc jumps right in with the questions, while their mum sits quietly, blinking rapidly, trying not to cry.

"Well, little darling sister of mine. They have very loud alarms here, to wake you up, and very small beds, the size of your doll house beds. And the rooms are smaller than your doll house."

His sister giggles, "that's just silly. You wouldn't fit if they were that small."

"Oh, it's very true. Teeny tiny barbie beds. The first day here I was not expecting the alarm, it scared me so much I fell right off the bed. Just splattered on the floor, like a human pancake."

His sister is laughing now, a huge smile splitting her face in two. His mum on the other hand, is wearing a mask of sorrow, a dark look in her eyes. Like she knows it's bad inside and this fake charade for Luc is just that. Fake.

Sitting quietly in her chair, his mum does not speak. Izz wants to reassure her he really is okay, but can't do that in front of Luc, without upsetting his sister. She's an innocent child who doesn't need to know how dangerous it is in this cage.

He tries his best to convey what he's thinking to his mum, willing her to see it in his eyes. He's not sure the message is being received or believed.

"I drew you this, Izzy," Lucia announces, thrusting a page into his chest. His breath huffing out with the impact—his sister is surprisingly strong.

He looks down to find a drawing, containing a little house and people—the three of them. Their home.

I will not cry.

That will seriously downsize his reputation. Not that he could possibly have a tough reputation. He probably has a crappy rep' after that fight. The corridor had been filled with other inmates by the end. And even if there had been only one, gossip in prison spreads faster than in a girls' dorm. He's sure everyone in this cage heard about him getting his ass kicked within five seconds of the start of the attack.

"In case you miss us, so you don't forget what our home looks like."

Izz fights back tears, he doesn't want to kill the moment by turning on the waterworks. "Of course I miss you, Luc, and I'll never forget any of it. This is perfect. I love it. It'll give me something to look at other than the brick walls and my cell—roommate's—ugly face," he tries to make her laugh, to lighten the mood.

Lucia sighs in frustration, crossing her arms over her chest. "Why do you have to stay here? Why can't you come home already? You're a nice person. You're the best. Nicest."

How to explain it? The reasons he's here are not for Luc to know. It is not her fault she became sick and the doctors charged so much for her life-saving treatment. You would think keeping people alive would be a higher priority than money—it is not. Never had been. Taking and taking—from those who have nothing left to give.

Izz chose to do what he did. That's on him, not little Luc, who never chose to get cancer. Never has a choice in the treatments that saved her life. It isn't fair that someone so young—a child—had to go through all those tests and treatments just so she could live a normal life. A life the

CAGED IN

other children around her take for granted, they don't know the harsh reality of life.

Of course, he would not wish his sister's illness on anyone, he just wishes she never had to suffer it and could live like the other children in the neighbourhood. Free of sickness, free to live their childhood without worry.

"Because I broke the law, Luc. I have to make up for it. So I have to stay here until I make it right," Izz smiles at her. He hopes his smile doesn't convey the sadness trapped inside his heart, the grief for the sister he loves dearly.

Izz sits back and listens to the stories his sister recites. Her best friend's new crush. The homework from school being hard and taking her forever to complete. A new girl who's moved into the neighbourhood with curly red hair, who never stops talking, and is staying over to have a movie night on the weekend—reminding Izz that he has no idea what day it is today.

The list of stories goes on and on. He's delighted to hear them. At least it takes his mind off how terrible he's been doing in here. How depressed he's been. This is the perfect medicine for him, exactly what he needed and hadn't known it until it showed up—happy and smiling and chattering away like there isn't a care in the world. Like she should be, without the worries and burdens of her illness.

Please God, don't let the illness return. Don't take this happiness away from her. She's so young.

The visitation time eventually winds down, a guard giving him a wrap-it-up warning.

Izz utters his goodbyes—it's tougher than he anticipates. He is not thrilled to be going back to his new life. This place is a death trap waiting to happen. Sooner or later he is going to be thrown into another fight-for-his-life situation, and he won't have anyone close by to save him like the last time. Reni and Zidie can't be with him 24/7, they have to worry about their own survival. Their schedules don't revolve solely around Izz and protecting him from harm.

He knows he's going to find himself trapped alone one of these days—it's just a matter of time.

"Lucia, wait over by the door for a moment," Izz's mum speaks softly for the first time during the visiting period, "I'd like to talk to your brother for a sec."

Luc frowns but doesn't protest, wandering off to stand by the door. Her keen eyes tracking their movements as she waits.

Izz looks deep into his mum's wise eyes. There are dark shadows under them, revealing the strain of the past few weeks. She's exhausted and heartbroken.

"You're staying safe? Not doing anything to get into more trouble?" his mum whispers, even with Luc too far away to hear anything.

"I'm keeping my head down," at least he's trying to, "and I'm fine. I've made friends, we watch out for each other. It's going to work out fine. I'll be out of here before you know it."

His mum's concerned expression does not lift, "I hope so," she softly replies. They say tender goodbyes and his mum goes to join his sister.

CAGED IN

He watches them walk down the visitors' corridor—lined with glass windows—all the way to the end. His family slipping out the door, back into the real world.

When Izz arrived, he'd been taken past the front entrance, around to a side door, he has no idea what the visitors see when they enter the prison for the first time. Maybe a bunch of fake plants, some inviting chairs with soft pillows, photos of beautiful scenes covering the walls—

"Move it, inmate."

Izz rolls his eyes—he's not facing the guard so he is free to express his disdain. What they don't see won't hurt them. And if it does, they kind of deserve it. He has yet to meet one who is actually nice or at the very least treats him like a human being and not some low life degenerate.

He follows the guard back out into the corridor heading to Gen-Pop and all its assholery—is that a word? Doesn't sound like one. He's going to use it regardless, it fits the bill perfectly—

"You can't take that back with you," the guard's grating voice invades Izz's ears like an unwanted parasite.

And there it is—*reality*—slapping him on the ass. His blissful bubble—created by his wonderful sister—not so much popping but exploding into a million pieces.

"What? Why?" Izz clutches the drawing closely to his chest, trying to protect it from the a'hole guard.

"It's contraband," the guard smiles, literally smiles.

What an asshole.

"No it's not. It's a picture drawn by a child."

There is no way this is contraband. You are allowed photos of family members, he's sure a drawing of your family is allowed too. This guard is waving their dick around, trying to get an ego boost.

"Do I look like I care? It can't come with you," the guard sneers, that messed-up smile not leaving his face.

Izz's shocked. Stunned. Outraged. Is this guard serious? Are they going to enforce it and take away the drawing? They surely can't do this—

What is he thinking, of course they can. Because no one cares about prisoners, no one will care if Izz put in a complaint. The only thing complaining will get him will be more notice from the guards', and that is something he does not want. He does not want an entire prison of guards' gunning for him.

The sinister smile spreads across the guard's face, right before they snatch the image out of Izz's hands. He releases his hold immediately so the paper doesn't rip.

"Unless . . ." the guard drawls.

"Unless what?" Izz snaps, irritated by this guard abusing their powers.

". . . you suck my dick."

Crass and disgusting.

Izz cringes and moves back, "the fuck is wrong with you? You're seriously asking that? For me to keep a child's drawing? Are you kidding me?" Izz throws his hands up in astonished outrage.

This guard is more than an asshole, they are a rapist asshole. There is no way he is going to do anything for this prick. They have another thing coming if they ever thought he would—

Izz's eyes widened as the guard shrugs, lifting the picture up, holding it between two hands to rip it in half—

CAGED IN

"No. Wait. Stop." Izz surges forward, but doesn't dare actually touch the guard.

He knows the cancer could return and he could still lose his sister. It might be the last picture she ever draws for him. The last gift she ever gives him. He can't let this ego-swinging a'hole take it away from him. He can't let them destroy it—

Izz must have paused for too long, the guard raises an eyebrow, moving his hands to show he'll do it.

"Okay. Okay." Izz holds his palms up, in a surrendering gesture, "I'll fucking do it. Just give me the drawing."

Is he truly going to do this? He regards the drawing in the guard's clutches—his sister's face flashes before him, her loving smile as she presented the drawing to him. How proud and happy she was to give it to him. Her joy when he told her he loved it.

"You can get it back after," the guard's sinister smile thickens.

Izz wants to throw up.

When the guard turns to leave, strutting off down the corridor. He has no choice but to follow, gritting his teeth to keep his anger in check. It's the only thing he can do. The guard holds all the cards over Izz. There's nothing he can do, no moves he can make. He's completely helpless.

Completely . . .

. . . Alone . . .

18

They arrive outside a door marked *'Filing Room'*—must be the one the counsellor was talking about, it feels like years ago since the first time he'd been to the counsellor's office. He'd thought things had sucked back then, he was wrong. He never would have guessed his life's path would have driven him to this moment in time. These events unfolding right before his eyes, an avalanche he can no more prevent than he can stop from burying him alive.

The guard unlocks the door, using one of the many keys attached to the uniformed belts' all guards' wear. Shoving the door wide, and stepping back, flicking his head to indicate Izz's to go inside.

Yeah, that's obvious, you asshole. Izz elects not to voice his displeasure—this doesn't need to be worse than it's already going to be.

The room's filled with row after row of shelves, holding stacks and stacks of boxes. If he has to guess he'd say the boxes are filled with files. There had to be more files in here than inmates in the prison.

CAGED IN

Are these files the documentations of every single person who'd ever been stuck in this cage? The history of the prison, boxed up in this airless cramped room.

He swivels back around at the sound of the door clicking shut. The guard's hulking frame taking up the space in front of the door.

"I'm going to do it," Izz states, holding his hand out palm up towards the guard. "I just want the picture back . . . please." He pushes the last word out through gritted teeth. He hates having to beg. But he wants to be sure it isn't going to be for nothing. He needs the image to be in his possession by the end.

The guard doesn't move, doesn't waver, doesn't appear to have heard Izz. He completely ignores Izz's words, not fazed in the slightest.

He tries again, executing a different approach. "At least put it down over there," Izz points to one of the shelves with a space between boxes, "so it doesn't get ripped or scrunched up."

He's thankful when the guard complies, he doesn't appreciate how the guard tosses the drawing down, but at least it's away from the a'hole. The one solace in this crappy situation—

Izz's gripped by the shoulder and shoved down onto his knees. The hard concrete flooring offering little cushioning as his bones meet solid mass. He winces, unsure if it's the pain or the degrading position.

I don't want this. I can't do it.

He wants to stay strong. To steel his emotions and do what has to be done. But he can't . . . he can't pretend like this is okay, like it's not affecting him.

It isn't okay, this scumbag's forcing me.

He doesn't want to cry, doesn't want to give this a'hole the satisfaction.

Is he really doing this? Is this what his life has become?

Is this who I have become? Who I've chosen to be.

No. He has a choice. And the drawing is safe, at a safe distance. Far enough away that the guard can't grab it. If he plans this right, executes the plan correctly—

One misstep in timing and Izz will destroy the picture he is here to protect. He isn't a fighter, that has been proven. But he's also not about to bow down to rape—

Izz attacks—he's sloppy and uncoordinated—trying out an under the arms and over the shoulders tackle he's seen in movies. It works—taking the guard by surprise is in his favour. He now has the guard flat on his back. And Izz's out of ideas, he hadn't thought this far ahead in the plan. He's surprised he made it this far—

The guard solves the stagnant pause, fist snapping out to take Izz's head off. He barely manages to duck out of the way. Grabbing at the arm before the guard can pull it back for a second strike.

Izz punches out, aiming for the fleshy muscles over ribs, hoping to break one—

Izz's sure he broke his fist instead—who knew it hurt so much to punch someone. Even with the adrenaline pumping through his veins.

Izz has the advantage, he is on top, it's easier for him to control the guard and swing blows down at the a'hole. And it's clear the guard is struggling to swing a decent punch up at him. He also has more room to dodge and weave. Punching down with uncoordinated fists, trying to hit the

CAGED IN

guard's face, being blocked every time. His pummelling blows end up hitting the guard's arms more than anything else.

He's not letting up. He keeps punching. If he stops, he's dead. There is no getting out of this. He knows attacking a guard will have dire repercussions, worse than The Hole—

Izz's knocked off balance, a surge from the guard throwing him backwards and out of the dominating position. Not good.

He quickly scrambles up—

Get on your feet. You hit the ground, you're done.

—grabbing the first thing he touches—swinging it forward, aiming at the guard's unprotected mid-section—

A broom.

The broom makes a nice cracking sound as Izz slams it into the guard's middle, followed by a series of grunts and curses. The prison's cheap wooden broom handle splintering.

Ha. I actually managed to break something. Granted it isn't ribs, but it still feels like a win.

Izz snaps out of the premature celebrations, his hands tightening above the shaggy end to keep his weapon in hand, swinging what is left of the handle—

The side of his knee is kicked out, toppling him into a shelf, knocking boxes off and scattering them over the floor—

The guard charges, grabbing at the broom Izz holds in an iron grip—he is not about to let it go—he shoves into the guard, using his shoulder like a battering ram to drive the guard back into the opposite shelves—

E.P. WRITER

The broom's scruffy end catches in the bracing of the shelving unit and, with a crack, it snaps off, the brush landing somewhere in the scattered paperwork. His weapon is shrinking, soon he'll have nothing left to defend himself with.

The guard strikes Izz in the stomach, doubling him over. Winded, his lungs screaming at him for being hit again in so many days. His body is still recovering from the last beating.

Izz stands strong by force of will. Kneeing up into the guard's side, shoving him back against the shelves. Trying desperately to knock him over. To plant him on the floor, to keep the larger man from regaining his footing—

The guard tugs at the broom chunk in Izz's hand, trying to yank it away from him. Izz wraps both fists around the splintered wood. Curling himself around it, twisting to the side to shake the guard's hand free—he can't lose his only weapon. Can't let go of his defence—

The guard's grip is strong and unrelenting. So Izz does the next best thing—outside of pulling away—he drives forward. Intending to wind the guard, ignite some pain, to make him let go—

Izz feels a sickening squelching wet pop and a soft giving resistance at the end of what's left of the broom handle. It's an outcome he hadn't intended. An outcome he doesn't want to accept—

The resistance Izz's up against falls away, the guard's mass slipping free, slumping onto the floor with a sloppy thud—

Izz stares ahead at the shelf in front of him. He knows deep down what just happened, but his mind doesn't want

CAGED IN

to acknowledge it. He can't look down, at the broom handle still gripped tightly within his hands. He can't look at the floor below the wood, to the . . .

Izz drops the handle, stumbling away from the shelf, away from the weapon, away from the . . . body . . .

Oh, God.

He falls back on his ass, disbelief welling in his chest, staring at the guard's slumped, motionless body . . . at the pool of crimson gradually spreading over the floor, the puddle darkening as it becomes deeper and deeper. Thickening to the point of black sludge.

What have I done . . .

Izz's mind snaps into focus—he's in a locked room, with a . . . with a dead guard—He can't stay here, he can't be caught. He wants to run and keep running, but there's nowhere he can run to in this cage.

He's beginning to shake, the combined effects of adrenaline and shock spearing into his core. Closing his eyes, he breathes. Forcing himself to calm and to think.

What can he do . . . ?

Grabbing the hem of his shirt, Izz wipes off the broom handle to remove his fingerprints. He does the same to the boxes scattered over the floor in case he touched any of them. He rubs over the shelves nearby before checking his clothing for blood—finding no blood he sends up a prayer to whoever's watching over him. If anyone is. He sends his prayer anyway. You never know.

Moving carefully around the blood, Izz snatches his sister's drawing off the shelf. Relieved it remained safe in its resting place. Holding it carefully in one hand, he hopes the guard didn't lock the door. He doesn't want to reach into the puddled mess to find the keys on the guard's belt.

Using the inside of his shirt once more, Izz treats the handle the same as the rest of the room. Wiping it down—he sighs, relieved when the handle moves under his palm, twisting open with ease.

He wipes the outside handle off before snapping the door shut—he can't remember if he touched the door on his way in. Better safe than sorry.

Izz rushes down the corridor, moving swiftly. Constantly glancing over his shoulder to check if he's being followed. Who would even be following him—

Did anyone see him enter the room with the guard? Did anyone see him leave? Or hear the fight? Was there a loud noise to draw attention to it? How much time does he have until the bod—until the guard is discovered . . . ?

Stop. You're acting suspicious. You're going to draw attention to yourself.

Relax.

Relax.

Slow down . . .

Izz forces himself to slow down, to keep his shoulders squared and his head straight. No more looking over the shoulder. No more rushing movements. Nothing out of the ordinary.

Act normal, or you're going to get caught.

If someone didn't already see you—

Stop it. Izz reprimands his inner voice, it is not helping the situation. In fact, it is making everything worse—

Shit. Shit. Shit.

CAGED IN

He's a murderer now . . . This death is his fault. He can't blame it on the serial killer. He can't blame it on anyone. He can't dismiss it.

I did this . . .
It's all my fault . . .

19

Izz drifts in a numb haze through the corridors. His mind floating free of his body. It's a surreal dream, coating him, consuming him. His spirit torn, his soul fragmented.

Is this truly happening . . . Is this where my life has led. . .?
Is he really a murderer now . . . ?

What is he going to do? He's killed someone, a guard. He has no idea how to cover up something like this. What if he left his prints on the body—

Murderer.

Izz wipes frantically at his eyes, he needs to keep it together. He needs to hold his head high and not let anyone know something's terribly wrong.

Because it is terribly wrong. I'm terribly wrong. I've killed another man. How could I—

Hold it together Izz. Izz's inner voice hardens like it's trying to gather all the frazzled strings floating around his head. Trying to tie his sanity back together.

It will never be put back together. He will never be the same. How can he be? When he did . . . When he . . . He . . .

CAGED IN

Murderer

Izz needs to do something, but what? How can he be sure he left no traces behind? Is that even possible? Or is that only something you can do in a movie . . . ?

He needs someone to talk to. An expert or something—someone . . . Someone who's done this before . . .

Is he really going to do this? Is he delusional . . . ?

He may be incredibly stupid, but Izz's going to do it . . . . He's going to find a serial killer. Find a serial killer to ask for help in a murder he's committed. He never would have thought his life would come to this. Not in a million years would he have pictured this scenario. Seeking out a serial killer for advice . . .

While The Gang and the entire prison is off at their assigned jobs, he is tracking down a serial killer. And hoping the rumours are actually true, and the mohawked inmate has experience in this field. Otherwise he isn't sure what he'll do, who he can approach.

He can trust a serial killer to keep his secrets . . . can't he?

It's an hour into the search when Izz comes to the realisation the killer is probably at a prison job. Complicating his plans. How is he going to find where the killer works, let alone get him somewhere to ask for help. It's not as if he can walk up to the male and be like *'Hey, I need a little help with this guard I left in the filing room.'*

He sighs, rubbing the bridge of his nose. Who knew murder could be so stressful. He's pretty sure he's in the denial stage of his grief or depression or whatever it's called.

Giving up, resigning himself to his inevitable—and well deserved—fate, Izz trudges back to his Wing, to his cell, to sit and dread what will come next. Where does killing a guard place him . . . ?

Did the guard have a family? Children . . . ?

It's too quiet in the corridors—in the prison. It feels like death. His mind is chaotic, if only he had his headphones, some loud music to drown out the screaming fear in his head.

The world is too silent.

Alone . . . He feels so alone . . .

A-Wing is empty when he arrives. Barren. A wasteland of barred skeletal rooms filling him with unease and dread. This cage is so much creepier when it's deserted. He thought it would be better not having so many criminals lurking about, fearing they will stab him in the back. But no, it is way worse being alone. He hates quiet loneliness on the best of days—out in the real world. Today, however . . .

It had never been so eerie on the outside.

He cannot feel his body, it's disconnected from him—from the world. Somehow he moves up the stairs, his body a liquid mass. His slip-on prison-issued shoes scuffing and thumping, announcing their presence to the second floor. The metal clanging and echoing through the empty Wing.

Izz finds his way to the top, without giving in to his impulse to scream. He's hanging on to his sanity by his fingertips, sliding closer and closer to the edge by the second—

A flicker of movement seizes his attention in the opposite direction to his cell—

CAGED IN

Maybe fate is trying to make up for all the crap he's been dealt.

At the end of the second-floor platform—leaning casually against the wall—is the mohawked male. Smoking with no care as to whether or not a guard passed by. White roll flaring orange with each draw.

Guess the serial killer doesn't have to go to a prison job.

Izz turns towards the killer, his back to his own cell. Sucking in a deep breath, he slowly shuffles to the far end, scuffing his shoes when his feet lag behind. Nervous energy rolling off him in waves.

Years pass before he's standing in front of the killer—the male has not shifted a single muscle. A frozen statue of dangerous intent in the path of Izz's life. Granted Izz has a good reason to be here. He also isn't foolish enough to leave himself vulnerable while alone with the one individual everyone in this Hell-hole fears.

His eyes dart everywhere but to the killer's face, he can't look the male in the eye, scared he might recognise himself in the killer's eyes.

He, too, is a murderer now . . .

His eyes land in the last cell, shocked at the sight before him. It has two bunks, like any other cell, but the similarities end there. Only one bunk has mattresses on it—and he means mattresses—there has to be a stack of at least half a dozen hidden under those sheets.

What catches Izz's eye more than the nice soft bed are the walls. All over the white-washed cell walls are pictures, cut outs, photos. Pages and pages of . . . Satanic drawings. Monsters, demons, devils. Pentagrams. Pages ripped from books, with upside down crosses or triple six drawn in thick black letters over the pages of whatever book it once was. The deep blacks and dark reds, mixing and mingling, to form a kind of wallpaper . . . a Satanic wallpaper . . .

The second unoccupied bunk holds a treasure trove of items. Shoes, clothes, books, pencils, food. The little cupboard's doors hanging open, spilling out its contents all over the bunk.

On top of the opposite cupboard is a small baggie of weed, rolling paper, and a lighter—an actual silver flip lighter, not the battery foil combo the stoner in the yard used—are laid out in the open. Disregarding the potential threat of The Hole if a guard were to see it.

The floating shelf above the messy bunk has lines and lines of chocolate bars, books, and other snacks. Unlike its counterpart—above the human occupied neatly arranged bed—immaculately stacked with papers, pencils, pens and sharpies—

Where did the killer get those last items? Do they sell those in Commissary? He's sure he's never seen pens or sharpies available for purchase. Wouldn't inmates use them as weapons—

"You here for a reason." The deep voice behind Izz thrust him back into his body. Without realising it, he'd walked inside the killer's cell.

He throws a glance over his shoulder, to the killer through the bars, the male is in the same casual laid-back position against the wall.

He isn't sure what he's supposed to say. Now that he's found the killer, he is lost for words. Not sure it was a smart idea on his part to seek out this type of help. Is it true that this male's a serial killer? He has no evidence. No proof.

CAGED IN

Only the rambling rumours of gossipy bored inmates. He has no idea if the killer shivved Levis—or anyone else for that matter. Perhaps he's letting his imagination run wild.

Izz recalls the look on the male's face, the slight nod the killer had given him in the cafeteria. He doesn't want it to be true, would be happier to never know the truth. To never know if he is to blame for Levis's demise. He's already a part of death, even before he took it with his own hands.

Izz takes a step back, so he isn't in the cell anymore. The cell he doesn't need to be told belongs to the killer. Who else would harbour a Satanic worshipping cell?

"Your cell?" Izz enquires anyway, pointing into Satan's lair, well aware he's stalling.

The killer nods in way of answer. Inhaling the joint pinched between his fingers. Its orange flames working hard to consume the last of the paper, racing to his fingertips, threatening to burn them.

"It's . . . unique." Izz has no clue why his mouth is spouting small talk. Is it small talk?

He has no idea how to ask what he came here to ask. He's struggling to hold himself together, to not blab every random thought crossing his mind, to delay the inevitable question.

How does one ask a stranger for help covering up a murder?

He's an amateur. He isn't a hardened criminal. Not like the drug dealers and gang members who handle these bloody events all the time. He's never had anything remotely close to a murder to deal with. Breaking into empty houses doesn't result in cleaning up dead bodies.

He must have been pulling some sort of wincing expression because the killer chuckles. Straightening up from his casual lean to his full height. Towering over Izz, in both height and experience. And everything else.

"Not a Satanic fan," the killer observes, his dark eyes roaming over Izz's face.

Izz gulps down his nervousness. He can feel the black irises on his skin, pinpricks of sensation following their path. He feels himself heating up and shivering at the same time, a strange combination of sensations.

"I'm not really religious. But I hold nothing against those who are. It wouldn't surprise me if the Devil exists." With all the evil in the world, it has to come from somewhere, doesn't it?

The killer hums in a way that could be anything from agreement to disapproval. Izz worries that he's pissed the killer off, destroying his only chance to get help—

That is until the killer offers Izz the last dying end of his joint. He takes the offering, relieved he has an excuse to not speak. Although, he can't pretend to be engrossed in the smoke's relaxing hold for too long. There isn't much left of the white roll of blissful delight.

Dragging the smoke into his lungs, he watches the end flare to life, eating away the white paper in seconds. The killer raises a brow at him, as he makes quick work of the remainder. He is sure he looks like a rattled mess. But why wouldn't he be? With everything that's happened. With his messed-up thoughts, the gut-wrenching fear, the helplessness . . . the guilt . . .

God . . . The guilt.

CAGED IN

It's crippling. He wouldn't have thought he'd care, considering what the guard had tried to do. He does care though, he cares and he hates himself for what he did. His conscience is gnawing at him, consuming him with remorse for the killing. He knows he hadn't intended to stab the guard—that knowledge does nothing to ease his regrets.

He sucks down the last of the joint—nearly burning his lips—discarding the ashes into the small metal bin near the cell door. Watching the very last lick of life flicker out of the smouldering tip. Wishing the wisps of grey would reveal the answers to his problems.

Glancing back down the second-floor platform, Izz checks to ensure they are alone. That the whole prison hasn't discreetly snuck up on him. He is faced with an empty line of cells. No commotions. No voices. No one else in sight.

He's exposed out here. In the open. With what he's about to ask, he doesn't want to risk anyone so much as hearing a whisper of it. He does not want to be seen with the killer. He has blood on his hands. Blood he can't physically see. Blood he can't wash off, no matter how many times he scrubs himself clean. Blood the other inmates will see. They'll know—

As if the killer senses Izz's unease, he steps around Izz to move into his cell, blending in flawlessly with its Satanic decor. The whole room an extension of his essence. Flicking his head to indicate Izz should join him.

Izz follows him awkwardly. If he felt alone with the killer before, he's utterly isolated and helpless now. This could easily go south, and he knows he doesn't stand a chance if this inmate decides to kill him. His lack of experience and fighting skills leaves him vulnerable and defenceless, unable to protect himself against a serial killer who will crush his attempts to fight back.

The male lifts his chin to the bunk, indicating Izz should sit down. He obeys, choosing to sit on the far end, as far away from the killer as possible, settling gingerly on the edge of the soft mattress.

It's surreal . . . He's alone in a serial killer's private quarters. A killer's territory. Their domain. He's pushing his luck, how many chances is fate willing to give him. Is this the last straw? Is he about to find out how bad it can get in this Hell-hole—

No, he has already found out how bad it can be. Already seen how vicious they are in here. And not just the inmates, the guards are just as bad, if not worse. This killer is his only chance to get out of this horrible situation without being beaten to death by the other guards when they find out what happened—what he did . . .

"I-I . . . You kill people, yes . . . ?" Izz enquires timidly, keeping his eyes downcast. Wishing he still had the joint to fiddle with, to give him something to pretend to be doing. So he doesn't have to focus on the killer's gaze eating away at him.

Is this the right move to make—

He shouldn't be here. This is a mistake. He needs to leave, pretend he never came here searching for the serial killer in the first place—

"What happened," the deep voice demands an answer, an answer Izz finds he cannot withhold.

CAGED IN

"It was an accident—I mean . . ." How is he supposed to explain. How does someone talk about this?

Coming here was a mistake—

"Where is it," the male's low rumble carries throughout the cell.

—he shouldn't have come—Wait?

Izz's head jerks up to gaze at the killer—had he heard that right?—the male is calm and rock steady, completely collected, like they're talking about where to go for lunch, not where a body is located. And the killer has to know that's what they're talking about, why else would he ask the question?

He knows. He has to know, But how . . .

Izz has to be reading into it, coming to conclusions he's made up in his head, with zero evidence. How would the killer know? Maybe it's a guess, based on his antsy behaviour? The killer is impossible to read, he can't tell what's going through the male's head. He prays it's a guess on the killer's part. Prays he doesn't have blood over himself that others can see and he can't—

Izz glances down at his body, to double-check he isn't covered in blood—nope still the orange prison assigned uniform. Bright orange, no bright red. No metallic, rapidly cooling blood anywhere in sight . . .

. . . '*It*' . . .

The mohawked inmate had said '*it*'. The guard is not an '*it*'. The guard is a human, a man. Albeit a terrible one, but still a human. A human Izz . . . killed . . .

Oh God, he really did kill someone. This isn't a messed-up nightmare, this is reality. It's his reality.

"The—um." Izz takes a shuddering breath, reaching deep down into his willpower. He's started down this path, opened this door, there's no turning back. He has nowhere to turn back to. "The filing room, down the corridor from visitation."

What have I done.

It's out there now. Good or bad, he has to deal with the consequences. He's no longer the only person who knows what he did.

Izz perceives a hand squeezing his shoulder. A comforting gesture completely at odds to what he thought he would receive from a serial killer. He welcomes the human contact openly, taking in the reassuring touch.

"I'll take care of it. You stay here." It's not said as an order, but the tone suggests it is. The firm hand squeezing down on Izz's shoulder also suggests it isn't up for argument, he is staying here no matter what he says, and he is okay with it. More than okay with it. "Right here. Until I get back. You understand."

Izz nods. He's not sure what else to do. He couldn't stand up even if he wanted to. His legs are too numb to hold his weight. He can barely feel them, let alone send signals from his brain to his legs for them to move. His mind's as foggy as his body. Far away and near impossible to see or connect with.

20

He's not sure how much time passes before the killer returns—his thoughts are a blank haze. He's slumping over, staring at the floor, when his ears pick out the soft footfalls lightly thumping over the second-floor platform. Heading for the cell he is numbing out in—turning into a stone statue.

A random thought pops free as the killer's shoes step into view, he blurts it out, "what's your name?" He was told the killer's name once by Reni or Zidie, but he can't remember.

"Sinn'ous."

Oh, yeah. That's it. Izz can't believe he'd forgotten it. It's a unique name, one you'd think would be memorable and impossible to forget.

Izz can see the killer's—Sinn'ous's—shoes in his peripheral vision. Filling the space in the cell's doorway. Like he's trying to give Izz space and not overcrowd him—a naive thought, why would a serial killer care if they made someone feel scared or unsafe?

"You were given that name at birth?" he isn't entirely sure why he asked. Maybe hoping the small talk will bring him out of the numbness.

"Is it relevant."

Clearly Sinn'ous isn't big into chit-chat. Or he doesn't possess the emotional awareness to know Izz's talking to ease his worries? To distract himself. It's well known that serial killers enjoy their kills, don't they? They wouldn't need emotional support after a kill. Unlike him—barely holding it together.

"No, I suppose it's not . . ." Izz mumbles, darting his eyes away from Sinn'ous to the other side of the cell, so he can no longer see the male.

The small grace of not having to look at the other inmate doesn't last long. Sinn'ous moves to sit on the edge of the bunk. Effectively placing himself in Izz's line of sight.

Izz can always leave. If he truly doesn't want to look at Sinn'ous. But right now, he does not want to be alone. He doesn't want to be near Reni, or Zidie, or even Blake. Those three would see right through him and see something is wrong. They wouldn't stop until they dragged the secret out of him. He can't deal with their questions and their caring compassion. He doesn't deserve it, doesn't deserve to feel better. He's murdered someone, he deserves to suffer for it.

Will suffering make it better? Izz's inner voice questions.

No, nothing will make it better. How can it? Not unless he can turn back time and stop the events unfolding in the first place. What would he do to change it? He has no idea. But maybe if he'd known, he could of . . .

CAGED IN

He won't ask, he will not ask Sinn'ous what has been done. He doesn't want to know what Sinn'ous has done to the body. What can really happen? It's not like the body can be dumped in the woods or buried. They are locked in a cage, with surveillance cameras all around. And guards patrolling the fence lines and corridors, always watching—they hadn't seen what occurred, otherwise Izz would already be in cuffs, dragged to The Hole.

One thing he's sure of, if he ends up in The Hole, he won't be making it out alive. Not with what he did to a guard, the other guards' will surely kill him for it—

Oh, God. I'm responsible for the body. For the death. It's all my fault.

He isn't aware he'd started crying until he's pulled up against a solid body. Tucked in under a comforting arm, a hand rubbing little circles on his back. He leans into the hold, squeezing his eyes shut as he cries in a prison cell, against the chest of a serial killer, over a murder he committed.

Where has his life taken him . . . ?

When Izz calms down enough to breathe without choking back sobs, he pulls away, not enough to dislodge the comforting arm, but enough to not be completely reliant on Sinn'ous to hold him up. "Thank you . . . For helping me with this. And for . . . everything else."

"It was no problem."

"I can't pay you back. I have no money." Izz has nothing, he doesn't even have the clothes on his back—they belong to this Hell-hole, not to him. He has nothing. Absolutely nothing. He's lost his freedom. He's lost his humanity. He is nothing but another killer now. A terrible irredeemable murderer.

Another murderer in prison. Where we deserve to be.

"I don't need your money, or want it. I have plenty of my own—which is sitting around attracting dust while I'm in here. May as well use it on something."

"Then what do you want?" Surely Sinn'ous isn't doing this out of the goodness of his heart. Serial killers don't have that capability, do they?

"I've told you. You intrigue me. I savour gifting you things. I like watching your reactions to them."

Izz snorts, a genuine laugh bubbling up. Pushing away from Sinn'ous, he rights himself, "you've been spying on me. Stalking me. Reni was right about the stalker type."

"Stalking . . . I suppose, in a way. But there is little to do in this place. I'd call it more . . . observing a fine creature. A fascinating creature."

Izz rolls his eyes, failing miserably to suppress a small smile, "stalker."

Sinn'ous chuckles, a bizarre sound coming from a serial killer. Izz's surprised serial killers laugh. It seems odd—then again, they are still human, so why wouldn't they laugh—

Izz's stomach lets loose a strangled noise. Demanding food before it dies—or a threat it's going to eat itself if Izz doesn't feed it instantly. His stomach at odds to the rest of his body. Everything else is nauseous.

Sinn'ous stands and moves around the cell, collecting different items to place on top of the cupboard next to the sleeping bunk. A metal pan, with some kind of makeshift heating device clipped onto it. Water added from a bottle,

CAGED IN

ramen packets going into their water bath. Flavouring added to the boiling prison stove.

It's absurd, watching Sinn'ous cook. Not only is it weird to see someone cooking using such a peculiar contraption, but to know a serial killer is doing it. It's a normal thing to do, yet completely at odds to what he expected. He clearly has a lot to learn, and can't base his knowledge of how serial killers act from movies.

Sinn'ous hands him a bowl filled to the brim and watches as Izz greedily scoffs down the noodles. Mumbling, "thank you," as he continues stuffing his mouth. Ignoring the half smile Sinn'ous gives him. He's starving, sue him. His nervous energy needs to be expressed somehow. And eating is his outlet.

As Izz forces himself to slow down—and reminds his mouth to chew to avoid choking—he eyes the paper and envelopes neatly stacked on the floating shelf above Sinn'ous's bunk. Maybe . . .

Well, Sinn'ous did say he isn't shy in handing out his money. And he definitely implied that he likes Izz . . . ? He has to, why else keep giving out gifts.

It can't hurt to ask . . .

Swallowing the noodles coating his tongue, "would you mind if I borrowed some of those?" Izz points to the papers and envelopes, "I'd like to be able to write to my sister."

Is it weird to ask? Out of line?

"Help yourself," Sinn'ous answers nonchalantly, as he cleans the cooking pot—prison stove?—whatever you call it.

E.P.WRITER

Izz shyly slinks back into his cell, he doesn't want anyone finding out where he's been—who he's been with. His stomach warmed with food, a stack of papers, envelopes, stamps and pencils, crammed under his arms. His sister's drawing still nestled safely in his pocket. With everything that had happened, he'd almost forgotten about what had started it. Glad he hadn't set the drawing down somewhere in his weird numbed out state. He would not want to go out searching for it. Or lose it, when it cost him so much to keep—

Don't think about it.

Throwing the supplies onto his bunk, Izz crouches down to make some room in his cupboard for the collection. Carefully laying them out on one of the shelves, he shoves the snacks and clothing aside. He can live with crumpled clothes, he can't live with sending his little sister letters on scrunched-up paper. He doesn't want her to know anything about the terrible conditions on the inside of this Hell-hole.

His sister's drawing is the last thing left, sitting in the middle of his bunk. Perhaps he can find something to hang it up with. Sinn'ous would have tape or pins or something? He must have, to hang all those pages on his cell walls—

"Hey Izz, we missed ya at dinner, you all good?"

Reni's abrupt disturbance startles Izz to such an extent that he unintentionally slams the cupboard doors shut. Unsure why he jumped out of his skin, as he has nothing to hide—nothing in this room to hide at least. Reni already

CAGED IN

knows about the gifts, and who they come from, and he's already made his disapproval clear.

"What?—oh." *No, I am not fine,* "I'm great, sorry. Visitation was hard, I came back here to get away and clear my head."

Not strictly true, though it is close enough to the truth to be believable. No way is he ever uttering the words out loud to Reni or his other friends about what he'd done—

Stop thinking about it.

"Yup." Reni sits on his bunk across from where Izz's kneeling on the cold floor. "Lots of inmates tell their people on the outside not to come, to move on and live their lives. Because it's depressing and hard to see them. To hear about the world moving along without us. It's easier not to see anyone, to forget the outside world exists."

Izz settles onto his bunk, picking up his little sister's drawing, he can duck back down to Sinn'ous's cell and pinch some tape, there is still time before lights out. Though he isn't sure what he'll say to Reni about it. He's not ready to divulge that he'd spent the afternoon in Sinn'ous's cell. Reni had told him to stay away from the dangerous inmate. Good thing he didn't listen or he'd have been screwed today.

"Cute drawing."

Izz regards Reni, who's leaning forward to study the picture. "My little sis drew it. She's big into the art side of things. She wants to be an artist when she gets older." Izz winces at the memories of what transpired after his sister left. He turns away from the picture, placing it down on the bunk once more, hoping the drawing won't be tainted forever with terrible memories. Fearing that it might be, for a while, until it isn't so fresh in his mind.

Will he ever get the images out of his mind's eye? The events are seared into his brain, vivid in their visual accuracy and saturated colours—

Izz fights to regain control of his thoughts, locking them away in their little box of denial. Deliberately focusing his mind on other activities, like writing to his sister. He'll do it tomorrow, pack some stamps into the envelope as well, so Luc can write back. He doesn't want to worry about them spending money on stamps. He might ask her for some more drawings in the letter, so he won't have only this one to look at, with its sickening baggage attached—

A shrill alarm shrieks through A-Wing, slamming into Izz's eardrums and rattling his skull. He cups his hands over his ears, trying to block out the piercing noise.

Does it need to be so loud. Izz's inner voice screams. Not helping the ringing in his ears.

"Lockdown," Reni bellows over the alarm's screech, cupping his ears the same as Izz. "Someone's got their ass shivved."

Reni laughs—Izz can't hear it over the screaming alarm, and his own inner screaming, but he can see Reni's ecstatic expression—

Izz barely makes it to the toilet before puking up the ramen he'd consumed.

21

Day two of lockdown.

Another frickin' day, stuck in a tiny cell, with nothing to do. Nothing but listening to Reni gossip about anything—and everything—that's been going down in prison. Including the new perfume of the guard, Missy, who works in Med-Wing. Apparently they have specifically allocated guards who look after Med-Wing and nothing else. One of the guards is shady and you can buy shit off him. Izz kind of zoned out at that point. There is only so much gossip he can take before he'll breakdown and start screaming.

The guards allow the kitchen inmates to leave their cells to cook for the rest of them. Dragging trolleys through the Wings to feed everyone in their cells. The library is also still open, guess the guards want the inmates to be occupied and not strangle their cellmates. Commissary and the library inmates working together to deliver reading material and goods. If you paid for them of course, the prison still wants to make their money, even when one of their guards is killed.

E.P. WRITER

" . . . must have been a guard. Bet it was that psychopath who did it," Reni muses from his bunk, hanging upside down over the edge as he plays collect the dust bunnies on the floor.

Guess again.

Izz winces at his cellmate's obsessive chattering. He knows Reni is referring to Sinn'ous. He also knows it's wrong. It hadn't been Sinn'ous who did it, isn't any of the known murderers in here. Nope. Just one sad pathetic excuse of a thief . . .

He scrubs at his face, trekking over to splash some water on himself. Trying to wash away the sin he committed. It doesn't help. The guard is still dead. He's still a murderer.

Did the guard have a family? Children? People who care about him—

"Yo, Izz man. Got you something." Erik is standing outside the cell door, a trolley filled with books and commissary items by his side.

"What?" Izz hadn't ordered anything, he has no money and he certainly isn't borrowing any books. He'd rather watch the paint fleck off the walls than read a long droning book—or novel—or whatever the bookworms call them these days.

Erik holds up a deck of cards, slipping the stack between the bars for Izz to take.

He stays frozen by the sink, sceptically scrutinising the paper cards. "I didn't order anything."

Erik must have made a mistake in the deliveries. Has to be . . . right?

"They're for you, from . . ." The side glace Erik swiftly flashes down the platform fills Izz in on who they're from.

CAGED IN

Sinn'ous.

Izz wanders over, plucking the cards from Erik, ignoring the sad look Erik gives him. He's not interested in anyone telling him it's a bad idea getting so close with a serial killer. For one, he is well aware he's playing with his sanity and his life. And secondly, how does he even know Sinn'ous is a serial killer? There is no evidence, and Sinn'ous had helped him with the guard . . .

Who is he trying to fool? You only have to look into Sinn'ous's eyes to see the darkness lurking beneath. The obvious cold danger prowling right at the surface, waiting for the next naive innocent fool to walk by.

Izz hopes it's not him.

Sinn'ous said he likes you, he's intrigued by you. He's not interested in killing you. The little voice in Izz's head tries to reassure.

Who's to say Sinn'ous didn't lie. Serial killers lie, don't they? If they didn't lie, they wouldn't be able to hide their secrets. And that's an important talent to have—when you kill people—you have to lie so you don't incriminate yourself. He's guessing, he has no idea. He's never been in a real murder investigation, or an interrogation. He's only ever seen it on TV. Who's to say they don't have mind-reading robots questioning you these days?

He's becoming stir-crazy. There is no stimulus in this cell. He can't stop his mind running and ruminating over everything that's happened to him, and what's going to happen to him—if anyone finds out. How much longer will he survive in this Hell-hole?

"You want to play a game?" Izz jostles the cards in Reni's direction. Needing something to focus on.

Reni grins, clapping his hands together like he's about to win big. "Hell yeah I do."

The days are blurring together. Time melding and mixing into a disarray that Izz can't distinguish. His sleep patterns are off. His appetite is practically non-existent. Even with the snacks Sinn'ous has been sending his way. His stomach is a twisted mess, unable to hold anything down before it comes back up to say hello. Like some twisted morbid game his stomach is playing with his mind.

His throat is killing him, probably to do with the stomach acid burning its path out. His cellmate thinks he has a virus, he has no intentions of correcting the facts.

Guilt. Izz has guilt. No virus bug going around. Just your old-fashioned guilt. Nauseating and thick, filled with dark thoughts and a depressing realisation that he is capable of murder.

He's not a hardened criminal. If his behaviour over the past—however long it's been—is any indication, he would make a terrible mob member. No Mafia wants a guy who falls off the deep end over a murder some would say was self-defence. How would he survive a murder in cold blood? An innocent target he was sent to kill—

This line of thinking is not helping Izz's anxiety and every other crappy emotion racing through his psyche. His emotions are a ticking time bomb. One he fears will end in a confession. Words he never wants to utter. Not when it will surely end his life. No way will any of the guards let it slide. He will be another *'tragic prison suicide'*, which no

CAGED IN

one will investigate. It will be brushed aside, the public won't care, and the guards will get away with killing him.

It isn't helping with Reni spitting out different types of conspiracy theories. Going on and on about who could have done it. Hits from gangs, drug deals gone sideways. A love affair coming to an end—he has to give his cellmate credit on that one, it is very close to the truth. A little too close for comfort.

During the long stretch of lockup, the only upside to Reni being his cellmate is how easily he can be distracted. Izz doesn't want to hear about the murder, but he fears he'd sound suspicious if he flat out told Reni to stop talking about it. So he keeps quiet and resorts to playing card games to try to divert his cellmate off the topic. Ninety nine percent of the time it works, and his cellmate forgets about the guard's murder. Too engrossed in winning the games to focus on the *who-done-it* side of things.

If only I could forget so easily . . .

Izz convinces Erik to deliver Sinn'ous a message, He'd had to write it down, as the skinny inmate refused to talk to the serial killer. He'd found the little joint he'd completely forgotten about, stashed away in its little hiding place. Ready to numb his mind for an hour or two, all he needs is a way to light it. And so, he sends a message to Sinn'ous to politely request one.

It's been a week. A week since Izz . . . murdered . . . He's finding it hard to sleep, every time he closes his eyes or the lights shut off, he can see the guard. Lying in a puddle of blood. Unmoving. Lifeless. Dead.

No matter how many times Izz tries to save the guard in his dreams, he can never do it. The guard always dies. The dreams always end in blood. He always wakes up in a panicked frenzy covered in a cold sweat. The only upside, in the—some could argue, self-imposed—lockdown is his new clothing. No longer the stand-out orange newcomer. He is an official member of the prison crew. A criminal home among other criminals. A murderer behind bars . . .

How long will the guilt last?

Will it never leave? Is this his life from now on? Never able to sleep without seeing the guard's face. Without reliving the events that transpired in the filing room. Without wishing and hoping for time to rewind and the incident never to occur.

Will the guilt leave if he confesses? Or will that only make it worse? He needs someone to talk to. Someone to help him make sense of everything he's done, everything he's feeling—

He cuts off his thoughts. Demanding them to focus elsewhere. He's desperate to take a proper shower. Sick of having to wash in the sink. He would give almost anything to take an actual shower. He feels tacky and gross.

How did people survived back in the days before showers were invented? He couldn't have done it, he'd have found a waterfall or something—anything—to wash the icky sensations away. He's unsure if it's the lack of a shower, or that he can still smell the metallic stench of blood on his hands—

CAGED IN

A clunking bang signals the cell door opening, for the first time since lockdown started. The bars sliding back, the prison beyond awaiting the inmates' return.

Does this mean the lockdown has lifted? Does this mean they didn't find any evidence to link him to the murder? Surely he would already have been dragged out of his cell by now if they found anything on the body to incriminate him. Surely?

Izz wants to sprint straight to the showers, firstly however, he has someone he wants to talk to.

He follows Reni out the door, his cellmate paying little attention, talking a mile a minute about going to the Rec-Room—must be the room with the TV they played cards in a lifetime ago? He can't believe he hasn't been in here for a year, it isn't even close to six months. Too much has happened in too short a time.

He has only one destination in mind, and it isn't the Rec-Room. Ignoring Reni's yelled attempts to gain his attention, Izz manoeuvres himself past the inmates heading in the opposite direction. Elbowing his way down the platform to the cell on the end. The Satanic cell that holds an inmate who he can talk to. To throw everything off his chest. He needs to expel it before it corrodes his soul further than it already has.

Legs numb and cold, breathing uneven and skin clammy. Izz edges down the line of cells, neither recognising nor taking note of the inmates he passes. His focus solely on his targeted goal . . .

He discovers an empty cell. The Satanic artworks hanging in all their glory. But their owner . . . The occupant of this particular cell . . . Gone . . .

Where could Sinn'ous be? The cells literally just opened. And the only way out is the stairs. The stairs Izz had passed on his way here. He had not seen Sinn'ous.

Had Sinn'ous been let out early? Or was Izz completely unobservant and walked right past him?

Guess I will take that shower after all.

22

The warm water flowing over Izz's skin is calming his nerves. A cleansing to wash away his sins. He prays it lasts, prays his guilt washes away alongside the water swirling down the drain. He shouldn't hold guilt over what happened, what he was forced to do, to a bad person who wanted to do bad things to him.

But he does. The guilt is there and it's a hard thing to live with. He wants it gone. He wants to go back to how he used to be, before he was caged up. He fears those days are long gone and he will never return to who he once was.

"Hello, Beautiful." The hand on Izz's back would have caused him to break out into an anxiety attack—and scream like a girl—if he hadn't recognised the deep voice.

A soothing presence he welcomes with theoretical open arms. Sinn'ous is the only inmate aside from Reni and Zidie, and maybe Blake, who he trusts. He shouldn't trust anyone in prison. But he can't help it. He needs to hold someone close, needs the human connection. He will go crazy if he doesn't have someone to talk to.

Izz watches Sinn'ous through the water's flow as the male stalks around him and leans against the tiled wall. He needs to say something to open up to everything else he wants to get off his chest. But what?

Act normal. Be polite. Say anything—

"Ahh—hi." *Wow. Great work Izz. You nailed that one.* He's like a clueless teenager who has zero vocabulary.

Sinn'ous's eyes run up and down Izz's front. Making him squirm. Not from fear, rather a primal desire he refuses to look too closely at.

Izz had been secretly hoping the killer would come here. He'd tried not to think about how vulnerable he is in the showers. How alone he is—metaphorically speaking, as the showers are packed with inmates in his same mindset to get clean, only he trusts and knows none of them. And his experience last time . . . when he was without The Gang . . . He does not want another guard scenario transpiring in the prison showers. He doesn't want to add to his guilt pool *'shivved man in prison showers'*.

"Heard you were looking for me," Sinn'ous folds his arms over his broad chest, "you enjoy what I gifted you."

How did Sinn'ous hear Izz was searching for him? Does he have eyes watching? Or is it more along the lines of him spotting Izz at his cell?

Should I ask, or let the subject drop? Do I really want to know?

He decides to let the subject drop. He doesn't want to know, he has enough on his plate, he doesn't need to add more to it.

"The cards were a Godsend, I was going stir crazy. But my cellmate's a terrible cheat, so there was that."

CAGED IN

Sinn'ous's eyes narrow ever so slightly at the remark. "He didn't cheat you out of anything—"

"No, no. Nothing like that. We weren't gambling with anything, just messing around." Considering everyone else who's done anything to Izz has been killed, he's not about to say anything bad regarding his cellmate. He has zero proof Sinn'ous murdered all those inmates... It could be a coincidence... couldn't it?

The inmates who attacked him in the corridor were killed and no one could figure out how or why. And there was Levis's death after he was an asshole to Izz. If vomit-dragon tattoo—or is it a snake? It's hard to tell what the tattoo is supposed to be—turns up dead with his slimy friend, Izz will be sure Sinn'ous had something to do with it. If he hadn't killed them himself, then he hired someone to do it. He doubts Sinn'ous would hire someone to do the deed. It isn't something serial killers do. Is it?

"Very well," Sinn'ous relaxes against the wall, his scowl disappearing from his face.

"You going to shower too? Or just stand there staring at me."

That earns him a devilish smirk from the male. Who deliberately runs his dark eyes down Izz's body, making a show of it. Izz manages to suppress his own grin, turning his face up into the spray to keep it at bay. He doesn't want others seeing him grinning at a serial killer, while naked in the showers. Not a reputation he wants.

"I missed my birthday," Izz mutters, while deliberately not looking over at Sinn'ous. "I overheard some guards on my way here. They mentioned it's the ninth today. I wish

I could have seen my sister on my birthday. First one I've had since she was born where she hasn't been with me."

Why is he talking about this? To—arguably—a stranger.

He feels obliged to talk, and not stand in silence while showering next to the other. Izz also, kind of, maybe, wants Sinn'ous to know when his birthday is. He's very aware how much of an idiot it makes him.

"When was it."

"The sixth." Izz peeks through the water's clear flow, trying to catch a glimpse of how the other is reacting—without catching water droplets to the eyes.

"You're what, twenty."

Doesn't particularly sound like a question. Does Sinn'ous already know? Search Izz's criminal records or something? Sounds like he has been stalked. Should he be terrified, or ecstatic, that Sinn'ous wants to know him?

Perhaps the serial killer is doing their research on their next victim—

Stop. Izz fights off his invasive inner thoughts. His paranoia is not welcome here.

"Yes. How old are you?" Izz's on a roll now with the information sharing so why stop.

"Twenty-eight," Sinn'ous answers off-handedly, as if he doesn't care, doesn't understand why it's important for Izz to know, but will indulge Izz anyway.

He's not sure why he needs to know either. It isn't really important. Especially considering he's supposed to be staying away from the dangerous inmate. According to everyone else at least. Izz's not sure about staying away from him. Isn't sure the male is actually a threat.

The entire prison fears him . . .

CAGED IN

"How long have you been here?"

Maybe Sinn'ous has lived here for years and years and that's why the rest of the prison is terrified. Because Sinn'ous has built a reputation over the past decade, and rumours have been spread and changed. As it went with word-of-mouth stories, each person adding details or leaving things out, morphing and changing the stories until they become unrecognisable. Maybe Sinn'ous is misunderstood, the rumours faked because of the Satanic nature of his cell.

"Since last year."

Well, there goes that theory right out the window.

"Oh, the way everyone acts I just assumed you'd been here for years." Izz pushes his wet hair back off his face, annoyed it's clinging to his skin.

I'd hoped you'd been here for years, that way I could justify hanging around you when everyone tells me, no.

Why does he trust this male as much as he does? Someone who can be in prison for such a short time and have the entire place cowering in the corner isn't someone a sane person would stand comfortably next to—while naked.

"They're terrified of you. Everyone told me to stay as far away from you as possible. And never be anywhere alone with you."

Good to see I listened.

"And you failed to listen."

"Oh, I listened. I just don't think they're right about you. You don't seem so bad . . . Don't seem like you've done the things they say you have."

I hope.

E.P. WRITER

Although. If Sinn'ous has, at least Izz's protected with the male right next to him. That's if said male doesn't decide to kill him first.

"I'd never hurt you," Sinn'ous states.

Sinn'ous isn't answering the question, but Izz will take it. And ignore the unspoken confirmation on the killing part. Sinn'ous isn't denying the murder accusations ... innocent people tend to protest against it, when accused of murder.

Izz's surprised how easy it is to talk to Sinn'ous, considering the other inmate is said to be a serial killer. Considering Izz's naked, right alongside the male leaning casually against the tiled wall.

He finds it comforting. Showering with Sinn'ous watching over him. He knows he shouldn't. How naive it is. However, his nerves are easing and his breathing calming. His body is telling him this male is trustworthy.

Can he allow himself to trust his instincts? Or are they flawed and broken with the traumas he's suffered locked up in this cage? A cage in which he is powerless, where he will be stuck for years to come.

Slapping the shower off, he pads his way over the tiles to get dressed. Sinn'ous trailing behind, which boosted his confidence. He feels untouchable. Because no other inmate will come within a mile of Sinn'ous so they steer clear of Izz by proximity.

It's a rush. If Izz was a king, this is how he'd feel. Untouchable. Unstoppable. Invincible. *Immortal.*

Izz hides his little secret smile by pulling his grey shirt over his head, composing himself before emerging from the neck hole. He will never get use to the scratchy materials of the prison clothing. Plastic sandpaper,

CAGED IN

rubbing his shower-kissed skin the wrong way. He longs for the day he can choose what he wears—

It also wouldn't hurt to shower in a place that doesn't smell like a dozen rats died in it.

Sinn'ous walks Izz back to his cell. It's a silent stroll, with his imagination running away from him. Almost as if they are two people coming home from a date night. It's a weird thought to have, but his forbidden emotions make him feel like a giddy teenager sneaking home, desperate not to be caught by disapproving parents. The parents in this instance being his cellmate and very loud best friend.

Back in Izz's cell, he throws the towel onto his bunk to fix later. Turning to face Sinn'ous who is waiting, toeing the line between in and out of the cell. So close Izz could touch . . . if he leaned forward a fraction . . .

Swallowing down the strange impulse to touch Sinn'ous, Izz shuffles his feet anxiously. Attention anywhere but on the other's face. He's nervous and does a terrible job to pretend otherwise.

"I'm ah . . . going to skip breakfast tomorrow to shower again . . . if you wanted to . . . do this again."

And there you have it. Izz has officially asked a serial killer out on a date—of sorts. If only his mum could see him now. She'd slap him, not that she's ever done that. Seeing her son with a serial killer, she'd lose it. Probably faint. Die. Come back to life to slap him again.

Sinn'ous smiles, a little upturning of his lips. Which manages to flutter Izz's heart—definitely feeling the teenage first crush vibes. Sinn'ous nods—a barely noticeable dip to the chin. But it happened, Izz had seen it.

Is that a yes?

Before he can demand a verbal confirmation the male glides back down the metal stairs and off into the prison below, swallowed up by the sea of inmates. Leaving Izz wondering if the encounter actually occurred.

23

Izz hides out in his cell until lunch, replaying the encounter in the showers and what happened afterwards. And he is thankful for it, it keeps his mind off . . . other events he doesn't want to think about, let alone reminisce over.

He is late to arrive at the cafeteria. Standing alone in line, and being served isn't too bad. His mind consumed by thoughts of an inmate he shouldn't be thinking about. He hardly notices anyone around him until he makes it to his table, joining The Gang in mid conversation.

" . . . that's nothing, hardly an adequate conquest," Sinj laughs, slapping Erik on the back. "If anyone's got some conquest stories, it's Izz. Ain't that right? Little buddy."

Izz blinks at Sinj, he isn't entirely sure what they're talking about. Conquests? Conquests of what? And why is he part of the conversation?

Sinj grins. "I saw you and a certain . . . *serial killer* . . . moseying out of the showers this morning. You were quite cosy and shit."

Izz flops down onto the awaiting bench. His entire body becoming a furnace under The Gang members' curious and shocked expressions. And he had been worried about only Reni or Zidie catching him. Now the whole Gang knows.

It's not as if he and Sinn'ous did anything. Or spoke much. Or touched. It was only . . . Izz doesn't even know what. A friendly greeting? or . . . something else . . . ? A date—

Shut up about it, it wasn't and never will be that word.

"We were just walking. Nothing happened," Izz can hear the panic in his own voice. No way the others can't hear it too. He sounds guilty as hell. How he hasn't been caught yet—for the guard's . . . murder—is a miracle.

"Uh-huh. Sure," Sinj winks at Izz, which makes Izz sink further into the bench trying to disappear into the table.

"Lay off, Sinj," Blake scolds, "Izz is smart enough to not get involved with the likes of that . . . murderer." Izz can tell Blake's being nice with his wording. Choosing not to curse out the dangerous inmate in front of the entire cafeteria.

Izz drifts away from the conversation—his mind blocking them out, as they continue to bicker amongst themselves—pushing his food aimlessly around his tray. He isn't that hungry. He hopes his appetite comes back soon, or he's going to become skin and bones if he keeps skipping meals—

The hairs on the back of his neck stand up, prickling. He looks out from under his lashes—to the far table. Sinn'ous is there, and is openly staring at Izz.

Man, this relationship—or whatever it is—is going to get him killed. What are the chances of a serial killer attaching

CAGED IN

themselves to Izz purely out of innocence, and not a rooted desire to draw in his next victim.

This cage is going to be the death of him. He won't survive long enough to be a free man. He'll throw himself a party if he makes it past a year—nah, if he makes it to six months, he'll punch the Warden in the face. He knows he'll never win the bet. He's leaving this Hell-hole in a body bag—if the prison has body bags, they probably class it as a waste of money. No doubt they bury the deceased inmates in a hole out in the yard, and make the living inmates dig it. No money spent on a funeral for the forgotten prisoners.

This place brings out Izz's dark and depressing thoughts. Things he didn't know lived in his mind. His mind will be the first thing to die in here. His sanity lost, his soul corrupted. Will he be forever changed? His very essence becoming nothing more than a walking breathing dead thing. Forever lost . . . A death that cannot be physically seen.

Thumping his head down in his palm, Izz gives up any pretence of eating. He's not hungry and playing with the food on his tray will not magically bring back his appetite. Along with his other problems he's developing an eating disorder.

Terrific, what I always wanted. Not.

Movement to the side tugs Izz out of his depressive spiral. Sinn'ous is leaving, packing up his tray and sauntering off in his predatory way. An inmate who isn't going to allow this cage to change him. Izz envies him that. Sinn'ous is put together. Not scared of anyone or skirting the boundaries of sanity.

E.P. WRITER

Perhaps I should take notes from him. See if he can teach me.

Izz tries his best to wait an appropriate amount of time. To not draw attention to his going after Sinn'ous. To spend some time with the male in his Satanic cell.

When Izz's sure he has left an adequate amount of time, he excuses himself from The Gang. Letting them know he needs to piss and he'll catch up with them later. It's a lie but he doesn't stick around long enough to see how many of The Gang know it. They seem pretty engrossed in whatever topic is being discussed. He'll meet them at dinner, or perhaps not even then. He may skip the laundry work and dinner to chill with Sinn'ous until lights out.

If Sinn'ous wants to. Maybe Sinn'ous will hate the idea. Or maybe the other will encourage it and he'll find himself bleeding out in a supply closet. Right alongside the guard's body—

Izz's instincts flare to life—three seconds after he rounds the corner to pass B-Wing on his way to A-Wing. A three second warning, time enough for his adrenaline to jump start, and zero time for his body's reactions to kick in—

Izz gets jumped.

For the umpteenth time, he is attacked. Though this time, it's swift and his attacker silences him fast. Hands clamping down on his arms and mouth, thighs and waist—too many hands to be one attacker—as he's carried back down the corridor, towards B-Wing.

The inmates lugging his flailing body are stronger than him, and their grips are stable and powerful. He can't wriggle free. He can't yell for help—not that anyone will come to his aid either way. He's not getting lucky again

CAGED IN

with Zidie and Reni. They are back in the cafeteria. Eating and chatting away. None the wiser.

And Izz . . . He doesn't know where he's going. Has no say in the matter. He never does—

The hands release him in a coordinated move, and Izz finds himself falling. His arms shooting out to try to break his fall—

He needn't worry—at least, not about the landing—a mattress breaks his fall, half-heartedly cushioning his impact with the bunk below. He's in a cell. Not his own, and not one he recognises.

There's a sheet too, hung over the cell's entrance. Hanging open far enough for them to walk in. And it is them. Four of them. Four snarky smug-looking inmates squished together in a cell built to hold two prisoners.

One of the four inmates crowding the cell, pulls the sheet's corner, effectively blocking them off from prying outside eyes . . .

The eyes of the men leering at him send cold shivers down Izz's spine. Their snide expressions, menacing smiles, eyes twinkling with delight . . .

Oh, God . . .

He can feel his face draining of colour. His chest caving in on itself. Dread seeping into his stomach and twisting his insides. Deep down he knows what is happening. Knows what the men want. He refuses to allow the thoughts airtime. He refuses to acknowledge them. If they aren't there, then it won't be true. It won't happen to him. He'll be safe, so long as he doesn't acknowledge the dark truths rattling his skull—

Izz darts up, to make a break for the door. His body operating on pure adrenaline-fuelled terror. The cell door is blocked by four inmates who each have more muscle mass than Izz could ever dream of possessing. Fearing he is prey, all his panicked mind wants is to flee. He is barging straight through—

He's easily grabbed and thrown back down onto the bunk. Then they're on him. Hands grabbing at his legs. His forearms. Pinning him to the bunk. Holding him down as easily as if he isn't struggling tooth and nail to break free. His lungs screaming, his breathing coming in irregular gasps as his entire body flips into extreme panic mode.

"Please, don't do this. Please." Izz tries begging. He isn't getting anywhere with his struggles.

"Shut up," the shorter of the four men spits out, "no one gives a shit, bitch. Someone gag him."

Izz's expecting a sock, shirt, dirty old cloth. Being dragged backwards over to the end of the bunk, so his head hangs over the edge, is not what he expects. And it only gets worse. When one of the inmates steps around behind him, their legs on either side of his head. An evident bulge pushing at the front of their grey prison pants.

"N-n-no. NO. NO. GET OFF ME." Izz kicks his legs as hard as he can. Nothing budges, he can't knock them free, whoever's pinning his legs is an immovable wall—

Izz's eyes fill with tears at the feeling of his pants being tugged down, the rough hands cold as ice on his exposed hip. The sickening touch is something he's never going to forget. If he lives after they're done with him. They could beat him to death.

CAGED IN

Why is this happening to me. What did I do to earn this much ill intent?

"Get off me. LET GO."

Izz screams. He pulls at his arms, twists his hips. He tries everything to pull free.

"I said gag the bitch, hurry up," the angry inmate giving the orders shoves Izz's shirt up, displaying his lean figure to the entire cell.

The man by Izz's head grabs his hair, wrenching his head back. He isn't having any of it. He twists his head to the side. Turning every time the man tries to get a good grip in his hair.

"He won't stop fucking moving, the angle is off."

Izz tries his hardest to pull his arm free, focusing every bit of his strength into one arm. If he can get one free he has a chance of fighting back—

Izz's field of view spins, the hands on his body releasing and grabbing hold once more as he is flipped onto his stomach. The coordination of the movements, the lack of conversation between his attackers—they've done this before. To have a system with little to no words required.

How many victims have come before me—

Cold fingers press between his ass cheeks, slick with something gross and slimy—

Izz grunts, crying out as two fingers force their way inside. His tears falling, sliding down his cheeks as he's violated by a complete stranger in a rank prison cell. He completely forgets he's fighting to keep his head out of the other man's grip.

A harsh tug in his hair pulls Izz's head up, his lapse in concentration working in the man's favour to pin him where the other wants. The straining on his neck is stretching his muscles beyond their limits.

He's greeted with an inmate's revolting . . . *thing* bobbing in front of his face—

He clamps his jaw shut, he can't see much through the wavering of his vision as his tears flow. But he can see enough to know the inmate is holding that disgusting . . . *thing*, and stepping into Izz's space.

"Open up, whore. Jay-Jay, open the whore up."

Izz doesn't have time to process the words, before an excruciating pain shoots up his spine, radiating down the backs of his thighs, as a third—or fourth—he can't tell, it hurts too badly—finger shoves its way inside. He cries out, opening his mouth—

A mistake he can't correct in time. The inmate at his head takes advantage of Izz's parted lips, shoving their way down his throat. Causing him to choke and squirm. Trying to pull away as he gags on the salty length invading his throat. Shoving all the way down. He can feel his muscles straining. The pain in his throat colliding with the agony further down his body.

Izz's legs are shoved apart, the invading digits unceremoniously pulled out. The sting followed by a warm trickle down the inside of his thigh. He's bleeding, it has to be blood. What else would it be.

He already knows what's about to happen. As much as he prays for it to never come. He knows what's about to unfold. And he can't do anything to prevent it.

He tenses up—he shouldn't, he knows he shouldn't, tensing will only make it hurt worse—he can't help it. He

CAGED IN

can't stop his body's instinctive reaction to protect itself and he can't prevent this from happening.

He's weak.

A disgrace.

How can he call himself a man if he can't defend himself against something like this?

I'm a weak coward.

The hold in his hair tightens as the inmate groans, shoving in deeper. Choking Izz more. He can't breathe. His body's panicking. He's gagging. He wants to pass out. He doesn't want to feel anything.

If he stops fighting. If he stops trying to prevent this, it'll be over faster. They'll be done with him faster. He has to stop resisting or it's only going to drag out longer . . .

Izz waits—tense and suffocating—for the inevitable burn to sheer through his entire existence. Yet . . . nothing's happening—

The invasion never comes, instead, a sickening crack—loud, wet and horrendous—echoes throughout the entire cell—

A solid heavy weight slumps over Izz's legs—

A gurgled gasp—another meaty crack—seconds after the first—

Izz can breathe again. His airways cleared. Sucking in sobbed gasps, as another snapping sound rings out, a solid thud of something heavy hitting the concrete floor—

Sinn'ous's face appears in Izz's wavering vision. He's sure he's hallucinating. Certain Sinn'ous is not in fact crouched down in front of him, with lips moving to form words. Words the ringing in his ears refuse to allow him to hear.

The blazing anger in Sinn'ous's eyes has Izz questioning his resolve on the image being a figment of his imagination. He could never envision such cold hatred in anyone's expression. Let alone the handsome eyes of the male who caught his attention the moment he arrived in this cage.

Izz bursts into tears, ragged, raging, girly-girl tears. Reaching out to grasp his hallucination—

A warm comforting embrace greets him. And Izz knows it's real. He's not imagining a scenario as he's being used by four inmates in a tiny cell. He really is saved.

He allows the male to help him to his feet. Clinging to the comforting lifeline that by some miracle has appeared before him. Standing strong and secure for him to take hold of. For him to use as an emotional escape.

Please, God, don't let this be in my head.

He'd break—if he woke up to find the four inmates huddled over him—he'd break. Crack in two. Fall apart, dive headfirst into insanity that would never be cured.

He blinks, slowly clearing his vision so he can see the chaos laid out in the cell. The bodies strewn over the concrete floor—

Wait . . . This is . . .

Izz shifts his gaze around the cell, peering past Sinn'ous, who he clings to like a Kevlar vest—

This is my cell?

When had they arrived back here? He doesn't remember leaving . . . He doesn't remember walking anywhere. Had Sinn'ous carried him? Or had he walked on his own, in a numbed-out haze?

CAGED IN

He's back in his cell now, curled up on his bunk. A blanket around his trembling body, and a solid saviour pressed up against his side. He's practically seated in Sinn'ous's lap. A warm hand rubbing slow circles over his back. The gentle touch comforting after the vicious violation . . .

Izz closes his eyes, tightening his grip on Sinn'ous's shirt. To keep the male from leaving. He can't be alone. Not right now. He can't. He's falling apart, he needs this lifeline to keep his mind. He can't lose his sanity.

I can't let this place take away who I am.

The next time Izz becomes aware of the prison around him, it's to the clanging noise of multiple inmates. The hustle and bustle of the work period being over and done with—or is it the ending of lunch? And the inmates are clearing out of the cafeteria?

It feels like a lifetime has passed, yet at the same time, it feels as though mere seconds have flashed by.

He hears the sound of his cellmate's cheery voice. Reni beginning a conversation with Izz before the other is even in the cell. It must be the end of the meal, why else would Reni sound perfectly normal. Izz's mind is too fried to string his friend's words together into a meaningful sentence. The familiar tone is reassuring. A soothing, safe, familiarity.

He watches the cell's entrance as his friend barges in. Watches the smile fall off his friend's face quicker than a gasp. Reni freezing solid in the entrance way.

Izz would laugh—at the shocked look on his friend's face—if he had the willpower to. It must be a scene—his pale, tear-stricken face. Shaking body curled up in

Sinn'ous's lap, seated on his bunk, with the serial killer gently rubbing his back.

"You okay, Izz?" his cellmate grits out, his eyes flicking to Sinn'ous and narrowing in contempt.

Izz's not sure he can answer, his throat feels like he's sculled boiling water filled with thumbtacks—

"He's fine," Sinn'ous takes over, answering for Izz.

"Wasn't talking to you. With all due respect," Reni speaks in a way that screams bitter, spiteful, disrespect, "was asking Izz."

"And I have said he is fine. You. May leave." Sinn'ous isn't looking at Reni. Izz can sense the male's eyes on him. Can feel the concerned gaze checking he's okay. Sinn'ous's tone of voice, however, implies there is no room for argument. Reni is to leave or be thrown out.

"I'm not going anywhere. This is my cell. You're the one who should leave," Izz's surprised Reni's standing his ground. After that talk—a lifetime ago, on Izz's first day—to run from Sinn'ous and not look back.

He has to smile. Reni may be shitting himself with terror but he's not abandoning Izz. Not like those wankers in the kitchen.

Izz jerks as Sinn'ous abruptly stands, the coiled-up danger trapped in the ever-tightening fibres of the male's muscles—

Reni backs way off, but stays in the cell, glaring at Sinn'ous like he's about to take the male on, "too many witnesses for you to do anything here," Reni straightens up, fists clenching, ready for Sinn'ous to attack him, "best you leave."

Sinn'ous moves to surge forward—

CAGED IN

Izz shakily reaches out to grab Sinn'ous's arm in an uncoordinated effort to still him. Surprised when the killer halts in his tracks.

"Don't—" Izz coughs, choking on the burning syllables, his throat protesting the action, "don't . . . He's fine . . . He can stay. I trust him."

Sinn'ous's intense gaze shifts back to Izz who finds himself soothed by the male's protective presence. A deep sense of safety floating over him at the possessive look in the male's eyes.

"What did you do to him?" Reni growls out the accusation towards Sinn'ous.

Izz chips in before Sinn'ous does something to his cellmate that can't be undone, "he didn't . . . do anything. He saved me from. . . others . . . who . . ."

Izz curls in on himself, struggling to perceive what has been done to him. Snuggling into the blanket further—as Sinn'ous takes up the space beside him once more. He would love nothing more than to cuddle into the male, however, with Reni there glaring, he is reluctant to reveal his vulnerabilities and emotions. Even to Reni. He'd give nearly anything for his friend to not see him in his current state.

Reni opens his mouth, gearing up for a bombard of questions. Enquiries Izz doesn't want to answer—

The shrill alarm crashing through the prison is a gift he's thankful for. It works to cut off Reni and smother his questions. For now, Izz has time to work out his answers to the inevitable interrogation he's bound to receive from his friend. He knows Reni has good intentions but right now he doesn't have the mental stability to relive what occurred.

Their cell door slides across with a deafening clang, effectively locking the three of them in together. Izz knows from the other lockdowns the guards' will be around soon to count them.

Sure enough, guards are pulling inmates out to move them back to their own cells. They don't even try it with Sinn'ous. The guard on Count for Izz's cell, takes one look at Sinn'ous before moving on to the next cell to evict those inmates trapped in the wrong sleeping quarters.

Guess the inmates in this prison aren't the only ones who fear the black and red mohawked male. Izz wouldn't be surprised if no one stopped Sinn'ous if he decided to walk out the front door.

He is grateful for Sinn'ous staying. It means he can nestle into his bunk, with a protective saviour stretched out behind him, a comforting arm tucked around his waist. He wouldn't be able to fall asleep without it.

He's not a fighter. He decides he's ditching the fight or flight. He can't protect himself. He's a flight or freeze. A run or panic. He's a failure as a man. A failure as a male in general.

"Not everyone was born to fight, some were born to be protected. You have other skills," Sinn'ous speaks quietly into Izz's ear, to prevent Reni from overhearing.

Oh . . . He hadn't realised he'd spoken out loud. How much has he been muttering out loud?

CAGED IN

"Don't worry about it. Get some sleep. I'll be right here."

Guess he said that out loud too. . .

Sinn'ous pulls Izz in close. Forming a shield at his back. Protecting him from the cell, from the prison beyond. He wonders what Reni is thinking? He doesn't have the energy to explain. He is glad his friend has stopped pushing for answers.

Izz drifts off, into an empty sleep, clutching at the serial killer who saved him. Safe in the warm embrace.

24

The next morning, when Izz wakes, he finds himself alone.

Sinn'ous is gone. Where to? He has no clue. The cell doors are open, guess he missed the wake-up call. How he slept through the alarm is beyond him. Those bells are loud as a marching band stomping away on his eardrums.

Reni is here, so there's that comfort. He isn't completely alone. He would have liked it to be Sinn'ous. He feels protected with Sinn'ous. More than he does with anyone else in here. Even with Reni taking The Hole as punishment for stepping in on the fight with the bald gang members. When Izz was having his ass handed to him. He still feels safer to be close to Sinn'ous. Maybe because Sinn'ous won't hesitate to kill anyone to protect him.

Izz leaves with his cellmate once they finish their morning routine—getting dressed and ready for a new day in this Hell-hole. Surprisingly, he'd slept like the dead. No nightmares or dreams of any kind. A black, welcoming abyss had consumed his night.

Where did Sinn'ous vanish to?

CAGED IN

He's surprisingly naked without Sinn'ous next to him for protection. He's barely been in the other's presence, yet he feels as though he's missing an essential part of himself while walking the corridors alone—save for his cellmate.

Reni's uncharacteristically quiet this morning, does he know? Or simply suspect?

Arriving at the cafeteria, he finds an empty table in Sinn'ous's usual place. It amps up his heart rate, not having Sinn'ous here. His mind running away from him with thoughts of where the male could be. His imagination blurting out scenarios of death, with Sinn'ous as the victim. Lying alone in a back prison room, having been ambushed and shivved by several inmates . . .

You need to pull yourself together.

He's so far off the rails he isn't sure he can come back. His life is forever changed. He is forever changed. So much death has taken place in here. So much suffering and pain. So many events have stabbed at his sanity. Brutally destroying who he once was—a far-off distant self he can never reach ever again. He is a forever-changed man. And this Hell-hole has done it to him. He'd come here as a decent man, he's leaving as an unseemly disgrace. There is nothing he can do to stop it. The events have already taken place.

This is who I am now.

Izz sits—like every other meal—with his cellmate and The Gang. At the same table. In the same spot.

He should change it up. Do something spontaneous and different. Like . . . sit on the floor. If only to break out of this repetitive existence. Maybe the change in routine will stop his downfall into madness.

E.P. WRITER

He fears it may be too late, fears he's reached his lowest point. And he's standing at the bottom, looking up the dark tunnel to the person he used to be. The person who's hovering far away at the top of the gloomy cavern. Forever unreachable.

He keeps his head down. Ignores the entire table. He doesn't want to join in on The Gang's discussions. Doesn't care if they are talking about him. Doesn't care if they notice something is wrong with him. He doesn't have the energy to pretend he's alright. When he's not. He's breaking. He's dying inside. A disgusting disturbed . . . thing . . . that doesn't deserve to be treated the same as before.

He is not the same. He's a murderer. A criminal. A disgusting weak individual who can't defend himself. He deserves everything he got. Deserves what they did to him. It was karma—if he believes in that type of thing—for what he had done . . . to the guard . . .

So much blood . . . There had been . . .

. . . So much blood . . .

It took Izz a long time to realise the conversations have dried up and died off. A thickening silence clouding the table. The calm of the forest as a predator stalks. No sounds made, in fear of being caught, of being discovered. It's self-preservation.

He frowns in confusion at the others seated around him. He's sitting at the end of the row, allowing him to see the entire Gang without turning his head. Everyone is staring at him, their eyes wide.

What's everyone looking at? Does he have something on his shirt?

CAGED IN

Izz glances down at himself, finding nothing out of the ordinary. His new, grey, prison assigned clothes, in tidy order. Clean and neat. His eyes observing zero discrepancies in the colouration of the crisp grey material—

A tray clicks down beside him, brushing against his own tray with its close proximity. A large body taking up the seat next to him—

Izz freaks. His mind short circuits and spazzes out for a second before it resumes working, and everything clicks into place. He already logically knows who it is. Why else would the table have gone dead silent?

He turns his head, thrilled to see Sinn'ous is not lying dead in a forgotten prison cell. He smiles softly as Sinn'ous settles down beside him. Then—because he fucking can, why the hell not after what Sinn'ous did for him—he leans into the male, his side flush against the larger frame—

A sharp intake of breath—is the collective response from The Gang. You can hear a pin drop. He's sure they aren't breathing. Come to think of it. The entire room seems to have come to a speechless pause. As if everyone is collectively noticing that the most-feared inmate—who usually sits at his own table—just sat down next to a bunch of inmates.

Next to Izz.

All the prisoners and guards are holding their breath for the serial killer to attack.

Instead, Sinn'ous places a chocolate pudding cup and a little bowl of soup, down on Izz's tray. Fingers brushing Izz's arm as Sinn'ous pulls his hand away.

E.P. WRITER

He would thank his saviour, but his throat is killing him, he does not want to talk. Doesn't want to remember why.

Instead, he picks up the pudding, taking hold of the cold plastic cup. Discarding its floppy top, he scoops out its contents. Stuffing it into his mouth. This must be where Sinn'ous had vanished too. Collecting pudding and soup. How? He hasn't a clue. Threatened a kitchen worker? Most likely. He can't say he feels sorry for them. He hates the kitchen staff. Hates most of the people in here, they are assholes.

His body permits the food to stay down. It doesn't immediately evacuate it out. His stomach settles and relaxes, happy with the meal. A gift from Sinn'ous that Izz's body doesn't want to disappoint him by throwing it back up.

The cold chocolatey treat soothing his burning throat. He takes comfort in it. He is sick of the constant tightening burn whenever he swallows or moves his head. The cold treat helps to neutralise the sensations he doesn't want to look at too closely. He never wants to relive those experiences. He wants to forget. Wants it to be a long-lost memory.

Dementia would be nice right about now.

Sinn'ous stands, apparently satisfied with Izz eating, or finished in the task he set about completing—the delivery made and accepted.

He would like Sinn'ous to stay. But he doesn't voice his wants. Isn't sure they will be reciprocated. Just because the other inmate saved him and gifted him with a heavenly treat to ease his pain. Doesn't mean the male isn't a serial killer. Who could very well be keeping him alive to have

CAGED IN

the pleasure of killing him later. He doesn't want to make it any easier for the hypothetical death to become a reality.

But as much as he tells himself not to trust the dangerous male, he finds himself falling deeper into the realm of true faith. Faith in someone everyone else told him is untrustworthy.

All the eyes—from the entire cafeteria—are on Izz. The conversations slowly starting to pick back up. Whispered and murmured. As though the whole room is trying to guess what the interaction was. But no one's brave enough to risk their words being overheard by Sinn'ous.

It takes a little while for The Gang to collect their hearts from the floor and begin chatting. The tension is still hanging thickly over their heads. They had already finished their food—eaten while Izz was sitting in his head, before their unexpected interruption. Leaving Izz as the last one with a full tray.

The soup is lovely, a cool soft mixture. Easy for him to stomach. He wouldn't have been able to eat it if it'd been hot. Sinn'ous really had been thoughtful with this gift.

When he's asked by Zidie to join his team for the first card game in the Rec-Room, he politely declines. Fabricating an excuse, he walks off to empty his uneaten food into one of the bins and return his tray. He hadn't even tried to eat the prison meal. Sinn'ous's gift is all he needs and all he wants.

Izz connects his eyes with Sinn'ous from across the room, waiting for the male to acknowledge him . . . He receives a small nod, figuring it means Sinn'ous understands what he's waiting for—

Sure enough the mohawked male rises, making his way over to return his own tray, setting it down on top of the tray Izz left.

They exit the cafeteria together, Izz following along close behind as Sinn'ous leads the way. He's not exactly sure where they're going, but he follows, nevertheless. Completely trusting in the male not to be holding ill intentions. He may regret it later, if it turns out he is merely the naive prey.

Izz wants desperately to forget he's caged up with so many violent untrustworthy criminals. Trapped.

He doesn't want to discover any evil intentions coming off the male he's placed his trust in. The one inmate everyone else fears. A ghost of death in their midst. They avoid him, and hold their breaths, terrified to be caught in Death's cold clutches.

Turns out, their destination is Sinn'ous's cell. The religious Satanic markings something Izz's becoming used to. They don't scare him, as he thought they should. Maybe because he is on the other side now. He knows what it's like to take a life. How easily it can happen—how easily it can happen to anyone. That killing someone isn't always planned out. Sometimes it's a deeply regretted mistake. An accident that, no matter how much you want to rewind time, cannot be undone.

Despite his aching throat, Izz finds himself opening his mouth to talk, to drive his thoughts away with a distraction, "I'm surprised the guards let you leave this up. Wouldn't it be considered . . . *Evil*—or something," he whispers the words, running his eyes over the painted walls, the scriptures and book pages interlaced with

CAGED IN

symbols and markings. It's neat, tidy and well crafted. An artistry of work. The cell a tapestry for the Devil's marks.

"A lot of them think stepping foot in here will condemn them to Hell—"

Izz burst out laughing, a rasping choked off noise, his throat protesting. He can't help it. His nervous energy is letting itself out. It's a ridiculous laugh verging on hysteria. Now he really does resemble a man teetering on the edge of insanity.

"They think you're the Devil?" Izz's injuries make it hard even for him to understand his words. He won't be surprised if Sinn'ous can't decipher them.

"I've never asked. Don't care," turns out Sinn'ous can hear the question just fine.

Izz wants to end the conversation he started, every syllable causing pain to his healing throat. If only it would hurry up and heal, he'd like to erase the memories, and have no physical links to bring them back. Too many traumas piling up, creating a wall of issues which will require years of therapy to knock down. If he ever can.

"I see," Izz eyes the soft inviting bunk. It's cushioning of soft blankets and enticing mountain of pillows . . . It would be so nice to lay down on it—

"You can relax, if you wish. Get some rest."

Izz nods, slipping his shoes off to settle down on Sinn'ous's bunk, curling up and tugging the blankets around himself. The soft mattresses marshmallowing his body in a gentle embrace. He scoots over, close to the wall, pressing his front to its bricks, the blankets shielding him from its harsh cold. Hoping Sinn'ous will take up the empty space behind him and cuddle with him.

E.P. WRITER

He's aware he should not be relying on Sinn'ous for safety or reassurance. Especially when he knows little to nothing about the male. With only the whispered rumours from fellow prisoners to go on. No way of knowing how many of those stories are true, and how much is false.

He should ask. Should get to know Sinn'ous, the one he's laid so much trust in. He's too exhausted to try now. He will. One day . . . At some stage. Possibly . . .

He worries about discovering the truth, not sure he wants to know why the male is in prison. If it's spoken by others, Izz can write it off, ignore it. But if Sinn'ous tells him, in person, that the rumours and whispers are true . . . He isn't sure he's ready to handle it. Isn't sure he can deal with Sinn'ous being a soulless serial killer . . .

Izz figures Sinn'ous can't be wholly what people say—a cold-hearted killer. He's protected Izz, has saved him. A cold-hearted killer wouldn't do that. Wouldn't risk their own life, risk being caught, risk having a witness. Just to save someone they don't know.

Sinn'ous has to be good. He has to be a decent human being . . .

Izz slips into unconsciousness, in the company of Sinn'ous—an inmate he associates with safety—watching over him. Awash in a sense of calm, choosing to believe in the saviour who will never harm him.

Izz wakes to someone nudging him, it takes him a moment to remember he'd fallen asleep in Sinn'ous's cell, in the male's bunk . . .

CAGED IN

His body hurts. His throat's a ball of agony. His joints, old rusted hinges who refuse to work without complaint. His eyes, would burn less if they were stuck open in a desert heatwave, they sting so much.

Flopping over in his heavenly warm cocoon of blankets, he blinks up at Sinn'ous. The male is perched on the edge of the mattresses. A small bowl held in steady hands. He can see the triple six tattoos on Sinn'ous's wrists. A dark branding on otherwise flawless skin.

"Sit up," Sinn'ous instructs, presenting the bowl, "I have pain meds for you too."

Izz doesn't ask where they came from or how they'd been acquired. For either the soup or the medication. He's appreciative of both. Bracing his elbow into the mattresses to cradle the cold sustenance in weak hands. Setting it down to balance on the prison bunk, in order to accept the pills without spilling anything.

He keeps his words internal, smiling a thank you to Sinn'ous. Pinching the three little pills between his fingers, plucking them out of the offered hand. He doesn't hesitate to scoff them down, using the soup to swallow them.

The nourishment is bland, tasteless, yet he's thankful for it. No spices to irritate his throat, or any chewing required.

Izz snuggles back into the bedding once he finishes the soup, Sinn'ous taking the bowl from him to place on the floor out of the way. The meds are already working, his battered and exhausted body drowsy and sluggish. A combination of his physical exhaustion and the drugs are demanding his eyes close and his mind rest.

E.P. WRITER

He's brought to consciousness by a nice smell wafting throughout the cell. Sinn'ous has more food awaiting him. Where the meals are coming from, Izz does not know.

Did Sinn'ous leave to collect them? Or have someone collect them for him? Would anyone do that? They all fear him . . .

Does he have a guard to do his bidding? Does Izz really want to know either way? It's probably safer not to know. In fact, it would have been wise not to eat meds from Sinn'ous in the first place. Especially with the luck he's having so far around inmates . . . and guards . . .

I know nothing about him.

But he can find out. "Why the Satanic stuff? Were you born into the religion? Or did you take it up on your own?" It's as good a time as any to ask. He's curious to learn more about Sinn'ous.

"Something I picked up as a teen. It was easy for me to relate to," the mattress shifts with the weight of Sinn'ous sitting on its edge. Handing Izz a dish of rice, with little chunks of vegetables mixed throughout. And three more little pills.

Do I want to know why it's relatable? Do I need to know the details?

"Do you sacrifice virgins?" Izz mutters, picking through the rice with a slim spoon, to inspect the types of vegetables it houses.

"You watch too many movies, Beautiful," Sinn'ous strokes his fingers through Izz's hair. Chuckling softly as

CAGED IN

he hands Izz a small cup of water to take the pills with. "A misconception. Satanism isn't based on sacrifices and deaths. It's being true to yourself and not apologising for it. You can be a nature lover and a Satanist. I, on the other hand, use it for the former. I'm true to myself and who I am. I will never apologise for what I've done. Or will do."

Whoa. That's a lot to take in. Izz hadn't known Satanism is deeper than sacrificing people to the Devil.

Sinn'ous clicks his tongue lightly, "you could be a carer for your family and a Satanist. If it's true to who you want to be. You don't have to get on your knees and pray to Satan."

"So you don't believe in Satan?"

All the paintings and markings over the walls present as someone who worships the Devil. As offerings to an out-of-this-world deity. The admiration clear in the carefully constructed wall of arts.

Sinn'ous tilts his head, scanning over Izz's features, "Jasper Marcelo. Yet you go by Izz, why is that."

Whoa. He's asking a question in return.

Is this the first time Sinn'ous has asked him a personal question? Enquiring into who he is as a person. Granted, it was spoken more along the lines of a statement, but it's the closest to a question he's heard from the male, so he'll take it as such.

Sharing personal information with someone who everyone believes is a serial killer . . . Stupid on his part. He's half witnessed murders committed by Sinn'ous. He'd heard two—or perhaps three—of the four inmates who'd assaulted him—die. He'd witnessed their murders. He can't remember if he'd actually seen Sinn'ous kill any of them, his memories are foggy from that day, but it's obvious.

Izz draws in a deep breath . . . and jumps off the ledge . . .

"My sister had brain cancer. She used to have a toy horse. Her favourite," Izz closes his eyes, the memories visually dancing over his eyelids. "During one of her seizures—in the beginning stages before we knew it was cancer—she fell down next to the fireplace. Her little horse fell over the rails and went in."

She'd been more upset about her horse than the seizure she'd suffered. It was a gift that she didn't remember the uncontrollable seizures. Izz was scarred enough for the both of them, by the image of her little body flailing on the floor.

That day had been horrifying. He hadn't known what was wrong, why she was convulsing on the carpet. He'd never seen someone in the middle of a seizure. Waiting for the operator to answer his call for an ambulance was the longest three seconds of his life. He can still hear every syllable of that ringtone.

"I found her a new horse, the same colour and everything but she knew it was different. She didn't want it. Wouldn't accept the new toy."

Her tiny fragile body lying in the huge hospital bed, wires and tubes sticking out of her and snaking around the bed and the IV pole. She'd been as pale as the white sheets wrapped around her.

"Her horse's name was Izzy. Lucia had trouble speaking, after the cancer grew, j's and p's were a few of the letters

CAGED IN

she struggled with, so I became Izz." He takes a deep breath, searching for his inner strength.

"Apparently I was really good at horsey-back rides—they weren't to be called piggy-back rides, it was horsey-back rides. I'd give her one around the hospital, to take her to the different rooms where they'd . . . with all the testing and treatments. . ."

The testing and treatments were extensive. Not something any child should have to go through. Being poked and prodded, drugged and medicated. He would have taken her pain in a heartbeat, if he could have. He still would. He'd endure it if it meant she would live a normal happy childhood.

"That's how I got the nickname. Her absolute favourite animal is a horse, said I was her favourite, better than any horse. It sounds weird when I say it out loud, but it was the sweetest thing at the time."

When Sinn'ous doesn't say anything for several moments, Izz chances a look over at him.

Sinn'ous is staring at the wall across the cell, as if caught in deep contemplation. "I never had any siblings so I can't relate. Nor do I feel anything for others." Sinn'ous's dark eyes flick over, boring into Izz. "I can understand how you mean. What would be there. The love you share with her."

"You really don't feel love for anyone?"

"No. Not in the way I've seen others," Sinn'ous turns his full body to face Izz. "I . . . enjoy things, maybe you could call it love but not in the way most people do."

If he doesn't love, why is he so nice to me?

"So what do you feel for me?"

Sinn'ous has to feel something, right? You wouldn't step in and save someone if you hold no feelings for them. Especially when you are a psychopath. And Sinn'ous is a psychopath, he killed people, how can he not be?

Izz can't deny it, that Sinn'ous is a psychopath. Not with the death of the inmates or the confession he'd made about not feeling anything for anyone. That's one of the traits of a psychopath, no regard or empathy for others, isn't it?

But he saved your life . . .

Sinn'ous can't be completely rotten. He is protecting Izz. He's given him many, many, gifts. Made certain Izz's not going hungry. Wasn't bored during the lockdown. Isn't hurt by others.

It's beginning to seem as if Sinn'ous will never answer. " . . . Protective. I do not want anyone else to be near you, to touch you. I want to keep you."

Izz blinks up at the male. He should be creeped out, or at the very least slightly alarmed. Yet he is the opposite. He feels delighted—butterflies fluttering in the stomach, delighted.

Sinn'ous wants to keep me . . .

Why does the thought have him buzzing lightly? His heart fluttering right alongside his ribs.

"You'll protect me . . ." Izz whispers, more to himself than to be heard.

Izz curls over to rest his head on Sinn'ous's lap. Human contact has been lacking since he arrived in prison—the warm kind, not the punch-you-in-the-face revolting-skin-crawling type—and he craves its warmth.

CAGED IN

"Is this your version of loving someone?" Izz would guess it's the closest Sinn'ous has come to the feeling. With how the male is describing his emotions. Although it is hard to tell. Sinn'ous doesn't wear his emotions on his sleeve like Izz does, making it impossible to read the male's inner thoughts.

"Perhaps," Sinn'ous runs his fingers through Izz's hair, "is that what people do, who care for each other."

Is Sinn'ous enjoying the contact and close proximity? Izz sure is. It's nice, normal, helps him forget where he is.

Why are you pushing so hard to have him express his feelings . . . ? Izz's inner voice questions and answers. *Maybe because you're lonely and afraid?*

"I guess," Izz's not sure how to answer, he can't tell someone how to express their love for another. "I feel safe with you around. Best sleep I've had since I arrived here. 'Cause I know you'd never let anything happen to me while I sleep."

I'm also attracted to you and wouldn't object to you touching me. Or . . . doing more than touching . . .

"I would not."

Izz bites his tongue on his inner revelation, keeping it to himself. "But what about when you're not around? Everyone in this place seems hell bent on making my life a living Hell."

He can't go through what happened yesterday ever again. He cannot endure more of the same treatment. To feel so weak and pathetic . . .

What kind of a man can't stand up for himself and stop . . . what happened . . . from being done to them?

"I could mark you."

. . . mark him?

What does Sinn'ous mean by *'mark him'* . . . ? Like some weird animal marking their territory type of thing? Izz's not sure he's on board with any . . . What is it called? Waterboarding—no, isn't that a torture technique?—Whatever it's called, he isn't sure he would like it.

He's experimental, yes. But he isn't *that* experimental—

Maybe if he's wasted drunk—nah, not even then. It's not his thing. And kind of weird for someone to raise so casually . . . Humans also don't have a sense of smell like dogs so how would peeing on someone do anything to mark their territory.

Izz must have pulled a face because Sinn'ous clarifies, "I can have my mark tattooed on you. No guards or inmates will dare touch you, they'll know whose wrath it will invite, if they so much as disrespect you."

Ohhhhh . . .

A tattoo.

Izz's cheeks light up as if it's their sole job to warm the entire prison—the entire country—

He's glad Sinn'ous can't read minds. With where his thoughts immediately jumped to . . .

Why had his mind gone so dirty?—probably because he hasn't touched himself since he got to prison. He's pent up and his mind's eating away at itself, finding ways to turn anything dirty.

A tattoo makes sense.

A tattoo would be logical. An easy way to show others he's untouchable. He'd be safer, less on edge, and not scared shitless every minute of the day. No more walking backwards to watch who's following him, or hiding away

CAGED IN

in his cell, or using The Gang as a shield to avoid getting caught alone—although it had helped save him in the past. Kind of.

This would be different. Sinn'ous is different. A type of protection nobody wants to fuck with. And Izz wants the defensive shield. If he bears the mark of the prison's notorious serial killer. . . no one will attempt to mess with him.

Decision secured in his mind, Izz smiles softly at Sinn'ous, "yes. I'd like that."

25

Breakfast.

Similar to previous days. It's a time of gossip among the inmates, and The Gang is not above it. Everyone shares stories they learnt from their cellmates during the forced hours locked up in their cells. Today is no different. However, today the gossip is a little more interesting. Izz's stunned into silence as Sinj continued with the bombshell he'd dropped.

"Guards are calling it a pact-suicide. The evidence to link them to the death of that guard was in their cell. The knife that killed him, wrapped in a shirt hidden under their mattress."

Izz can't believe what Sinj is saying. It's absurd. The suicide of two inmates, who killed—only they didn't. They didn't kill the guard they are being accused of killing. He killed the guard. And he sure didn't use a knife to do it.

So why are these two random inmates being called murderers? Why are they being blamed for the guard's death? They hung themselves in their shared cell, but

CAGED IN

why? He knows they didn't kill the guard and they surely knew they didn't do it.

So why are they dead? And why is the knife found in their cell being called the murder weapon?

The guard was killed with a broken wooden broom handle. Not a knife—how did they even get a knife in prison? Did they steal it from the kitchen?

"Mark and Harry killed the guard?" Blake's exasperated voice chimes in like he, too, cannot believe it.

"Who are they?" Izz ponders out loud. Who are they blaming for the death he had caused?

Izz hadn't expected an answer, Reni fills him in anyway. "Those two from our Wing—dude with the ugly dragon tattoo and his friend. They didn't have the balls to kill a guard, if you ask me, it was . . . Well . . . You know," Reni glances over at Sinn'ous.

Guess again roommate.

Sure, Sinn'ous may have framed the inmates—he'll ask when they're alone again—but Sinn'ous sure as shit did not kill the guard as Reni is insinuating.

The Gang went back and forth discussing the suicides and guard's death. Theories are tossed around with others dismissing them. Meals eaten absently between banter. It's not long until they are done and ready to head off to start their day in the prison yard.

"I'll catch up with you guys later," Izz doesn't wait for a response, ditching his tray and rushing off in his excitement to find Sinn'ous.

Turns out to be easy. Sinn'ous is already waiting for Izz, leaning back against the corridor wall. Much to his relief, he did not want to wander around the prison—alone—to find Sinn'ous. Not after what happened the last time . . .

"You sure you still want to do this?" Izz's mildly surprised Sinn'ous cares enough to ask.

Rubbing his mouth to hide a little smile—Izz doesn't want Sinn'ous to think he's crazy or clingy . . . or something equally embarrassing. He's excited to get a new tattoo, that's all there is to it—well . . . maybe he is extra giddy because it's going to link him to Sinn'ous.

Sinn'ous holds out a miniature water bottle to Izz—it's half the size of the ones he used on the outside. He frowns but takes the offering, opening his mouth to ask what it's for—the male opens his fist to reveal two white pills nestled in his palm.

Oh, pain killers.

"The pains not so bad," Izz murmurs, gathering the medication as he twists the bottle's lid off.

Only two this time? Why three before?

Izz shrugs off his inner question, pushing it to the back of his mind. It's not important. He trusts Sinn'ous.

Sinn'ous prowls ahead, leading the way, Izz falling in step behind him. Dumping the near empty miniature bottle in a bin as he hurries to keep up with the male's long strides. Watching the predatory male gliding through the corridors like he owns the place. Dangerous and not someone to fuck with. Other inmates clearing a path, scrambling to move out of his way.

Powerful.

The cell they arrive at is plain and boring, no personal belongings on the shelves. No photos or posters hanging on the walls. Smaller than the cells in his Wing. The only

CAGED IN

thing in the one-prisoner cell—apart from the skeletons of furniture—are two boxes, nestled on top of the knee-high cupboard, filled with a collection of little glass bottles—must be tattoo ink?

A free-floating chair—rare, considering the prison has a thing for bolting everything to the floor—is pushed against the cupboard, holding a gun like device—*the tattoo gun*—

Are they called tattoo guns? Or tattoo machines?

This must be the place inmates come for their tattoos. It doesn't appear very . . . legal . . . Do the guards not know inmates are tattooed in here? He'd never thought if they are allowed to get tattoos or if it's strictly prohibited. The equipment to do it would have to be classed as contraband, wouldn't it?

"Where are we?" Izz whispers, stepping in close behind Sinn'ous, attaching himself to the male's personal bubble. His anxiety is rising at how silent this Wing is, he'd gotten use to how loud prison is, now that the noise is gone, he notices it.

This Wing . . . Is dead.

There are no other souls in the area, no inmates, no guards. He is effectively isolated, in a room with . . . a serial killer . . .

This better not be the time everyone says 'I told you so' as he's lying in a forgotten prison Wing dying . . .

"I-Wing. It's unoccupied, no guards will bother us here," Sinn'ous explains, stepping further into the cell.

The answer does not lessen Izz's anxiety—

"This your bitch you want inked?"

E.P. WRITER

Izz startles at the new voice behind him, spinning to face the intruder, and backing up into Sinn'ous space, leaning against the male's solid frame.

Who are they?

The newly arrived inmate is leaning against the cell's barred door. Cocky grin in place over slightly chubby features. His face is clear of any ink—the same can't be said for the rest of him. Every fleck of skin Izz can see is covered, including his ears. His prison shirt is worn out and torn in places, revealing inked skin underneath.

Wait . . . ? Bitch . . . ?

Is a *'bitch'* all he is to Sinn'ous?

Does this mean he'd have to . . . to *be with Sinn'ous*—he's not against the idea, he merely wants it to be his decision. Not based on conditions for protection—

Sinn'ous surges forward, grabbing the inmate's shirt collar, shoving them up against the cell wall, pushing his face in tight to the other's mug. "You'll refrain from ever referring to him in that manner."

The chubby inmate nods, eyes bulging like they're liable to pop out of their sockets. Izz's sure his eyes are doing the same. He's never witnessed Sinn'ous this way. Never seen how aggressive Sinn'ous can be. How quick the aggression erupts to the surface.

"This is Izz," Sinn'ous continues, flicking his head back over his shoulder to indicate where Izz's standing—without taking his eyes off the man he has pinned.

Guess Sinn'ous is true on his word, regarding the *'not needing to pay for protection'*. He hadn't given Sinn'ous anything, yet here the male is, protecting Izz's honour.

CAGED IN

Sinn'ous leans in, to breathe something into the other's ear. Izz could have sworn it was, "and he's mine," but he's sure his ears are interpreting it wrong. No way is Sinn'ous being possessive over him. That is too out of this world to believe. No serial killer is going to do that for anyone . . .

Sinn'ous backs off, and the other inmate straightens up. Skirting around Sinn'ous to a small stool next to the tattooing supplies. This must be the artist, he should have figured it out sooner, but his mind is a little preoccupied. He's not entirely sure he trusted his body in the hands of someone who'd just been threatened. He's liable to wind up with a dick, or something equally unpleasant, inked into his skin.

"Take a seat, please, Izz." The guy's attitude sure has changed—polite and then some.

Izz follows the instructions, perching on the edge of the bare bunk. Watching Sinn'ous pull a neatly folded piece of paper from his pocket. Handing it over to the artist, who flattens it out on their thigh.

Izz can't see what is on the page, the angle the artist is seated at keeping whatever is on it out of his sight. Guess it will be a surprise for him when it's finished.

The artist scans over the paper as he clicks together various parts of the tattoo machine—or gun. "Easy enough. Where am I putting it?"

Izz opens his mouth to answer, only to find the artist hadn't directed the question at him. Instead they are focused directly on Sinn'ous.

"Above the hip, will suit him . . . Is that okay with you." There's a brief pause during which Izz takes his time studying the floor, the little rocks and dust clumps scattered over it.

"Izz?"

Izz blinked, peering up at Sinn'ous. "Huh?"

Both sets of eyes in the cell are staring at Izz, waiting—the last question must have been aimed at him. He'd thought Sinn'ous was talking with the artist. "Oh, yeah. The hip is fine. Yes."

I mean I had been thinking the thigh or calf, but if Sinn'ous says it will suit me there . . . I'd like it there. I can always get another tattoo on my thigh later.

Turns out the *'calling card'* is Sinn'ous's name. Red splatter ink highlighting the bare skin around the curving letters spelling out . . .

Sinn'ous.

It very much resembles a blood splatter. Quite similar to the tattoo Sinn'ous has at the small of his own back—a miniature version of it, and less masculine. Petite letters curling above Izz's hip bone. Flowing perfectly with his body shape—

I feel like a girl, with the delicately written name of her boyfriend on her hip.

Izz can't choke back the laugh. He is aware the others in the cell are no doubt considering him a crazy person, who's lost any hope of presenting as normal. For him, and his weird thoughts, it's the funniest thing in the world.

CAGED IN

He has to physically beat his giggles into submission. Before Sinn'ous decides to leave him in I-Wing with the rest of the Psych inmates joining the prison population.

He smiles softly at Sinn'ous who is smirking at him. Maybe the male can actually read minds. At this point, it wouldn't surprise him if the mysterious mohawked inmate can enter his thoughts.

He turns towards the artist to break the eye contact, "you're very skilled. How long have you been—never mind." Izz doesn't want to appear as if he's prying.

"Don't worry about it, and several years now. Was a hobby on the outside, became my thing in here."

Izz nods. The inmate may have indulged his curiosity, but he doesn't want to push it. He isn't entirely sure the artist hadn't answered in self-preservation. To not piss off the serial killer hovering close by.

He pulls his shirt back on after the artist places a patch over the new ink. He's given a tube of something to apply to the fresh ink, to help with the healing process. He will be keeping this tattoo the cleanest he has ever kept one. He's not messing up the ink work. Not when it means so much to him.

This new ink holds a power to it. A burning stinging shield against the world—the prison world. A reminder he does in fact have someone in here who is taking care of him. Who won't allow anything bad to happen to him.

The walk back to A-Wing had been quiet and uneventful. His scratchy prison clothes irritating his skin—Izz's weirdly conscious of his new tattoo even with the patch over it.

"It suits you, Beautiful."

"Thank you," Izz shifts shyly on Sinn'ous's bunk, "I like it—" Izz freezes, words cut off mid-sentence—

He is uncertain how he came to be in this situation. He'd walked back with Sinn'ous to the Satanic cell at the end of the second-floor platform. Sat down on the mattress-stacked bunk . . . and the rest is a blur. What steals his focus and fizzles his short-term memories is Sinn'ous's lips. Hot, smooth, pressed against his own . . .

Izz's motionless. Unsure what he should do next—

The kiss is over before it starts. As quick as a gasp, Sinn'ous is pulling away. Snapping Izz out of his dazed shock.

Did that truly happen?

"Forgive me. You're perched there delectably, I couldn't help myself."

Izz's eyes dart over Sinn'ous's features. Over his black eyes, his coloured hair, his . . . lips . . .

Leaning back in, Izz brings his own mouth down onto delightfully full lips. Kissing Sinn'ous with a growing hunger.

He weaves his hands into Sinn'ous's hair. Deepening their kiss. Groaning at the exquisitely silky strands, a welcome delight. He'd half expected the mohawk to be stiff and crispy with hair gel—unrelenting to match its owner. It's as if his hair grew upright in its styled glory without a need for hair products.

Izz opens up into the kiss, drawing Sinn'ous down to him. He likes this, it's not rough or unwelcome. He doesn't feel

CAGED IN

as if he has no control. He is secure, protected. He knows Sinn'ous won't hurt him—

Izz gasps as his world flips, his back hitting the foam bedding, the prison mattresses contorting to his and Sinn'ous's combined weight. His lips part in shock—digging his fingers into Sinn'ous hair—chasing the tongue probing to enter his mouth. He lets Sinn'ous in. Opens up to the larger male. Welcomes the sparking heat surging through his veins.

He exhales as the connection is broken, his protest turning into a broken-off cry as those talented lips work their way over his neck. Licking and nipping at the delicate skin—

Izz grunts softly as the bites turn sharper. A steady hand gripping his chin as those teeth sink in. The sting of pain shooting down his nervous system like a highway carrying hot energy—aiming for his crotch. He is rock hard in a split second, throbbing in his confinement. His neck exposed to the male above him, vulnerable in the best possible way.

I never knew I had a biting kink . . .

He sure does now. It's amazing. The licks of pain. The sparks burning his arousal deeper into his flesh.

He's hot, needy. Arching up into Sinn'ous. The bite isn't hard enough to break skin—but there's no doubt it's left a decent mark. A branding . . . different from the tattoo. This one is made by Sinn'ous, not in dedication to the male.

Izz's in heaven. *Delectably*—to steal Sinn'ous word.

Through his burning haze, he can feel hands working their way under his shirt, shoving past prison greys to brush bare skin. Licks of sensation following the fingertips working their way down his abdomen. Dipping under his waistband—

Izz sucks his stomach in, hollowing out his hips to allow access. Sinn'ous takes full advantage of the invitation, fingers wandering further inside . . . closer to the place he's begging to be touched.

Izz digs his nails into Sinn'ous's hips, trying to urge the other on. To hurry up and touch him—

Teeth clamp down on his neck further down than the last bite. The sharp stinging pain jolting his body off the mattress—

This new kink is driving him crazy . . .

Fingers brush over his inner thigh, so close to their goal. He needs Sinn'ous to touch him, needs to feel the heat of hands on his sensitive skin.

The first brush of flesh on flesh is electric, drawing a rattled breath from his chest—

Everything shifts at once. Like an ice-cold bucket tipped over his head. It is no longer a welcome touch. No longer soft and careful—he is thrust back—back in time, to a different cell—a cell with four inmates leering at him. The unwanted touches—

Izz cries out—this time in fear, not reciprocated pleasure—shoving at the heavy weight on top of him. His mind filling with images racing all around. Too many faces flashing past. Too many hands, too much contact—

He scrambles away, his back hitting the wall, pulling his knees tightly into himself—

He can't breathe—

His lungs don't work—

He's going to die—

CAGED IN

"Relax."

A soft faraway voice whispers into his downwards spiralling void. His body spinning and twisting with present reality mixing with past. Swirling in a knot of pain and fear.

"Breathe."

Izz follows the instructions. Concentrating on his breathing. Stamping out the images trying to take over.

"It will pass."

He's aware he's in the throes of a panic attack—doesn't make it any less real. Or any easier to pull himself out of. The whispered reassuring words are helping him. Slowly easing him out of his mind's downwards spiral.

"You're fine. I'm right here."

He's not used to this. It's so real. As if he has actually jumped back in time and is helpless once more, in the clutches of those . . . degenerates. Logically, he knows it is all in his head. The inmates who had hurt him are dead. They can never harm him again.

"I'm right with you. You're not alone."

Izz grabs onto Sinn'ous's voice, using it to calm his breathing enough to force out an explanation. Knowing he owes one to Sinn'ous. "I'm sorry—"

"Don't be. You can choose to stop any time you like. It's your choice. And I will respect it. We can wait until you're ready."

Izz blinks into his folded arms, he hadn't been aware just how tightly he's hugging his legs. Holding himself in a safe embrace, clutching onto himself so he doesn't collapse, doesn't sink into the tornado of emotions and memories.

"How are you so nice?" Izz mumbles into his knees. "You're a serial killer. How are you like this? So kind and gentle with me."

"You intrigue me," Sinn'ous offers in way of explanation, the same thing he'd said to Izz in the showers. He pauses for a brief moment before choosing to elaborate further, "closest I've come to *feeling* anything towards someone, outside of what it's like for them to . . . no longer be around . . . but don't call me that. I am not a *serial killer*. I am only me. Who I have always been. Not some make-believe-thing *normal* people invent to allow themselves to feel better about living boring sheltered lives."

'*No longer around . . .*'

Does Sinn'ous mean when they die—when he kills them?

Sinn'ous's explanation leaves Izz with more questions than answers. He will have to consider how to put all the things he wants to know into words. To ask at a later time.

Izz smirks when his mind catches on to the last of what Sinn'ous said.

"Something amusing?" Sinn'ous obviously clicking on to Izz's shift in mood.

"You can live a perfectly eventful life without killing anyone," Izz smiles over at the male. Watching Sinn'ous's face spark with delight and something . . . sinister?—he can't quite put his finger on what it is.

"We'll have to agree to disagree."

Izz laughs. His body loosening from its tight defensive ball. The panic attack receding as fast as it came on. A lingering unease is left in its wake. An easy thing for Izz to shove to the back of his mind. Especially with the stinging pain in his hip and neck. The brandings of the male who's

CAGED IN

shown him compassion and kindness in a sea of manipulation and lies. Someone he wholeheartedly trusts.

"You're strange," Izz playfully mocks, his smile broadening.

Sinn'ous shows his own form of amusement, his usual stone-cold face cracking with lines of emotions, "is it a good or bad thing."

Izz's not entirely sure. He likes Sinn'ous. Enjoys the other's company. But he is a killer. One who enjoys killing. Dangerous.

You can't trust someone who feels nothing for others. Who desires to kill, holding zero remorse.

He knows he shouldn't be so trusting, yet he finds himself embracing it with open arms.

Why do I feel this way about this male? Am I safe . . . or will this be how I die?

"Haven't worked it out yet," Izz murmurs in response.

And it is the truth. He has no idea why he is this way. Why he is willing to trust his life in the hands of a psychopath. Which is what Sinn'ous is, isn't it? An unempathetic killer . . .

26

Izz's late for work. He'd lost track of time, the hours having passed in a blur while he was with Sinn'ous. He'd missed lunch and almost completely forgotten about his assigned job.

Sinn'ous said Izz could stay in the cell with him but Izz declined, stating he should get to the laundry room or the guards will get pissy. He remembers all the trouble it caused missing his shifts in the kitchen. The lifetime ago when he worked there. His prison stay is going to feel like a million years before he is released. Already it feels as if he has been in here for a solid year.

How can it be only twenty-eight days? Too much has transpired in too little time.

He's regretting saying no. He should have stayed in the cell. And damn the consequences. Sinn'ous is able to arrange for things to happen or not happen. Maybe he can get him out of working in the laundry. Probably not, but here's to hoping—Izz mock salutes a beer glass in his mind. Snickering like a crazy person to himself.

I'm already going mad in here.

CAGED IN

Going? More like *gone.* His mind is gone, his body is trapped in a cage. On the plus side . . . he may, possibly, perhaps, have an itty-bitty crush. Not that he is catching feelings or anything for a serial killer.

Nooooo, that would be crazy.

He is in his own head, his own little happy bubble. He isn't stupid though, he can feel the inmates in the laundry room watching him. Constantly sneaking glances at him, whispering about him. He's sure they know he's become close to Sinn'ous. This place is gossip central, you can't scratch your ass without someone—from a different Wing, you've never met—hearing about it.

His hip is not helping. It's itchy and irritating. He'd removed the patch to let it air out and heal quicker—not healing fast enough for his liking. Is a stinging reminder of how correct everyone is. He does belong to Sinn'ous — who'd had an uncanny twinkle in those black eyes as he watched Izz clean the tattoo before heading to the laundry room.

I wonder what he was thinking?

Izz rests a hand over his hip, gently cupping the fresh tattoo hidden under his shirt. It's a comfort for him. Knowing he is protected. If anyone tries anything with him, he can play the protection card. No one will dare cross Sinn'ous.

Izz hasn't been here long, doesn't know much about the ways of prison life, yet even he can see how much they all fear Sinn'ous. How they step on eggshells around the red and black mohawked male.

Hefting a bundle of sheets, Izz stuffs the load into a machine. Clicking the dials to start the washing process.

Listening to the steady flow as water fills its belly, drowning the dirty sheets in fresh liquids. Dry prison blankets becoming a soggy soapy mess, churning and spinning their way to cleanliness.

His ears perk up, his subconscious sensing he is the topic of conversation for inmates hidden behind the stacked machines. They can't see him but he can hear what they're saying. Unknowing that he is listening in—or not caring. As they discuss bets on how long he is going to last. Talking about Sinn'ous's new *plaything* not living to the end of the week before he's found gutted in a back corner. Or shivved in the showers. Strung up and suffocated—

He turns away, scurrying off to machines further away, so he doesn't have to listen to their gruesome descriptions of how he's going to die . . .

He wants to stay in his happy love-struck cloud, but his surroundings are threatening to dampen it and disperse his newfound happiness. His mood is close to plunging into despair at the other inmates discussing his murder, as if his life is nothing to them other than a chance to have fun on the side taking bets.

Apparently the universe doesn't want to give Izz a break. He can now hear the hushed voices of The Gang. Voices he easily recognises.

"He's got a frickin' serial killer around us now," David's voice drifts from behind a machine. Anger laced through it.

Izz's not sure he's ever heard David's voice without anger in it. Perhaps the man doesn't have any other settings, anger being the only one.

CAGED IN

He's sick of it, sick of David and his attitude and hate—before Izz can talk himself out of it, his mouth is opening at the machines in front of him, the ones hiding The Gang from his view.

"Well," Izz growls, loud enough to be heard from the other side, narrowing his eyes at the inanimate objects, "I would think you'd be grateful. 'Cause now you don't have to worry about '*protecting*' me. Or *'gangs'* targeting you for it. Or *'going to The Hole to save his ass, 'cause he couldn't fight to save his life'.*" Izz makes a bad mockery of David's voice to emphasise the wording David used in the corridor all those weeks ago. After Zidie and Reni were carted off to The Hole.

A burst of laughter erupts from behind the machines, Isco's voice booming out. In no way trying to quieten his reaction, or prevent anyone overhearing him, "I knew there was a reason you pissed off out of The Gang when Reni was in The Hole. You heard big mouth here. Didn't you?" Not a question, the answer is obvious.

Izz marches around the machines, with a scowl on his face, directing it at David. He's in time to see Isco elbow David in the side, a smile on his scarred face, "told you Izz wasn't someone you would have to worry about. The guys been here what? A day. And he's already got himself protection from the most feared fucker in this shit hole. Maybe you should be the one on your knees for him, eh, Davy."

David scoffs, crossing his arms over his chest, "he hasn't got protection. Sinn'ous is keeping him around as a plaything—"

E.P.WRITER

There's that word again, Izz officially hates the terminology.

"—until he gets bored and kills him. Then we're going to be a target 'cause we've got Izz in our group. That serial killer's going to be watching Izz who has turned the rest of us into a target for the *'most feared fucker in this shit hole'*. Ain't nothing to celebrate about that—" David mimics Isco's description of Sinn'ous, and it rubs Izz the wrong way.

Izz's sick of this piece of shit thinking he's better than him. Why? Why is *high-and-mighty* David so up himself?

"You're kind of an asshole, you know that right?" Izz snaps at David, throwing his distaste into his tone, "I've only ever been nice to you and everyone in here, and all you do is make shit up, bite my head off with your negative nancy crap. And mock me. Like I'm some child who's not in prison with the rest of you assholes. Serving my time and trying to survive. You people have made me a target and act like you're better than me. Newsflash, you're in prison just the same as all of us. Like me. Like him," Izz jabs a finger at Isco, "like everyone in here. You're not special and you're not better than me. We're stuck in the same fucking place. The same cage that society—and circumstances—put us in."

Izz storms off, to find an empty machine away from David and his negative energy. That's it, he's done with them. Done with this whole day. He should have stayed in the Satanic cell with Sinn'ous.

He has no idea why David's been such a prick to him. But there you have it. Izz knows who the asshole in the group is—

CAGED IN

He throws his arms around a pile of clothing, bear hugging the scratchy cheap material towards a machine. Strangling the life out of the innocent prison greys in his hand. Stuffing them into a machine in the far corner. Away from the other inmates in the laundry room. He came in here with a full heart, happier than he's been in a long time, and David effectively killed it. Slaughtered it. Murdered it with no hesitation.

Who's the killer now, you pompous ass—

Izz's done. His emotions are surging, his anger seething. He no longer cares about the guards and potentially getting stuck in The Hole.

Slamming the washer's door closed, he holds his head high as he storms to the laundry room exit.

He's done. He's not in the mood for work, doesn't want to be in the same room as David. Or any of the other inmates. Not even Reni or Zidie—who thankfully haven't bothered him so far. He's done with the lot of them. He should have listened to Sinn'ous and stayed in the male's cell.

He's rectifying the mistake now.

"Hey, where are you going?" Reni's voice calls out to Izz from somewhere behind him but he doesn't stop, or look back.

He ignores his cellmate, continuing to the only way in or out of this room. To the guard taking up space beside it.

The guard straightens up, opening their mouth to say something—

He is not having it. He is done with the guards' shit too. Pulling up his shirt, he exposes the mark—Sinn'ous's branding. He doesn't falter at the door, continuing his storm out, slamming open the double doors. Exiting the laundry room like an unhappy bullet shooting out of its barrel.

I'm done with this whole fucking place.

27

Izz storms back to his own cell after leaving his job early. He doesn't attempt to find Sinn'ous. With the mood he's in he's liable to complain to Sinn'ous to get the asshole killed. So, instead, he throws himself on his bunk and seethes at the ceiling.

Frustrated at how he's stuck in here—circumstances which were of his own making. And hatred at everyone he is trapped with—not a result of his own choices.

It took him way too long to pass out. And when sleep wants to claim him, he doesn't resist it and is grateful for the distraction from his own mind.

His sleep sucks. Restless, tossing and turning. Waking constantly.

Halfway through the night his stomach growls him awake, furious at him for missing two meals.

He finds food waiting for him on his cupboard. The moonlight seeping through the baby window allowing him to see the wrapped sandwich. Sinn'ous had clearly stopped by to check on him sometime before the nightly lockup. He must have been out cold.

E.P. WRITER

The morning sun couldn't rise fast enough. Pacing the floor in front of his cell's bars waiting to be sprung free. His mood hasn't improved much. Reni is sitting on his own bunk, thankfully keeping quiet and not pestering him.

At long last, the doors begin clanking open, running along the lines of cells. Izz's out as soon as the lock clicks, shoving free—free of the cell, but screaming internally at the thought of the years before he's free from this cage.

Thankfully, Sinn'ous is waiting for him. Leaning against the stairs' railing, blocking the only way off this side of the upstairs cells. It's amusing how the other inmates hang back, no one daring to pass Sinn'ous to get to the exit.

Izz feels immortal, the only one to set foot near the Satanic male and live to walk away from the encounter.

He grins, his mood instantly shifting as he approaches Sinn'ous, yesterday's anger and frustration gone—shoved behind him without a second glance. It's a fresh day. And he can choose to spend the entirety of it with whomever he wants.

He squares his shoulders, strutting his ass closer to the stairs, and the male awaiting his arrival. The one everyone else is desperately trying to avoid. He can feel their judgemental looks boring into his back. He. Could. Not. Care. Less.

Izz stops in front of Sinn'ous.

"Morning," the male greets—pushing off the rails to stand at his full height.

CAGED IN

"Good morning." Izz boldly leans into Sinn'ous's space, chest to chest with the taller male. "Thank you for the sandwich."

He can get used to being treated like a special someone. Being greeted in the early mornings. Sinn'ous waiting for him to come out of his cell. Walking him down to the cafeteria for breakfast. Which is what the male is doing, why else would Sinn'ous be waiting?

"You left the laundry room early. Made quite the scene," Sinn'ous tilts his head, scanning Izz's body.

Izz's brows furrow. Unease settling over him. How does Sinn'ous know?

Is he spying on me? Had he watched the entire scene unfold?

"You heard about that?" *or did you watch it?* Izz keeps the last bit to himself, he doesn't want to accuse Sinn'ous of anything. He can't risk pushing away the only person in here who genuinely cares about him—who takes care of him.

With his anger subsiding, he feels stupid and embarrassed about how he acted. Like a tantrum-throwing child, not a fully-grown man capable of regulating his emotions. In the laundry room, he had not been thinking rationally, instead he allowed his emotions to run rampant.

"Your storm-out is the talk of the prison. You showed a guard my mark to get out of work."

Izz sighs, relief washing over him at the realisation Sinn'ous isn't annoyed with him. The male is amused, Izz can hear it in his voice. Izz's beginning to see the little cracks in the cold demeanour he portrays to the rest of the prison. Izz's sure it's an act, to prevent people from getting too close to him.

"I suppose I did. I hadn't thought about it at the time. I just didn't want the guard in my business. I was pissed," Izz shrugs, rocking nervously.

An understatement. He'd been seething, ripe-shit furious. Guess he knows how much he can handle before he snaps. And he had snapped, a rubber band let loose, uncaring what it hit, or took out, in the process. It was everyone else's issue to get out of the way in time.

Sinn'ous raises a brow in question. Reluctantly, he fills Sinn'ous in—on all the bets being taken to do with his lifespan and a recap on everything else said about him. There is a lot, and the recap is threatening to spoil his refreshed mood.

Sinn'ous opens his mouth to say something, but Izz cuts him off, remembering the talk about two inmates going down for the guard's murder. The murder Izz had committed. And isn't that a happy memory—Not. This morning is turning sour real fast.

"You framed those guys for the guard's . . . murder?" Izz squeaks softly, in a voice barely loud enough to carry to Sinn'ous's ears. Hoping no other inmates on the periphery will catch what he said—not that they're standing close by, he could scream and they wouldn't hear him with how much distance they're keeping between themselves and Sinn'ous.

"A guard's death is always investigated thoroughly. Best not to leave them an open case," is the only explanation Sinn'ous gives.

CAGED IN

Not much else to say on the matter. It was Izz's fault. Those inmates are dead to cover up a death Izz caused. He may as well have done the deed himself.

Trailing Sinn'ous down the stairs, he can't help but think about the *deed*. Had it really been a suicide . . . He doesn't want to know . . . At the same time, he needs to know, "did you only frame them? or did you . . ."

Do you truly want him to answer . . . ?

It sucks either way. And the outcome is the same. The inmates are both dead. Knowing or not knowing isn't going to change anything.

Wouldn't it be better to not know? To assume . . . Yet not truly know . . .

The brief moment of eye contact between them tells Izz what he needs to know. Sinn'ous doesn't need to answer. He can already see it. His gut telling him Sinn'ous killed those two creeps.

He can't say he's upset about it. He is sure they were going to have another go at him one of these days. Now they will never have the opportunity.

Izz can't control where his thoughts drift. All the inmates who had threatened him or hurt him in any way are dead. Killed, or dying under strange circumstances. Including those bald gang members who had attacked him. Who had died in The Hole and in Med-Wing.

Is Sinn'ous responsible for killing all of them?

That many people dying can't be a coincidence.

You need to tread carefully, you have a serial killer obsessing over you. Izz's inner voice warns.

E.P. WRITER

Sinn'ous will never kill him. Will he? How far does this possessive behaviour go? Will it turn into an *if-I-can't-have-you-NO-ONE-CAN.*

Please, God, don't let it turn into that. I don't want to die because of a killer who won't take a break-up well.

What's going to happen when the time comes for Izz to leave prison? Will Sinn'ous kill him to prevent him from leaving—

He knows you killed that guard, he could turn you in for it, have you locked up in here with him forever—

No, Izz dismisses. That's ridiculous. Besides, he doesn't even know how long Sinn'ous has left in this cage. He could stress over it . . . Or he can—

"How long do you have left on your sentence?"

"Ten months."

Oh, so Sinn'ous will be out before him. Great. Now Izz has more to fear. Like what will happen to him when the other leaves. He never should have asked. His stupid paranoia getting the best of him. Now he's on a ticking time crunch before Sinn'ous is gone, and he's stuck in here alone. Without protection . . .

Or perhaps not alone. Not fully. Glancing subtly over his shoulder, Izz confirms his instincts that he is being watched. Reni is behind them—at a safe distance, but nevertheless, right behind them. And his cellmate's scrutinising gaze is burning holes into their backs. Shooting daggers at Sinn'ous, no doubt.

If looks could kill . . .

Smothering a grin at his friend's antics, Izz jogs to catch up to Sinn'ous. Turning to join the end of the queue—

CAGED IN

Sinn'ous takes hold of Izz's upper arm, redirecting him to the front of the line. Dragging him straight to the trays—he'd forgotten Sinn'ous never stands in line. Kind of has him feeling like a famous person. Some famous VIP, holding royal privileges, with none of the peasants daring to mock or slander him.

Collecting his meal goes the same as it always does, and completely different. He participates in the same pick-what-you-want game. Only difference being his portion sizes are extra. His food is carefully selected and placed on his tray with delicate precision. Given the choice of extra items, extra drinks. Extra anything. He's even offered salt. He hadn't a clue you could get salt on your hash-browns.

Having everyone think you're the serial killer's prison bitch comes with some nice perks.

He is planning on sitting with Sinn'ous at the . . . Sacred Table. Where no other inmates dare touch, let alone sit on. Instead, he gets lightly nudged towards The Gang's table by Sinn'ous's body.

"Sit with your friends, it will do you good to have a social circle. You thrive off social interactions," Sinn'ous pulls the plug on Izz's plans, and Izz doesn't possess the strength to go against him.

How did Sinn'ous even know Izz was planning to sit with him and not The Gang? Is he such an open book he can't hide anything from the male?

He wishes he could read people as well as Sinn'ous clearly can.

He isn't thrilled about sitting with Zidie and the rest of The Gang because of David. He had been ignoring David throughout the previous weeks. He's not sure why it's different now, why he's tense and sick to his stomach at the thought of being near the asshole. David has always been an asshole to him—nothing has changed on that front.

But he won't protest and make a scene arguing with Sinn'ous. And he does like the rest of The Gang. Except maybe Isco . . . the man gives him bad vibes. As if Isco would be happy to kill someone in front of the entire cafeteria just for looking at him for too long.

And chances are high Sinn'ous prefers eating by himself. Izz will ask later, when they're alone.

He hangs out with The Gang through the downtime before lunch. Playing card games in the Rec-Room, to Zidie's evident delight. His best friend is all over him with questions, grilling him about Sinn'ous and the tattoo.

Izz gives little away. He doesn't have much to give away on the subject in the first place. He isn't sure what the two of them are either, so Zidie's guesses are as good as any.

Are they a couple? Friends? Acquaintances?

He has little clue. Not sure what he wants. Though he is sure on one thing. He is only here with The Gang because David had left right after breakfast. So he doesn't have to look at or be anywhere near the guy—

He may not be over his anger as much as he thought he is. Underneath, he is still seething.

CAGED IN

Lunch had come and gone. Uneventful to say the least. He'd spent his time wondering why Sinn'ous was absent.

As everyone gathers their trays and heads to their jobs, Izz splits off from the group. He wants to stock up on candies and other treats to eat while in the laundry room. Hoping the sugary treats will help him live through the ordeal it is bound to be. And a small part of him wants to check on Sinn'ous.

Why? He doesn't have a valid reason. Sinn'ous is more than capable of taking care of himself. Either way, it is part of his reasons to stop by his cell.

Scaling the steps two at a time, he lands at the top of the second-floor platform. Stopping short when his eyes lock on the male leaning back against the far wall.

Sinn'ous is smoking outside his Satanic cell.

Izz lets his grin shine, skipping over to the male like a love-struck idiot. He may be locked up in a cage with a bunch of criminals but he is happy. The first time in a long time, he is genuinely happy. The stresses of the outside world are non-existent, and the stresses in here had been cleared away due to the *alliance* he's formed with Sinn'ous.

"Don't you work?" Izz asks curiously, stopping just shy of colliding with Sinn'ous.

"No."

To the point. No explanation. Izz wants to know. "How come you get away with it?"

He can visibly see Sinn'ous's internal sigh. And he isn't the least bit concerned he may be irritating the male. He lets his grin widen and his eyes puppy-dog at the black ones watching him.

"People are too scared to say anything against it." Sinn'ous inhales half the joint pinched between his fingers. The orange tip eating through the end to race up towards his lips.

Izz had been on his way to his own cell to stock up, but . . .

Glancing into Sinn'ous's cell, he scans the items taking up so much cell space . . .

It would be unjust to leave it like that, to not relieve Sinn'ous from the burdens.

Besides, the treats in Izz's own cell are also Sinn'ous's. It wouldn't matter if he simply nicked the stuff in here, instead of having to walk *all* the way back to his own cell.

Izz enters the Satanic space and goes to the cupboard with its doors hanging open. The chocolates and other goodies are on full display, ripe for his picking.

Crouching down, he takes his time sifting through them and stuffing his pockets.

"By all means . . . help yourself," Sinn'ous's sarcastic tone fills the cell, Izz can hear his underlying amusement. So he's not worried he might have gone too far.

"Don't worry, I am," Izz laughs as he stuffs more chocolates and bars into his prison pants.

He pecks Sinn'ous on the lips on his way out. Watching the small smirk pulling at the male's lips.

"I'll see you after work," Izz throws over his shoulder, as he hits the top of the stairs.

Man, it's good to be alive.

28

Izz chooses to work alone, away from everyone else. He wants to clean and eat and not have to worry about being in any conversations. He especially wants to be as far away from David as possible, he doesn't want to overhear another blow up about his *'protection'*. Not that David has the guts to talk directly to him—only talks about him to others.

He starts his work on the other side of the laundry room, loading machine after machine. Snacking on chocolates between each bundle of clothing.

Izz's joyous mood is holding strong against the unruly tangle of sheets he's manhandling into an empty machine—the load not giving up without a fight. It's as if it has a deep-seated phobia of being clean. He concentrates on the task at hand, ignoring the inmate he can sense approaching.

His wishful thinking *if-I-don't-acknowledge-you-you'll-leave* is sucked down the shitter when they open their mouth. "I'm sorry." A voice Izz recognises, not one that's usually directed to him personally.

E.P. WRITER

He really doesn't want to say anything, he grits his teeth and reluctantly faces David.

Why is David here? Can he not tell Izz doesn't like him?

David shuffles his feet, blurting out, "you were right. I was being an asshole. You hadn't given me any reason to say those things about you. I shouldn't have said anything. So I'm here to apologise and hopefully hit a restart on us."

Fool me once . . .

Izz's not convinced, "I'm not interested. You said what you did. Put out how you feel about me, without knowing shit about me. That's on you. I'm not interested in having anything to do with you."

Why would he stoop so low as to befriend someone who clearly hates him and judges people without knowing them. He's open minded about making friends with all types of people, but a person who blatantly pokes fun at others, bullies, spreads around made-up shit . . .

Nah, he's good. He'd rather befriend this pile of wet clothing he's about to manhandle out of one of the old machines—which is beeping its demands to be empty, the urgency unnecessary—it's not going to explode if it isn't emptied immediately. Whoever invented this machine should have known how annoying it is to beep louder the longer you ignore it.

Demanding machine and its high pitch whining.

"Look, I'm sorry, okay."

Why is he still talking? It's not as though I hedged around my answer, the message should be clear.

Izz ignores David. Stuffing his hands into the machine's belly to heft out the wet load, ready to switch it into a dryer and finish the process. Other inmates will do the folding

CAGED IN

after it's dried and load the trolleys to do the deliveries to all the cells.

They run shifts, for who's on what, changing each day. But because he's new, he winds up with the harder job of loading machines. It's heavy as fuck when it's wet. Though he's not complaining, it's the only form of exercise he gets now.

"Can we just restart—"

"He told you to fuck off," a deep voice interrupts their little conversation.

Izz jumps out of his skin. Dropping the bundle in his hands. The pile slopping wetly onto the floor at his feet. Both he and David spin around. Neither had heard him prowl up on them—

Sinn'ous has materialised out of nowhere, his menacing presence sucking the air right out of the room. Izz recognises the death glare Sinn'ous is sending David. Last time he saw Sinn'ous look at someone like that, it was Levis . . . and the server had been killed not long after.

Izz steps over to a very pale David. Holding his hand out—yeah, he knows, no handshaking. But this is a unique circumstance.

David looks at Izz, and back at Sinn'ous briefly before accepting Izz's hand.

"We're cool. But it doesn't mean I'm going to be your friend anytime soon." Izz drops the hand and turns away.

Watching out the corner of his eye as David flattens himself against the machines, to squeeze past Sinn'ous, without so much as touching the serial killer with the ripples in the air from his movements. The entire time Sinn'ous's narrowed eyes are following him, burning holes in his skull, until he's retreating to the other side of the laundry room.

"Don't even think about it," Izz scolds, scooping the wet mass off the floor, to move it to the dryer. If it's dirty, it's dirty, he's not rewashing it.

"About what?" Sinn'ous's edgy tone suggesting he knows exactly what Izz's referring to.

"You know what," Izz pegs Sinn'ous with a knowing stare. Rolling his eyes when the male smirks, a spark in those predatory eyes at odds with what one should see when murder is on the table.

Izz had shaken David's hand for the sole purpose of the inmate not becoming the next victim. He doesn't need more bodies of inmates who are linked to him. Dead because they cross him—and the possessive serial killer obsessed with him kills them.

Supposedly, you don't actually know. Izz's little voice denies, refusing to see Sinn'ous in any form of bad lighting.

"What are you even doing here? I thought you didn't work."

"Got bored. Thought I'd come help you out," Sinn'ous leans back against the dryer Izz's loading. Eyes scanning the room as he studies Izz clicking the controls.

Izz doesn't buy that excuse for one second. But he doesn't complain. Work will be a lot more enjoyable with Sinn'ous to keep him company. Help him pass the time. And it will keep the rest of the laundry room occupants from talking shit about him. None will dare with Sinn'ous in the room. In fact, it is exceedingly quiet in here, the only noise is the soft whirring of machines.

CAGED IN

Sinn'ous's helping out is more along the lines of reclining against the dryer, arms folded as he watches Izz work. Occasionally copping a feel when Izz wanders within arm's reach—Izz may have deliberately started walking closer to Sinn'ous after that.

He is aware he's crushing. A love-struck idiot is the term coming to mind when he peeks under his eyelashes at the male who is hovering over him.

He knows he's in trouble. Developing feelings for someone who is incapable of love is a dangerous game—

Can serial killers love?

29

His whole body is agitated, restless, as Izz leaves the laundry room. Eating all those sugary treats hadn't been a hot idea. His blood is pumping in his ears and he's fighting the urge to sprint down the corridors for no reason other than to run.

Looks like I can still get hyped up on sugar.

He jogs back to A-Wing. Stomping his way over the second-floor platform to the cell at the end. Throwing his arms wide, "I'm home," he exclaims at the empty Satanic cell.

Izz's inner crazy is reviving. Now that he isn't constantly glancing over his shoulder and worrying about someone shivving him, he is beginning to come out of his protective shell. To show his true colours . . . his true personality.

"Remind me not to feed you chocolate."

"You're just jealous 'cause I'm having fun, while you brood around all . . . broody," Izz grins, spinning to face the other as he steps backwards into his second cell. He's sure he spends more time here than his actual cell. He has basically moved in—

CAGED IN

Maybe he can? Sinn'ous doesn't have a cellmate—

Nah, he likes living with Reni, the man is funny and a good friend—and what if mister serial killer is a sleepwalker, huh? He doesn't want to wake up in those conditions, especially if *Sinie* kills in his sleep.

"I'm going to call you Sinie," Izz declares. Practically bellowing the nickname in his excitement.

"You will not."

"Ugh, fine. How about . . ." Izz taps his chin in thought. ". . . Sin? Yeah. That's it. You are now officially Sin—"

Izz's back hits the wall faster than he can blink. The side of his leg pressing up tight against the sleeping bunk. Sinn'ous's hand pinning him to the wall by his chest. Holding him flat to the cold bricks—or whatever is under the whitewashed uneven paint job.

Swallowing hard, Izz tilts his head back staring directly into dark eyes. Watching the brown flecks dance within black irises. The sheer danger lurking at the surface . . .

Izz's guts churn, his lungs constricting in their caged confines. His body terrified he's pushed Sinn'ous too far. Overstepped.

"Are—" Izz releases a shuddering breath, "are you going to kill me?"

Sinn'ous's head tilts to the side ever so slightly. A spark of excitement flashing through his eyes. "Perhaps." He leans in, bringing his chest flush with Izz's. "Or perhaps . . . I'll do this . . ."

Izz can see Sinn'ous is moving in to kiss him. It's deliberately slow, he is given enough time to turn his head away or tell Sinn'ous to stop. He doesn't. He allows the contact. Allows the soft lips to press against his own. He would not have guessed a serial killer could have such soft warm lips.

He hums as the kiss deepens, opening up to the tongue licking over his lips for entry. Smooth and silky. Their tongues moving together as one. Like he's been kissing Sinn'ous for years. Their tempo matching perfectly . . . Addictively.

Izz breaks the kiss, his body heating with anticipation. "I want it. With you." Izz breathlessly whispers to Sinn'ous, gripping the male's hips to draw him in closer.

"You sure . . ." Sinn'ous lazily stretches his arms out, caging Izz in against the wall. "You don't have to do anything. I'll protect you either way."

"I'm sure." And he is, he has wanted it for some time now. "Hell, the first time I saw you I thought you were hot as fuck. I would have introduced myself, only my cellmate told me . . ." He gestures vaguely around with his hand, to indicate Sinn'ous's reputation within the prison, ". . . You know."

Sinn'ous makes a noise that could be anything from a *'yeah I know what I did'* to a *'yeah, those rumours are vastly over exaggerated'*.

Izz's starting to think maybe they are. He's seen nothing but nice intentions from Sinn'ous. Surely he's not all bad—

Izz gasps in alarm as he's unceremoniously thrown onto the bed, bouncing on the mattresses as they protest his harsh invasion.

"Hey," Izz yells, sitting up, "what did you do that for—"

He's cut off by a hand wrapping around his throat, shoving him back into the bunk, pinning him down as Sinn'ous braces over him. Looming above him—he would

CAGED IN

be terrified at the look on the male's face, if he doesn't trust Sinn'ous with his life. Trust Sinn'ous not to kill him.

"You're mine," Sinn'ous growls, his hand tightening around Izz's throat. "All mine. No one else can touch you."

It's difficult to breathe. Wheezing in shallow pulls to try to draw air inside his lungs. His mind screaming at him to give it more oxygen. His body begging him to arch his back and rub up into the heavy weight over it, to relieve some pressure—who knew being choked would turn him on so much.

Sinn'ous bites Izz's lip, relinquishing the hold on Izz's neck just enough so the smaller inmate doesn't pass out, "you're gorgeous when you're helpless."

Is he supposed to answer? Or is it an involuntary confession Sinn'ous didn't mean to say out loud?

All he knows is he wants more, he craves it. "Please," he moans, giving in to his body's urge to arch. Digging his nails into Sinn'ous's sides.

His head is forced to the side, a soft velvety tongue sliding over his hot flesh.

"Roll onto your stomach," Sinn'ous murmurs into his ear.

Izz doesn't hesitate to follow his order. Squirming his way over. Sinn'ous is no help, staying put, not budging an inch to give him room to move. He has to manoeuvre in the tight space between the prison mattresses and the male's thick coiled muscles.

He's a hundred percent a bottom. He loves this feeling. Loves the heavyweight pinning him down. Loves how dominated he feels. How overpowered, yet he isn't completely helpless. He trusts in the male holding him down. Knows Sinn'ous will stop if he asks.

Izz grips the sheets above his head as his pants are slid down. Two large hands grasping his ass, massaging it roughly. He bites the bed to hold back his cries. He doesn't need the whole prison hearing him fall apart. It's bad enough he can hear their loud voices bouncing off the cell's walls', he doesn't need them knowing what he and Sinn'ous are up to.

The hem of his shirt is tugging up, and he assists to throw the grey fabric across the room—to land wherever. All he cares about is it being off his body and out of the way so Sinn'ous has access to him. Access to all of him.

Frustration growing at his pants still clinging to his legs. Covering his legs. Blocking the skin on skin contact he desperately craves. Desperately needs.

Sinn'ous takes care of it. Shoving backwards to strip everything off Izz's lower half. From his prison pants to his socks and shoes. The whole lot thrown off in one sweep. Leaving him completely bare to the male's hungry eyes.

Izz nervously glances over his shoulder, feeling self-conscious—

His thoughts dissolve as he watches Sinn'ous removing his own clothes. Tattoos flashing in all their glory. Bright in the dim cell. Standing out against his flawless skin.

Whoa, I forgot how good he looks without his clothes on.

Izz had tried not to look at Sinn'ous in the showers. Tried to avoid studying every detail. Now though . . . he can take it all in.

The blood splatters littering Sinn'ous's body. From the blood pools on each shoulder dripping crimson down his upper arms. To the deep red ink spreading out over the

CAGED IN

inside of his thighs—splattering, to dust the tops and backs.

Izz tucks his arms under himself, pushing his upper body off the bunk so he can turn over. He wants a better view of Sinn'ous—

"No," a sharp order, followed by a hand pushing Izz back down, "I want you like this."

"O-okay. . ." Izz surrenders, stretching his arms out once more. Keeping himself in the position Sin wants him in. He wants to appease Sinn'ous, wants to impress and do whatever pleases Sin.

Izz whimpers as hands tug his hips up, obediently keeping his chest on the mattress. His ass on display for the male behind him. He can't see what the other is doing, he can, however, hear small clicking sounds—

Slickened fingers trail between his ass cheeks, telling him Sinn'ous has some form of lube. Something Izz completely forgot about in his strung-out state. At least one of them can think clearly enough to do the prep work. Because he sure can't.

He tenses as a finger brushes over his entrance. He can't help it. Yes, he wants this, but he's so nervous—is it going to be painful?

"Relax," Sinn'ous orders softly, his other hand massaging Izz's hip to calm him down.

He tries his best, tries to be good for Sin. To do as he's told—

All thoughts cease as a finger works its way into his hole. Pushing past the tight rim. The lube helping it slide inside with ease. It feels strange. Burning its way inside. His muscles contracting around it as he tries to breathe through the strange sensations plaguing his body.

The stretch isn't painful. Tight and hot. But not painful. Sinn'ous is slow and methodical, gently pushing in the intruding digit. Rubbing Izz's insides delicately with the smooth pad of his finger.

Working him into a frenzy. His back arching, his muscles relaxing to open up. Allowing Sinn'ous to enter with less friction—

The second finger sings, Izz hisses and tries to pull away—

A hand grips his hip, holding him firmly, keeping him still as the second finger slides in to join the first. The stretch intensifying as Sinn'ous slides his fingers in and out. Building to a rhythm which has Izz panting and rocking back to meet each intrusion.

"Don't stop. Feels good," Izz gasps, shifting his knees, widening his legs to move into a more comfortable position.

It's over all too soon, the fingers retreating to pop free. He would have protested, if the mattresses didn't shift. Indicating Sinn'ous is moving in closer behind him.

"Fuck. . ." Izz breathes out, his arms stretching out in front of him to grip the edge of the bed. His entire body shaking in anticipation.

This is really happening.

His ass cheeks are spread open, and a blunt head nudging at him. He tries his best to relax. To not tense. It's harder than he thinks. His body automatically tightening in defence—

CAGED IN

Izz grits his teeth as Sinn'ous pushes, the head popping past his first ring. A burning pain following the penetration. Heat radiating along his spine and down the insides of his thighs.

His grip tightens, white knuckling the bed below him. It's a lot to take in. The burn, the stretch, his whole body lighting up to an inferno of sensations, making it hard to breathe.

"You alright." Sin sounds as if he's holding on by a thread. It must feel incredible to him, tight and warm.

Shit. Izz never realised how much it burns to be penetrated. Did it feel like this to everyone he'd been with?

"It burns. Can you—can you give me a minute?"

"Take your time. Relax. You're doing exceptionally," Sinn'ous flexes, shifting his position, which results in pushing him a little further in.

Izz rocks forward to ease the burn, to prevent Sinn'ous sinking deeper—but the grip on his hips keeps him locked in place. Holding him still as he tries desperately to relax. To stop his muscles tensing around Sin who is barely inside him.

"You're taking me so well," Sinn'ous praises. Pressing forward with his hips to slide in further. More of his length entering Izz.

"D-doesn't feel like I am." Izz grits out, his arm muscles shaking with how hard he's gripping the mattresses. He feels as if Sinn'ous is beyond his capabilities to handle. Way too big, and he knows Sin isn't even close to being halfway inside.

He hears Sinn'ous chuckle, feels the vibrations through the cock buried inside him. Sin fists his hands by Izz's head, holding his weight off Izz's back as he leans over him. Shielding Izz from the world, caging him in. Keeping him pinned.

"Get up on all fours. The angle change will help you adjust."

Izz does. His back hitting Sinn'ous's chest. He's so much smaller than the other when he's under Sin like this. He's utterly aware of their size differences. Of how much muscle mass Sin holds over him. How easy it would be for Sin to take whatever he wants from Izz.

"It's not helping, Sin . . ." Izz whines, as the change in position moves Sin deeper, tugging at his straining hole. A fire igniting its way through his stomach, twisting and flickering.

"Helps take your mind off it," Sin sounds way too amused by this whole thing.

Izz scoffs, his arms shaking while trying to support his weight. His whole body damp with a sheen of cold sweat.

"Liar," he accuses, letting his head hang on his shoulders, too weak to hold it up any longer. He feels as though he is going to collapse at any moment.

"Allows me to do this," Sinn'ous bites onto Izz's shoulder, causing Izz to cry out, the stinging pain at odds with the burning between his legs.

And Sin is right. The sting helps draw attention away from the cock breaching his entrance and rearranging his inside. But it doesn't dull the pain. Doesn't help the stretching.

He pushes up against Sin's chest, trying to find an angle to help him cope. His body filling with a mixture of too

CAGED IN

many sensations to name. He isn't sure if he wants to moan or start crying. Maybe a bit of both.

Turns out Sin is correct—somewhat—with the position change. The pain level is gradually subsiding, pleasure building to take its place, slowly becoming bearable. It may have more to do with his body adjusting to the stretch and not so much to do with his change in positions. He doesn't mind either way, he's just glad it isn't a blazing fire anymore.

"You alright for me to move," Sinn'ous licks over the bite mark he's put in Izz's shoulder.

A soothing gesture? Or possessive demand?

"Yes," Izz breathes out. Choking on his breath as Sin shifts. Kissing up his neck to lick and suck under his ear. Is Sin trying to comfort or distract him? Either way, the affectionate touching is helping Izz deal with everything else.

"Let me know if it becomes too much," Sin nips gently at Izz's ear lobe, "I'm not into rape."

Before Izz can decipher what Sinn'ous said, the male is rising to grip Izz's hips. Starting at a leisurely pace. Rotating his hips with each shallow thrust. Entering slightly deeper each time. Inserting more of his cock with each forward thrust.

Izz's skin is clammy. His body shaking. His mind fritzing out. He can't determine if it is pleasure—or displeasure—to the unnatural sensations. His eyes drift back between his legs, to see his erection bobbing. At least his dick is taking the feelings to be pleasurable.

His mind isn't so sure. He's not sure he's enjoying it. Is he overthinking it? Is it years of society saying this is wrong? Or is it his own mind telling him he isn't into it . . . ?

But it feels so good. . .

Shit.

"W-wait. Wait," Izz gasps. Sticking his arm back to grip Sin's thigh. As if his weak noodle arm will stop anything.

To Izz's relief, Sinn'ous stills, "you need a minute to adjust?" Sin asks, as he leans back over, to brace his fist on the bed. His other hand rubbing up and down Izz's side, stroking. Trying to loosen him up.

"No—yes. I mean. I don't know," he doesn't know how to describe what he's minds going though—

"You feeling overwhelmed," Sin nips at Izz's neck, sucking on the delicate skin.

"A little," Izz confesses. His muscles tensing as his mind and body fight to control his reactions. His body says yes, but his mind . . .

The caressing from Sin is helping him. Helping connect him to his body, keep his mind focused. But he still feels . . . off . . .

"We can go at your pace. It's natural to feel overwhelmed the first time."

Is it? He doesn't know. How is it supposed to feel? His mind is splitting into two different thought processes. One screaming at him to keep going, to give in. The other one is huddling in the corner trying to hide away.

"I don't think I like it," Izz blurts, pinching his eyes closed. He doesn't want to disappoint Sin. But he can't shake off the weird feelings inside himself. "I mean, I do. But I . . ." How does he describe what is in his mind?

CAGED IN

Sinn'ous kisses his shoulder blade, then shifts, carefully pulling free. Causing Izz to grunt as he slowly eases his way out. "You need time to adjust. Mentally."

"But I—"

"I'm not angry," Sinn'ous reassures. "Or surprised. We have time. I'm aware of who I am and how others view me."

"I don't see you that way," Izz protests. He's still relieved when he no longer has to battle with the stretching burn between his legs. Even as he sort of misses it, his hole squeezing around nothing but air.

He feels empty now . . .

Sin hums in answer. Which could mean anything from *'I believe you'* to *'you're an idiot'* to *'are you lying to me or yourself'*.

He's not sure. He can't distinguish his thoughts, they are too muddled. Too hard to read. He doesn't know what to think. How to feel.

Izz and Sin lie down side by side. Sinn'ous tucking Izz into his chest, turning him into the little spoon. He doesn't mind. Being held is comforting. He feels protected with Sin at his back. Safe.

It doesn't mean he forgets about his erection. Or that the thing gives up on the idea of getting off and goes away. No, it stays right there. Demanding and hard as stone. Aching to be touched, not allowing him to forget its presence.

It's making him restless. No amount of snuggling into Sin is giving him any semblance of relief. He's trying his best to keep it to himself, so Sin won't know.

But what if I just . . .

He discreetly slides his hand down, biting his lip to hold back his moan at the first contact of his hand with his hot flesh—

Izz fails to hold back the choked hiss as Sin grazes teeth over his throat. The arms caging him in squeezing tighter. Holding him flush against a solid chest.

"Would you like me to help you with that," Sin's deep voice murmurs from behind.

Yes, please pleasepleaseplease . . .

"I . . . But what about you?" He feels bad, calling it quits and now wanting to cum while Sin is no doubt sporting blue balls.

He doesn't want to be greedy or weak in front of Sin. But he is horny and he is hard. Needy. With Sin pressing up against his back, it's turning him on.

He might be regretting stopping so early.

Sin repositions behind him, unfurling his arm, letting his fingers slide down Izz's bare stomach. "Don't worry about me. Let me take care of you."

"Yes . . ." Izz whispers, removing his own hand from his aching member. Closing his eyes to the sensation of Sin's hand closing over him. Stroking him.

It's incredible. He's never felt something so good in his whole life—or maybe it's because it has been so long for him since he's had someone else's hand on him—or his own for that matter. He's been too stressed. Since he marched into prison, he hasn't been anywhere remotely private or safe to touch himself. Hasn't had the opportunity to let off any steam.

And never like this. Never with someone so . . . dangerous . . .

CAGED IN

The slow unhurried motion of Sin's hand is driving him mad. His breathing rapidly increases, to the point where he is close to passing out. His vision blacking around the edges.

"Mm, so close . . ."

To passing out, or cumming? He can't tell. Doesn't care.

He's already needy and worked up. He can't hold back. His body is on the edge of the cliff. And he doesn't want to delay his free fall into bliss.

Within minutes his back is arching against Sin. His release thundering out of him. Coating Sin's sheets. His thighs twitching with the pulsing pleasure radiating through him.

Coming down from his high is a task in and of itself. His mind floating back down. Grounding him to his body once more. To the prison. To the cell. To Sin . . .

"Thank you," Izz murmurs in a tone riddled with sleep. His body slackening in Sin's arms. Consciousness slowly seeping away from him.

30

Izz momentarily freaks out when he stretches and discovers he's not sleeping alone in his bunk. His eyes shoot open as his heart jackhammers under his sternum. Until his eyes latch onto a wall littered with devil drawings, and he recalls the night before.

How is he still in Sin's cell? The guards' surely know, they do Count every night.

Izz groans at the thought of the Count guard seeing him passed out in Sin's bunk. He hopes he wasn't naked. He does have a blanket over him now, it would stand to reason Sin put it on them before the guard showed for Count?

Izz peers behind him, to a sleeping serial killer. He has to admit, Sin doesn't look deadly while asleep. With all his features relaxed, his dark eyes closed. It's easy to forget who he is. And everything he's done to others.

Slowly, Izz extracts himself from the other's arm, shuffling off the bed, to use the metal toilet—

Stopping short when he catches sight of his reflection. He is littered with bruises. Leaning into the fake mirror, he

CAGED IN

probes the ring of bruises circling his neck. His shoulder is likewise black and blue, turning at an angle he can see the purple and red bite mark Sin put in his skin.

His hips are showing the same treatment. Finger sized bruises—he hadn't realised just how hard Sin had been holding him. He was aware the grip was strong at the time, but hadn't expected to be heavily bruised from it.

Izz resembles someone who's had their ass ploughed. There is no way to mistake the markings. If he went to the showers with the rest of the prison population they will all see them, and know exactly what happened. Well . . . Maybe not exactly. If he hadn't known better, he would think the bruises came from a victim who was forced into the act.

I was the opposite of forced.

Izz quite likes the bruises, they look hot on him. He loves wearing the claiming marks Sin has given him—

"You feeling alright," Sin yawns from his bunk. Sheets flapping as he shifts around to a different position.

"Huh. Oh. Yes, I'm good. Was inspecting what you left behind," *and imagining what it will be like to add more to the growing collection.* The bruises, the tattoo . . . He wants more.

"Regrets," Sin questions in his usual way, a statement to be answered.

Do I regret them?

Twisting to get a better look at the bite on his neck, Izz runs his hand over the marred flesh.

Nah, he doesn't regret any of them.

No, I definitely want more.

"No. No. Nothing like that. It's actually pretty hot, if I say so myself. I'm looking rather fine," Izz half jokes, splashing water over his face to wake himself up. He's still pretty groggy, but not as fatigued as he usually finds himself in the mornings. As if for the first time since he arrived in this Hell-hole he's had an undisturbed nights rest.

Although his ass is throbbing. A dull little tingle which has him remembering everything he and Sin did together . . .

"I'm sorry I passed out after you got me off. Do you want me to return the favour?" Izz asks, walking over to use Sin's toilet. It would only be polite and he also sort of, kind of, wants to . . . He wants to see if he can make Sin feel as good as Sin made him feel.

The last part of their activities. Not the first bit. That hurt. Is still hurting. How is he going to be able to stand going the whole way with Sin? He can't even handle taking half—

"No," Sin's response is short. Sharp. Almost bored.

"You sure? I could like . . ." Izz rubs the back of his neck, unable to look in Sin's direction, " . . . blow you—or something."

Why is he so awkward and shy around Sin? It's not as though he'd never been with anyone before. It just feels . . . different with Sin. For some reason. Though he can't figure out why.

Is it because Sin's so dangerous?—according to the other inmates. Or is it because they are in prison?

"No," Sin repeats in the same nonchalant tone.

Is Sin mad at him?

CAGED IN

Izz washes up after relieving himself and walks over to the bunk, perching on its edge. He hates this feeling, like he's letting Sin down. Not good enough. Not what Sin needs him to be.

Sin is facing the wall, broad back bare to Izz's eyes—

Whoa, Sin has a pentagram tattoo behind his ear, Izz can't believe he's never noticed it before. Maybe because he's always too busy staring at Sin's hair? Or into his dark eyes . . .

He wants to touch, to run his hands over Sin's smooth skin. He's not sure he's allowed, not confident in whatever it is they have between them. He would like to call it a relationship. But what does Sin call it?

In the end he keeps his hands to himself. Deciding to play it safe. Especially if he's done something wrong and Sin is displeased with him.

"Why? I um. Did I . . . Did I turn you off me, 'cause I stopped it?—" he rushes to add on to his own question, "—I mean I'd like to try again. It was just a lot all at once. But I—"

"I wasn't with you for my own satisfaction."

Wait . . . What?

"What? What do you mean—Oh. Can you like not . . ." Izz does a few vulgar hand movements to indicate cumming, even though Sin can't see him.

Sin chuckles in the way he does, deep with little to no emotion in the sound. Rolling over to face Izz. His smile is actually warm. Well, warm for him. "I can't '*get off*' without certain aspects being met."

"Like?" Izz's curious to know. He wants to know everything there is to learn about Sin. All his likes and dislikes. His desires. Favourite colour. Everything.

Sin doesn't answer. Rising to his full naked glory, drifting over to pee in the toilet. Izz stares without apology—not at him peeing, 'cause that would be weird. But his eyes eat up the body on full display before him. All the tattoos, smooth skin, and scars here and there.

The killer's triple six tattoos on both his wrists match exceptionally well with the whole Satanic vibe the male's ink is portraying.

The black tattoo coating one side of his abdomen is a circular figure eight cross of a solid black design—Leviathan cross?—with animal skulls and barbed wire interwoven throughout. A similar-looking design covers the back of one calf, from the look of it the skulls are human, and the solid black design is more a triangular Satanic witchy thing. This one Izz's sure is the mark of Lucifer, he remembers it—from back in his rebellious school years when researching dark things was popular.

The word written at the small of Sin's back is a larger version of the one on Izz's own hip. Only Sin's are thicker, bolder—the complete opposite to Izz's more feminine curvy piece.

He's disappointed to see Sin doesn't have any bruises or anything from their time together. He would have enjoyed seeing those left behind. To signify their first dip into the waters of their relationship. To show others they are together.

I like calling it a relationship. Makes it sound . . . real. And not a figment of my imagination.

CAGED IN

"Come on," Izz whines. "I won't blab to anyone or laugh at you or anything. I promise. Tell me . . . Please," Izz adds on the last plea as an afterthought. Trying to sway the male to divulge the information. Divulge any information. He will take anything, any small snippet of who Sin is as a person as opposed to a serial killer. And all the fearful rumours. Rumours he has yet to prove factual.

He didn't actually see Sin kill those inmates who had attacked him. For all he knows Sin may not have been the one who did the deeds. He was so out of it, he can barely remember what happened. A memory lapse he is grateful for.

Sin hums, cold eyes locking on Izz. Contemplating his answer, "I need blood—"

"What, like a vampire?" It's blurted out before Izz can think it through—he clamps a hand over his mouth as Sin's eyes narrow. Opening his fingers to mutter, "I'm sorry. I wasn't poking fun—a stupid joke—ahh, you were saying?"

Man, great way to get Sin to shut up and never reveal anything about himself.

Sin pivots back to finish up with the toilet. Washing his hands. Brushing his teeth.

Izz's sure Sin is done with their conversation. Let down he's wrecked his opportunity to know Sin a little better. His heart sinking with disappointment the longer the silence stretches out, with no answers forthcoming.

Good job. You screwed that up.

Sin's voice drifts over to Izz. Calm, deep. "Blood is my thing, I'd have to draw blood from you to find my own satisfaction."

Izz pales, half aware of how fast he stands up. "I . . . umm."

He isn't sure why he's freaking out. Or surprised. It's not as though he hasn't heard all the rumours, and he knows everyone fears Sin.

Izz has nowhere to go, Sin is right in front of him, the cell is small. And locked. His mind reeling with the bombshell a serial killer dropped on him. Heart racing so loudly it has its own echo in his skull. He's sure Sin can hear it.

"Have you heard of knife-play, Gorgeous," Sin drawls, stepping in closer. A predator moving in for the kill.

Izz shakes his head as he's backed into the wall, Sin prowling closer until they are chest to chest. Sin has to know he's freaking out, panicking internally. Too scared to let out his inner scream.

Sin's lips brush over Izz's ear, "you've enjoyed me biting you . . ." Sin emphasises his words by grazing his teeth over Izz's neck, causing a shiver to run down his body. "Well. Knife-play holds a similar pleasure . . . I promise you'll enjoy it . . . I know you will," Sin drawls.

Izz shudders at the tongue sliding over his throat. His body pressed firmly against the wall. Sin trapping him in place, with no way to break free—

Except he isn't fighting back. He's not trying to push Sin away. And he can feel his resolve dwindling by the second as Sin continues his ministrations on Izz's skin. Kissing and sucking hickies to join the countless bruises.

He wants Sin to press closer. His desires are flaring to life. Being placed in such a dangerous position shouldn't turn him on as much as it is . . .

CAGED IN

Sin grips Izz's jaw tightly, shoving his face upwards, exposing his throat. "Only I'll use something slightly sharper, to mark your smooth . . ."

Sin's other hand runs over Izz's uncovered body. Reminding him how naked he still is. How vulnerable he is to the male touching him.

". . . Clear. . ."

Nails faintly digging into his skin, to leave red lines over his abdomen. Sliding . . . Dragging . . . Electrifying the sharp pin pricks of pain surging through his nerves.

". . . Skin . . ."

A hand cups Izz between his legs. His erection hard and throbbing in the others hold. Sin's hand lazily moves up and down. A rhythm which does nothing but amp up his desires.

The prospect of being cut . . . Of Sin using a blade on him . . . The thought shouldn't be leaving his soul an aching mess. Begging wordlessly for Sin to do what he promises.

What is wrong with me?

31

The yard is surprisingly nice today. The Gang's laid back on the soft grass, enjoying the calming peace. Erik is practically asleep curled up by Phelix's side. No cold wind or bitter rains to disturb them. And the sun isn't scorching, merely a warm comforting embrace.

It has been raining on and off the past couple days—and the few days before that it was as hot as shit—not that it matters too much in here. The rain that is—they have to spend most of their days indoors anyway. And the prison is surprisingly well acclimatised. The day's heat, or the cold winds, you would never know until you walk outside.

Downside, the yard is only open to the inmates for a small window of time after breakfast and during the work period. Although there are the rare occasions it's closed off for the entire day. The changes aren't common. And he's not entirely sure why they occur.

He finds it strange that they open the yard during the work period. As the vast majority of inmates have jobs— he supposes it makes sense for the inmates who work the kitchen, after all, they work three shifts a day for an entire

CAGED IN

week. Gives them time away from the rest of the criminal elements in here when the kitchen staff have their week off—when it switches to the second set of kitchen working inmates. So they can chill outside without the hassle of the rest of the prison filling the yard.

Although Levis had been running a contraband gig out of the kitchen, so they wouldn't truly be away from the criminal elements. And they are criminals too.

Wonder who took over the business after Levis died?

Even under the whirlpool of strange prison thoughts, Izz's relaxed. Comfortable. A Zen warrior about to embark on some hippy ritual of peace of mind—*inner peace? Is it called inner peace? Or is that from a movie he'd watched with his sister . . . ?* It sounds familiar.

His calm composure has little to do with the weather, and more to do with the fact that he and Sin are officially a couple. No, Sin hasn't called him boyfriend or held his hand and confessed his undying love. Nothing has really changed with Sin's behaviour.

In Izz's mind, however, it is official. They hang out all the time. They talk about random stuff. They kiss and make out. They do intimate things together—

Izz scoffs at himself, "*intimate things.*" He mumbles under his breath, "say it like it is, Izz, you had sex."

—it's official in the way they'd fucked—well, sort of. Does it count if you haven't been filled with their entire length or you stop after a few penetrations?

"What's up with your neck, man?" Zidie helps himself to grabbing Izz's shirt collar, pulling it down to reveal more bruising.

Izz shoves his friend off, rearranging his shirt to cover the marks—watching Zid throw out a hand onto the ground, to catch himself, a grin splitting his cupcake face in two.

"Nothing," Izz bites out.

He likes being bitten, so sue him. Doesn't mean he wants to talk to Zid about it.

"Doesn't look like nothing. Looks like you're auditioning to become a canvas for some CSI show." Zidie throws a handful of grass in Izz's vague direction—payback for the shove.

Trust Zid to turn it into a big issue. It's not bad. It looks worse than it feels. And Izz relishes them. He wouldn't take any of it back for anything.

"Nothing to it," Izz mutters, his best friend pegging him with an *I'm-not-buying-it* expression. So Izz reluctantly adds, "it was consensual."

He watches Zidie's face light up like a Christmas tree—with a bunch of presents under it waiting to be unwrapped. Izz needs to cut that train of questioning off before they're set free. "No. I am not talking about it."

"Don't be a buzz kill, Izz. Not like there's much else to talk about in here. Spill."

He would rather talk about a million other things which don't involve his newly discovered kinks. Like the grass, and how long it's *not* grown, it is literally the same length as when he arrived in prison. And he's never seen anyone mowing it. Is this grass even real? It presents as real and feels pretty real. Maybe they have a night shift of prisoners who came out with a pair of scissors and a ruler, to trim the stuff—

You're surely not thinking about grass to avoid the question?

CAGED IN

Maybe he can change the subject—except, knowing Zidie a subject change won't work. The man is tenacious and ruthless when he wants to pry into someone's business.

"Yeahhhhh, Izzy, my man," Sinj bellows from across the yard as he saunters over to The Gang. Arriving late as usual, "look at them battle scars."

Sinj holds his fist out to Izz, waggling his eyebrows. Izz grumbles under his breath as he reaches up to pound his knuckles with the red-head. Why is Sinj so mellow about these things? Whereas the rest of The Gang are liable to pop a haemorrhage over it.

Sinj's nonchalantly open with everything sexual. Including giving it up for items or protection. He's always bragging about blowing someone for expensive Commissary products or contraband. And he's completely on board with Izz and Sin's relationship dynamics. In fact, he encourages it. Telling Izz it's a good deal, *'why bother protecting yourself when someone else is willing to do it for you'*.

"Well well well," the soft voice cutting in is God-sent, giving Izz a reason to avoid Zidie's inevitable torrent of questions.

That is, until he turns to the voice and finds a familiar feminine inmate swaggering over.

"If it isn't my favourite smoking buddy," the small inmate purrs. Hips swaying with exaggerated movements.

Vince.

Izz celebrated the interruption too soon. Why does it have to be Vince? Of all the inmates or guards who could have jumped on the interrupting train. Why does it have to be this one?

He's not sure why he's on edge. Maybe because Vince made it clear he's into selling his body to get things—except Sinj does that too, and Izz's not on edge around the red-head.

It could be something to do with Sin? Perhaps Izz doesn't want word getting back to Sin regarding him talking with the prison . . . prostitute . . . ? Escort? Hooker? What do they call themselves these days?

"Hi," Izz pulls out his polite self-defence, restraining his urge to snap at the small female-presenting inmate, "haven't seen you around."

Can you please fuck off. Izz's itching to say, holding the words in by his fingertips. It's hard work being so polite—some days he wonders why he bothers. It's so much effort. Wouldn't it be easier to blurt out the truth?

"You haven't been looking very hard, Sweetness," Vince purrs, moving too close for Izz's comfort, standing to hover over Izz. "I'm where I always am."

Great, another pet name from a random inmate. Why can't they use *'Izz'* or even his real name. Which at this point he probably won't register if someone is talking to him. He hasn't been called Jasper since the counsellor mentioned it. Everyone calls him Izz—except for those with ulterior motives—and Sin—but Sin doesn't count. He actually likes it when Sin calls him *'Beautiful'* or *'Gorgeous'*.

"You care to have a chat," Vince smiles, in what he no doubt imagines is seductive—to Izz it screams fake intentions and artificial flirtation.

CAGED IN

He's into one—and only one—inmate in this cage, and it is not this overly feminine cute inmate before him. His is a rough dangerous alluring male, with zero tolerance to anyone near Izz.

Not really, but if it gets rid of you quicker. Izz answers in his head. Deciding against telling Vince outright. He picks a more friendly approach. He doesn't need to make more enemies.

"Sure. Talk away."

And then leave. Izz adds silently.

Where is Sin when Izz needs him. If the feared male—who everyone avoids—was around, he wouldn't have to deal with Vince. No one bothers him when Sin is nearby.

In fact, they studiously make a point to avoid looking anywhere within Izz's vicinity. Even the guards tiptoe around him. It's . . . eerie.

"Elsewhere," Vince flutters his eyes at Zidie—and the rest of The Gang reclining close by—reminding Izz of a bitchy girl in a reality show. All *I'm-the-best-one-here-and-I-know-it.*

Sucking in the strength to deal with Vince. He begrudgingly rises to his feet, trudging off, separating himself from The Gang. He doesn't wander far. Out of earshot, not out of sight. He doesn't trust Vince. And Sin isn't here to protect him. He knows Zidie and Reni will jump in to help, if he needs it. The way the two of them are outright staring reveals they are already considering it.

Love those two.

"I have someone who's been in my business. Says I owe him money. I don't care for it. If you would be so nice as to ask Sinn'ous to deal with him, I would be much obliged."

Vince doesn't mince his words. Straight to the point as soon as they are out of hearing range. "I know you have sway with him."

What came out of Vince's mouth is not what Izz had been expecting. Or prepared for. Standing in front of the feminine inmate, he waits for his mind to catch up. To fully grasp what he'd just been asked.

"You want me to ask Sin to *kill* someone for you . . ." He's so caught off guard he accidently uses the pet name he's given Sinn'ous, in a sentence with a stranger—not sure Sin will appreciate it.

"Yes, Sweetness," Vince purrs, placing a hand on Izz's chest, he's too stunned to react to the contact. "I can owe you a favour . . . Anything you wish . . ."

Vince is really offering—

For a—

What?

"Ahhh." What is he supposed to say in this situation? His mind is blanking. He's doubtful he can remember his own name at this point.

What . . .

"I—ah, need to—I have somewhere I need to be . . ." Where? They're literally locked in the same cage with the same schedules. No one has anywhere they need to be right now.

"Alright Sweetness. Come find me later."

Ha, yeah. That's not happening.

Izz watches numbly, filled with confusion, as Vince swaggers his hips off. Deliberately swaying his ass for Izz to gape at.

CAGED IN

The only reason he's watching Vince walk off is because his mind isn't connecting with his body to tell him to move. He's glued in place, going nowhere fast.

"Seriously, did that conversation just take place?" Izz whispers into the wind. No one else is around to hear or answer him, and the wind doesn't seem interested in answering either.

Izz's in a weird mindset for the rest of the day. He ran through his laundry duties on autopilot. He barely remembers any conversation he had with Zidie or the rest of The Gang.

He's unsure if he's weirded out by the conversation with Vince or worried about what Sin will do if he finds out.

He decides to skip dinner and wait in the Satanic cell for Sin to return from the cafeteria. He perches on the edge of the thickly cushioned bunk. His thoughts are too erratic to consider eating. He's way too anxious to try, he may throw up if he does.

"You didn't show up to eat," Sin's voice demands answers without the need to ask.

Does Sin already know? Or is this a greeting to be polite and enquire why he isn't eating?

Is he reading more into it? And freaking himself out, when Sin doesn't know anything . . .

Should he breeze over the implied demand or pretend he hasn't noticed it? Which will be worse? Feigning ignorance or telling the truth. If Sin doesn't know, he could get away with the lie. But if Sin does know, will the serial killer be angry enough to hurt him?

No, Sin will never hurt me.

Be honest. Lies never stay hidden anyway. It will be worse if Sin finds out from someone else.

"I . . . Um. I have something to tell you . . ."

Where did all the air go?

Sin is a dangerous statue filling the cell's entrance. Unmoving, save for each deep breath.

Is Sin tense? Sin is tense, isn't he? He must already know.

Stay calm, you're panicking over nothing. You don't know if Sin knows anything.

Izz takes a deep breath and jumps off the cliff, "Vince offered himself in exchange for me asking you a favour."

Izz's anxiety spikes when Sin doesn't react to the news. Does it mean he already knows? Or he doesn't care?

The overwhelming need to fill the silence has Izz opening his mouth to explain further, "he has an inmate who he owes money to . . . he wanted you to . . . k-kill them. Asked me to ask you . . ."

Izz fiddles with the prison sheets under him. Twisting the material between his fingers, he's too nervous to continue holding Sin's gaze. Using the lapse in conversation to study the surprisingly clean floor—considering no one vacuums it.

"What did you say." Sin's voice is cold. Devoid of any emotion.

Izz's sure Sin heard him correctly and doesn't actually want him to repeat it. Is more astonished someone would brazenly ask this of Izz. He assumes. He can't read

CAGED IN

anything from Sin's voice and he can't bring himself to look at Sin's face.

"I didn't really answer him. I wasn't expecting to be asked such a thing. It caught me off guard." Not like he isn't caught off guard all the time. When is he ever ready for the crazy things this Hell-hole throws at him.

"He touched you," Sin's voice is dark, riddled with dangerous intent. Sucking the air right out of the cramped cell.

Izz's terrible at reading people, and even he can tell Sin is fuming. Pissed enough to indicate he probably hadn't known about this incident until five seconds ago.

Might have been better to keep quiet and not divulge this titbit of information.

"No—Well. Yes. But it wasn't—"

Sin strides off. Disappearing out of sight down the second-floor platform. Izz can hear his heavy footfalls clunking on the bare metal platform.

"Wait," Izz bellows after Sin, "where are you going?" He jumps up to rush after him—

Only for his feet to tangle in the sheets, taking him down to the cell's hard floor. His knees erupting in a pained protest to the harsh landing. He's going to have bruises over the entire expanse of his knees. Zidie will find a million reasons to tease him for it.

Using his hands as leverage he kicks his legs around. Little noises of frustration escaping his throat as he tries to fight free of the twisted sheets.

How did my legs get so tangled?

With a final shake, he breaks free. Scrambling up to chase after Sin—

E.P.WRITER

There is no one on the second-floor platform. Clapping his hands on the railing, he leans over the side, checking out the level below. He can't see Sin down there either. No inmates with red and black hair, a sea of colours, but not the one he is looking for.

Sin is gone.

This is bad. This is really, really bad.

Stumbling down the stairs, Izz runs through the grey sea—the other inmates moving out of his way. With no destination in mind, he sprints down the first corridor he reaches. He has to find Sin before something terrible happens. His stomach is knotting with dread the longer he runs with no sign of Sin.

Throwing his body around another bend in another corridor, he spots Zidie further down the other end. A relief.

Izz cups his hands around his mouth to help his words travel—not that the echoing empty corridor needs the extra support. Bellowing to Zid, "have you seen Sin—Sinn'ous?"

Zidie indicates the corridor off to the side. "C-Wing. He looked pissed. What's going on?"

Izz doesn't answer. He sprints down the corridor Zidie pointed towards. Hoping it leads straight through to C-Wing. He doesn't know his way around well enough to find C-Wing in time if he becomes lost. There isn't time to be thrown off course. And in his panicked state he is very likely to run aimlessly in circles.

If he doesn't make it in time, Vince will die. He doesn't want anyone else to join the list of inmates to die because

CAGED IN

of him. To die because Sin killed them in his possessive territorial claim on Izz.

"My Izz isn't interested in your scams, little con artist," Izz can hear Sin's growling voice down the corridor.

Izz's so close, relief flooding him, followed by a constricting sense of doom.

I'm nearly there. Sin has to be around this next bend.

Please don't be dead. Please don't be dead.

"I-I-I w-wasn't—"

He skids, nearly colliding with the wall as he overshoots the corner. His eyes locking on the scene before him—as he braces his hand on the wall to steel himself—his lungs and legs threatening to give out.

Vince is pinned against the bars of one of the cells in a suspiciously empty C-Wing, his feet dangling off the floor. Sin holding him aloft by the throat, gripping his neck tightly. Vince's eyes are bulging from their sockets and his face is bright red, and deepening in colour by the second.

"Save it. We all know you were. I don't kill for hire—I don't kill, at all. There is no evidence. No proof. And there never will be."

Izz's frozen.

As he watches Vince struggling to free himself. Watches the inmate desperately pushing at Sin. His pathetic attempts to break free becoming weaker and weaker. All Izz can do is stand there, his eyes wide, praying for Sin to let the other inmate go. Incapable of voicing it, his throat too dry to form the words he desperately wants to say.

"Keep away from Izz," Sin snarls, leaning closer to Vince's face, "and you and I won't have a problem that needs . . . solving . . . Understood."

Through his choking and whimpering, Vince drops his head slightly, nodding. Unable to utter a verbal reply. His lips are changing colour, growing an unnatural blue tint.

Sin steps back, and Vince hits the floor. Gasping and wheezing. Choking on air. His face a deep red to match his equally red neck.

Izz still can't speak, he wants to do something—anything. But he's stuck. Unable to move. Trapped in his own body ... Frozen. This would get him killed—if he was an animal, seizing up in the face of danger.

Sinn'ous doesn't look Izz's way. He doesn't acknowledge Izz in the slightest. Merely saunters off in the opposite direction. His head held high, his shoulders rolling with every step.

Sinn'ous doesn't look back.

Before Izz has a chance to find his voice and call out, Sinn'ous is disappearing behind the far row of cells. And Vince is staggering to his feet, using the cell's bars—catching Izz's attention.

"Are you okay?" Stupid question to ask someone who was almost asphyxiated by a serial killer.

Vince holds his hand out, as if he wants to fend Izz off. "Leave—"

Another violent coughing fit engulfs Vince. The feminine inmate sliding back down to the floor, gripping the bars for dear life as he hunches over on the ground.

Izz reaches forward to try to assist Vince. "Let me help—"

The cute inmate shies away. Keeping out of reach, avoiding Izz's hands. "Leave."

"But I—"

CAGED IN

"Please," Vince's voice is straining to form the words. His rasping tone cut off with wheezing noises.

Izz hugs his arms around his middle. All he wants is to help. To tell Vince he's sorry. Instead, he swivels away. Sprinting from the man he almost got killed. So he won't cry in front of them. His eyes prickling with unshed tears.

He hadn't meant to cause anyone to be hurt. He never wanted Vince to be attacked. Or any of the others . . .

Why is this place filled with so much violence?

So much death . . .

Izz doesn't stop running until he finds himself back in Sinn'ous's cell. He hadn't consciously thought about coming here and his legs are too weak to carry him anywhere else—he lets them collapse. Falling onto the empty bunk. Hugging the pillow to his chest.

Where did Sinn'ous go? Why isn't he here?

Is he angry at me?

Is it me? Am I so broken I bring death to everyone?

All he's done since he arrived is make a mess out of everything. Get his friends thrown in The Hole. Get people killed. . . And . . . He'd murdered too . . . A guard who will never go home to their family . . .

He's worse than everyone in here. His body count is growing with every passing day. He should be locked up for the rest of his life. They should throw away the key. Never let him out. How can he live normally in the outside world when he has done so many bad things in here?

He will never be the same.

He thought he enjoyed being around people, but in this cage it always results in violence. In fighting. In death . . .

His friends punished for something they shouldn't have been involved in. People dead who had years left to live. Families who've lost loved ones. All because of him.

He is a curse to them. Maybe he should go to The Hole. It would protect everyone else from him.

And worst of all, Sinn'ous hadn't looked at him. Had walked off and left him behind. If not even a serial killer will have him, there must be something wrong with him.

I'm broken.

32

It's rapidly approaching lunch time, and Izz still hasn't seen Sinn'ous since the . . . incident yesterday. His mind is filled with the nagging thoughts he's screwed up and Sinn'ous is done with him. As much as he should rejoice, all he feels is rejection. He and Sinn'ous had been getting along well. Things were doing great.

Turns out he was very wrong. Sinn'ous hates him.

Izz's with The Gang in the Rec-Room purely out of self-preservation. If he has indeed pissed Sinn'ous off, hanging around a group would be wise. To protect him from other inmates, but also to protect him from Sinn'ous. Even if he truly believes Sinn'ous would never—*will never*—raise a hand in aggressive violence towards him.

I still believe this. I still believe Sinn'ous will not hurt me.

And there is the other matter . . . He feels like shit and doesn't trust himself to be alone. He's never been a self-harmer but a lot has happened to him in this Hell-hole. He doesn't want to risk taking up a new hobby, so here he is. Pretending to have fun with this card game he is barely tracking.

E.P.WRITER

He wants to sit down and cry. He's alone and helpless even surrounded by his friends. Sinn'ous is the only one in here who helped him feel different. Who combated the dark depressing life as a caged animal. Who gave him a strength he can't find now that Sinn'ous is gone—

"Ow. What the fuck," Izz snaps when Zidie slaps the back of his head.

"I said it's your go. Are you even paying attention?"

No, I'm not. Izz flops his cards down, "I fold."

Zid purses his lips, but doesn't say anything. Getting back into his own little zone. A hundred percent invested in the game, trying to beat out Isco. Who usually wins every game.

Izz settles back into his chair. Observing the other inmates scattered around the room. It's packed in the small space today, because the rain is heavy, drenching everything outside. So the guards closed off the yard, forcing them to stay squashed indoors.

They're just lazy and don't want to watch inmates out in the rain and get wet themselves. It's not due to some nonsense about inmates being cold. He doubts they give a shit if their captives come down with the flu.

The hairs on the back of Izz's neck prickle in warning, agitated by an unseen threat. The rest of the table doesn't appear to have noticed his unease. They haven't sensed whatever has his instincts flaring to life. They're too engrossed in their game.

His eyes land on the doorway, drawn to the grey-clad presence which is filling the entire space. Izz's reaction is a jumbled mix of emotions—of dread and excitement.

CAGED IN

Sinn'ous is scanning the Rec-Room. His eyes roaming over all the bodies which are stilling in their actions and conversations. A hushed silence falling over the room, as everyone slowly comes to grips with the predator gracing their presence.

Sinn'ous's eyes fall on Izz. Hard cold gaze drilling into his very soul. He isn't sure what he's expecting to happen. If he is still in Sinn'ous's good graces. Or if he's another prey among the many.

He's stressing. Extremely worried Sinn'ous is angry at him. Fearing his presence around the male is no longer welcome.

Sinn'ous strides over. Inmates vacating the space in his advance. No one wanting to be caught in the predator's path. Everyone watching. Waiting. Trying to figure out why the carnivore is in their presence and who will be on the menu.

The Gang catches on. Their game pausing as they swivel to watch the predator prowling closer, his eyes locked on their table as his destination.

Sinn'ous stops directly behind Zidie's chair. The cupcake-tattooed inmate's eyes blown wide as he stares right at Izz, not daring to turn around. Izz would have laughed at Zidie's expression if he wasn't so anxious about where he stands with Sinn'ous.

Sinn'ous's cold gaze runs over the occupants of the table Izz sits at—

The Gang clears out. Quickly departing—except Zidie, who's stuck between the table and a serial killer up against the back of his chair. With no way to slide his seat back without touching Sinn'ous in the process.

E.P. WRITER

Izz watches his best friend hunch forward trying to disappear from view. Maybe hoping to teleport out of the room.

"You alright. You look a little pale," Sinn'ous asks Izz in his usual way, expecting to be answered, arms folding over his chest. He must know Zidie wants to leave and he is blocking the exit.

A power play? Or is Sinn'ous fucking with Zid because it amuses him how much he scares others?

"No—yes. I mean. . ." Izz studies Sinn'ous's face for any signs of anger. "I was worried you were angry at me. You stormed out pretty fast."

He can literally feel Zidie breathing down his neck for answers. His best friend is trying way too hard to appear as if he's not listening in on the conversation. While he's clearly hanging onto every word.

"I wasn't annoyed at you. You've done nothing wrong," Sinn'ous states, his tone all matter of fact, hiding nothing.

"You sure?" Izz's a little sceptical. And he's fishing for more confirmation. "'Cause you still seem tense."

And I desperately need to know that we're okay. That our relationship is okay.

He can see the room slowly draining of occupants, as the inmates make their retreat. No one wants to be stuck in a small confined space with the serial killer.

"Not directed at you. Had to restrain myself, which I've never done. Could do with a distraction."

Sinn'ous is referring to not killing Vince, isn't he?
Does this mean he pulled back because of me?
Did I save Vince's life?

CAGED IN

What does it mean? If Sinn'ous really stopped and didn't finish the kill because of him, what does this make Izz? Does this mean he holds influence over the most feared killer within these walls?

It's a jittery feeling to have. One of relief and a swelling sense of pride in himself—for stopping a bad deed from occurring. His mind lightening with the knowledge he isn't all bad. If he's thrilled about preventing someone from dying, he can't be all bad? Can he? Not a completely terrible irredeemable person who deserves to be locked away for life.

It's a relief. The weight lifting off his shoulders.

"Zid, seriously," Izz can't hold back his grin. Half because of his friend, and half at his relief that he and Sin aren't over, "if you couldn't ask any louder, you'd be screaming."

Zidie laughs, throwing his hands in the air, in an innocent gesture—like he hadn't been silently begging Izz for details—which dies as soon as Sin's eyes land on him.

Izz would rather have this conversation in private. Lord knows what Zid must be thinking it's about. He happily shimmies his chair back, springing to his feet. He may also be seeking privacy so he could reaffirm, in his mind, that he and Sin are good.

We're still together.

Even if, technically, he has not asked Sin if they are *together* together.

To me. We are together and no one is going to change my mind.

Izz's much better now that he knows Sin isn't irritated with him. Isn't going to stop hanging out with him. Stop talking to him. He still has his escape out of this shitty prison. Into a happy little bubble where only he and Sin are allowed.

They stop at the top landing—Sin crowding up against his back—instead of walking down to the cell on the end—to spend time in Sin's space. Izz strolls off in the opposite direction, making his way to his own cell. With Sin trailing behind him.

He sits on his bunk, patting the space beside him for Sin to join him. He smiles when Sin does so, the mattresses dipping inwards under the extra weight. Drawing Izz in closer, his weight at a disadvantage to the other's.

"I, um. Was thinking last night." Izz rubs at the back of his neck. Unsure why he's so nervous, he knows Sin won't laugh at him or judge him. Or spread gossip throughout the prison. "I would like to . . . try again. If you would like to—" His voice cracks and he cuts himself off.

Stuffing his hands into his lap, refusing to look at Sin. It's embarrassing, how much of a virgin he's acting like. It's not as though he's never been with others. He has had relationships before. This isn't the first time he's had sex or kissed someone.

So why is he acting like a fumbling newbie to this whole thing? Why is it different with Sin? Is it because it's the first time he is the bottom?

A light touch brushes over his jaw, and he leans into it. Sin's fingers curling under his chin to bring his face up to meet black eyes. The dark colour shining with more

CAGED IN

emotion than Izz's used to seeing in the other's masculine features.

When Sin leans in, Izz opens up to him. Allowing the other's tongue inside. To penetrate his body. Their tongues intertwining within Izz's mouth. A claiming of ownership.

He's not so sure who's owning who.

Izz doesn't resist as he's manoeuvred—while keeping their mouths connected. Sin making quick work of Izz's clothing. The chilling cell air prickling over his skin. His hands working under Sin's shirt. Seeking skin on skin contact. His body sprawling out under Sin, who is completely dressed. While Izz lies vulnerable and bare—

Izz gasps as a finger pushes inside him. His legs parting to give Sin complete access to his body. Tucking his feet in behind Sin's knees, using the leverage to rock into Sin. To fuck himself on Sin's finger.

His body is thrumming with desire. Only half aware Sin has added more fingers. Is scissoring inside him. Stretching him open.

Sin breaks the kiss, "you okay," he asks while curling his fingers inside Izz.

He nods frantically, groaning, "y-yeah. Feels good."

Sin forces Izz's head back with a firm grip on his jaw. Exposing his throat. He's barely holding on to the edge. His body tightening as Sin's fingers work their way deeper. Probing inside, searching—

A sharp tingle shoots up Izz's spine as those exploring fingers brush against something within him. His back arching as he curses. His hands slapping down onto the mattress, gripping the sheets tightly, grounding himself as his mind floats away from his body.

What is that?

Whatever it is, he doesn't want Sin to stop. It feels amazing. How did he not know this part of his own body? Would have made his times alone a hell of a lot better. Though he has a feeling half of his reaction is due to who is doing it to him.

His jaw is released, followed by a snarled order not to move. Which Izz willingly obeys.

Sin slides down his pants enough to release his erection. Removing his fingers in favour of hefting Izz's legs. Resting them over his shoulder.

Izz's glad he has some flex in him, or this would hurt. His body being pretzeled under the other's weight—

His breath rasps out of him as Sin begins to push his way inside. His shaft slick, sliding in without too much of a burn. Sin must have applied lube of some kind—

All his thoughts fizz out as Sin drops his weight. Forcing half his cock directly into Izz. White fills his vision as he forgets how to breathe. The stretch bordering on agony. A mix of pleasure and pain swirling and clashing inside him. He isn't sure if he wants to scream or moan.

"Breathe. You're doing well," Sin tilts his head to the side, studying Izz.

He would give anything to hear what's going through the male's head right now. The spark in those dark eyes growing in intensity by the second.

"I'm going to try something," Sin resettles his weight into his legs, the mattresses dipping with the change, "I want you to hold out as long as possible, and longer. When you

CAGED IN

feel like your vision is slipping, tap my leg three times. You understand? Three times."

He's not sure what Sin's talking about, but he agrees either way. His hands white knuckling the bed below them as Sin sinks in deeper. He isn't sure he can fit much more.

Sin's hands curl around his neck, and before Izz can fully grasp what he's agreed to, his airways are cut off. The grip tightening to the point where he can no longer suck in oxygen.

"Relax," Sin orders. "You can hold out. I know you can hold out," Sin's hands squeeze tighter, his pupils dilating as he watches Izz closely.

Izz's panic at being deprived of air is quickly shoved aside as Sin drops his entire weight onto Izz. Sinking in to the hilt, reaching places inside he didn't know he has. Their hips flush together.

And then Sin moves.

The slide is electric, helping the stretch. However, when Sin snaps his hips forward and drives back in with a brutal clap, it burns and shoots a sharp pain into Izz's thighs.

He shoves his hand up against Sin's chest. Trying to push him off. Not to stop what's happening, but to ease it. His body is filling with so many sensations it's overwhelming him. And the pleasure racing through him at being used in this way is almost unbearable.

The asphyxiation is not helping. His body pumping with adrenaline. With pleasure. With lust and . . . and . . .

Izz cums. He didn't intend it. He hadn't known he was about to. But there is no stopping it. His body tightening, his muscles gripping the cock inside its walls. His throat constricting on its own, without the assisted aid of Sin's hands.

His vision blackens, and he hits Sin's thigh. He's pretty sure he does it more than three times, but Sin gets the message and his throat is freed. Air shooting down into his lungs as he gasps through his release. His cum shooting out to land on his own chest.

Sin doesn't stop thrusting. His pace as brutal as it started out. Taking everything he can get from Izz. Demanding all of it.

Lips close over Izz's shoulder, teeth sinking in, drawing blood he can feel trickling over his skin. He barely registers the pain over the overwhelming pleasure as he continues riding the high of his release.

His vision clearing. His ass oversensitive. His body weak. Finally he can feel Sin's thrusts sputtering out. Sin's getting close—Izz groans at the thought of Sin claiming him. Of marking him inside to match the exterior brandings. A marking only they will know of. A secret between the two of them.

"I want you to cum inside me," Izz grits out between each penetration.

Which evidently is all Sin needs to push him over the edge. The male shoving in one last time, deeper than ever. His cock kicking inside Izz as he growls, cumming within the tight confines. Marking Izz as his own.

Which is a nice time for Reni to walk in on them.

While Sin is balls deep, coming down from the high of release, Reni makes the mistake of entering the cell. Eyes blown wide, he stops dead in his tracks.

CAGED IN

Izz can't help but grin as his friend's pale face retreats right back out, as if he'd been burnt. The mental image forever implanted in the mind. As unwelcome as it may be, Reni is stuck with it for the foreseeable future.

Izz holds no regrets. *Sorry Reni*, but he wouldn't change anything that happened between him and Sin in this moment.

Sin stays deep within Izz, as they both pant, catching their breaths, until the bells for lunch ring. Announcing another meal for the prison population.

Sin pulls out, and Izz expects them to follow everyone else to the cafeteria—not that he can walk with his legs completely numb—only to be flipped over. And before he can ask Sin what he's doing. He's shoving right back in. Pulling a choked off whimper from Izz's lips.

He has no objections to being fucked from behind. His body pressing flat into the mattress as Sin uses him once more. Biting down on the sheeting as his ass is taken again. Grunting and cursing as Sin seems to be filled with energy to go all day. Izz's so exhausted he doubts he can manage to stand at this point.

Does not mean he doesn't want more, needing Sin to fill him. "Harder," Izz begs.

The chuckle Sin produces reverberates through Izz's back—

His hips are pulled up. Forcing him to his knees. But as he moves to get his hands under him, a firm hand between his shoulder blades forces him down. To keep his chest pinned.

Izz stays where he collapses. As large hands grab his hips and his ass is used as a toy for Sin's pleasure. The pounding bordering on painful. Yet pleasure is all he feels. All he knows. The pain is intoxicating.

Until the dangerous male is cumming into him a second time.

Izz's sure he came more than once during Sin's ministrations. His body is so wired out it's like a long line of pleasure. Sin had been relentless with hitting the spot inside him that had him seeing stars. He can't tell if he came or if it's simply mind-blowing pleasure.

Izz continues lying on his bunk, trying to catch his breath, as Sin leaves. Throwing a thin sheet over him on the way to the cell door. He thinks Sin said something about getting food. But his mind's a muggy mess and he can't be sure.

He must've passed out, because he's woken by Sin sitting down, with food in hand. A sandwich of some description, he barely tastes it as he practically inhales the thing. His stomach has never felt so empty.

His ass throbbing deliciously, demanding him to take notice of it. A phantom feeling of Sin still deep within him. It's turning him on again. His body lighting up with excitement. His dick too spent to even twitch.

Sin leaves as Izz's stuffing the last morsel into his mouth. The bell for all inmates to return to their cells' for the nightly lockup is chirping through their Wing. An annoying sound Izz resents—he doesn't want Sin to leave.

He's disappointed to see Sin's back disappear from sight. He may be alone in the quiet cell but the aches all over his

CAGED IN

body have him feeling cared for. A small smile spreads his lips at the thought.

Peeking around the corner before entering, Reni walks in hesitantly, a little more cautiously than he had the first time. A quizzical look washing over his face as he sits across from Izz on his own bunk.

"What?" Izz frowns. He's high on endorphins and doesn't want Reni raining on his post-sex bliss.

"Nothing. Just be careful. I know it's a good deal and all. The best protection in this shit-hole, to belong to an inmate with his status. But he's still a psychopathic serial killer."

Why does everyone assume he's doing this for protection? Sure it's a bonus. But he isn't sleeping with Sin to get it. He's sleeping with Sin because he . . . finds the male attractive. End of story.

Still . . . He understands where Reni's coming from. His friend is only looking out for him. Concerned with his safety. It's kind of touching.

"Awww. You're so sweet and protective of me," Izz teases, grin widening at his friend's expression of annoyance.

Reni scoffs at the mockery—at the lack of sincerity and teasing tone. "I just don't want to come in here one day to see your mangled remains," he teases Izz back. "And we both know the guards ain't cleaning that shit up, so I'm gonna have to bucket and mop your sorry ass up."

Izz burst out into a full-blown laugh. Trust his friend to pull out some morbid scene, over sex.

Sin might be a serial killer but he'd never once hurt him, or done something he didn't want. The same can't be said for other inmates in here—well, they aren't here anymore, are they . . .

33

Two weeks have come and gone since the day Izz had sex for the first time with Sin. And he's not referring to the attempted time. No, the first time Sin had pinned him down and taken him until his legs were jelly and his ass was aching.

Since then, Sin has become more and more assertive, rougher—aggressive. Pushing Izz further each time they fuck. Or rather, each time Sin fucks him. He's always the bottom, and he doesn't mind. In fact, he revels in it.

He's able to hold his breath longer, or rather, when he's deprived oxygen, he could take it for longer and longer each time before his vision blurs. And he loves it. There are no limitations to how much it turns him on. To be held down and overpowered by Sin.

His body's covered in bruises. In a whole range of colours. He can literally compare bruise colour ages in his skin. He has the whole healing colour chart mapped out on his body. And he couldn't be happier.

Other inmates stay away from him. The whispers about him being killed by Sin are declining. The rest of the prison coming to terms with Izz sticking around to be Sin's . . . plaything?

They are calling him the serial killer's bitch boy. And he has no issues with it. He loves bottoming for Sin and he doesn't care what the rest of the prison thinks about it. Just because he likes to be dominated doesn't make him a coward or weak.

Sin's opening his eyes to many darker sexual games he hadn't known existed. Allowing him to accept who he is and not apologise for it. It doesn't help that whenever he voices his annoyance with being called lesser for being the submissive in their relationship, Sin will pin him down. And he'll forget all about why it's a bad idea to let a serial killer dominate him.

He's learning more and more every time. About himself and how much he can take. Learning new terms and experiencing new levels of pleasure. And he must say, he thoroughly enjoys breath-play. As soon as Sin places a hand around his throat, he's hard and begging to be bent over.

He also learnt what a drop and aftercare are. Sin taught him it's normal to feel a stinging emptiness sometimes after submitting. Sin holds him and rubs his back during his drops. It's a weird feeling, but he bounces back fast.

Sin explained to him how enjoyment derived from pain is nothing to be ashamed of. He's learnt that people this way are known as masochists. And many people are into pain-play and other forms revolving around it.

Izz's never in charge of their couplings—sure he can say no, or give the safe word, or action, to let Sin know he's been pushed beyond his comfort zone.

CAGED IN

But ultimately, Sin is running the games. He is in charge of how they play out. He controls how harsh, how brutal, how *sadistic* he will be to Izz.

Sadism is another term Izz has learnt. Dom, sub, the list goes on. He never knew there was such a vast variety to sex. So many terms and levels of play. Ranging from people who get off on being cut, or burnt. To people who want to be tied up, or humiliated in public.

Sin has expressed his interest in the darker kinks. The ones involving blood and pain—on Izz's side of the deal, inflicted by Sin. He's spoken of his enjoyment in watching the deep reds run over Izz's tanned skin—his bites often break skin.

Izz's on the fence with the whole slice and dice, playing with blades, side of things. He isn't comfortable with Sin attempting it, he's nervous Sin will cut too deep and hit an artery or something equally unpleasant.

"Sin," Izz groans, frustration building as the male sits over him, straddling his thighs. Refusing to touch him. And Izz can't reach out to touch, with his hands firmly tied behind his back—a shirt torn to strips forming a makeshift rope, effectively binding him in place. Arms trapped under his body. Pinned to the male's bunk in the Satanic cell, with Sin hovering over him fully clothed while Izz is completely bare to the room's cold embrace.

"I'm going to try something new with you." Sin leans down biting at Izz's vulnerable throat. "You're going to have to trust me."

E.P. WRITER

Izz gasps. Squirming in his bindings. "I do trust you. Please." He is so hard he's liable to burst open.

Sin pulls something out from behind him. At the same time gripping under Izz's chin to push his head back. Preventing him from seeing what is happening. What Sin is holding.

Izz exhales his breath, his lungs working overtime to match his rapidly increasing heart rate. His entire body tingling with anticipation, associating Sin with pleasure—

He jumps a little at the cool touch—smooth, cold, some type of metal pressing against his skin over his ribs—

Sin takes his mouth in a surge of dominance. Kissing into him. Claiming him . . .

Izz's mind leaves whatever object is cooling his skin, in favour of hungrily devouring Sin's lips—

Sin bites him, a firm pressure on his lips which has him whining and arching, trying to press closer. He loves when Sin bites. The sharp licks of prickling pain amp up his desires.

A tingle in his side has him sucking in a sharp breath. The strength of the sting growing, working its way into his overwhelming lust. A small burn blooming—

Izz hisses a curse as the burn registers. The sting in his side building in intensity. Turning his head—as best he can with Sin's hand holding his jaw—breaking the kiss.

"What . . ." Izz's breath is too far gone to get his question out. Swallowing hard to try his luck again—

"Relax," Sin commands. His voice level and soothing, "you're okay. You trust me."

He nods but still tries to look at why his side is stinging—

Sin leans a hand on the same place in his side—

CAGED IN

A title wave of agonising pain flares to life, killing his blissed-out arousal—

Izz screams. His body jacking off the mattress as he pulls at the bindings, tears pricking in his eyes. "Red. Red. Red," his voice laced with hurt, wheezes the safe word Sin had given him.

The pressure lets up. Sin removing his hand. The pain remains, sharp and intense. His side twisting and knotting. Angry at him for the distress it's in.

"Untie me please. I don't like it. I don't—" Izz shakes his head. He's never used the safe word before. Sin's never pushed him this far—hurt him this much.

"Calm down," Sin keeps Izz's head pinned back, so he can't see what he has done to him. The other hand coming up to stroke through his hair, "deep breaths. You're not in any danger. Calm down."

"I want to stop. It hurts."

"You like it. Your mind is merely experiencing a survival reaction. You need to let yourself know you're not in any danger. Repeat it in your mind."

It hurt too much for him to concentrate on Sin's words. He's close to slipping into a panic attack. The sensations are bringing back memories of other violent attacks he's suffered in this cage. His mind is having trouble grounding him to this moment. In this cell. With this male.

"I don't—" Izz cuts off as Sin drops down on top of him. The male's heavy weight encasing his entire being. . .

Izz's hard. His erection making itself known by pushing up against Sin who smirks down at Izz. Rotating his hips to drive the point home, to show Izz how much his body is responding.

He forces himself to come back. To be in the moment with Sin. To kill the panic attack before it takes root. He silently repeats what Sin told him.

You're not in any danger. You're not in any danger. You're not in any danger.

He closes his eyes. Focusing on his breathing, on the pressure rubbing over his dick. It feels good. He is fine. Sin's not hurting him. Sin will never hurt him. Sin protects him, gives him safe words.

Sin's your safe zone. He's your safe place.

"There you go," Sin praises, fingers stroking through Izz's hair, "you see, you're doing well."

"It feels better." The burning in his side is only throbbing a little now, the same kind of ache the bites Sin gives him leave behind. A bearable pain he is alright with. One he is used to. "Can you let go of my jaw now."

"No." Izz frowns at the response. Sin has never told him no before, especially when it comes to their intimate times together. "You're doing well. I want your mind to stay in this zone. We don't want you to panic again."

"Why would I panic?" Izz can feel his heart rate spiking, he can hear his blood pumping faster.

What is Sin hiding? Why isn't he allowed to look? What has Sin done to him?

"Repeat what I told you. You're spiralling again," Sin's other hand dips past the curve of Izz's hip, sliding down to rest on his length. Using the soft skin on skin contact to help ground Izz.

You're not in danger. You're not in danger.

CAGED IN

He focuses on the touch. On the hand slowly stroking over his sensitive skin. Allowing it to wash over him. To coat his mind . . . His mind . . .

Does he truly want this? Or is he acting out of pure fear?

Fear at what will happen without protection in this Hellhole. The other inmates have proven how foul and brutal they can be. How their humanity is all but a distant dream, a dream they don't want to remember.

He's been attacked, groped, forced into situations he didn't want to be in. Treated like nothing, like a thing to be used by anyone who wants him.

But with Sin . . . He has a powerful ally, protection from the mass of the prison population, from the guards. And Sin listens to him. Treats him well. Kindly. With respect.

Except . . . What has Sin done to his side? And why isn't Sin letting him see?

He doesn't like it. Something is off. He's not in this a hundred percent. His mind is racing too much, he can't concentrate. "Red. I'm done. Let go. Please, Sin."

Izz calls the safe word. He needs to step back. To give himself time to figure everything out. He's come too close to a panic attack and he is still feeling off.

Sin pulls his hand free, releasing Izz's hard cock. "You sure?"

"Yes."

Izz's body is rolled over, and the bindings cut off. However, when he moves to get up, Sin keeps him pinned with a hand on his back. Preventing him from sitting up. From checking why his side is paining him.

"Sin—" Izz's plea is quickly cut off, Sin speaking over him.

"Relax. I'm letting you up. I need you to stay calm. It's not deep. It hasn't gone through all the layers of skin. You trust me, yes."

All the layers of skin?

"What do you mean? I don't understand." Izz stops trying to sit up. Allowing Sin to keep him down. He's not so sure he wants to see anymore.

"You remember our conversation, to do with different forms of play."

"Yes," Izz nods along with his answer. Sin's hand leaves him, now that he has ceased trying to get up.

He still trusts Sin. It may have hurt and been overwhelming, but Sin stopped when he asked him to. Sin respects his boundaries.

"The one mentioning knife-play."

Knife-play . . .

Izz slowly rolls his torso, to see what was done . . . Eyes wide as his side is revealed—

And now he feels like a baby. Sure, he has a slice in his skin, just under his ribs. But it's a nick. Barely longer than half his pinkie, and thin, paper-cut thin. He purses his lips. Probing at the slice, the tiny trickle of blood.

"That's it. It felt like . . ." Izz punches Sin in the chest. "You're an asshole. You freaked me out more than this would have," he gestures to the injury, as though they aren't both clear on what he's talking about.

"Mind's a powerful thing, isn't it." Sin laughs. Actually laughs.

Izz's completely caught off guard by the sound, his anger evaporating. He's never heard Sin laugh before. Not like

CAGED IN

this. Like an average amused person would do. A loud, spontaneous laugh.

He can't help but smile at Sin. The male's amusement rubbing off on him. He enjoys seeing this part of Sin. The playful side, the more . . . human side—with emotions. As opposed to the dangerous cold air Sin normally carries around—a shroud of death.

The frequently recurring prison bell rings out. The calling card for the next meal. Lunch is starting. Inmates noisily making their way to the cafeteria. He's hungry too.

"I wanna shower first." Izz swings his legs off the bunk, gathering his clothes which are scattered around the Satanic cell. "You joining?"

"Not much else to do."

"Wow. Don't get too excited to spend time with me." Izz smirks, wiggling his legs into his grey pants. Is it sad that he's already used to the scratchy material?

"You're developing an attitude," Sin informs Izz, crossing his arms over his chest as he watches the smaller inmate dress.

"Nah, I'm becoming comfortable with you. Enough to open up as who I've always been . . . Well, who I was on the outside—"

Except now I've killed someone.

I'm a murderer.

He's dealing with it. Slowly coming to terms with the fact that he isn't a bad person, he's just been dealt a bad hand. Sin's collection of Satanic pages on the walls has actually helped him. Who knew the Satanic culture is so easy to understand. Helpful too, it's allowing him to process what transpired with the guard. How much it hadn't been his fault.

Two passages he read over a week ago, he keeps close to heart, bringing them forth whenever his mind wanders into dark places. Texts he recalls clear as day in his mind's eye. The printed words branded within his mind. A comfort to hold onto.

```
One's own body is sacred, and is subject
to one's own will alone.
When in open territory, bother no others.
If others bother you, politely ask them
to stop. If they do not heed your words,
destroy them.
```

Passages he finds himself repeating over and over, when he's lying awake at night, unable to sleep.

It hasn't left him since he read it. It's a comforting blanket to inform him he did the right thing. He isn't to blame for all the attacks, the assaults . . . the deaths . . .

Those inmates brought it on themselves. They suffered the consequences of their own actions. They are the ones to blame for what events transpired and the outcomes to befall them. He is the victim. They chose their own paths and sealed their own fates.

It wasn't my fault.

"—Kind of. Can we just drop this subject? It's depressing," Izz brushes aside his thoughts. He is in a good head space and doesn't want dark thoughts clouding his mind.

He may be slowly healing from his traumas, but it doesn't mean he isn't still holding a little guilt, feeling sad for them. They were people after all. Granted, they were bad people, but they were still someone's son.

CAGED IN

A hand runs down his spine as he leans forward to pick up his shoe. Bringing a smile to his face. He's used to Sin touching him. Since the first time they did it, Sin's always looking for excuses to get his hands all over Izz—

Izz hisses when he bends too low, his side stinging its protest. He'd forgotten about the cut—will he need stitches?

Standing in the middle of the cell—shirt in one hand—he probes the injury. It's a neat clean cut, a thin line. A little slice with no rough jagged edges. It's not bleeding very much anymore. Seeping a little but it seems to have closed up on its own.

How much practice has Sin had? How many have been sliced open under his blade . . . ?

Izz's compelled to know why Sin treats him differently. Why he's allowed to become so close to a psychopath who enjoys killing—no one kills as many as Sin without enjoying the act.

"Why do you care about me, and no one else?" Izz stares directly into Sin's eyes, watching them flicker as the question sinks in.

"Don't know. I just do." Sin's trying to dismiss the subject. Why?

Izz's not going to allow that to happen. He wants to know what goes on in Sin's mind. How Sin views the world. "But why am I different?"

"Do you want me to treat you like I view others," Sin raises a brow.

A threat? Or playful teasing? Sometimes it's hard to tell.

He decides to play it safe, especially on this subject. He doesn't want to provoke a reaction.

E.P. WRITER

"No," he mutters. Pulling his shirt on, refusing to look back at Sin once his shirt is covering him. He's a little hurt that he hasn't received an answer to his question.

"So what's the problem," Sin questions in his usual *you-will-answer-me* fashion.

Why is Sin pushing for an answer now? It's clear Sin doesn't want to talk about his thoughts or feelings.

Izz shakes his head, shrugging, "never mind." He can already feel his emotions shutting down, to protect him from the rejection.

Sin stays silent.

Izz steps around him on his way to the cell's door. His excitement about them showering together has evaporated. His feet heavy and his heart dropping along with the rest of him. It doesn't feel like a sexual drop, more like an emotional hurt. It sucks either way.

Sin grabs Izz's forearm, before the smaller inmate can squeeze past him. Sighing long and low—a curse of breath filling the tense atmosphere, "I can't tell you because I don't know. I've never cared about anyone before. People . . ." Sin trails off, mulling over his words.

Izz patiently waits for Sin to continue. His breath held in his throat. Hanging onto every word.

"To me, people are simply animals, or . . . the way you would view an apple. Some you want to slice. Others look repulsive, you don't touch them, but you would slice them open, if needed, without care."

Izz's not sure he's following the explanation . . .

"You on the other hand . . . I care if you feel pain—unwanted pain. I don't want to inflict injuries on you which you're not comfortable with. And I don't want to treat you

CAGED IN

as the apple, I care if you were to be sliced open, I do not want it from you. I would like you to be in one piece."

So . . . Sin views people as unthinking unfeeling plants? Like crushing a grape—the emotions Izz would feel if he squished a grape is what Sin feels to . . . squish a person . . .

Izz can't say he relates to the feelings. It's strange to him, to view people—or any living creature—as nothing more than an apple, as Sin describes it. With no guilt over a human's death . . .

It would actually be kind of nice to hold no guilt. He'd be able to sleep a full night without nightmares of dead people plaguing him. Without seeing the guard on the floor . . . All the blood . . .

Izz blinks the images away. Shoving them into the back of his mind. He isn't sure how to respond to Sin. So he nods, taking Sin's hand to lead the dangerous male out of the Satanic cell to the shower room.

He may not understand why Sin views life as meaningless, but he does understand one thing. Sin holds him above everyone else. As a prized possession to be taken care of. Protected.

They walk side by side down the corridors to the showers. With every inmate—who is unlucky enough to be stuck in the same corridor—turning and swiftly retreating back the way they came.

Izz finds it amusing how everyone avoids Sin. And here he is, clinging to the male's side. Letting Sin fuck him—

No, *begging* Sin to fuck him.

I truly am insane.

34

Izz's naked under the shower spray all by his little lonesome. Sin's still in the separate area where you leave your clothing when you enter the massive communal shower room—a word one would think doesn't belong in front of showers. *Private* or *singular* shower stalls would be a million times better. Less nasty, less horrifying, less leering creeps watching you.

He doesn't have to worry about the last part, not this time. The entire shower room is empty. There had been one inmate about to get naked and come in, Sin's narrowed eyes in their direction had them hastily scurrying out.

Which leaves Izz alone, under the warm spray. With his erection raging and demanding attention. He's still pent up over their activities in Sin's cell.

And he is alone . . .

Glancing around, he takes a deep breath, and before he can talk himself out of it his hand is wrapping around his cock. Stroking his length as he pinched his eyes shut. He wants to get it over with as quick as possible so he doesn't

CAGED IN

get caught wanking in the showers. Not that he hasn't seen multiple men in here shamelessly touching themselves. He, on the other hand, is extremely shy when it comes to this and would probably die of embarrassment if he were to be caught.

The slice in his side is throbbing under the warm spray. Reminding him of its presence. He's reluctant to admit that the pain feels somewhat good. The small tingling throb . . .

Izz tentatively hovers his other hand over his side. Lingering mid-air for a moment before applying pressure—

He gasps as sparking sensations radiate down his side, traveling over his ribs to fan out inside his stomach, shooting into his cock.

He drops his forehead against the tiled wall. Working his hand up and down his shaft as he plays with the slice in his side. His thighs trembling. Rapidly approaching his release.

Several strokes later he's biting his lip as an explosion of pleasure splinters him apart. Rope after rope of hot cum spurts out of his twitching length. Spluttering on the tiles to be quickly washed away by the water's flow.

He stands there, alone, shuddering, as his body pulls itself back together. Slowly blinking his eyes open—

Sin's leaning right next to Izz, a smirk gracing his lips. And he holds no apology for sneaking up on Izz to watch him pleasure himself.

Izz fights back the urge to drown himself out of sheer embarrassment. "O-okay, so I like knife-play. Leave me be."

Sin's smirk only grows, a full-blown sinister grin spreading across his face. He doesn't say anything. He doesn't need to. Izz can feel the hyper excitement radiating out of him. Knows he's pleased. Knows he must be thinking about how much further he can take it. Now that he's confirmed Izz enjoys the new kink . . .

Izz's eyes drag to his wound . . .

Will the cut leave a scar?

A new brand to go along with the tattoo he wears. The bruises his body bears. A scar to show he belongs to Sin . . .

Perhaps he should get some more tattoos, to represent himself, before he's covered in marks from another . . . Don't get him wrong, he loves the bruises and bites marring his flesh. He'd just like something to portray who he is.

"I think I'd want another tattoo." Izz flicks the showers spay off, finished with his rinse and scrub routine. "When I get out." He'd need to find a job first, and make sure his family has food, shelter, warmth—

"I'll get you one in here." Sin stalks Izz out, his massive body pressing close behind as Izz stops in front of his clean clothes.

Izz picks up his towel. Rubbing it over his warm damp skin. "I can't keep sponging off you."

Sin's already buying him food and treats, and card games, and mattresses—which cost so much in here, he'd have to sell a kidney to afford it on his prison job's meagre pay.

"I don't mind."

"But I do," Izz snaps.

CAGED IN

Sin doesn't seem to care about money. Treating it as one would an apple core—throwing it away with no regard. Izz would love to have so much money he could afford to throw it at people.

"Why." Sin seems genuinely puzzled by Izz's refusal. "It's my money to spend on whatever I want."

Because I want to earn my own keep in the world, and not be reliant on others . . .

It would be nice though. For once. To be the one someone gifts money to, and not the one who has to earn it for the family.

"I-I—it just matters," Izz doesn't know how to explain it. How to word his past—how he is supposed to be the responsible one, and it feels weird to have someone else in the role.

Sin chuckles, in his usual dry humourless way, "your mind's a curious thing, isn't it. So caught up in others, you're not taking the time to get what you want. Denying yourself. For what. Social standing. Because society says it's wrong to sponge off someone who's doting on you."

"It's called a gold-digger," Izz mumbles. He doesn't want to be one of those either.

When no reply comes back, he looks over at Sin, who's smirking at him. A playful light glinting in his black eyes.

"You can always say I *'demanded it of you, for my protection',* if it makes you feel better."

Izz scrunches his nose at Sin, impulsively sticking his tongue out—

He ducks his eyes. Regretting the childish act. It doesn't help his whole I-can-take-care-of-myself monologue.

E.P. WRITER

"Come, we're leaving," Sin commands, fully dressed and prowling to the door without waiting for Izz's replay.

Izz hops after him. Trying to move and pull his last shoe on at the same time. He calls it an accomplishment for not tripping and face planting.

"Where to?" Izz questions, stomping his heel into his shoe as he obediently follows after Sin.

"You have a tattoo to receive."

"W-what? No—" Izz stutters, trying his best to think of some sort of protest.

Sin ignores him, speaking right over the top of him as though Izz hasn't said a word, "you want one, don't you."

Well, yes. He does. But . . .

What's the difference between a tattoo and all the gifts he's already given you . . . ?

"Yes . . ." Izz gives in reluctantly.

It is true, Sin's been buying him things since the moment he walked into prison all those weeks ago. And he's accepted them all. Hell, he sleeps on one of those gifts every night and his back is grateful for it.

He truly does want a tattoo. Not sure why it feels a little off to have Sin buying it for him—he assumes Sin will be buying it? He's not sure how the payments for tattoos go down in prison. Is it favours? Cash? Commissary goods?

He can't recall if Sin had given the artist money the last time. He doesn't think so. He'd been pretty out of it when he got his first one. Way too excited to be getting inked, he barely remembers anything else happening around him.

CAGED IN

And that's how Izz finds himself in the same cell in I-Wing. With the artist . . . he can't remember his name—if the guy had told Izz his name the first time?

Sin's in a chair by his head as Izz lies on his stomach on the tortuously bare prison bunk, his pant leg bunched up above the knee. The artist's back is to them, sitting in another chair, hunching over Izz's exposed leg.

"I don't know why you pay for this stuff," Izz winces as the needle passes over a particularly sensitive place on his calf, "it's not like I do anything in return for it."

Sin smirks, the only warning Izz receives before he opens his mouth in reply, "so you don't bend over for me. I was imagining you sprawled out on my bunk—"

"Oh, my God. Stop," Izz frantically looks back at the artist. He's never felt so embarrassed in his entire life—

"Satan," Sin sits up in his chair, leaning closer to Izz.

"Huh?"

"Your *God* reference is repulsive," Sin slides his fingers through Izz's hair, tugging lightly, sending an immediate response to Izz's cock, "*oh, Satan.* Is the term you should use . . . If you want me to do sin unto your body."

Fuck . . .

He is now officially getting a tattoo with a raging hard-on digging into the metal bunk below him. No squishy relaxing tattoo chairs in prison, to cushion his raging erection.

He's ashamed of his body's reaction. Of how easily Sin gets inside his head . . . How much of a hold Sin has over him . . .

You truly are ruined . . .

35

Izz's not sure if he should be worried by the look on Sin's face.

He'd agreed to allow Sin to try again with the knife-on-skin action—he'd actually spent the night in Sin's cell. Sin had woken early and, in turn, had woken Izz up to play with.

He's slightly put out by the shine in Sin's eyes. But he's more interested in stepping off the ledge and into a darker realm. His experience with it in the showers had been euphoric.

"Close your eyes. Let yourself feel it. Don't over think," Sin instructs, and Izz follows the orders. Closing his eyes, he relaxes on his stomach, bare to sin's eyes, arms tucked under the pillow his head is resting on.

Sin's hands stroking up and down his thighs. Massaging the muscles in a calming rhythm. He lets the sensations consume him. Giving in to his body's desires, his lust.

Hands caressing. Rubbing. Massaging his flesh . . .

He sighs as his muscles slowly unlock. The fearful tension seeping out. His mind flowing into the moment. His dread leaving . . .

The first cut is tentative. A delicate move of blade through skin. A small sting, and it's gone. Sin's lips working his neck—kissing, sucking . . . biting. Taking his mind away from everything. And it's working. His body is opening up to Sin's ministrations. Wanting more. Needing more.

The next slash is sluggish, dragging over his thigh before sinking into skin. Warmth trickling down his thigh—his breath hitching—then the blade is gone once more. Hands kneading his ass, teeth grazing his shoulder. A distraction he clings too.

He sucks in a breath as a finger pushes inside him. Working its way in deep, sliding over sensitive walls—

He arches his back into Sin when the finger hits the place inside that has him seeing stars. His breath ragged. "Fuck . . ." He grits the word out on an exhale.

"Your body responds deliciously to me," Sin practically purrs, pushing down on Izz's sweet spot.

The leisurely way Sin pierces Izz again, with the blade, has him digging his hands into the sheets. Begging, "please." *I don't know what I want.* "It hurts."

Sin pushes a second finger inside. "Do you want me to stop . . ." his voice holds an amused undertone to it.

"N-no. Please." *What do I want?*

I can't think. I can't—

"Didn't think so," Sin removes his fingers, lining his cock up with Izz's entrance. Pushing in. Penetrating with a

CAGED IN

sluggish air. In no hurry to finish. Wanting to drag this out for as long as possible.

Izz whimpers, his breath hiccupping, his body overstimulated. His sweat slickening his burning skin. His core heating up, shearing his insides.

It takes him a moment to realise he's right on the edge. He's so close. "I'm going to cum—" He barely has the word past his lips before he's biting the pillow under his face to muffle his scream. His body spasming with the intensity. His mind fogging and clearing, fogging and clearing.

He's vaguely aware of Sin cutting into him. Slicing . . .

Izz sobs. His oversensitive nerves sending pain signals through his lust. "Please—"

"Hush, now," Sin shifts above Izz, gripping his hips to sink in to the hilt. "You'll beg when I tell you to beg. Not before."

Izz complies, his breathing shallowing. Small gasps following each deep penetration, hitting the place within, sending sparks throughout his nerve endings. His pleasure building and growing with every push and pull of Sin's cock.

Izz flinches at the kiss of the blade, running up his spine. The promise of what's to come. . . What he's begging for . . .

His breath hisses as Sin grabs his hair, tugging his head back, exposing his throat. His internal voice sparks with warning—warnings he ignores—flooding his body with adrenaline. His lips part and he does nothing to prevent the blade pressing under his jaw—

How many people have died under Sin's blade? How many have felt the deadly pressure promising pain, promising death. Unable to move away, to pull back, their throats slit. Delicate skin giving way under a sharp blade.

Sin handles the weapon as if he's performed this manoeuvre a thousand times. Confidently and with controlled purpose . . .

The pressure increases . . . A burning sting registering before the tell-tale warmth follows. Blood trickling free. . .

How deep is the wound . . . ?

How much blood is he losing . . . ?

How much can he afford to lose . . . before his body gives out?

. . . Am I going to die today. . . ?

"You're mine," Sin growls, pressing deep inside as he claims Izz at his throat and between his legs. "To do with as I desire. . ."

36

Izz moves slowly down the stairs. Using the rails to do the majority of the work of holding him off the floor. His body is aching and throbbing in various places. Including his thighs and ass.

Under his prison-issued clothes he wears an array of bandages. Sin is a rather good little nurse, with the patch-up job. Applying something which stung like a bitch, and is supposedly to prevent infections.

Izz had weakly accused Sin of using it out of pure sadism. He'd been teased for not being able to handle the pain. It had been a relief once the bandages were applied to the injuries to give them a reprieve.

Though it doesn't help him walk. He also isn't a baby, and he is starving. So here he is, gritting his teeth as he takes the final step off the stairs.

He feels like giving himself a pat on the back for making it without falling down.

He's sporting a noticeable limp he tries his best to disguise. Shuffling along slowly with Sin by his side. The male slowing his strides so Izz can keep up. Glancing over at Izz every second to check on him.

"Quit staring. I'm fine. Just a little stiff." And he is fine. Sure he aches somewhat, but it doesn't take away from his enjoyment of what he and Sin have done.

Sin hums, not believing Izz for a second, "you sure you're not bleeding or—"

"I'm fine, quit worrying." Look at him, telling a serial killer not to worry about his health. Not a place he would have envisioned his life being at—to be comfortable enough to order around a serial killer.

What has my life become?

He never would have remotely guessed his life would have come to this. To be limping inside prison because his serial killer— . . . boyfriend . . . ?—has used his body as a carving canvas and Izz begged him to do it—

Is Sin his boyfriend? Or are they only fuckbuddies?

I'd like it to be more than merely a hook up . . .

"You keep grunting when you walk," Sin grips Izz's elbow when Izz wobbles to the left slightly more than intended on his next step.

Oh.

My bad.

He hadn't been aware he's showing his hurt. He thought he'd been doing a bang-up job hiding his discomfort. Masking it.

"Am I? I hadn't noticed," Izz tries to play it down, brushing off Sin's concerns, even if they do give his stomach butterflies from the care Sin shows him.

Izz discovers it's rather difficult to walk and not utter pained noises. He tries his best, with Sin eyeing his every

CAGED IN

move. He wants to show the other he can take it. He's tough and not a weak pushover. He wants to impress Sin. He's aware it's a weird thing to want to impress someone about—not being in pain after their activities involving sharp objects—nevertheless, he wants to.

They step into the cafeteria together. And he's thrilled with the VIP status, he isn't so sure he could have stood in the line. His legs are already starting to give out, struggling to keep him upright.

He parts ways with Sin to sit—or rather wince down onto the bench—at The Gang's table, between Sinj and Blake. With Zidie, Isco, Phelix and Reni on the opposite side, staring at him from across the table's scratched surface.

The whole table is giving off the vibe of concern, worried at Izz's harsh breathing. Erik is the only one not looking shocked or concerned, like he somehow knows what's going on.

He catches the moment the rest figure it out. Sinj positively beams, grinning so wide his cheeks are liable to split. Zidie joins in on the grinning smirk. Reni's face falls with concern. As does Blake's. And Isco . . . well, Isco portrays indifference to the whole thing, right alongside Phelix.

He makes a point to not look David's way, the man is sitting on Izz's side of the table at the far end. With Blake and Erik between them, so he doesn't have to see David unless he leans forward and intentionally tries. Which he has no plans of doing.

Izz doesn't bother addressing their questioning expressions or easing any worried minds. He grabs his spoon, and uses it to shovel down the prison food he doesn't hold in his mouth long enough to taste. Cramming it right into his barren stomach.

"Was it *that* good?" Sinj elbows Izz in the ribs, luckily missing hitting any of the countless slashes hidden away from view.

"Better," Izz mumbles around a mouthful of food. Zero pause in the next spoonful he shovels in. He feels as though he hasn't eaten in weeks.

Zidie laughs along with Sinj, his cupcake face boldly glancing over his shoulder to sneak a look at Sin in the usual place—sitting in the shadows of the far back table.

Izz glances over as well, his eyes connecting with the black ones already boring into him. He smiles softly, refocusing back on his meal.

The food helps with his light-headedness. The woozy sensations easing away. He's better now that he has some food in him. His aches are dulling too or perhaps he's merely getting used to them?

Either way, he's well enough to be on board with following The Gang to the Rec-Room to play some card games. Slow and steady, with Reni by his side and the rest of The Gang well and truly ahead of them—

"Izz. You 'right, my man. Ya bleeding," Reni stops Izz in his tracks, a hand gripping his arm.

Izz follows his friend's concerned gaze, down to his side—blood is seeping through his shirt.

CAGED IN

Guess this one is a little deeper than he thought. He double checks the rest of his body . . . none of the others are bleeding through their bandages.

Does this one need stitches? He should probably have someone check it out. If it is bleeding enough to have soaked the bandage and is coming through his shirt, it would be a good idea to have a professional take a gander at it.

"I might need to go to Med-Wing," Izz voices his thoughts. Tugging at his shirt, as if pulling it away from the injury will somehow stem the bleeding.

"I'll take you," Reni not so much offers, as states. Already pulling Izz in the direction of Med-Wing.

"I can get there myself," Izz complains as he's tugged along after his friend. Not that he knows where it is. He has a vague idea but he's never been there before.

"No. You're pale and already wobbling. How much blood have you lost?"

A good question. One Izz can't answer as he doesn't know.

He lets Reni lead him with hurried steps to the professionals. Watching the blood patch growing in size as they swiftly make their way through the corridors. With Reni muttering all kinds of things along the way. Mostly cursing out Sin under his breath. Izz ignores it, knowing Reni is only worried about him.

Med-Wing is surprisingly clean—neat, tidy and sparkling clean. With the smell of disinfectant lingering in the air.

E.P. WRITER

The nurse is nice and cheerful. Showing him over to an examination table. Which he sits on voluntarily—

The doors to the room snap open, clanging against the wall, announcing Sin's arrival. The male striding right in like he owns the place. The guard by the door—who nearly became one with it and the wall—like a grotesque pancake—doesn't try to stop Sin.

"What the fuck happened," Sin growls, eyes locking on Reni—who steps back, pressing against the exam table and Izz's legs.

Wow, Izz's not sure he's ever heard Sin curse before. He should probably redirect the menacing male who's terrifying the entire room. The poor nurse looks close to breaking down into tears or an anxiety attack, her face pale as she hides behind Izz and the exam table. He can't say he blames her, she's small, young, and no match for a muscle-clad serial killer with murder written all over his face.

"It's fine. Chill, you're freaking out the entire room," he smiles, gingerly stretching out onto the exam table. Lying down is a good idea, his head is a little foggy. "It's just bleeding a bit."

Sin reigns in his anger. Concern showing in his eyes, something Izz's sure only he can see. The sparks of emotion in the male's eyes would not be obvious unless you have spent as much time with him as Izz has.

Izz peers over at the nurse, who is wide eyed and frozen in place. "You're fine. He won't hurt you," he addresses the nurse, reassuring her. She doesn't seem to buy his story but does begin to collect equipment to use on him.

CAGED IN

Constantly looking back to make sure she can see where Sin is the whole time.

Sin on the other hand ignores everyone else, jerking Izz's shirt up to get to the bandages below. Inspecting what's bleeding.

Izz can hear Reni's sharp intake of breath at what's revealed. The countless bruises. The older cut on his side. The new bandages covering all the fresh ones. The larger bandage, soaking wet with dark red blood—

He has to look away, the blood's making him nauseous. He focuses on Sin, meeting the dark eyes scanning his body. He gives Sin a smile, to ease the male's worry about him.

He's jittery to have a serial killer expressing concern about his wellbeing. To be fussing over him. It's surreal. Not something he would expect from someone like Sin.

The nurse walks over, keeping her distance from Sin, "I-I, excuse m-me. I need to get t-to him. To assess his injuries."

Izz feels bad for her. She doesn't deserve to be terrified in her own workplace. There isn't much he can do to help her. He can't really promise Sin won't kill anyone in here, because he would be lying. He has no way of knowing, and isn't confident enough to say with certainty, that Sin won't do it.

He can ease her mind a little though, "he won't hurt you for helping me. You're okay," it's not strictly a lie, he knows Sin is protective but won't attack someone who is helping him.

Will Sin kill the nurse if Izz dies on the exam table? Most likely. However, she doesn't need to know that.

He pegs Sin with a look, to wordlessly reprimand the male and tell him not to harm her. Sin smirks, knowing exactly what Izz's thinking.

Reni's hovering, wanting to leave Izz in the hands of the professional, but not wanting to leave with Sin here. His mind clearly stuck in-between not intervening and wanting to punch Sin and kick the male out.

Izz reaches out, gripping Sin's wrist to tug him as best he can despite the growing fatigue he's experiencing. "Can you stand on the other side . . ." *So I don't have to worry about Reni doing something that ends in everyone's deaths.*

Sin does as Izz asks. Prowling behind the table, pulling a chair over and sitting by Izz's other side. Leaving a full table between him and the innocents in the room. As the nurse works on cutting the soiled bandages away.

Izz grunts when something cold touches his side, his breath hitching at the throbbing sensation igniting from his injury.

"S-sorry. I need to clean it," the nurse stutters nervously, her eyes flicking between Izz's injuries and Sin.

"I'm okay. The pain's not so bad," he lies as he pinches his eyes shut. Turning his face in Sin's direction. To use the male's presence as an anchor to help ground him.

Sin grips Izz's arm with both hands, fingers tracing over Izz's skin. He's probably watching the nurse work. Which is no doubt not helping the woman concentrate.

"I'll have to go shallower next time," Sin murmurs at Izz's ear, loud enough for only Izz to hear.

He nods—gritting his teeth as a needle pierces his stomach. Relief soon following as his side begins to numb.

CAGED IN

"I'll stitch him up. His side is deep but nothing life threatening." Guess she must be addressing Sin? "He will need to take it easy for a few days, to allow the injury to heal. Does he have any others or just what I can see?"

He would feel annoyed—at having the nurse speak to Sin about him like he's a child who needs consent from an outside source before anything can be done to him—if he wasn't in so much pain. As it is, he is perfectly fine with Sin carrying the conversation.

"More on his legs and back—"

Reni's voice cuts through the room, "you piece of shit. How could you do this to him? I thought you were supposed to be protecting him."

Izz pushes his pain away to answer, not wanting Sin to lash out. Peering at his friend through half-opened lids. "Reni. It's fine. It was consensual—"

"How the hell is that—" Reni gestures at Izz's body "—consensual."

This is going to end badly if his friend keeps pushing, "Reni, please leave." *Before Sin silences you with his usual methods.* "I'll talk to you about it later."

Before Reni can open his mouth to add onto the growing tension, the nurse interjects, her bravado coming back with a vengeance, "Jasper is correct. You are not helping in this situation. I'll ask you to step out of the room or be escorted out."

It's weird. Hearing someone say his real name. Nobody uses it anymore. She must have pulled up his records on the little tablet she has leaning against her hip.

Reni scowls at Sin but he does as the nurse asks. Storming out of Med-Wing. Izz guesses Reni won't go far, probably waiting in the corridor outside the door—pacing back and forth, no doubt cursing them all out.

"Alright," the nurse takes a deep breath to ground herself, "I'm going to need him to undress so I can look over his entire body. If that's okay with you. It will benefit his health to do so."

It's quite strange—the nurse still talking about him to Sin. To get Sin's permission. He doesn't blame her, if he didn't know Sin, he'd want the male's permission to touch anything belonging to him—

Izz inwardly beams at the thought of belonging to Sin. Which he does. The entire prison is constantly gossiping about it. And he doesn't mind. In fact, he loves the idea.

Izz gets naked in front of Sin and the nurse. Moving where told, to let the nurse poke and prod at the cuts Sin made in his skin. He has a lot of them. He hadn't realised there are so many before now. And the worried look in the nurse's eyes isn't helping him feel okay with his new kink.

After the external exam, he's being stitched up as the nurse explains hygiene practices—to Sin—for cleaning the wounds. And keeping the stitches away from any direct water flow. And more boring instructions Izz zones out of. It's not like she's talking to him anyway. And he trusts Sin to listen, to collect any pills or whatever he needs to heal.

37

Turns out, whatever pills the nurse gave him are the pick-me-up he needs. Izz's raring and ready to go. Or, more like, not in pain and able to function properly.

He arranged with Sin to have lunch together, so he can talk to Reni alone and he also wants to beat Zidie in The Gang's card games. He was so close to achieving it last time. He knows he can do it. He wants the gloating points.

"Hey," Izz greets his friend as he emerges from Med-Wing's doors. He isn't sure where to start in his explanation.

"Are you alright? They cleared you to leave?" Reni's mother bird is firing up and fretting over Izz, circling him to check he has all his parts attached.

"It wasn't that bad." At Reni's sceptical look, Izz adds, "I only needed a handful of stitches."

"I'm going to kill him. Why did he—"

"Stop. It was consensual. I had the choice to stop it at any time. I liked it, okay," and Izz does enjoy it. He wouldn't take any of it back. It's an experience he's never been through and one he wants to do again.

And again.

Just thinking about it is getting him hard. He hopes his friend doesn't notice his pants tenting. If Reni does, he doesn't mention it as they slowly make their way to the Rec-Room.

"What do you mean you *liked* it. Is that what he's got you thinking?"

How to explain it to Reni . . . without coming across like a crazy person . . . "You know how Sinj is into all kinds of weird sex things—"

"Yeah, but that's Sinj, he's wacked and a masochist— ohhhhh . . ." Reni's voice trails off as what Izz's hinting sinks in.

"Mm-hmm," Izz hums, a little embarrassed having to explain his newfound kink enjoyments with his friend. He fears being judged harshly for it, "I've figured out I'm one too."

Izz doesn't understand it. But it turns him on when he has a blade against his skin. Threatening, pressing up against his throat. Cutting him . . .

"Oh," Reni mulls over Izz's disclosed claims. Walking in silence for a time as they edge their way through the corridors to their destination. "You're careful with it? He stops if you ask?"

"He gave me a safe word and everything. It's consensual. Trust me." Izz holds his hands out in a reassuring gesture. Trying to convey to his friend that he's one hundred percent cool with what went on between him and Sin.

"Alright. But if he steps out of line, scary motherfucker or not, I will mess him up. Even if I die in the process, I will make him hurt."

CAGED IN

Izz laughs. Nudging his friend playfully. "Thanks. You know. For having my back since I got here."

"Don't mention it. It's what friends do."

They walk in silence the rest of the way to the Rec-Room. Izz's mind wandering back to Sin's cell. To the bunk, and the . . . activities they do on it—

"You self-harming?" Zidie blatantly asks, as soon as Izz walks through the door to The Gang's table.

"No," Izz bristles, sitting in one of the empty chairs. He hates prison in this way, there are no secrets kept in this cage. Everyone knows everyone's business. Especially the stuff you want to stay hidden.

"You sure?" Blake enquires, like he doesn't believe Izz for a second.

Izz slumps a little in his chair, waiting for the game to end so he can be dealt in and have something to occupy his hands . . . and his mind.

"Yes, I'm sure" Izz snaps, irritated with both of them. He would prefer not to talk about his sexual activities, thank you very much.

He receives a scrutinising look from everyone at the table . . . Speaking of everyone, David isn't among them. Perhaps the inmate died on the way here? He doesn't want anyone to die but if he has to daydream about someone hitting the gravestone early, it will be David.

No, he doesn't actually want the man to die. He just doesn't like him. At all—

He's definitely still holding a grudge. He isn't sure why. David has long ago eaten his words. The Gang is rapidly becoming the most feared among the prison population. No actual prison gangs mess with any of them. For fear of the repercussions they will face. With Sin in their corner no one bothers them.

Might also have something to do with the rapidly decreasing number of creeps in here—the creeps who touch Izz. He's sure some of the men in here have done things he does not want to know about.

The Gang's judging Izz, their sceptical looks boring into him. Their game on pause until they hear all the gossip from him. Not satisfied with a vague answer.

He sighs dramatically, deciding it's not worth the fight. "Sinn'ous was careless. He went a little too deep with a blade, I needed a few stitches in my side. No big deal."

Can you all drop it now, and get back to focusing on the cards.

"Your shirt has a lot of blood on it for '*no big deal*'," Zidie points out, with nods of agreement from all around the table.

"I know," Izz mutters. Maybe he should head back to his cell. They're all way too nosy for their own good. He should have seen it coming.

"Apparently he's into it," Reni takes it upon himself to share the details, "says he is anyway. I think that serial killer is messing with his head. Manipulating him—"

"Sin has never forced me to do anything I don't want to do. It's my choice." Why can't they respect his decision? Why does it have to be him getting manipulated?

I'm perfectly capable of making my own decisions.

Blake rests his hand on Izz's shoulder, giving it a reassuring squeeze. "You shouldn't let him do that to you," his older brother vibes coating his entire demeanour.

CAGED IN

"Like he has a choice," Isco butts in. Re-stacking the cards to shuffle out a new game, after everyone abandoned their cards in favour of focusing on Izz and the latest gossip.

"It's consensual," Izz all but yells, other inmates in the room turning to look their way. Dropping his voice back to a reasonable level he adds, "and it's really none of your business—"

Isco cuts in, deep voice rasping right over Izz's building annoyance like Izz hasn't said a thing, "with his protection being the motivator."

"No," Izz protests, trying to defend Sin, "it isn't like that."

He has a choice. He's not under duress. Or scared of Sin and doing it out of fear the male will be angry. He does it because it feels good. He likes it. Likes the way Sin treats him. The way his heart flutters when he's under Sin's thickly muscled body, looking up into his dark eyes . . .

"Nobody judges you," Sinj interjects, smiling warmly at Izz. "It's a reasonable motivation. Hell, I do it all the time to get things."

"He doesn't give his protection for that. He'd protect me either way," Izz knows Sin, knows he's safe, he's respected, he's cherished.

Sinj shrugs nonchalantly. Unbothered either way. Why can't the rest of The Gang be as carefree about it? Instead of the judgement coming off them. The pity. As though Izz's trapped in a predicament he can't escape.

He's grateful when The Gang lets the subject drop. Isco dishing out cards. Games firing up. Izz's losing rapidly faster each round. His mind not in the games. He can't concentrate, their conversation on repeat in his mind. Swirling around his skull.

He's glad when Sin shows up. The male appearing in the Rec-Room's doorway. Meaning lunch is just around the corner. It also gives him an idea . . .

He's the only one facing the door. The rest of The Gang hasn't noticed Sin entering the room. And there is a seat right next to him . . .

His smile threatens to split his cheeks in half it's so wide. He grabs Sin's eyes with his own and flicks his chin at the chair. Watching the male raise a brow in question.

Sin prowls over and slumps into the empty chair. If The Gang wasn't tense before, they sure are now. All of them stiffening when they realise who just sat down.

Izz makes a point of looking every single one of them in the eye, before stopping on Sin. Who has questions written in his black eyes, but doesn't voice any of them, "I choose if we fuck, yes?"

He can feel the entire table stop breathing. You could cut the air with a butter knife with the amount of tension thats in it.

Izz's been around Sin enough to see he's intrigued by this line of questioning and the events unfolding. Amusement lingering in his eyes, his lack of facial expressions giving nothing away.

"You do," Sin's eyes stay locked on Izz, ignoring the rest of them.

"You'd protect me? Even if I told you right now that I don't want to fuck, ever again."

CAGED IN

He watches the faint smirk pick up the side of Sin's lips, a barely noticeable change in his static expression. Sin's caught onto what Izz's doing.

Sin's leg brushes Izz's as he leans back in the flimsy chair, crossing his arms over his chest, "why would I be so shallow as to exchange sex for protection. Only a naive fool would think that way."

Izz can't hold in his amusement. Waggling his eyebrows at The Gang, who are staring with wide eyes. A real *I-told-you-so* smirk spreading over his face. He has to bite his cheeks to stop the laugh bubbling up in his throat from escaping.

"As much as this consent conversation has been thrilling," Sin states dryly. "I'm getting food. You coming." Izz can tell Sin's not asking a question, and is only framing it in such a way for the table's benefit.

Izz follows suit as Sin rises to his full height, his aura of power coating the air around him as he strides back out of the room, with a jittery Izz hot on his trail.

Izz practically skips down the corridor. His body light. His mind clear. He's better than ever. With zero aches or pains.

"Care to share what your little stunt was all about," Sin grips Izz's elbow to still the jumping movements. Corralling Izz to his side to avoid colliding with a wall.

"They think I'm gullible and being manipulated by you into sexual acts I don't want to do," Izz frowns, staring at his elbow, wondering why Sin has grabbed him.

"You seemed pretty fond of what I was doing to you," Sin states, releasing Izz's arm.

Izz steps in closer to Sin, leaning on the male as they walk down the corridor together. Ignoring the side glances he receives from passing inmates.

"Oh, I am," Izz sticks his hand into Sin's pocket, earning himself a weird look from Sin—cross between puzzlement and amusement. "And I want to do them again. The guys were being dicks about it, that's all. And no, you can't kill them."

At that, Sin chuckles, "wasn't planning on it."

"Oh please," he draws out the last word, voice dripping with sarcasm. "As if you wouldn't spontaneously kill someone." Izz rolls his eyes, muttering under his breath, "making out like you need a plan."

Izz stumbles as he trips on something. His shoe? The floor? Air? Who knows.

"I think those drugs you took are working," Sin advises softly. Redirecting Izz from walking right past the cafeteria doors.

"What? Why? What makes you say that?" He feels fine. Completely normal. No pain or nothing.

Sin raises a brow, lightly shoving Izz towards the doors when he stops moving. Encouraging him without words to continue. So he does. But not before waving a hand in Sin's face, dismissing the mohawked male.

"Pfff. They are not. I'm completely normal."

Totally normal.

Drugs or no drugs, he's as he always is . . . Is. Is . . . ?

What was I thinking about again?

"Indeed," Sin states flatly.

38

The unease in the room is palpable. Sitting with Sin is immediately taken note of by the entire room. He isn't sure why, everyone already knows he and Sin are fucking. Or rather they think Sin is using him. Either way, they shouldn't be surprised. They do call him the serial killer's bitch boy, after all.

His side is beginning to hurt once more, the pain meds wearing off. A dull ache taking their place. It's bearable, a little discomfort he can live with.

"I feel like I'm doing something I shouldn't be," Izz whispers. As if he's in a forbidden part of the prison. It's quite strange. Nobody sits here except for Sin. And now, apparently, Izz. "I kinda like it. Like I'm sitting on a throne or something."

Sin smirks. Pressing his thigh against Izz's under the table. The contact can't be seen by the rest of the room. Not unless they walked close. Which no one is ever brave enough to do.

Izz's tucking into the start of his meal when a guard catches his eye. The guard is rocking on their heels.

Hovering close by. On the periphery of the last tables holding inmates, before the bare table in front of Sin's own. It's almost as though they are building up the courage to do something . . .

The guard drags a hand through their hair. Then approaches. Staring at the ground the entire time. "You have a visitor, inmate A-18910." Swiftly retreating now that the message has been relayed.

Izz peers at Sin. He wants to see his visitors. He knows it will be his mum and sister. At the same time however, he doesn't want to leave. He wants to stay and finish eating next to Sin.

"We have other meals to do this again. Go see your family."

He can't handle waiting days to eat with Sin again. "Dinner," he insists, squeezing Sin's thigh with his hand under the table.

Izz's grown more and more confident with touching Sin. And why shouldn't he? They have sex all the time. They spend hours each day together. If anyone is allowed to randomly caress Sin, it should be him.

"Dinner," Sin repeats, agreeing.

Izz dumps his tray and wanders off to visitation all by his lonesome. With no fear he'll be attacked by anyone. They all fear Sin too much to try anything with him.

The visitation room is packed with inmates in dull plain colours and guests in brightly coloured clothing of all types. And scents, all manner of perfumes filling the space, a bouquet of flowers competing for approval.

CAGED IN

Through the crowds he spots a familiar face. His mum waiting at one of the many tables. His sister isn't there. Perhaps she's in school? He can't recall what day it is.

His mum's wearing one of her casual, yet respectable, outfits. A lavender purple shirt, the softness of the colour complimenting her features. Her long ankle length skirt is a pale blue with a spiral pattern of flowers.

I miss this. I miss my family.

"Hi." He greets, sitting opposite his mum, her floral perfume a happy reminder of home. "Where's Luc?"

"Waiting outside the room. I have to speak with you first, alone."

Oh, God. Something's wrong . . .

Is it—

Is the—

Please don't let it be back. He can't lose his sister. She can't be out there, going through it alone. All the appointments—

No. The cancer can't be back.

If he refuses to acknowledge its presence, his mum won't say it. Please don't say it.

"We had an offer. For a house to live in," his mum speaks softly, her eyes bleak.

Izz sags into his chair. While his body is flooded with relief, he experiences a pang of unease. If they have a house offer, why is his mum acting so odd? Why does she appear so put out and . . . wrong . . .

She pulls a letter from her coat pocket, slipping the pages out from within its folds. Presenting it to Izz. Who stares at it without reading, the words blurring together, his mind unable to focus.

E.P. WRITER

He tentatively takes the letter. "What is it?" He brings the paper closer, trying to overcome his unease enough to read it.

"It says he's a friend of yours. He has a home we can stay in rent free. Is this true? And why is he offering it? What's going on?"

"I'm not sure . . ." Izz's eyes skim over the neatly handwritten letter. The contents not making sense, even as he can read the handwritten letter just fine.

The page does not contain a name of the person who wrote it. However there is a single letter inked at the bottom. Izz doesn't need a full name to know who wrote it. But why . . . ?

Dear Miss Mariana

You will not know me, but I know your son. Jasper Marcelo is a kind hearted soul who speaks fondly of you.

I feel as if I know you, your daughter too. Her hardships often come to light in Jasper's worries. His nature to care for you both is unable to be met in a place he does not deserve to be.

I understand you are in need of a more accommodating residence. I humbly offer my home to yourself and your daughter. It is not in use and will benefit greatly from occupants to care for it, as it returns the favour with a roof over your head.

I do not wish to be your landlord. Merely a friend helping a friend. I will not be asking for any money or anything in return.

This is a gift. One I hope you will make use of.

24 Flynn Street, Damson Alone, Florence, QLD, 4114

S

E.P. WRITER

"I didn't know . . . He never . . ." Izz trails off, staring at the initial on the bottom of the page.

Why would Sin contact Izz's mum and offer her his home?

Without so much as mentioning it to him? For that matter, *how* did Sin contact her? Izz has never shared her address with anyone. Maybe Sin has seen the address written on one of the many letters he sent Luc? It's the only possible explanation.

"Are you okay?" His mum looks closely at him, her loving concern written all over her face, "is this person doing something to you? Blackmailing you with this," she points to the letter.

"Um. No. He's not." Izz blinks at the letter expecting it to disappear, a figment of his imagination. It stays right there, clear as day. "He didn't tell me. I'm not sure why . . ."

"This offer would help us. We're barely managing with you in here," he feels a pang of guilt at her words, even while knowing she hasn't said them to hurt him—she is only stating facts. "But I will not put my son in danger—in some terrible situation, for a house. We will get along fine without any handouts."

Her eyes reveal that they won't be fine. He can tell when she's lying. It must be bad out there. And if this is the truth. If Sin has offered . . .

"I'll talk to him. To make sure this is real. I'll call you no later than tomorrow, to let you know either way."

If it is real . . .

He can never repay Sin for this. He already can't repay Sin for everything the male has done for him. Given him. Protected him from.

CAGED IN

"You won't give him any hold over you. I will not have my son . . . for a house. It's not happening." She stares at him sternly, contemplating everything, "I shouldn't have brought it up. Forget it. I'm not taking the offer." She grabs across the table for the letter. Is she going to rip it?—

Izz quickly stills her hands. "No. Don't."

He doesn't want her dismissing this, he can tell they need it. He would—will—give everything for them to be safe. And they can be safe, with this gift, they can be safe.

"I, um," he sighs. He needs to tell her something so she will take the house and won't lie awake at night thinking he's being raped for her to live there rent free.

He can't tell her the truth. He doesn't want her to know anything bad has happened to him. All the people who have died . . . Doesn't want her to know why Sin is offering them his home—not that he actually knows why. Or who Sin is . . .

There is one angle to work from. One that's not completely a lie, but at the same time isn't strictly the truth. But it will explain the situation to her, without telling her everything.

Izz leans in closer to his mum, dropping his voice to barely above a whisper. So she's the only one to hear what he is about to say, "I . . . we're kind of dating." He finds himself hesitant to speak the words, "he's sort of my boyfriend—but you can't say anything. To anyone."

He wouldn't mind if it is the truth. He would love to be in an actual relationship with Sin. But he's not naive enough to think it will continue once they are free. Living in the outside world.

I can still pretend while we're locked inside.

He isn't ashamed to be seen dating another man. He can't, however, let the rest of the prison learn what he and Sin have is more than Izz offering it up for protection. It has never been that way for him. And never will be.

And one day he will gather the courage to ask Sin if they'll continue their—whatever it is—on the outside. Their . . . relationship, he supposes. He isn't sure if he can call Sin his boyfriend just yet.

His mum smiles, "oh, I see." She sits back. Holding the letter delicately. "This changes things . . . I'm glad you've found some happiness in here."

"Thanks, Mum. Me too." He loves how accepting his mum is with everything. She's completely open-minded and supporting of his relationships—

Just not one to a serial killer. She probably draws her line at that.

"I will want to meet him."

"I don't know." How to turn this around . . . ? She can't see Sin. Not if they aren't technically boyfriends—although he can probably ask Sin really nicely to lie and play pretend long enough to put her mind at ease. Sin had played along with his little thing back in the Rec-Room.

Except that hadn't strictly been lying . . .

"I'll ask but . . ."

What?

He's a dangerous serial killer and I don't want you finding out those little details about him. Don't want you judging what I have. How I know I shouldn't, but I do . . . love him—

Izz cuts his inner thoughts off, unbelieving what they just said . . .

CAGED IN

"He's shy, and isn't open about being . . . you know," he insinuates about being gay. Knowing his mum will take it that way.

She nods, giving Izz a warm smile, before standing to go collect his sister from where she's waiting outside the visitation room. While he waits at the table. He's shocked to the core at his own realisation.

I love Sin . . .

Izz locates Sin on his bunk in his Satanic cell. Propped against the wall. His face blank, eyes locked on the wall opposite him—filled with pages of Satanic scripture and devil artwork.

Izz doesn't hesitate for a second. He marches in, climbing onto the bunk, straddles Sin's legs, sits right in the male's lap, and kisses him.

Running his hand down Sin's chest as he deepens the kiss, his eyes closing to enjoy the sensation of soft lips against his own. It's the first time he's initiated a sexual encounter with Sin. First time he's the one in charge—to an extent.

Breaking the kiss, Izz clings onto Sin, pressing his face into the solid chest as he hugs the warm body against his own.

"I can never repay you for any of it," his voice is muffled by the prison shirt's fabric.

His debt to Sin is too great to be repaid. Especially since he has no job and no money. The prison jobs don't count, a few coins aren't enough to do anything with.

"I'm not asking you to," Sin calmly states. Slipping his hands around Izz's waist to hold him in place.

"Why did you . . ."

It's one thing to help Izz in here. But another thing entirely to open his home on the outside to people he's never met. All because they are Izz's family.

Sin doesn't even play as though he isn't fully aware of what Izz's referring to, "you care for them, and I'm in a position to help them for you. It's not as though I'm using the house."

Do not cry. You're a grown man, you will not cry.

"Thank you," Izz kisses down the column of Sin's neck. Sliding his knees backwards to slip further back. His hands working into Sin's pants, gripping the waistband.

He wants to try something, something he offered back in the beginning but has never had the opportunity to try. Sin's always wanting to use his ass . . . But what about his mouth . . .

In all their explorations he's never sucked Sin off. Never licked him or worked his length down his throat. He's not sure he can even take the whole thing in.

Only one way to find out.

He shuffles back further. So he can ease down, to position himself to get to Sin with his mouth. Pausing briefly in his task of slipping Sin's pants down.

"What did I do to deserve you? You're so kind to me," Izz studies Sin's dark eyes, watching the sparks of life racing through them. "I love you. I know I shouldn't. But I do. I love you."

He needs Sin to hear it. Needs to let Sin know how he feels. He doesn't want to keep it bottled up. He doesn't

CAGED IN

want what they have together to only be a relationship of convenience in this Hell-hole.

He wants more.

Wants to be more when they're both free.

The serial killer smiles down at him. A genuine, gentle smile. Pulling Izz up into a deep kiss.

NOTES

Don't worry the story doesn't end here. The next one, Caged Killer, overlaps this timeline and continues on from it.
You will enter the prison world through the point of view of Sinn'ous. You'll see what he sees and what Izz didn't. There are many things that happened behind the scenes that Izz was completely unaware of. Events that paved the way to what was to come.
Sin's viewpoint will show you what Izz missed and answer many of the unanswered questions and missing pieces.

Does Izz actually have friends? Or was he fooled from the start? Who can really be trusted?
Poor little naive Izz, what did he get thrown into?

And a side note: Caged Killer will have several chapters (located at the end of the book) that will continue from here—chapter 38—and give you Izz's viewpoint of events.
To be read after Caged Killer, can't have any spoilers for Sin's story, now can we.

SINN'OUS'S LETTER

(for anyone who couldn't read the font)

Dear Miss Mariana

You will not know me, but I know your son. Jasper Marcelo is a kind hearted soul who speaks fondly of you.

I feel as if I know you, your daughter too. Her hardships often come to light in Jasper's worries. His nature to care for you both is unable to be met in a place he does not deserve to be.

I understand you are in need of a more accommodating residence. I humbly offer my home to yourself and your daughter. It is not in use and will benefit greatly from occupants to care for it, as it returns the favour with a roof over your head.

I do not wish to be your landlord. Merely a friend helping a friend. I will not be asking for any money or anything in return.

This is a gift. One I hope you will make use of.

24 Flynn Street, Damson Alone, Florence, QLD, 4114

S

UPCOMING SERIES

If you're interested in serial killers, this series is for you.

Where you follow the life of a serial killer, Zayne, as he discovers who he is and hones his skills. Embracing his true self, he holds nothing back as he takes apart his victims to build a name everyone will fear. SKhorpion.

A Serial Killer's life Series

SKhorpion Adolescence
SKhorpion
SKhorpion Obsidian Blade
SKhorpion House of Blood

This series will be linked with the Caged Prison Series. An overlap that won't take away from either story if you don't want to read the other series.

Feel free to follow my social media pages (see front of book) to keep an eye on their progress.

SKhorpion Adolescence

Released October 2024

Follow the life of a young man as he discovers who he is.
A serial killer.

SKhorpion

Released November 2024

Follow the journey of a young serial killer as he learns the ropes of the trade. Working for the Mafia.

ABOUT AUTHOR

I am a bin rat. A rubbish raccoon. I spend my days in a dark boxed in den. A hollowed-out tree amidst the discarded remnants of life. Hissing at anyone to disturb the dark sanctuary of death.

After a day spent scrounging the trash cans, I come home to my chasm of fortitude to write stories from the darkest depths of the soul.

Writing is the easy part. Editing is the challenge, to suck the will to live right out of the soul. I never realised how much work goes into a single novel, until I wrote one.

Staring at the screens until words blur, swirling around to suck me into their pit of chaos. Dragging me down until I'm one with the words, the story playing over the backs of my eyes with every blink. To become one with the characters. One with their world. One with their lives.

Enjoy.

Or don't.

This world of serial killers and criminals is not for the faint of heart. Read it if you dare.

E.P.Writer

P.s. keep your hands clean and stay out of prison my fellow raccoons. The real thing isn't pretty.

READER INTERACTIVE PAGE

I have seen—and am a part of—a lot of fan pages, where many fans ask lots of questions and theorise together. Like characters favourite colours, or why they did something. So, I thought, why not make an interactive page?
This is where I'll answer story related questions.

If you have a question, leave it in your review and I'll do my best to answer all of them in the back of the next book in the series. You can also get in touch through my social pages with questions too. Otherwise leave those questions in Amazon or Goodreads reviews.

I think this will be a nice way for author / reader interactions.

Side note: Names of who asked the question will not be shared. Only the question will be shared.
Some questions won't be answered here if the question is answered in the next book or a spoiler.

READER INTERACTIVE PAGE QUESTIONS ANSWERED

Where is the heavy surveillance?
This is a minimum security prison, and Caged Killer will go into detail as to why the guards leave Izz alone.

The serial killer is the owner of the prison?
He isn't. People leave him alone because they fear him. Caged Killer shows why.

Izz makes friends so fast? It's out of the ordinary.
Does he? Are they really his friends? Those answers come in Caged Killer.

What happens when they get out? Do they stay together? Did one get out before the other?
These answers come in Caged Killer.

It feels like it just ends?
The story ends here because to go any further would give away too many spoilers for Caged Killer. I split the Points-of-view up into two books so you, as the reader, can enter into Izz's mind and feel just as clueless as him.

He is so naive, how does he not understand some of the stuff that happens?
Izz was a hard character to write because of this. When I write, the story plays like a movie in my mind and I write what I see. Him being clueless had me saying, why? Why are you eating those random pills you found? Do you want to die?
The frustration was real. *facepalm*

47% into the book is an odd place for them to meet/speak. Why?
Without spoiling I can say there is a lot that happens that Izz was unaware of. And is that really when they first meet? Caged Killer holds those answers.

Printed in Great Britain
by Amazon